Also by Matson Taylor

The Miseducation of Evie Epworth

ALL ABOUT EVIE

MATSON TAYLOR

SCRIBNER

LONDON NEW YORK SYDNEY TORONTO NEW DELHI

First published in Great Britain by Scribner, an imprint of
Simon & Schuster UK Ltd, 2022

This paperback edition published 2023

1 3 5 7 9 10 8 6 4 2

Simon & Schuster UK Ltd
1st Floor
222 Gray's Inn Road
London WC1X 8HB

www.simonandschuster.co.uk
www.simonandschuster.com.au
www.simonandschuster.co.in

Simon & Schuster Australia, Sydney
Simon & Schuster India, New Delhi

A CIP catalogue record for this book is available from the British Library

Paperback ISBN: 978-1-4711-9087-2
eBook ISBN: 978-1-4711-9086-5

Typeset in Sabon by M Rules
Printed and Bound in the UK using 100% Renewable
Electricity at CPI Group (UK) Ltd

To Sarah, Pete & Bob – for making me feel cool

In memory of Barbara Hanson (1947–2022)

CHAPTER 1

Summer 1972

'I am the wind. I skeet across tarmac and whoosh over dale. Birds skate along my amorphous limbs and the sun bakes down on my back. I am a sirocco, hot as the desert sand. I fly. I ...'

'Yes. That's quite enough hot air for today, Evie.'

That's Pamela, my boss, the producer. I'm in the *Woman's Hour* recording studio at Broadcasting House and I'm sound-checking for an Extremely Special Recording. Princess Anne is coming in to do an interview. Amazing. Pamela (grey hair, jodhpur bothering, cruciverbalist) pulled a few horsey strings to get the interview and, ever since, she's been busy arranging everything with the planning and precision of a moon landing.

And who am I? I'm Evie, a silk-scarf rocking, Biba frocking, hollyhocking, cheesecloth smocking, spatchcocking, coloured stocking, list up-knocking twenty-six-and-a-half-year-old. I grew up on a small farm in Yorkshire (that's another story) but have been living in London for the past ten years, swinging my way through most of the sixties and hot-panting my way into the seventies. All that time, I've been working at the BBC, which makes me, officially, a metropolitan sophisticate who knows her way round an avocado pear and *The Observer* colour supplement.

I have everything I could ever want in life:

1. A career
2. A leatherette portfolio briefcase
3. An Ossie Clark poncho

When I first got to London, the only practical skills I had were knowing how to change a tyre (car *and* bike), tie a butcher's knot and milk a cow. But now I am a modern woman armed with a broad range of modern skills, fully equipped to cope with all forms of modern life (cafetières, continental quilts, flashers).

What I can't do, though, is keep Pamela happy.

'Can you do it again,' she says, huffing extravagantly, 'but this time don't lean into the microphone. It's Princess Anne who's coming, not Mick ruddy Jagger.'

Pamela's standing with her arms folded, watching me through the studio glass. She has the nervy energy of an aerosol can and doesn't look happy (she never really does). She's in full battle-dress: tailored jacket and matching skirt. The skirt looks like it doesn't really know how long it wants to be, so has settled on a compromise around the knees, exposing two heavily deniered mahogany shanks. I've opted for mustard trousers, white blouse, and a stirrup-themed silk scarf (in honour of our guest) but have been thoroughly reprimanded by Pamela because, apparently, *trousers aren't what one wears around royalty.*

I pull back from the microphone and lick my lips, making them nice and moist. 'Round and round the rugged rock the ragged rascal ran,' I say, going a bit Cheltenham Ladies' College.

As I speak, I can see Pamela playing around with the recording console. She's frowning but this isn't necessarily a bad thing as she frowns pretty much all the time. She flicks her eyes, cracks out a quick *again* and then gets back to fiddling with the various dials.

'Round and round the rugged rock the ragged rascal ran,' I repeat, this time giving it my best Glenda Jackson.

'Yes. Good. We're done,' clips Pamela, sitting back and fingering her giant upside-down apostrophe glasses. She glances at her watch. 'Eleven-thirty!' She lets out another monumental huff (Pamela seems to spend all her time breathing out and never breathing in). 'I need to see Marjorie and run through the questions. Can you get a jug of water and a glass for the Princess? And make sure the studio's clean and tidy. We don't want her thinking she's walked into a garden shed, do we?' She snatches her handbag from the recording console and bristles out the door.

The studio actually *is* a bit like a garden shed. The walls are panelled with wood (the same shade as Pamela's tights) and there's an underlying mustiness, caused by a damp patch in the carpet tiles (which I tackle with the occasional squirt of *Rive Gauche*). Non-garden-shed touches include a round table with three fluffy microphones, a photo of Lord Reith, and a door with a couple of coloured lightbulbs over it, each signalling Pamela's likely reaction if you come in: green, semi-smile; red, death by a thousand tuts.

I think about all the things I have to do before Princess

Anne arrives. The main one is practise my curtsey (there's not much call for curtseying in 1972, even at the BBC) but there are other things too: make sure the recording equipment is ready, get a jug of water and *clean and tidy* the studio. Pamela's also asked me to sort out the bookshelf in the editing room and make it *suitable for our royal guest*. By this she means get rid of the Germaine Greer (well-thumbed) and our review copy of *The Joy of Sex* (even better-thumbed) and then pad out the remaining books with a couple of Jane Austens and a Brontë she brought in earlier. I've decided not to bother doing this, though, as I can't really see Princess Anne paying much attention to a bookshelf.

But before any of that, I'm going to sit and have a quick ponder. I love to squirrel away moments on my own, a consequence, I think, of being an only child. I'm often to be found lost in thought, weighing up debates and contemplating the important issues of the day, giving my head the feel of the *Guardian* letters page (the EEC, equal pay, crocheted cheesecloth crop tops).

I look down, staring at the table. Before I know it I'm tracing my finger along its gnarly old grains, picking up a conspicuous squiggle of dust. I smile, thinking of all the people in my past who'd be deeply unimpressed by this (in my village, dust is an evil greater than Satan). The dust worm stares up at me accusingly. I play with it for a while, rolling its squishy greyness between my fingers before flicking it on the floor.

Bugger *cleaning and tidying*.

I am a modern woman with a terracotta chicken brick and

a desktop diary, living in the dirtiest, grubbiest, messiest city in the world.

And I wouldn't have it any other way.

My dusty reminiscences are interrupted by some loud knocking and a face squashed up against the glass. It's Joyce, a very nice BBC colleague. There are two important things to know about Joyce:

1. She comes from Canada
2. She works in television

Something that I quickly learnt when I started at the BBC is that it's very tribal. There's the radio tribe and there's the television tribe. Each looks down on the other – radio looks down on television because it's the Populist Opiate of the Masses and television looks down on radio because you'll never get Bruce Forsyth on the radio. Joyce and I, though, have managed to cross this divide, bonding over a pair of green-and-silver-zigzag platform sandals – hers, not mine.

'Are you free?' mouths Joyce through the glass.

'Yes,' I mouth back (doing a thumbs up for good measure). 'Why?'

She doesn't say anything but just waves her handbag in the air mysteriously.

'Where's the old battleaxe, then?' she asks, as I step into the editing suite.

'She's gone to speak to Marjorie,' I reply. Marjorie (lovely nails, cribbage queen, watercolourist) is the *Woman's Hour* presenter. She is the extremely nice yin to Pamela's always crabby yang.

'Great. So you're free?'

'Well, free-ish. Why?'

She gives her handbag another quick wave. 'It's arrived!'

A little thing inside me chafes.

'Oh. Right. I see.'

'Yeah, it came in the post this morning,' she goes on. 'I'd have gotten here earlier but we've had temper tantrums in studio three again. Bloody *Gardeners' World.*'

What's arrived is a home pregnancy test, a piece of Canadian magic that will change the world for ever (like stretch fabrics and colour telly). Joyce asked her cousin to send one over from Canada on account of me missing my time of the month. My GP, Dr Walker, is a lovely sweet old man who I'm happy to talk to about sore throats or a rabies jab but not about anything *down below* (especially involving sex). The specific sex was with Anders*, a very handsome intern at the Swedish embassy. I met him at a party, where, after quite a few *akvavits*, he told me that I had great legs (amazing) and that he was going back to Stockholm in two weeks' time (not amazing). We exchanged numbers and the next morning, I phoned him. And that was that.

'Evie?'

Joyce is staring at me, head fully cocked.

'Sorry, I was miles away. Yes. I'm ready.' I clench my fist and stick out my upturned arm.

*

> Name: Anders Engström
>
> From: Sweden
>
> Appearance: blonde hair, blue eyes, strawberry Mivvi lips
>
> Job: intern at Swedish embassy
>
> Seen for: two weeks
>
> Amazing: lovely nails, very good Strindberg joke, first fling with an umlaut
>
> Less amazing: lutist, a little dull, moved back to Stockholm

'What are you doing?' she asks.

'It's for the test. I thought you'd need to take some blood.'

'Blood? God, no.'

'Oh. What do we have to do then?'

'Pee.'

'Pee?'

'Yes, pee. Well not us. You.'

'What, just pee? How can it tell?'

'No idea. It must be Canadian magic or something. Come on,' she says, linking her arm through mine, 'let's give it a try before Pamela gets back.' And she yanks me out the door.

'Is that it?' I ask, trying hard to hide my disappointment.

We're in the ladies' loos down the corridor from the studio. Joyce has just pulled a small cardboard box from her bag (very dramatically – you can tell she works in television) and is waving it around.

'What do you mean *is that it*? This is state-of-the-art stuff. It's what science is all about. Never mind men and their bloody Apollo missions. It's about time science did something for us women.'

She passes me the box. It's about the size of a pack of Jacob's Cream Crackers. It's mainly white with stripy turquoise flourishes, making it look swish yet reassuringly clinical.

'You'll need to open it,' she says.

I hesitate for a second then pull open the lid.

We both peer inside.

You can't see much so I gently tip the box on its side and slide the pregnancy test out. Everything's held in a clear-plastic box: there's a tube with a blue lid, a pipette with a blue squeezy thing, and a little mirror angled across the bottom of the box like a periscope.

'Ooooh, fancy!' says Joyce.

'Okay,' I say, spreading the instructions out across an ancient basin. 'What do we do?'

It turns out Joyce was right. Peeing is involved. We need to put some of my pee into the tube (using the pipette) and then, a couple of hours later, check whether a red circle has appeared at the bottom of the tube.

'I'm going to need something to pee into,' I inform Joyce. 'I can't pee and pipette at the same time. It'd be carnage.'

'Can't you just hold the pipette in the stream and squeeze?'

'Squeeze what?'

'The pipette.'

We stare at each other blankly for a few seconds. Absolutely nothing in our lives up until now has prepared us for this moment.

'Hold on, I've got an idea,' says Joyce. And she dashes out the room.

I fold up the instructions and put them back in the box. The box is light, far too light really for something so important. Something that could change my life so completely.

I'd have to give up my job, of course. And platform shoes and miniskirts. Music. Parties. Trips abroad. And how could I tell Anders? In fact, should I tell Anders? And never mind all that – what would Dad say?

'Here we go,' says Joyce, walking back in and handing me a mug (a really lovely greeny-brown one I got last year on a trip to Hornsea Pottery).

'What am I meant to do with this?' I ask.

'Pee in it!'

'I can't pee in this. It's Hornsea Pottery!'

'Look, it's the first one I saw,' says Joyce. 'And it's either the mug or the pipette and a pair of Marigolds. You decide.'

I take the mug and go into a cubicle, leaving Joyce outside with the pregnancy test kit.

What I need is a fully panted test run to work out the logistics of it all. A dry run.

This isn't going to be easy. I'm not a great aimer at the best of times (as Miss McMinn, my school netball mistress, always used to point out) and, what with the added pressure of work and Princess Anne, the potential for urinological disaster is high. It's at times like this that I wish I were a man, although experience has taught me that men, despite obvious biological advantages, are nowhere near as good as they should be in the aiming department.

I look at the loo then at the mug then back at the loo.

'Are you all right in there?' shouts Joyce. 'What are you doing?'

'It's a bit awkward,' I shout back.

There's silence for a few seconds and then . . .

'Look, do you want me to come and help?'

'Help?'

'Yeah, I don't mind.' She sounds completely calm, like she's offering to put the shopping away or something.

'No, I'll be fine.' I close my eyes and take a deep breath. 'Honest.'

'Don't be daft. Look, it doesn't bother me. I helped deliver six Newfoundland puppies once – it can't be any worse than that.'

Two minutes later I find myself crouching over the loo, pants down and bum out. Joyce, strategically positioned beside me, is kneeling on the floor holding out the mug as if she's about to receive Holy Communion.

'Okay?' she asks.

'Okay,' I reply.

And off we go.

I had thought Joyce would be assuming the more junior position (Eric to my Ernie) but I actually think the roles were the other way round. In fact the whole thing reminded me quite a lot of my cow-milking days back on the farm, except with me as the cow.

'Well done,' says Joyce, as if I'd just broken the land-speed record.

'Oh, thanks,' I reply, pulling my pants back up with as much dignity as a shared loo cubicle allows.

'That's the hard part done. Now for the fun bit.' She passes me the mug and starts getting the pipette out of the clear-plastic box.

'It's just like being back in the lab at school,' she adds.

(Not a good advertisement for the Canadian education system.)

She gently lowers the pipette into the mug, gives it a good pump, then takes it out and waves it around between us.

A golden rod of glistening hormones.

'Have we finished with the mug?' I ask, trying to pretend it doesn't exist.

'Yeah, it's test tube time,' replies Joyce, busying herself with the box. 'Give your hands a quick rinse if you want.'

I open the cubicle door, pop the mug on a shelf, quickly wash my hands then dive back into the cubicle to see what magic awaits.

'What happens next, then?' I ask, rejoining Joyce in the cubicle.

'We wait and see.' She's already decanted my pee from the pipette into the test tube and is giving the tube and its contents a little swill round. 'If nothing appears after a couple of hours, it's negative.' She stops swilling. 'And if there's a little red ring at the bottom of the tube, well . . .'

Well . . .

My whole uncertain future summed up in one hazy, hollow word.

Joyce reaches out and holds my arm.

'Hey, you'll be okay.'

'Yes, I'll be fine.'

'Yeah. Absolutely fine. Of course. Yeah.'

Suddenly the big heavy door to the ladies' bathroom swings open, its creaks accompanied by some rasping heavily disguised as singing.

There'll be bluebirds over

The white cliffs of Dover

Tomorrow, just you wait and see-ee-ee-ee.

I quickly pull the cubicle door shut and we both freeze.

'Sssh,' I whisper to Joyce. 'It's Mrs Glazebrook, the cleaning lady.'

I know it's Mrs Glazebrook (hairnet, cockney, unreliable dentures) not only because of her distinctive singing voice (Vera Lynn by way of Les Dawson) but also because the singing is accompanied by an overwhelming smell of Rothmans. The singing continues for a bit and then stops so that all we hear is the clatter of a cleaning basket on the basins followed by the occasional knock of an Ajax tin and some perfunctory surface wiping. Not long after there's the sharp *tszzzz* of a cigarette being put out, more singing, a fair bit of clanking and – finally – the sound of the bathroom door opening and closing.

12

'Oh, thank God she's gone,' says Joyce. 'With singing like that, I'm amazed you guys got through the Blitz.'

I smile and take the test tube from her, then give it a little swirl and have a look at the bottom.

'What do you think?' I ask.

'You won't see anything yet, remember? We need to wait a couple of hours.'

I let out a sigh as long as a Tube train.

'Look, you get going and I'll take care of this,' says Joyce, taking the test tube.

'Yes, I'd better get back to the studio,' I reply. 'The last thing I need today is Pamela on the warpath.'

And I unlock the cubicle door, ready to embrace my future.

Whatever it is.

My future, it turns out, is waiting for me just round the corner.

Not a metaphorical corner but a real, parqueted-and-heavily-glossed BBC corner on the way back to the studio. As I turn it, several surprising things hit me all at once.

There's Pamela, smiling grandly, surrounded by various important-looking BBC men.

There's Mrs Glazebrook, smiling not-so-grandly (obviously struggling with her dentures), cleaning basket in one hand, my Hornsea Pottery mug in the other.

And there's Princess Anne, smiling prematurely, looking very modern in a pair of sky-blue trousers (Evie 1: Pamela 0).

Mrs Glazebrook is mid-curtsey. As she goes down, an arm goes up. It's the arm that's attached to the hand that's attached to . . .

Time slows to a dribble.

Princess Anne reaches out, thanking Mrs Glazebrook. She takes the mug with both hands – still smiling – and then regally, sedately, lifts it to her mouth, her hair piled high, her eyes alight and her mouth momentarily lost in a swirl of Hornsea Pottery green and brown.

CHAPTER 2

Summer 1972

'Sacked?'

That's Caroline, a magnificent Amazonian goddess in an emerald-green silk jumpsuit. It's hard to take her seriously, though, because her face is slathered in cold cream and her beautiful red hair is full of Carmen rollers the size of soup tins.

'Vicious old cow,' she goes on, taking a big draw of her Gauloise. 'I've always said you can never trust a knee-length skirt, darling.'

Caroline is my best friend. With her I have all the benefits of an older sister (clothes borrowing, advice acquiring, eyes opening) but without any of the drawbacks (bragging, ragging, nagging). She's the daughter of my father's old neighbour, Mrs Scott-Pym (the grandmother-I-never-had and a good friend to my long-dead mother), and I love her very much indeed. In fact Caroline is the reason I'm in London. She drove me down here in an open-top MG on a sunny, snowy January day in 1963, coddled in blankets and clutching a Thermos flask of hot tea.

She's the one who got me my apprenticeship at the BBC. And took me to the Albert Hall to see The Beatles. And bought me my first miniskirt and showed me how to apply mascara. In fact, Caroline has been responsible for introducing me to many things over the last ten years.

And what an amazing ten years it's been.

I've seen Beatles strolling, two Stones rolling, Coward Noeling, Quant-tights holing; great trains robbed, long hair bobbed, pop stars mobbed (hormones throbbed); white heat, dancing feet, plastic seats, groovy streets. I've watched a World Cup win, been to West Berlin, had a fridge built-in, dyed a coat (sheepskin), made a dress (sequin), met a Redgrave (Lynn). Motorways, a trim-phone craze, All You Need is *La Marseillaise.* Yellow Submarine, *Harpers & Queen,* no more scouring thanks to polytetrafluoro-ethylene. Flower power, *Woman's Hour,* revolving dates in the GPO Tower. Paris precarious, vexatious boyfriends (various), the age of Aquarius. Vidal Sassoon, tripped-out cartoon, women on a wage strike and a man on the moon. Power cuts, decimal nuts, shag haircuts.

Colour TV.

The Ford Capri.

Trousered princesses taking mugs and drinking pee . . .

'What? She drank your pee?'

'Well, yes,' I say, feeling very sorry for myself. 'It's not my fault. The cleaner picked my mug up from the bathroom and was taking it back to the studio. I had no idea.'

We're sat in Caroline's kitchen. She's getting ready to go out (hence the cold cream and Carmen rollers). She's meant to be consoling me about losing my job but she's far more interested in Princess Anne and my Hornsea Pottery mug.

'But what on earth was your pee doing in a mug, darling? Honestly, I can't keep up with the BBC sometimes.'

'Ah, that's my other news of the day,' I say, feeling like Kenneth Kendall. 'It was for a pregnancy test kit.'

'A what?'

'You pee in it and it tells you if you're pregnant or not.'

'Really! Like a Breathalyser?'

'Well, sort of.'

'Incredible, darling,' she says, taking another drag of her cigarette. 'They'll have us whizzing around in flying cars next.'

'Yeah, or rocket pogo sticks. Anyway, the test came out negative. I'm not pregnant.'

'Oh, thank God,' she replies, lifting a Gauloised hand to her forehead. 'That's such a relief.'

Is it?

'The little Swedish chap was very sweet,' she goes on, 'but he wasn't for you.'

She's right. Anders is sweet. And handsome. And has extremely nice teeth. But, if I'm honest, I got a bit bored of him even before he went back to Sweden.

'So you had to pee in a mug, then, for this newfangled pregnancy test?'

'Well, not exactly,' I reply. I'd hoped to avoid all the gory details but it's no good with Caroline. She always wants to know every little thing (the gorier, the better). So I just tell her, trying to make it all sound as scientific as possible, which isn't easy given Mrs Glazebrook, my poor aim and the Hornsea Pottery mug.

'Darling!' she laughs, throwing her head back (the Carmen rollers wobble). 'It could only happen to you! I do wish you'd be more assiduous in your pill popping, though.' She gives me a big-sisterly look. 'Anyway,' she goes on, getting up and walking over to a kitchen cupboard, 'after a story like that I think we both need a drink.'

I love Caroline's kitchen. It's a very stylish buffet of orange plastic and highly polished rosewood. Everything's fitted and there are clever hidden things all over the place that pull out, pop out or swivel out. The kitchen is German (amazing) and I can't help thinking that if the Germans had been as good at building V2 rockets as they are at building kitchens, we'd probably have lost the war.

Her whole house, in fact, is fantastic. It was built last year and is a very modern mix of exposed grey bricks, big metal windows and slat-less stairs. It's at the end of a picturesque Victorian mews, so it's like walking through a BBC costume drama and suddenly finding yourself smack-bang outside the Trellick Tower.

'Here you go,' she says, landing a huge brandy glass in front of me.

I sit for a moment, swilling the syrupy burnt-gold liquid around, watching it swell up and down the deep curves of the glass.

Caroline sits opposite me, finishing her Gauloise. She has one last drag and then casually puffs out a smoke ring. 'Well, look,' she says, stubbing the cigarette out on a stray saucer, 'I think it's actually very good news that you lost your job.'

'Thanks,' I say, taking a big swig of brandy.

'No, I mean it. You've become quite institutionalised.'

Caroline is brilliant in many ways but she has the tact of a dumper truck.

Unfortunately, though, she's right.

'Well, maybe I have been feeling a little stuck-in-a-rut-ish over the past year or so,' I say, my eyes locked on the brandy. 'But I didn't want this to happen. This morning I had a career. A BBC travel pass. Luncheon vouchers. And now look at me. Jobless.'

She reaches over the table and takes my hand.

'Hey, come on, darling. Where's your pep? Where's your Yorkshire grit? It's 1972. A clever young woman like you can do just about anything.'

'Anything?'

'Yes, anything.' She gives my hand a little squeeze. 'It's your chance to try something new.'

'Oh, I like the sound of that ... *Something new*,' I repeat, rolling the words around in my mouth, tasting their potential. 'Like what?'

'You name it. The world's your oyster!'

'Oh, I don't know. I think I'm too old to do anything new. I'm twenty-six.'

Caroline lets go of my hand. 'Nonsense,' she snaps, jolting backwards (the Carmen rollers jiggle again ominously). 'And if *you're* too old for something new, what does that make me? I'm thirty-six, darling. Hardly a pensioner.'

'It's different for you, though. You're always doing new, exciting things. You'd never get stuck in a rut.'

(Caroline works in fashion. I've known her for ten years but I still don't really have any idea what she does. She seems to flit around from one glamorous job to another but it's all very vague.)

'Darling, I'd never be seen *anywhere near* a rut, let alone get stuck in one. And I don't think you should, either.'

'But what could I do, though? I only really know about radio production and the odd bit of sound engineering.'

'Exactly,' she says, although I'm not really sure in reply to what. 'Something will come along. It always does.'

(This is true for Caroline – she's like a cat, always landing on her feet. The problem is I'm more dog than cat – and dogs tend to land in a big mess.)

She smiles her Hollywood smile, filling the room with infinite possibility. 'Look, if you could choose anything, *absolutely* anything, what do you think you'd like to do?'

That's a very good question. I wish I had a very good answer. Over the years, I've fancied doing lots of things (opening a bistro, winning a Nobel prize, presenting *Top of the Pops*) but now that I'm actually in a position to *try* doing something new, my mind is completely blank.

'I don't know ... it all seems so sudden. What could I do?'

'You're in London, darling. You can do anything.'

I look at her. Caroline definitely *could* do anything. But me?

'What a mess,' I say. 'I'm twenty-six with no job, no prospect of a job and no idea what kind of a job I actually want.' I have another swill of brandy. 'I don't even have a boyfriend.'

'Hey, come on,' says Caroline, reaching out and holding my hand again. 'London's full of boyfriends, darling. No need to worry about that.'

I sigh, a big, despondent, clock-is-ticking sigh.

'But I *do* worry. All the nice ones are getting married off. They're dropping like flies. I'm very close to being over the hill.'

Caroline gives me an unimpressed look (possibly for my lazy use of cliché).

'Everyone's married by the time they get to twenty-six,' I say. 'John married Cynthia when he was twenty-one . . .'

'Married twice, darling,' Caroline interrupts (unhelpfully).

'George married Pattie when he was twenty-two,' I go on. 'Ringo married Maureen when he was twenty-five. And even Paul had married Linda by the time he was twenty-six. And he's the sensible one. I'm going to end up an old spinster and live on my own for ever.'

She smiles and gives my hand another squeeze.

'You're not too old at all, darling. Just feeling a little sorry for yourself, that's all.'

I open my mouth to say something but she puts her finger to her lips and shushes me.

'Look, it's been a bad day. A very bad day, you might think. But you know what follows bad days, don't you? Good days. You're going to be okay.' She lifts up my hand and gives it a big, loving, cold-creamy kiss. 'Now, I know exactly what you need,' she says, standing up and walking over to the open-slat stairs. 'A little something to cheer you up. I have just the thing. I'll be right back.' And she slinks off, a cat with an abundance of cream.

I sit and stare at my brandy again, trying to digest the drama of the last few hours.

Jobs lost: 1
Lovely colleagues lost: 12
Horrible colleagues lost: 1 (Pamela)
Princesses caught drinking mugs of my pee: 1
Chances of ever getting an OBE: 0
Careers in tatters: 1
Pregnancies: 0

I don't know how I feel about the pregnancy test. I mean, I can hardly look after myself, let alone anyone else (especially some-one with nappy needs). But I must admit, just for a minute or two, while I was holding the mug of pee, I did begin to think that perhaps – possibly – it might not be such a bad thing. It might even, conceivably, be, well . . . I don't know, quite nice.

Maybe.

'Here you are, darling,' says Caroline, coming back into the kitchen. 'Something from an old girl to a young girl. Well, young-ish,' she adds, winking.

She passes me a battered Schofields bag (Harrods of the north).

'What is it?' I ask, taking the bag.

'It's something of Mummy's. I brought it down at the weekend. It was lying around up there and I wondered if you might like it?'

Mrs Scott-Pym, Caroline's mum, died almost three months ago now.

It happened very suddenly. One Saturday morning Caroline

had a phone call from her saying not to worry but she'd gone back to bed, feeling fatigued and slightly feverish. We drove straight up, of course, finding her lying on top of the eiderdown, staring out through the window, her translucent skin stretched taut across her cheekbones and her eyes, usually so bright, dimmed and cloudy. There was lots of hugging and kissing and then Caroline went downstairs to call the doctor. While she was gone, Mrs Scott-Pym reached out and we sat there, hand in bony hand, time moving slowly around us like mist on a moor. When Caroline came back upstairs, she said she'd be okay on her own so I left, going next door to see Dad and Élise (his lovely French lady friend). And then, just like that, Mrs Scott-Pym was dead. She fell asleep in Caroline's arms, their hearts singing and their cheeks wet with love.

I open the bag and see a plump, neatly folded bundle of beige.

'It's Mummy's old mac,' says Caroline. 'She'd had it years. It's probably as old as the two of us put together.'

I take it out. Its soft beige expanse is flecked with tiny pulls and splotches, marks of a life well lived.

'I just thought you might like it,' she goes on. 'It's far too nice to throw away. It's an old classic, just like Mummy.'

'Oh, thank you, but are you sure you don't want it?'

'Darling, I've spent the last couple of months sorting out the house and all Mummy's things. It's like the V&A up there. It never ends. There are more things than I know what to do with.' She smiles. 'I'm sure Mummy would love you to have it.'

(Caroline has already given me quite a few things of Mrs

Scott-Pym's. I've got her caramel-coloured mixing bowl – with all its memories of cake making, wooden spoons and buttercream – and the beautiful art deco silver hair grip she used to pin her hair away from her face. I've got the sleek wooden tray she filled with tea and cake (and sherry) and a small watercolour of Sadie, Mrs Scott-Pym's lovely dog, who died four years before she did. And I've got *A Book of Yorkshire Magic*, a very special book that Mrs Scott-Pym used to do some wonderful, extraordinary things.)

'I'd love it,' I say, holding out the mac and appreciating its Mrs Scott-Pym-ness. 'I can remember her wearing it when she was out on her walks with Sadie. And when she was doing the garden, too, whenever it was a bit chilly.'

'Yes, that sounds just like Mummy.' Caroline stares back through time. 'Who needs the BBC when you've got Rosamund Scott-Pym's old mac, eh? It's a very good swap if you ask me.'

'Definitely. Here's to Mrs Scott-Pym.' I hold out my brandy glass and toast my grandmotherly, cake-bakerly, magic-makery wonderful old neighbour. Caroline joins in, holding her brandy glass high.

'You see, darling, it's karma. You lose some, you win some. You're much better off without Pamela – you need to move on. *Courage, mon amie*,' she says, going all Joan of Arc (not easy with the rollers and a face full of cold cream).

'Exactly. And you're right – I'm still young enough to start another career, aren't I? Something exciting. Something new. Anyway, nobody's ever done anything by the time they're twenty-six, have they?'

Caroline runs her hands along the legs of her jumpsuit.

'Well, Mozart had done a few operas, I suppose. And I believe Shakespeare had written *The Two Gentlemen of Verona*.'

'Thanks. That's very helpful.'

'And of course Julie Christie had won an Oscar, darling.'

She knocks back her brandy and then thumps down her empty glass.

'Right, now, I'm very sorry but I'm going to have to get on with my beautifying. We've got this thing at the Courtauld tonight and I can't let the side down. Do you want to stay here and have another drink while I'm upstairs? Digby should be back soon.'

'Thanks,' I say, 'but I'd better get going. I've got my new life to plan!'

'You certainly have, darling.'

And she kisses me on the cheek, covering me with cold cream, gives my hand a final quick squeeze then glides off upstairs, a *grandeur* of emerald-green silk.

As I walk home through the tree-lined streets of west London, I feel pretty chipper. Caroline's right. Who needs the BBC? It's time for a new challenge.

A new Evie.

It's now or never. I'm twenty-seven next birthday, which is practically thirty, which might as well be forty – and forty means middle age, sensible shoes and dormer-bungalows, so I need to be quick. It's my last chance to be the woman I want to be. I can use it to do anything. Everything.

Out on the streets, I pass the familiar sights of London. Old ladies with tweeds and pink rinses. Young men with collars the size of model aeroplanes. Victorian postboxes. Ash-coloured dog poo. Grubby orange flashes of discarded cigarettes. The odd empty crisp packet gently blowing along the pavement.

London.

My dynamo, my spark plug, my home.

I skim over the pavement, long, rhythmic strides. As I walk I give my Schofields bag and its precious contents a good swing. Up in Yorkshire, everyone recognises a Schofields bag, but down here in London no one has any idea what it is. It's a foreign object, something alien, a bold northern invader.

Just like me.

Interlude – Winter 1971, Yorkshire

Rosamund Scott-Pym straightened her back, wincing.

It was there again. That pain. She rubbed at it with her non-trowel hand, feeling the soft folds of her old mackintosh under her fingers. The pain crunched down her spine. She strained back her head, sucking in a sharp blast of cold air through her teeth.

She was old, there was no ignoring it. Well beyond her three score years and ten. Aches and pains were to be expected. Part of life, that's all they were, like grey hair and capricious teeth.

She had a quick wriggle. She was kneeling on the ancient brown towel she kept for gardening. Beside her, a pile of spring bulbs waited to be planted. She loved spring; it always came with such a beautiful rush of colours and smells, just a few drops at first but then a great downpour, drenching the garden.

Spring would ease her back, too. The warm, dry air. The spirit-lifting blue sky.

She smiled, pulling her mac tightly round her and thinking of the promise of springtime. Lunchtime naps outside. Visits from the girls. Long, happy suppers on the terrace with Evie entertaining them with tales of her latest unsuitable man.

And then her back stabbed again, nasty rips of pain that tore straight through her. She squeezed her eyelids tight closed and waited for it to pass.

CHAPTER 3

Summer 1972

The kettle boils. The toaster pops. And Tony Blackburn gets extremely excited about a Motown medley and a three-mile tail-back on the A21 Sevenoaks Bypass.

It's nine o'clock in the morning, my first non-BBC weekday morning for almost ten years, barring holidays and ailments. I'm making the most of this by supplementing my usual breakfast (two rounds of toast and a pot of tea) with a strawberry Ski yoghurt, some Rise & Shine, and a Wagon Wheel.

It's very disconcerting suddenly not to have a job. I've worked pretty much since I left school and the BBC is all I know. Junior apprentice, apprentice, junior assistant, assistant, and finally the dizzy heights of junior assistant producer. Obviously, there were days when I would have given anything not to be at Broadcasting House (mainly down to Pamela) but on the whole I really enjoyed my time there.

And now it's all gone. For ever. Finito. Kaput. There's no going back, as Pamela made very clear when she marched me (oxymoronically) out the revolving doors.

Thoughts of what I should do with the rest of my life have been going round and round my head all night. A million whirling cogs, each one toothless and spinning pointlessly. I always think better when food's around, though, so here I am, sat at my kitchen table having an extra-large breakfast and making a plan. Or at least thinking about making a plan.

I've spread a selection of magazines out across the table, like a very easy jigsaw. I'm hoping to get some much-needed inspiration on the job front from the magazines, with their winning combination of articles, fashion shoots and endless adverts. Outside it's a glorious sunny day and when the sun streams in it shimmers across the glossy front covers.

A perfect day to start my new life.

The cover models stare up at me, each one managing to look sultry, happy and successful all at the same time (how do they do that?). I'm not sure which one to pick first, so I decide to go for a cover girl who looks like she's au fait with a commute and a work canteen.

This isn't easy.

Nova's June is wearing a sexy negligee (silky), as is *Cosmopolitan*'s July (lacy). The July *Nova* is even worse: completely naked but covering up her bits with her hands. July's *Harpers & Queen* is also naked except for lots of gold jewellery and a cat. The *Vogues* are very difficult to assess because they're nearly all close-ups of someone's face; all I can really make out are Apollonia van Ravenstein in a mass of feathers (May) and a serious-looking lady in pearls (July). June's *Cosmopolitan*, meanwhile, featuring a couple throwing back their heads laughing, looks like a scene from a below-par *Play for Today*.

The only two covers that look vaguely *Evie-gets-a-job*-ish are July's *Honey* (navy, businesslike dress with a large red tie and matching belt) and June's *Harpers & Queen* (floaty green wraparound plus yellow bangles and a nice tan briefcase).

I have a slurp of tea and pick up June's floaty green wraparound. The first few pages aren't very helpful, unless I want to be an estate agent, bag designer or make perfume (which I don't). I quickly flick past various social diary things and a feature on dry shampoo and then get to a few pages on 'How to Become London's Most Eligible Bachelor' (money and nice teeth, apparently). This is followed by a full-page advert for Barbra Streisand's new film. Two things in the advert temporarily distract me from thoughts of a job:

1. Barbra's lovely oversized tweed cap
2. Ryan O'Neal and his perfect hair

Perhaps I could work in the film industry? Then I'd get to rub shoulders with big Hollywood stars like Barbra and Ryan or at least British acting royalty like Larry Olivier or Twiggy. I could do something in sound. My BBC training would certainly help out: engineering, mixing, editing – I can do it all. But then I remember what Caroline said yesterday about the world being my oyster. About this being my chance to try something new. Something completely different.

I take a deep breath and press on.

There are more adverts then an article on Gerald Durrell and kangaroos. This brings to mind two jobs, both of which I think I'd be good at on account of my experience:

1. Writer (re. Gerald Durrell) – I'm always reading, which is basically writing for people who don't have much time on their hands
2. Vet (re. kangaroos) – I was brought up living with a herd of cows, which means I know my way round an udder clamp and rectal thermometer

I lean back on my chair, balancing precariously on the two back legs, and rummage through my 'everything but cutlery' drawer for a notepad and pen. I pull out a pad and a biro and turn to a clean page. At the top of the page I write 'JOBS?' and then start a list (which immediately makes me feel better).

1. Writer
2. Vet

Back in the magazine, there are a few pages about new restaurants (I add chef to my list then immediately cross it off) then more adverts ('French Line Cruises – Let 1000 Frenchmen* Show You The Best Way To New York'). There's a feature called 'Are You In Your Husband's Will?' (I add lawyer), followed by a ten-page Riviera travel special (ditto air hostess).

I pause for another slurp of tea and toast. Normally at this

Name: Hugo Archambeau

From: France

Job: banking

Seen for: one and a half weekends

Appearance: George Best with a Gallic twist

Amazing: lovely shoes, excellent wooing, accent as smooth as a Cadbury's Caramel

Less amazing: nasal hair, pompous, wouldn't countenance a Scotch egg

time, I'd be in the *Woman's Hour* studio, setting everything up for the day's show and trying to keep out of Pamela's way. Perhaps I'd be working on an interview or doing something tricksy with a tone oscillator. And now here I am. Sat at my kitchen table, eating toast and staring out over rooftops, pensive, uncertain, alone, contemplating something new. Something different.

I temporarily lose myself in daydreams (jobs, jumpsuits, Paul McCartney) until a swirling Tony Blackburn jingle brings me back to the kitchen. I have a couple of bites of toast then return my focus to the magazine. By the time I get to the final page (Next Issue: Beautiful lips, Epidurals, Scotland), I have compiled an impressive list of non-stuck-in-the-rutty jobs.

1. Writer
2. Vet

3. ~~Chef~~
4. Lawyer
5. Air hostess
6. Something arty (but not opera)
7. Nanny
8. Shop assistant
9. Legs model

This is quite exciting. I feel like I'm about to pick a ticket out of a huge tombola barrel. In my mind's eye, I see all the tickets fluttering, each one ripe with potential. Too many tickets, in fact. How do I know which one I should pick? What if I choose the wrong one? Having the world as your oyster is all well and good but it doesn't half make your head spin.

I sit back and have another sip of Rise & Shine. Outside, there's the music of London. Cars humming. Voices shouting. The occasional deep rumble of a passing delivery truck. When I first arrived here, the noise was oppressive. Always present. Buzzing. Scratching. But now it relaxes me, a great urban purr.

I begin to doodle (something involving curls and lots of shading) when suddenly there's the exuberant blast of a car horn on the street outside followed by a loud shout.

'Evie!'

It's Caroline. (As if it could be anyone else.)

'Evie, darling!' she shouts again, her deep gravelly voice punctuated by more car horn.

By now I'm at the kitchen window, sticking my head out of the open sash.

Caroline is sat in her lovely car, an Alfa Romeo Spider. It's dark orange (*amber, darling*) with a roof that is almost permanently folded back. Next to Caroline is Digby, Caroline's partner. Not partner as in Mr Marks and Mr Spencer but partner as in they've lived together ever since meeting in a Neapolitan bar in 1954. She's amazing. She works at the Arts Council and does something Very Complicated involving grants. Or buildings. Or actors.

'Oh, there you are,' Caroline shouts as soon as my head pops out the window.

Digby waves (an enthusiastic blur of navy).

'Come down,' Caroline goes on (a swirl of mint and fuchsia). 'We've got something for you.'

'Okay! Coming!' And I dash out the kitchen onto the landing then rattle down my whitewashed stairs.

(My flat sits above a small haberdasher's shop. The flat is only small but, because it's on a corner, it's got plenty of windows, making it feel light and airy rather than tight and cramped (which it is). My front door is down on the street but the rest of the flat is up on the first and second floors: on the first floor is a landing, the living room and a kitchen; and then up again to my bedroom, the bathroom plus a very small box room. Dad's favourite joke, the one he says every time he visits, is that I live in a two-up, two up again. I own the flat, bought with the proceeds of selling the farm back to Dad and Élise after my mum left it to me. A gift from beyond the grave.)

Caroline's car is parked straight outside my door, one front wheel mounted on the pavement and the rest of the car jutting out into the road at a very cavalier angle.

'Morning,' I say, walking up to the passenger door.

'Morning, dear,' replies Digby, her voice thick with Rs.

(Digby is Scottish and her accent – an Edinburgh burr – is the linguistic equivalent of being wrapped in a lovely soft blanket.)

'How are you doing, darling?' asks Caroline, sliding her giant sunglasses up onto her magnificent red hair. 'Everything okay?'

'It's a bit strange,' I reply. 'Not going to work, I mean. I'm not used to it.'

Digby grins. 'That's your protestant work ethic kicking in. You should try being Scottish!'

'Oi!' says Caroline, giving Digby's thigh a playful tap. 'We know a thing or two about hard graft up in Yorkshire, you know. You Scots don't have a monopoly on it!'

'Och, sorry,' says Digby, doing her best comedy Scottish accent and giving me a big wink. Then she turns to look at Caroline, eye locked on eye, and both their faces bloom into huge, glorious smiles. It's always lovely seeing them together. They are the happiest, funniest and most ridiculously romantic couple I know. Like Romeo and Juliet but with ruder jokes and less death.

'Anyway,' Caroline goes on. 'It's actually about work that we're here. You know how you were saying yesterday about you being a bit stuck-in-the-rutty?'

'Well I'm not sure I actually said that,' I reply. 'Not really.'

'Yes, you did, darling. And quite right you were too.' She flicks her glasses off her hair and points them at me. 'I was thinking about it last night. You need to branch out.'

'Spread your wings,' says Digby, leaning over the car door and making little flappy motions with her hands.

'Exactly,' says Caroline. 'So, I hope you don't mind but I've spoken to a friend who helps out in a sweet little art gallery in Mayfair. Nothing fancy. She says you can pop along for a few days and give it a go. I thought it'd be a nice way to try out something new.'

'Less rutty,' adds Digby, winking again.

'Oh!' I say, already imagining myself running the National Gallery. 'That sounds great. Thank you.'

'Excellent, here's the address,' says Caroline, reaching past Digby and handing me a small piece of card. 'You'll love Delphinia. I've told her all about you.'

(Nearly all of Caroline's friends have horticultural names – Poppy, Daisy, Flora, Blossom. When they're all together, it's like being at a very posh garden centre.)

The card is solid and consequential. I look at the address: The Apollo Gallery, 28 Dover Street, London W1.

'But I don't know anything about art,' I say, intimidated by the top-class stationery and starting to feel out of my depth.

Digby reaches out of the car and takes my hand. 'Evie, dear, when has not really knowing anything about art ever disqualified anyone from working in a gallery?'

'Yes, I wouldn't worry about it at all,' chips in Caroline. 'You'll be running the place in a few days. By the way, I told Delphinia you'd be there tomorrow.'

'Tomorrow?!'

'Well, I didn't want you moping around. It's not healthy, darling.'

Digby smiles. 'You'll enjoy it, Evie. A wee young thing like

37

you should be out living life. Who knows where the gallery might take you? And even if it takes you nowhere, you should make sure you have a fun time getting there.'

'Hear! Hear!' says Caroline, throwing an arm around Digby and kissing her on the top of her head (Caroline is much taller than Digby. She's much taller than most people in fact and is a well-practised top-of-head kisser). 'The wise old woman of the north has spoken.'

'Less of the old,' says Digby.

'Well, Evie was telling me yesterday that she's already practically a pensioner at twenty-six so you, darling, in your forties must be positively ancient.'

'Is that so?' Digby looks at me, her eyes twinkling.

'Yes, she was telling me about how she's becoming a tragic old maid,' Caroline goes on. 'Like a character in a Jane Austen novel.'

'I just meant that everyone seems to be getting married,' I say. 'That's all. We did a feature on modern marriage on *Woman's Hour* a few weeks ago. Did you know that the average age to get married last year was twenty-five? And I'm twenty-six and a half.'

'Well, who's bothered about average *anything*, darling?' Caroline positions her sunglasses back down onto her nose. 'Now, look, we need to get going. We're heading up to Mummy's.'

'Good old Rosamund certainly knew how to stuff a house,' laughs Digby.

'She was always such a hoarder,' says Caroline, smiling

a big, beautiful smile, before flicking her hand and starting the engine.

A cool, sweet hum fills the street.

'Oh, and by the way, darling,' she shouts, reversing back onto the road. 'Remember to wear something smart tomorrow. A *Revolver* T-shirt and a pair of borrowed boxers might be okay for Notting Hill Gate but they're definitely not for Mayfair.'

And with that, they're off. A great forward charge of wave and horn.

Back in my flat, I put the milk bottle I'd picked up from outside in the fridge and stick the kettle on. While I wait for the water to boil I pick up my job list from the kitchen table. There, sparkling like a set of Christmas lights, is

6. Something arty (but not opera)

Well, you can't really get anything much artier than working in an art gallery can you? I'm obviously meant to leave the sound monitors and headphone amps behind me and start a new life full of glamorous opening nights and penniless but handsome artists.

It's all very exciting.

Interlude – Autumn 1949, Edinburgh

Catherine MacLeod looked out onto the dark elegant curves of the New Town.

The proposal had thrown her.

She hardly knew Muir. She'd met him, what, less than a dozen times? And most of those had been in company. Friends. Family. Other doctors.

She took a sip of tea.

Of course he was a doctor; wasn't everyone in Edinburgh? Trained at the Royal Infirmary, like her father. Her father had loved that. All those endless shared stories of Lauriston Place, all the characters and in-jokes. And Muir came from a good family too, her father pointed out. An old family.

Weren't all families old, thought Catherine, watching a car saunter by. She was sat by a window at the top of the house; beneath her, floor after floor stretched down, grand and self assured. The house creaked with propriety. A place for everything and everything in its place, said her father. It was something she could imagine Muir saying, head up and chin out.

Was he handsome, she asked herself, this man she hardly

knew, this man who had asked her to marry him? Well, no, not really. His face was thin and nondescript and he had a rather insipid nose. At least he had nice eyes, she thought, blue-grey eyes that caught the flinty light of the city. And his voice? Well, it was not exactly kind but not exactly unkind either.

He'd taken her by surprise, going down on one knee like that in the drawing room. That was the emotion that came to her now, mulling over the events of the last twenty-four hours. Surprise. Not joy. And definitely not love. Just a wry, detached surprise.

She'd asked for a day before she gave him her answer. He'd looked disappointed but she'd couched it all in the language of etiquette and good breeding. Time to reflect. To talk to her parents. Talk to her father.

Her father, of course, had said that she'd been a fool not to accept on the spot. Muir was an excellent prospect and she should count herself lucky. They would be secure, comfortable. Respected. And happy, too, of course, just like her parents.

Her mother agreed, smiling, with her thin lips and dull eyes. Beaten down by life. *Your father thinks he's a good match, dear*, she'd murmured. Is that what marriage is, thought Catherine? A daily subtraction that leaves you mousy and unsure.

She finished off her tea. She was getting old, she knew that. Twenty-one. An age meant for marriage. And marriage would mean a new home and, God willing, a family of her own. Muir's job would keep him busy and out from under her feet. She would meet other young brides, other new mothers. There'd be coffee mornings, the WI and charity work. And nurseries, too, and – later – schools.

She looked out from the window again, watching the smoke curl free of the chimney pots.

She was going to have to marry someone, she was well aware of that, and so, yes, she supposed it might as well be Muir.

Chapter 4

Summer 1972

It's eight-twenty in the morning and I'm in the middle of a full-blown wardrobe crisis. Virtually all my clothes are out on the bed, tossed and tumbled into a huge mound so that the bed looks like it's about to give birth to twins: Carnaby Street and the King's Road. All I can think about is what Caroline said before she drove off yesterday: *remember to wear something smart tomorrow* – without doubt the least helpful phrase known to mankind (or, indeed, womankind). For the past hour I've been trying out as many types of *something smart* as I can think of:

1. City *smart* (high-waisted trouser with blazer)
2. Wedding *smart* (flowery shirtdress plus hat the size of a bicycle wheel)
3. Meal-out *smart* (something navy and acrylic, the best combination for spills)
4. Trendy-party *smart* (striped blouse and wide pleated trousers)

5. BBC *smart* (anything not involving a cardigan)
6. Glamourpuss *smart* (hot pants and thigh boots)

Nothing, though, strikes me as being Mayfair art gallery *smart.* To be honest, my experience of galleries is not extensive; they are not really my natural habitat and whenever I do fancy a bit of art I tend to stick to the National Gallery (big horses), the Wallace Collection (chubby cherubs) or the Tate (excellent scones).

I'm going to have to get a move on because I don't want to be late on my first day. I finally decide to look Modern and wear trousers but then change my mind at the last minute and opt instead for a dress.

I rummage under the pile of clothes on my bed, pull out a sky-blue, striped wraparound dress (already tried on twice), huff my way into it (again) and look in the mirror. Someone *smart*-ish stares back at me. I try to titivate it up a bit by teaming it with my Biba strappy sandals but I'm still not sure I'm Mayfair enough. I walk over to my chest of drawers and pull open the top one. There, wrapped in tissue paper, is my mother's French silk scarf, the Rolls-Royce of accessories. Swirls of cavalry officers in different shades of blue and red all bordered by a looping golden chain. I bask in its many layers of beauty. A priceless relic of an age I never knew.

I tie the scarf round my neck (as Caroline and Élise taught me years ago) and look back in the mirror.

Perfect.

*

'Hello, you must be Evie, darling. You look gorgeous.'

That's Delphinia. She speaks like Caroline and looks like her too. She is tall and slim and has big bouncy hair (blonde, though, not red).

'Come through into the back and I'll get us a drink,' she says, sliding out from behind a mahogany desk and gesturing down the room.

I've just walked into the Apollo Gallery and am busy taking it all in. It seems very old and grand. There are dark wooden walls with lots of gold fittings, a dark wooden ceiling with elaborately carved coffers and a dark wooden floor covered with a huge burgundy rug. It's like walking into Liberty but without the chintz and handbags.

'I'm sorry we're such a stuffy old place,' she goes on, ushering me through the gallery. 'If it were up to me, I'd strip everything out and replace it with wall-to-wall pine and a nice rattan sofa. But Charlie won't have any of it. He's the owner,' she adds, opening a dark wooden door at the back of the gallery. 'Lovely but stuck in the last century.'

'Well, it's kind of what I expected,' I say, following her through the door. 'Art-gallery smart.'

We've walked into a small room that seems to be both kitchen and office. There's a sink in the corner with a small water heater gurgling away above it and, next to the sink, a draining board with a kettle and a few neatly stacked cups and saucers. Against one wall is a Formica table and across from it, on the other wall, are four large filing cabinets, each with a cardboard box on top, except for the last one, which instead is home to a catering-size Maxwell House, a large box of tea and a big red tin of Family Circle.

Delphinia wedges open the door with an old chamber pot.

'Rule number one. We always keep the door open when we're in here.' She taps the chamber pot with her foot. 'Just in case someone comes in the gallery.'

'Oh, and what's rule number two then?' I ask.

'No denim,' she replies, heading for the sink. 'It's a drag, I know, but, I told you, Charlie is practically Victorian. Tea or coffee?'

'Coffee please. Black, two sugars.'

Delphinia busies herself with cups and kettles. 'He set up the gallery years ago, before the war, and I don't think it's changed much since. Oh, that reminds me. He's a sweet old dear but he can get a bit handsy.' She passes me a china cup and saucer. 'Harmless enough, though. Anyway, come on, darling,' she says, sliding the chamber pot away from the door with her foot. 'We'd better get ready for the morning rush.'

The morning rush, it turns out, consists of one little old lady coming in and asking for directions to Green Park Tube.

It's not what I expected.

I'd geared myself up for a busy morning talking to clients about Art and Beauty and the benefits of a professional hanging. Instead, it's just been me and Delphinia, drinking coffee (four cups), comparing scarf-tying techniques (Delphinia favours the *at the end of a ponytail* method whereas I am firmly a *round the neck* kind of girl), having a quick look at the art on display (flowers, horses, ships) and chatting about a number of Very Important Things (decimalisation, the price of cinema tickets, Edward Heath's teeth).

'Is it always this quiet?' I ask Delphinia.

'Oh, yes, we can go for days without having anyone in. I always make sure I've got a good book with me. And once a week a sweet young thing comes and does my nails in the kitchen.'

(I glance down at Delphinia's nails, ten perfect little lozenges of russet red.)

'And on Fridays,' she goes on, 'I generally close early and meet friends for a drink in Flemings. It's just round the corner,' she adds, waving a beautifully polished finger over her shoulder.

'But aren't we meant to be doing something?'

'Well, there's not that much we *can* do without clients,' she says. She opens a drawer in the mahogany desk and pulls out a leather notebook. 'Every few months I'll send a quick note round to all of these' – she flicks through a few pages – 'inviting them to a new show or telling them about a special piece that's just come in. There are hundreds of them. Honestly, it takes for ever.' She puts the book back in the drawer and shakes her head.

'But what about when someone does come into the gallery?' I ask. 'What are we meant to do then?'

She leans back in her chair and sighs.

'What are we meant to do? That's a very good question.' She begins to tap her fingers on the desk. 'Well, I suppose it's all very simple really. Our job, Evie, is to make very *rich* men feel like very *clever* men for buying very *expensive* art. Et voilà!' She does one final dramatic finger tap. 'Now, what would you like to do about lunch?'

Lunch is an egg and cress bap (me) and a cottage cheese baguette (Delphinia). We have them in the kitchen/office with the chamber pot holding the door open just in case anyone comes into the gallery. But nobody does. I don't know how Delphinia does it. She must get through a lot of books.

After lunch we take up our positions in the gallery again, with Delphinia sitting behind the mahogany desk and me in front of it, nestled in a brown leather armchair. There's a lot of chit-chat (jumbo jets, Bill Oddie, knees) but the main thing we do is sit around and wait for someone to come in . . .

We sit . . .

. . . and sit . . .

... and sit ...

... and sit ...

... and sit ...

... and still no one comes.

But then, just as I'm giving up hope of ever seeing another human being again, an extremely suntanned man with jet-black hair comes in.

'*Ciao, bella!*'

'Fabio!' says Delphinia, standing up. 'How are you, darling?'

'Oh, don't ask.' The man gambols over to Delphinia, a crescendo of flared white trouser and white sailor shirt. He looks like Mitzi Gaynor in *South Pacific*.

'I have *huge* favour to ask,' he goes on with a blast of vowel and arm.

'A favour? Yes, of course,' replies Delphinia, sounding very chirpy. 'How can I help?'

'Well, it's the gallery. Could you be a *marvellous* angel and look after it for ten little minutes?' He puts his hands together like King Priam pleading with Achilles for the body of Hector. 'I have an assignation.'

Delphinia smiles. 'Darling, you know there's nothing I'd like to do more than help you with your little assignation but I'm afraid I can't leave the gallery. I'm expecting a very important client any minute now.'

(That's the first I've heard of it.)

'But Evie could nip over and keep shop for you,' she goes on. 'It would give her something exciting to do.'

'Evie?' says Fabio, giving my name all the brio of sludge.

Delphinia nods towards me.

Fabio stares at me. His lips purse together and one eye squints. I feel like I'm in the judging ring at Crufts.

'It'll give you a little change, Evie,' Delphinia goes on. 'It's just over the road. Such a lovely gallery.'

Fabio purrs.

'Very modern,' she adds. 'Not like us!'

'*Modernissimo*,' fizzes Fabio, doing something Italian with a hand.

'Oh, nice,' I say. 'Happy to help. It's all good experience, isn't it?'

Fabio smiles at Delphinia. '*Bellissima*. Thank you.'

'Oh, don't thank me,' says Delphinia. 'Thank Evie!'

He makes a short noise, half coo, half grunt, and then gestures towards the door.

'Shall we?'

I turn to Delphinia. 'Are you sure?'

'Yes, darling. Go and enjoy yourself. You'll be back in two ticks. Have fun!'

An hour and a half later and Fabio still hasn't returned from his assignation.

Delphinia was right when she said the gallery is very modern. It's about as different to the Apollo Gallery as you can get. The walls are pure white, as is the ceiling. Colour is provided by the floor, a gleam of orange lino. The art itself is very different too. Instead of lots of expensive-looking oil paintings in expensive-looking gilt frames, the walls of this gallery are covered in raw canvases, many adorned with real household objects (colander, spatula, ashtray), giving the space the feel of a Woolworths homeware department. The gallery's called

La Divinità, although I think Fabio might be in trouble with the Trades Description Act because my closest brush with anything divine has been the half-eaten packet of Revels I found in the little kitchen out the back.

I've been on my own ever since Fabio left. We've had no customers (or clients, as Delphinia would say) and I've had to draw on all the resources an only child can muster so as not to get bored. This has meant lots of daydreaming, some intricate scab-picking (elbow) and an occasional wave across the street to Delphinia.

(Mayfair galleries all seem to have big front windows housing just one piece of art in, meaning that it's fairly easy to see outside providing that you poke your head round, in Delphinia's case, a painting of a man on a horse or, for me, a sculpture made out of broken old bits of television.[*])

I'm currently perched on the desk at the back of the gallery. I've exhausted daydreaming and scab-picking and am looking for something else to keep me going until Fabio returns. Scattered across the desk in messy little clumps are various flyers and postcards. I absentmindedly pick up a few and flick through them. Most seem to be for exhibitions at other galleries ('The Monumental Strain of the Soul', 'Light II', 'Transcendental Dimensionality') and have the attention-holding power of a block of lard, but a couple do look interesting (an arthouse cinema, a new magazine) so I pop them in my bag.

I begin to straighten up all the flyers and postcards, making neat little piles of colour. The rest of the desk looks like it could

*

> Name: Justin Alba
>
> From: Australia
>
> Job: television cameraman
>
> Seen for: three weeks
>
> Appearance: hearty, hunky, hairy
>
> Amazing: lovely glasses, cheeky banter, Tim Tam biscuits
>
> Less amazing: poor timekeeping, questionable underwear, grubby bathroom grouting

do with a quick tidy too (anything to while away the time), so I pop a stray biro in an orange plastic pen-pot then line up the large stapler and ruler so they're nice and parallel. Next is a notebook (straighten), a small remnant of orange peel (discard) and a lone fruit Spangle (eat). My tidying then moves under the desk, where I find a few flyers and a broken pencil. I put the flyers on the appropriate pile, sharpen the pencil, and pop it in the orange pot.

And then I notice that some flowers standing in a big vase near the front window have dropped large messy petals onto the floor. I'm in full cleaning mode now so I go through to the back of the gallery, find a dustpan and brush and get to work. The flowers themselves have long dramatic stems, stretching halfway up the wall, and they're standing in a big vase in the shape of Churchill's head (or it could be one of the Homepride flour men, it's hard to tell). Quite a lot of the flowers have seen better days so I deadhead them and then do my best to spruce everything up with some creative stem rearranging.

When I'm done there's a satisfying amount of dead flower-age in the dustpan. I stand up, dustpan in one hand, brush in the other, and glance at the art on the wall. It's something very jolly and abstract involving various shades of orange and yellow with a couple of yellow plastic eggcups stuck on. I glance across at the label next to it in the hope of finding out what it's meant to be but all it says is, '*The Absence of Life is Death*, Mixed Media, 1972'. I suppose it must have something to do with eggs.

As I'm pondering Life and Art, Fabio finally skips back in the gallery. He's got a definite spring in his step and navigates the floor with the balletic swoosh of an Olympic figure skater.

'*Ciao*, Edith,' he flings. 'Sorry I've been a *teeny* bit long.'

'No problem,' I reply, worried that a few hours in the art world has turned me into an Edith. 'I kept myself busy.'

He makes a noise – half grunt, half Broadway musical.

'My assignation was much longer than expected,' he says, wiggling his eyebrows suggestively (two elastic bands stretched to snapping). Then he points to the dustpan and brush in my hands. 'What's this?'

'Oh, I've been doing a bit of tidying. I thought it'd help pass the time.'

'*Grazie*,' he coos, looking straight at me, as if noticing me for the first time. He tries a smile, sending little Italian sunbeams round the freshly dustpanned room.

The sunbeams don't last long.

'What's this? What have you done?' he asks, dark clouds gathering beneath the perma-tan.

'Just some cleaning. That's all.'

'Cleaning?'

'Yes, look,' I say, waving the dustpan full of dead flowers at him. 'All this was on the floor. It's looking much better now.'

'But . . . but . . . but . . .' he says, sounding like a starting Vespa. 'You've ruined it.'

'Ruined what?'

'The art!'

'What art?'

'*The Absence of Life is Death.* Look!'

He points at the dustpan full of dead flowers.

'It's vandalism.' He snatches the dustpan from me; a few dead petals fall back on the floor. 'Vandalism.'

'But I don't understand. It's just some dead flowers. That's *The Absence of Life is Death*,' I say, pointing at the yellow eggcups.

Fabio looks like he might explode. His eyes are bulging and I can see the blue veins in his heavily tanned forehead throbbing like an animated Stilton.

'That's *Sunrise Over Rome*,' he says, pointing at the eggcups. 'This,' he goes on, jabbing the dustpan at the vase and flowers, 'is *The Absence of Life is Death*.'

Oh.

'Get out!' he shouts, sending spittle everywhere.

'I'm really sorry,' I say, feeling terrible. 'I had no idea. I thought I was helping.'

'Get out, you stupid girl.' He throws the dustpan at me, covering me with *Absence* or *Life* or *Death*. 'Go on. Get out!'

I hesitate for a moment then grab my bag and run out the door, a battery of Italian artillery exploding all around me.

I go straight over to the Apollo Gallery, of course, where I burst into tears, prompting Delphinia to throw her arms around me, say something about a *vicious old queen*, and send me home with a spare hanky, some Bourbon creams, and a miniature brandy bottle she got from the top drawer of the mahogany desk.

And so here I am, mid-afternoon, lying on my bed thinking about what a complete failure I am.

I'm hopeless. In just a few days, I've managed to lose my job at the BBC, vandalise a piece of modern art and watch the fourth in line to the throne drink a mug of my pee.

Delphinia did her best to cheer me up (*we can just get some more flowers, darling*) and said she's looking forward to seeing me again tomorrow, somehow implying that it would be different from today. Better. But what if it isn't? What if tomorrow is just as bad as today? What if tomorrow is actually even worse? I lie on the bed, staring up at the ceiling and see my future life stretching out in front of me, a long succession of failures, day after blundering day.

I dab at my eyes with a hanky (my third of the day) and give my nose a good blow.

And then the rain starts. Just a few drops at first but then the heavens open and soon it's coming down like stair rods. It hits the window in bursts. Short rhythmic waves, like Moondust bouncing off your tongue.

I get up and walk over to the glass door that leads out onto my creaky metal fire escape. I stand there, leaning against the wall, watching the drops of rain chase down the pane, fast then slow, randomly stopping then skating off again, running, sliding, following each other's path until they coalesce.

At my feet is the Schofields bag. I sit on the floor and pull out Mrs Scott-Pym's old mac, lifting it to my face and breathing in its scent, a wonderful mix of grass and dogs and Arpège.

The rain spatters against the glass door and I watch the drops meander and race. I wrap myself into Mrs Scott-Pym's mac, calming, comforting, pulling the mac tight round my fingers, folding in on myself. Alone.

Or not quite alone.

I shiver, not because I'm cold but because of something else, something warm.

In the window, there's my faint reflection. A leaning head nestled on a beige expanse. And, joining the two, around my neck, is my mother's silk scarf. A tender touch from another age.

The Absence of Life is Death.

Is it? Is it really?

There *is* an absence; I feel it. But I also feel a presence. Something reaching out to me across gaberdine and silk and time.

Interlude – Winter 1971, Yorkshire

Rosamund Scott-Pym emptied the butter, flour and sugar into her large cream mixing bowl and began to rub them together gently. This wasn't the Christmas cake. That had been made a while ago, sitting now in the pantry and fed every few weeks with brandy. No, this was the shortbread. For Digby.

She added a pinch of salt to the bowl and carried on rubbing.

Digby had become her second daughter, well, her third, really, with Evie. Obviously, it had been strange at first – Rosamund came from another age – but it had all worked out in the end and she wouldn't change a thing. She enjoyed Digby's company enormously, her conversation and social ease. And her kindness too. Plus, of course, her common sense was just what Caroline needed.

As she rubbed, she watched the mixture steadily solidify in the bowl. Taking disparate things and bringing them all together. Like Evie, she thought, smiling.

Evie was a great cake maker. Or rather, Rosamund corrected herself, a great spoon licker once all the cake making was done. How many times had she watched Evie sitting here, at this table, waiting for the spoon as Rosamund stirred her way through all those Madeiras and Victorias and Genoas?

Rosamund's smile grew, broadening out beyond her face and venturing back through time . . .

The rubbing was slowly becoming a kneading. Over and over, fold into fold. She paused, straightening her back and rolling her shoulders.

And that's when it came. Shooting down her spine, a sharp pain that took her breath away. She clenched her hands, feeling her nails digging into her palms, the shortbread mix squeezing between her fingers.

She stayed there for a few seconds, frozen, and then carefully eased herself down onto a nearby chair. She sat for a while, getting back her breath, then tentatively reached over for a tea towel and wiped her hands.

Then the coughing started. Great rough squawks of it. Rosamund pulled her handkerchief out from under her sleeve and held it up to her mouth. The coughing went on, a barrage of agonising jerks. When it ended, she closed her eyes and dropped her hands down onto her lap, relieved.

And that's when she saw the blood. She looked down at the handkerchief for a while, observing the pattern on the pristine white cloth. Abstract, like modern art. Postbox red.

CHAPTER 5

Summer 1972

I'm upstairs on the number 94 bus heading down Bayswater Road towards Mayfair.

It's the morning after I deflowered *The Absence of Life is Death*. I'm not sure about *Life* or *Death* but I'm definitely feeling a certain *Absence*. Absence of sleep. I had a terrible night, mainly caused by:

1. Various disturbing thoughts (no job, no boyfriend, no idea about modern art)
2. Various disturbing dreams (giant petals, Fabio, angry eggcups)

I spent most of the night feeling very sorry for myself and there was a fair bit of crying, mac hugging and scarf stroking. I was actually in two minds whether to go back to the gallery today. The easiest thing in the world would have been to telephone Delphinia and find an excuse not to go but I didn't want Fabio and his spider-leg eyebrows to win.

So here I am, Mayfair-bound, going back to the Apollo Gallery and my potential new career in the London art world. I'm going back for Mrs Scott-Pym. I'm going back for my mother. And I'm going back for me.

The upstairs of the number 94 is its usual smoky self. Normally this isn't a problem. I would – normally – have had plenty of time between getting up and leaving the house and so would – normally – have put my make-up on at home after a leisurely breakfast. But today I had very little time to play with because of sleeping badly (see above) and important wardrobe decisions (see below), which means I need to do my make-up here on the bus. The man in front (pinstripes, comb-over, dandruff) is chain-smoking Player's No.6; it's like being downwind of the *Flying Scotsman*. I've done the easy bits (blusher, lipstick) but now I'm on to eyes and this requires smoke-free precision – any wrong move and I could end up looking like Coco the Clown. The task is made even more difficult because my sleep-deprived eyes have shrunk to pinpricks, something I'm hoping to fix with a generous application of peacock-blue.

(Unlike most of the people on the bus, I don't smoke. I've tried many times but I just can't manage it – I think I must have the wrong internal piping.)

Clothes-wise, I am a vision in Quant. I've decided to up my fashion game just in case I run into Fabio. I spent a long time (again) choosing what to wear and finally went for an accordion-pleat skirt and puff-sleeved top (both in number-94-bus red) and have teamed them up with some orange tights ('mango') and matching Mary Janes. I am ready for anything.

I snap my compact mirror shut and put it and my eyeshadow back in my handbag. We're almost at the end of Hyde Park now; soon Marble Arch will be juddering past us. This is my signal to begin getting off so I get up, ding the bell and clatter down the wooden stairboards at the back of the bus, quickly squeezing past the conductor, who brushes himself against me with the subtlety of an automatic car-wash brush.

When the bus has almost rattled to a stop, I jump off, earning a wink from the conductor and a wolf whistle from a window cleaner outside Chelsea Girl. I brush myself down, take a deep breath and head off into Mayfair, mortal, guilty, but entirely beautiful.

'Evie!' says Delphinia. 'I'm glad you didn't let that tin-pot Mussolini put you off.' She lays a sympathetic hand on my shoulder. 'I'm *so* sorry about yesterday.'

'Oh, no problem,' I reply. 'I'm fine. And to be fair to Fabio, I did mess up his art.'

'Don't make excuses for him! He behaved terribly. After you'd gone, I marched over there and tore such a strip off him. Well, of course, he didn't like it, did he, being spoken to like that by a woman. *Stronzo cretino rompicoglioni.*' She gives her hair a quick flick. 'Anyway, come on, darling, let's get down to some work.'

Getting down to some work, it turns out, is basically shorthand for sitting around again doing not very much at all. Delphinia does a little bit of filing and I have a quick whizz round with a Ewbank but that's it. Nobody comes into the gallery. Not a soul.

I don't know how Delphinia sticks it day after day, week after week. If I'm absolutely honest, I'm almost missing the drama of Fabio and his perma-tan and, actually, the non-Fabio part of yesterday was (how should I put it?) just a little bit boring.

For most of the day we've been in our usual positions either side of the mahogany desk. We've exhausted I-spy, gone through this month's *Burlington Magazine* (a very poor substitute for *Honey*), and had a good crack at setting the world to rights (Vietnam, Edward & Mrs Simpson, Biba patterned tights) but we've currently hit a brick wall, entertainment-wise, so we're sat in silence gazing out the window watching London wander by.

Delphinia flicks her ponytail. The ponytail has a silk scarf woven into it and a big floppy bow at the end, making her look a bit like a dressage champion (horse not rider). 'Evie,' she says, still gazing out the window. 'Do you mind if I nip out for a few minutes?'

'No, of course not.'

'Thanks, darling.' She opens a drawer in the desk and pulls out a string shopping bag with hooped plastic handles. 'I just need to pick up a couple of things for supper. I won't be long,' she adds, trotting over to the door.

'Take your time!' I say, already thinking about my next foray into the Family Circle box. 'It's not like we're rushed off our feet.'

She gives me a little wave and then steps outside, leaving the words *you're an angel* floating cheerfully in the air behind her.

I sit for a while, feeling the weight of responsibility (again) of being left in charge of a gallery. Obviously, there's a clear no-touching rule, even though here, unlike across the road at Fabio's, it's very easy to tell the difference between art and non-art. This might be because the art here is quite frumpy. It needs sprucing up a bit with something modern (but not *too* modern). What else would I change if it were my gallery? I'd definitely add a few pot plants.* And a radio. And I'd paint the walls too. Maybe even get a couple of beanbags.

I'm enjoying my new-found (imaginary) power so decide to go and sit on the other side of the mahogany desk, Delphinia's side, the side with all the drawers and gravitas. I immediately feel extremely cultured, like Joan Bakewell, and consider using my time alone in the gallery to learn more about the paintings on display and the world of art in general. But then I notice that Delphinia's chair (also leather) is a swirly one, as opposed to the non-swirly chairs on my side. I have a gentle test swirl, pivoting left and right with my hips. And then I do what any self-respecting twenty-six-year-old would do and hurl myself round, spinning and turning, twirling and whirling. It's tremendous fun. I find that if I tuck my legs under the chair, I can go even faster so off I go again, round and round and round and . . .

'Er, Evie?'

I grab the desk mid-spin, jolting to a stop.

'It is Evie, isn't it?'

A man in a light blue suit is standing at the desk. He looks vaguely familiar but I can't be too sure because the blood in my head is still spinning round and I'm unable to focus.

'*Woman's Hour* Evie?'

*

Name: Gordon Johnson

From: Manchester

Job: Kew Gardens

Seen for: two days

Appearance: dungareed Marlon Brando

Amazing: horticulturist, double-jointed thumb, northern

Less amazing: surly, nose picker, Lancastrian

His head is cocked to one side and there's a hint of a squint.

'With the mug?' he adds, unnecessarily doing a drinking gesture with his hand.

'Yes,' I say (mortified). 'That's me.'

He smiles. A nice, friendly smile.

'Lolo,' he says, putting his hand to his chest.

'Sorry?'

'I'm Lolo. Short for Lorwerth. I work at the BBC. We're Broadcasting House buddies. Well, we were until . . .'

He trails off.

'Until I got the sack,' I say, helping out.

'Yes, until that.'

A small van rattles by outside.

'You're famous, you know, back at work. Everyone's talking about it.'

'Really?'

'Yes, I'm surprised they haven't had you on *Nationwide*.'

'Me and the Esperanto-speaking donkey, you mean?'

'And what a show that would be! We're just missing a yodel-ling cat. Do you mind if I sit down?' he asks, tapping one of the leather armchairs on his side of the desk.

'Yes, sorry, of course, please do.'

He unbuttons his suit jacket and sits down, an elegant crumple of sky blue.

'So, is this your new job?'

'Yes. Well, sort of. I'm giving it a try.'

'Oh.'

'Friend of a friend,' I explain, answering a question that hasn't been asked.

'I see,' he says, nodding slowly. 'And, are you enjoying it? Life in the art world?'

'Oh yes,' I lie. 'Very ...' (I'm searching for the right word) '... invigorating.'

'Invigorating?'

'Yes. Very.'

'Invigorating.'

'Yes, very invigorating.'

'I noticed,' says Lolo, swizzling his finger round and round.

'I was just testing the chair,' I say, mortified for the second time in less than a minute. 'It had a squeak.'

'Oh, a squeak? I see ... not a squeal?'

'No, definitely a squeak.'

'Right.' (More nodding.) 'Nasty.'

'What do you do at the BBC?' I ask, trying to wrest back control of the conversation (as befits someone sitting in a leather swivel chair).

'I'm a producer,' he replies. 'At Radio Three.'

Ah, Radio 3. Lolo is homosexual. All men at Radio 3 are. It's a BBC rule, like playing the national anthem at the end of the day and the Director General always being a man.

I immediately feel far more comfortable.

'Oh, lovely,' I say, smiling a very understanding, child-of-the-swinging-sixties smile.

'Opera mainly,' he adds.

(Of course.)

'Oh, I don't really get on with opera,' I say. 'I've got friends who love it but it's not for me. I think it must be something you develop a taste for with age, like sherry and gardening.'

'I'm not that old!' he says, grinning.

'Oh, no, I didn't mean . . .' I have a good look at him. He's got light brown hair (no grey) but is heavily receding. At a guess, I'd say he's hovering somewhere around thirty. 'Sorry,' I say, throwing in a 'sorry' face for good measure. 'Anyway, how can I help? Have you come to buy some art?'

'No, I've come to *collect* some art. You've been cleaning a painting for us.'

'Oh, do we do that too?'

'Yes, you do,' he says, nodding, 'but I suppose you've been far too busy to notice.'

'Absolutely, I've been rushed off my feet.'

We both smile (snap!).

'Actually,' I say, going all *sotto voce*, 'if I'm *absolutely* honest, I'm a bit bored. I thought I'd be meeting artists and all kinds of interesting people but you're the first customer to come in since I've been here.'

'Well, to be fair, anywhere'd feel pretty quiet after *Woman's Hour*,' he says, sitting back and crossing his legs. 'I hear it's like a Fellini film in there some days.'

'Not exactly,' I laugh. 'But it did have its moments.'

Lolo looks down the empty room. 'I think you *probably* need somewhere a little bit livelier.'

I follow his gaze; all the room is lacking are a few artistic tumbleweeds rolling around. I sigh. 'I think you might be right.'

'Why don't you give something else a try, then?' he asks. 'There's no point sticking around if you don't like it, you know. We're a long time dead, remember.'

A long time dead. I think of Mrs Scott-Pym, a short time dead, and of my mother, a very long time dead. I can't really imagine either of them stuck swirling on a chair in a Mayfair gallery.

'Mr Morgan!' It's Delphinia, galloping into the gallery with a string bag full of food. 'So lovely to see you again. I hope Evie's been keeping you entertained.'

'She certainly has,' says Lolo, beaming over at Delphinia and adjusting his tie.

I realise I'm sat in Delphinia's chair so stand up.

'No, sit down, Evie, darling. I'll go and put this in the back' – she gives the bag a quick jiggle – 'and get Mr Morgan's painting at the same time.' She starts walking towards the back of the

71

gallery but almost immediately turns round. 'Oh, I forgot,' she says, coming over to the desk. 'I got you a little something.' She has a quick rummage around and pulls out a light green paper bag. 'It's a Chelsea bun. I thought you deserved a treat.' She winks then slinks off into the kitchen/office.

Lolo smiles. 'A Fortnum's Chelsea bun. Very nice. You seem to have found a job with an excellent canteen.'

'*Much* better than the BBC's.'

'That's not hard! Those dry sandwiches.'

'And the rock-hard scones.'

'At least you get a decent cup of tea at the BBC, though,' he says. 'And you're never stuck for someone to talk to. Look,' he goes on, lowering his voice. 'Why not try coming back?'

Going back. Back to all the people I know and the jobs that I know and the machines that I know and the hours that I know. Back to the life that I know. It would be like going home.

'I could even have a word with a few people if you like?' he adds with a friendly shoulder shrug.

It all sounds very tempting.

But wrong. It's like when a crab grows out of its shell and needs to grow a new one. I'm that crab, in need of a new shell. Something grown by me.

'That's really nice of you,' I say. 'Thank you. But I think I'll be okay. Not here, perhaps, and probably not in a gallery, but I'll find something.'

He's just about to say something when we both spot Delphinia. She's carrying a big painting, so big that most of her face is hidden behind it. The painting is back to front meaning that all we see of Delphinia is a smoky blue pair of eyes floating above a brown rectangle of wood and canvas.

'Here we are,' she says, resting the painting at the end of the desk. 'Shall we have a quick look?'

'Well,' says Lolo, suddenly less enthusiastic. 'I'm sure it's . . .'

Delphinia has already turned the canvas round.

We all look at the painting, a beach scene, full of sunshine and light, a warm strip of sea next to a quiet beautiful sandy cove with rock pools and beach balls and assorted naked men.

'I think the flesh has come up very well, don't you?' says Delphinia.

'Yes,' says Lolo with a quick nod. 'Very well.'

'And what a marvellous sense of light,' she goes on, hovering her finger over a shiny buttock.

'Lovely,' I say.

Lolo coughs. 'Shall I, er . . .?' He makes various take-the-painting-and-leave gestures with his hands.

'Yes, of course,' says Delphinia, sliding the elaborate gilt frame across the desk towards him.

'Thank you.' He puts the painting on the floor, propping it up against the desk. 'Now, I believe we said £15.' He pulls a cheque-book out from inside his jacket and opens it on the desk.

Delphinia nods discreetly.

'There. We. Go. Fif-teen-Pounds-On-ly. And voi-là,' he says, signing the cheque with a flourish. 'Right, I'd better get this home.' He nods down at the painting. 'Tarquin will be desperate to see it.'

'Please pass on my warmest regards,' says Delphinia.

'I certainly will,' says Lolo, tucking the painting under his arm (canvas out, buttocks in). 'Bye, then, Evie,' he says, doing a smile-nod. 'It's been lovely chatting to you.'

'You too,' I say, giving him a big friendly smile. 'Watch out for those dry sandwiches!'

'Will do.' He's already halfway out the door. He turns, waves his non-painting-carrying hand, shouts *good luck*, and then steps out onto the street.

'Who's Tarquin?' I ask Delphinia as soon as we have the gallery back to ourselves.

'Oh, they dropped the painting off together. He seemed very nice. Lovely nails. Quite theatrical, if you know what I mean.'

Chapter 6

Summer 1972

It's two days later and I'm snuggled up on the sofa with my all-time favourite trio: Simon, Garfunkel and butterscotch Angel Delight.

The rest of my day with Delphinia consisted mainly of telling her that the art world wasn't for me. She was lovely about it. We had a real heart-to-heart and I told her that I'm just not cut out for working in a gallery. I don't have the patience for it. Plus I'm terrible at I-spy. I'm not great with a Ewbank. And I can't tell the difference between art and non-art. Delphinia flung her arms round me and said she completely understood and that it was *time to give something else a try, darling*. There was lots of hugging and a quick toast to my future (another miniature brandy bottle) and then that was that. Back on the number 94 bus and home in time for *Hector's House*.

And so here I am, again, trying to work out what *something else* might be. I feel stuck in a metaphorical sense (no job, no boyfriend, no prospect of either) but also in a very literal sense too (I've hardly moved off the sofa for two days).

Whenever I think of something I quite fancy doing (for example, book editor), my brain immediately conjures up all the good things (lovely authors, long lunches, free books) but completely ignores all the bad things (non-lovely authors, inky fingers, semicolons). I can easily imagine myself doing almost any job because every job I imagine is the rose-tinted version. Reality is something I can't quite manage to keep hold of; it just slips away, like a fried egg on Teflon.

I stare over at the LP going round and round and round. It's hypnotic. Soon 'Baby Driver' revs to an end and 'The Only Living Boy in New York' starts up (my favourite). The guitar strums, Tom gets his plane and I lie back and close my eyes, imagining walking round Central Park hand in hand with a handsome poet or folk singer (or someone with similar knitwear).

For the past couple of days, my only measure of time has been the brief crackling silence between songs. I have been lost in thought (and Angel Delight) and the world has been spinning for me at a steady 33 rpm. Bridge. Blue. Abbey Road. It's been a beautiful pause from life.

Life. Something I'm meant to know about by now. Something I should be on top of. My mind skips to *Blue Peter* when they're making something that involves scissors and tell you to get an adult to do it for you. That's how I feel about life.

And then, just like that, side two finishes (for the fourth time running). The record player arm hesitates for a few seconds, pondering its own dusty silence, then lifts up and takes itself back to the armrest, dropping down into place like me flopping back on the sofa after a trip to the fridge.

I crawl over to the stereo, flip over the LP then sprawl out on the floor, staring up at the ceiling. The piano of 'Bridge Over Troubled Water' tinkles in, little plinks and plonks of beauty that drift around me like snow. Are times rough? Am I in troubled water? Do I need a bridge?

I'm deep in philosophical pondering when the phone rings.

'Hullo,' I say, turning the music down.

'Evie, love? Is that you?'

It's Mrs Swithenbank, or Doris as I keep forgetting to call her. She's an old friend from my village up in Yorkshire. Indomitable and unsinkable. With a heart as big as an English Longhorn.

'Doris! Hullo. This is a nice surprise.'

'Well, I thought I'd try you at dinnertime, love – just on the off chance.'

'Yes, I'm on my lunch hour – I've just nipped home to pick something up.'

(I haven't told anyone back in Yorkshire about getting the sack because I don't want them to fret. Caroline and Digby were given express instructions not to mention it.)

'Is everything okay?' I ask, hoping to distract her from me being at home in the middle of the day.

'Oh, yes, fair to middling. My knee's giving me some gyp but I can't complain at this age, can I? What about you, love? Is everything all right?'

'Yes . . . everything's fine.'

'I hope you're minding yourself with all those Londoners. I know what they're like down there.'

(We speak on the phone at least once a week and the preamble's always the same: ailments, Londoners, and . . .)

'I'm still waiting to see you reading the news, you know, or doing a turn on *Call My Bluff*.'

(. . . the BBC.)

'I work on the radio, Doris, not television. It'll be a while before you see me reading the news.'

'Oh, I don't see why not. Happen you'd do a much better job than all those men, pompous young things. Anyway, love, I'm ringing because I've just got back from the churchyard. I took some flowers for Rosamund's grave – it made me think of you.'

'Aw, that's lovely, Doris. She'd really like that.'

'I took her some roses. White ones, from the garden.'

'Yes, she always loved roses.'

'Oh, these looked grand, they did. I was there quite a while, telling her about various things, keeping her up to date. And I said hello from you, too, love. Told her you'd be busy chasing around London, interviewing film stars and whatnot. She was always very proud of you, you know. Down there with a job, standing on your own two feet, showing 'em all how it's done.'

(I'm currently slumped on the floor next to the coffee table, jobless, surrounded by a sorry clutter of wall-to-wall snacks and mugs.)

'Thanks, Doris. I really miss her.'

'Aye, love. We all do. But she's up there looking down on you; you know that, don't you?'

I squeeze my eyes tight shut. Warm salty drops blot my lashes.

'Doris?'

'Yes, love?'

I pause. Standing on the edge of something.

'Hello, Evie, love, are you there?'

I cock my head back; silence crackles down the phone.

'Yes,' I say, quietly. 'I'm here. I think the line cut out for a second, that's all.'

'That's London for you. Nothing works down there. Except for you, that is!'

'Yes.' I smile. 'Except for me.'

'Anyway, look, I'd better get off the phone and let you get back to work. You've probably got all kinds of exciting things planned, you and your glamorous London life.'

'Oh, yes, you know me, Doris,' I sigh, staring at my half-eaten Angel Delight. 'Always busy.'

'Well just make sure you look after yourself, love. For Rosamund and for me.'

'I will, don't worry. And you too, Doris.'

'Thanks, love. Ta-ta, then,' she says, sending a big kiss down the phone.

'Ta-ta, Doris,' I reply, sending her a big kiss back.

I put the phone down and sit on the floor, propping my back against the sofa. Should I have told her? About me losing my job and being so hopeless with art? About me spending two days marooned on the sofa with a box of Terry's Weekend? Should I have told her that I'm feeling weary and small and tears are in my eyes? That I'm in troubled water?

I sit here for a while, thinking about Mrs Swithenbank. All the kindness she's shown me. All the times she's made me laugh. I'm here in my sitting room, bathed in sunlight, aware of the noises outside on the street, but I'm also somewhere else, in the past, in gardens or seafronts or armchairs, memories twisting and merging, going in and out of focus like a beautiful kaleidoscope. I reach over and take my handbag from the side of the sofa, delving into its inside pocket. I pull out a Polaroid photo, already starting to fade. There, in the photo, is Mrs Swithenbank with Mrs Scott-Pym and me, all three of us laughing, sitting on Mrs Scott-Pym's gravelly terrace, hollyhocks and foxgloves poking out behind us. Two different Yorkshires, the Dales and the Moors, York races and Sheffield steel, Bettys tea rooms and the cobbled Haworth hill, but both steeped in wisdom, common sense and love.

When I put the photo back in my bag, I notice the flyers I'd taken from Fabio's gallery: the arty cinema and the new magazine. I take them out and have a proper look. The one for the arty cinema is a hundred shades of orange, with large art deco writing announcing various films in a variety of foreign languages (the English translation relegated to brackets). It looks the kind of place that I would pretend to enjoy but would actually much rather be at the Odeon watching *Cabaret*. The best bit of the flyer is at the bottom, where it promises *Real Italian Coffee** at the cinema cafe – always good to know.

The other flyer is for a magazine called *Right On!* In the middle of the flyer is a photo of Marc Bolan's head and coming

80

Name: Marco Valentino

From: Italy

Job: waiter

Seen for: five days

Appearance: mini Warren Beatty

Amazing: dapper moustache, very white teeth, could do the splits

Less amazing: non-stop weather moaner, walked at snail's pace, rude about tea

out of it like sunbeams are things like Nelson's Column, a ballet pump, a double-decker bus, a model in a trouser suit, and a trombone. Underneath the Marc Bolan sun, in lovely swishy writing, is the question **what's going down in London town?**

It all looks very exciting.

What *is* going down in London town, I ask myself? Mrs Swithenbank seems to think I know but I'm not so sure. The most exciting city in the world is just outside my front door and all I've been doing is lying on the sofa pondering life and feeling sorry for myself.

What would Mrs Scott-Pym say?

I look at the beautifully coiffed model sticking out of Marc Bolan's ear. She looks fab. A besuited goddess in platform boots. And then, in the blackened screen of the resting telly,

I catch my own reflection, a blurry mess of flannelette pyjama and scary hair.

It's time to act.

An hour and a half later and I'm sat in the cafe of the arty cinema having an espresso and staring at the film listings board. I have transformed, phoenix-like, and am now a blazing glory of crocheted top, maroon knickerbocker and strappy leather boot.

I give my coffee another little stir and carry on staring at the listings board. It's full of foreign films. *Das* here, *El* there. It's like being at the United Nations or finding yourself in a particularly difficult round of *University Challenge*. Thanks to school, I can just about manage the French titles and, thanks to various flings, can also have a good stab at the Spanish, Swedish, Italian and German ones but many of the others are beyond guessing so I have to resort to the English translation. I have two clear favourites. *Un Flic* (A Cop), because, if I ever find myself at a French hair salon, it's good to know not to ask for a *flic*, and *Die Angst des Tormanns beim Elfmeter* (The Goalkeeper's Fear of the Penalty), because now I know how to say goalkeeper and penalty in German.

I have a quick sip of my espresso, sit back and look around. The cinema cafe is tiny, just a small bar crowded with sweets and snacks and, here, over by the large floor-to-ceiling window, a few barstools looking out onto Soho. In front of me, on a very narrow bench, is the flyer for the magazine, *Right On!* I trace my finger across the jaunty title while Marc Bolan sunshines up at me. I'm right on, aren't I? I have platform wedgies, a Le Creuset omelette pan and once kissed someone who once kissed someone who once kissed a Beatle.

I gaze out through the window, watching the people out on the street come and go, a great library of stories.

What's going down in London town?

I tap my finger on the flyer.

Working at a magazine would be exciting, I bet. You'd be surrounded by witty, clever people, people who know their way round an Anglepoise lamp, people with insight and ideas and flair.

At the bottom of the flyer, in tiny writing, is the magazine's address. It's in Soho (of course). Just round the corner, in fact.

I tap my finger on the flyer again.

I like words. Words are wonderful, beautiful, magical things. Working with words would be good. It'd make a nice change from working with transistors or sound decks or Pamela. And I like writing too (well, reading). And interviewing (well, chatting).

Plus, with all the magazines I get through every month, I must be a magazine expert. Practically a journalist, in fact.

I brush my fingers over Marc Bolan's head.

It wouldn't do any harm, would it, just nipping in and saying hullo? And maybe I could help out? I think I'd like that. It'd be a very non-stuck-in-a-rutty thing to do.

A chance to try something new. Something completely different.

I knock back the espresso, pop the flyer in my bag, give the barman a quick smile, and head out into the street, a happy breeze of Tiggerish bounce.

The *Right On!* office is on the first floor of a ramshackle Georgian terrace building, sandwiched between a lava-lamp importer (second floor) and a sex shop (ground floor). You get up to the offices via a street-level door next to the sex-shop window, which is a similar set-up to my flat, except instead of walking past a window full of haberdashery here it's all neon signs and PVC bodices.

I'm hovering outside on the street, trying to get my opening speech straight. I need to be friendly but professional. Natural but articulate. Knowledgeable. Experienced. And *Right On*.

Thank goodness I'm dressed for the occasion. I stand in front of the sex-shop window and check out my reflection. Knowledge may well be power but so is Biba. I get a bit closer to the window, leaning in and having a few practice smiles, trying everything from beam (Des O'Connor) to pout (Amanda Lear) and finally settle for something between Charlotte Rampling and Eric Sykes.

I'm beginning to feel a bit self-conscious hovering outside the sex shop, so I give my hair a quick check in the window then press the buzzer for the first floor. Nothing happens. I try again. Nothing. I give it a few more prods but it's dead. I'm just about to give the lava-lamp importer a try when the door opens and a woman, more or less my age, slips out then skips off into the grimy Soho streets.

I quickly stick my foot in the door before it swings closed, borrowing a move from Columbo. A second later and I'm inside. It's all quite narrow and dark, just a flickering naked bulb hanging from the ceiling and some bare wooden stairs going up to the next floor. I give my knickerbockers a nervous little brush, take a deep breath, and then up I go, a chorus of boot heel and beating heart.

On the first-floor landing, the door to the *Right On!* office is wide open. Through it, the ends of some messy-looking desks jut into view and, across from them, against the back wall, squats a row of filing cabinets. Somewhere in the room, a chair scuffs across the floorboards and a tinny radio is playing 'My Sweet Lord'.

I pop my head round the door.

'Oh, hullo,' says a man with a round friendly face. 'Who do we have here, then?'

'Hullo,' I say, giving him (hopefully) a nice magaziney smile. 'I'm looking for *Right On!*'

'Well, you've found it.' He's sitting on a chair with his legs outstretched. 'Here we are,' he says, opening his arms to the room. He's clearly using the royal 'we' as he's the only person here.

The room is a messy clutter of desks and chairs and papers and files, all bathed in light from three huge sash windows that look out onto Soho.

'How can I help?'

I have a quick rummage in my bag for the flyer. 'I came because of this,' I say, pulling it out and waving it in the air like Chamberlain promising peace for our time.

He beams. 'They were my idea,' he says, pointing at the flyer.

'I did some very similar for a Beckett at the Fringe and they really helped pull the punters in.'

'It's lovely,' I say. 'Very eye-catching.'

'Exactly,' he replies, nodding. He must be around my age but has the casual well-honed confidence of a sergeant major or WI bigwig.

'Well, I was just round the corner and I noticed you were nearby,' I go on, giving the flyer another little wave. 'So I thought I'd come and say hullo.'

'Hullo?'

'Yes, hullo. Well, hullo and can I have a job?'

I smile.

He smiles back.

'Well, actually, we do have a vacancy, funnily enough.' He scrapes his chair round to face me. 'We're a man down. Well, woman down,' he adds, in a tone that suggests women have the disposability of a Bic biro.

'So, you're hiring then?'

'I suppose we must be, yes. But it's a very specialised job, I'm afraid. Highly skilled. Not just for anyone. The last girl was a journalist, you see, and we'd be looking for someone similar.'

He scrunches up his face, almost looking apologetic.

Light streams in through the sash windows, broad blades of gold. Outside, a Lambretta fizzes by.

'I'm a journalist.'

(What am I saying?)

'A journalist?'

'Yes, a journalist.'

'For whom?' he says, pretentiously.

'For the BBC,' I reply, seeing his *whom* and raising it with a national treasure.

'Did someone say the BBC?' says another man, taller and more angular, walking in from a door at the back of the room.

'Yes,' says the first man, cocking his head in my direction.

'Really?' says the second man. He walks over to us with the relaxed, easy-going demeanour of a Prussian army captain. 'Which programme do you work on?'

'Woman's Hour,' I reply, relieved to be back on honest (ish) ground because, if I hadn't got the sack, this would not be entirely untrue.

'Oh,' they both say, two flat little sighs.

I can see I'm going to have to up my lying game.

'And a few others, of course.' (My mind flicks through the schedule.) *'You and Yours ... Scan ... PM Reports ... Just a Minute.'*

'Oh, I love that,' says the first man. 'Clement Freud is *so* good.'

The second man narrows his eyes. 'That's a strange show for a journalist to work on.'

'Well, the BBC likes to give us a broad range of experience,' I say. 'It keeps us on our toes.'

'Quite right too!' says the first man, winking.

'But aren't you very young to have worked on so many shows?' asks the second man (who must be around my age but, obviously, that's considerably more in man years). 'How come you want to work here if you've got so much experience?'

I pause for a moment, turning my head towards the sun-filled windows, feeling the warmth on my face.

'I'm looking for a change,' I say. 'Something new. Something completely different.'

And I smile, an extra burst of sunshine.

The first man smiles back but the second man just stares, his mouth as rigid as a stick of rock.

Somewhere in the building a loo flushes.

'Why not just give me a trial?' I say. 'What have you got to lose?'

The second man gives me a Look that suggests they'd have quite a lot to lose. 'What we really want is someone to take care of the listings,' he says. 'Someone who knows the scene. Someone who's with it . . .'

(Thank goodness I'm in my Biba knickerbockers.)

'. . . Someone au fait with the cultural life of our great city,' he goes on, sounding like a politician.

The first man, short and stout, gets up from his chair and goes and stands beside the angular second man, teapot next to coffeepot. 'You certainly look like you know the scene,' he says. 'What was the last film you saw?'

It was actually *Mutiny on the Buses* but that doesn't seem the best answer, all things considered.

'*The Goalkeeper's Fear of the Penalty*,' I lie, adding, 'it's German,' as nonchalantly as possible to make it sound like I go and watch German films all the time.

'Oh, Wenders,' says the nice teapot, going all wide of eye. 'Isn't he marvellous?'

'Oh, yes.' I nod my head in an appropriately Teutonic manner. 'Marvellous.'

'And what about the last art show?' he asks.

'Ah,' I say, feeling on much surer footing. 'I was at La Divinità Gallery a few days ago.'

'Oh, amazing,' says the teapot. 'I love *arte povera*. It speaks to us all.'

'Doesn't it just,' I reply, clasping my hands together in the hope of looking more intellectual. 'I was particularly taken by *The Absence of Life is Death*.'

'*So* clever,' intones the teapot.

'Ingenious.'

'And what about music?' asks the coffeepot, ramrod straight. 'Who have you seen recently?'

'Oh, loads. I'm always at gigs,' I say (semi-truthfully). 'Wings, Pink Floyd, Free ...'

The teapot nods enthusiastically. 'Great. And what about classical?'

I stare at the teapot.

The teapot's eyes urge me on.

Nothing comes.

I blink.

He smiles, encouragingly. 'Glass? Cage?'

'Oh, yes,' I say. 'Of course. *The Glass Cage*. Wonderful. I loved it.'

The teapot coughs.

'Great,' he says quickly, his voice skipping up a few tones. 'Well, I think everything's okay there. You certainly seem to know your stuff, er ...'

He cocks his head and holds out a hand towards me.

'Oh, I'm Evie. Evie Epworth.'

'And I'm Nick. Very nice to meet you, Evie.'

The coffeepot looks me up and down. 'A trial, then,' he says, still not cracking a smile.

'Fantastic!'

'Let's see how you get on, Miss BBC. You start tomorrow.'

Interlude – Spring 1953, Dundee

Catherine tossed her husband's shirt on the arm of the sofa, the button successfully sewn back on. She could have asked Nell, the help, to do it, of course, but she didn't like to. It seemed such an intimate thing.

She sat back, letting her eyes drift around the room, taking in the familiar accretions of married life, the china wedding gifts, the unremarkable paintings, the photos mushrooming up in small joyless clumps. Her eyes came back to the freshly sewn shirt, hanging over the sofa arm like the flaccid neck of a long-dead chicken. She thought of her husband, a dull buttoned-up shirt, one ironed to within an inch of its life, every last suggestion of a crease erased.

The wedding had been three years ago. A fairly sombre affair. No, sombre wasn't quite right, was it? Workmanlike, perhaps. Functional. Joyless.

They'd moved from Edinburgh to Dundee soon afterwards because Muir had been offered his own practice. They'd found a nice house in the suburbs, an old manse, dignified and assured. Muir had thrown himself into their new life, joining the local golf club and the Rotary up in town. Catherine had joined the WI and tried to busy herself with the church and suchlike but she had the feeling that the other women were wary of her – the young doctor's wife. It seemed to put an invisible something between them, like they were standing either side of a window, looking, smiling but never able to touch.

There had been no children. Not yet, anyway. She was still waiting. A monthly drop of emptiness swelling inside her, growing bigger, heavier. She wondered if it would get so big that there'd be nothing left of her. Just an absence. A dim outline of something lost.

There was a gentle knock on the sitting-room door.

'Come in,' called Catherine, turning to the door and smiling.

A young woman popped her head into the room.

'I'm gannae do the rugs outside now, Mrs Gordon. But can I get you a drink before I start?'

(Catherine had still not got used to Gordon; it sounded so solid, like a castle – something to keep people out. Or in.)

'No, I'll make it, Nell. You carry on with the rugs.'

Nell hesitated.

'Are you sure, Mrs Gordon? It's nae bother.'

'Honestly, Nell. I need to stretch my legs. I've been sat here sewing for the last half-hour.'

'Oh, I could have done that for you,' Nell said, inching into the room. 'You just had to say.'

'Thanks, Nell, but I wanted to do it. I'm getting out of practice!' Catherine smiled, feeling something warm and real. 'Now, milk, three sugars, isn't it?'

'Aye – and thank you, Mrs Gordon,' said Nell, leaving the room with a slight nod of her head.

You won't be sewing Mr Gordon's shirts, thought Catherine, straightening her skirt. She would do them herself, or send them into town. Nell's hands would be saved for her own garments. For a seam that needed fixing. A collar to be stitched. Stockings to be darned.

She stood up, buoyant in the morning air, and made her way through to the kitchen.

Nell came to the house two mornings a week. It had been Muir's suggestion, *someone to help* he said, but Catherine knew it was really about slotting into the cut-out hole of expectations. Muir dropped into place perfectly – tailor-made – but Catherine caught and snagged. Awkward. Misshapen.

Her week revolved around Nell's two mornings. She enjoyed her company, chatting while Nell's gentle hands folded clothes or dusted down a mirror. They talked mainly about Nell's family – her mother, Cora, who embroidered and did the pools, her father, Donald, working in a jute factory, and her brother, Malcolm, a few years younger than Nell and with his mind set on a life in the army. It was a world she soaked into, twice a week, like a comforting warm bath.

And she lent her books too. When Nell first arrived, she'd commented on all the books around the house. Catherine had just finished a Forster so she gave it to Nell to read. Nell brought it back the week after and Catherine had given her another and that's how it had started. Every week, without fail, a new book. Dickens, Agatha Christie, the Brontës, anything, really, with a good story. She'd held back Lawrence, of course, and other books too, her special books, books she kept hidden in plain sight, her Woolfs, her Halls, her Barnes, her Bowles. Maybe one day, she thought, pouring the boiling water from kettle to pot, smiling, thinking, content for a while.

CHAPTER 7

Summer 1972

Here I am again, checking my hair in the sex-shop window.

It's twenty-five past nine in the morning on my first day at *Right On!* and I'm determined to make a good impression. I'm sporting Mrs Scott-Pym's art deco silver hairclip for good luck and have teamed it up with a floaty Liberty-print dress and some block-heel boots. I'm aiming for professional but cool, a tenacious probing journalist with a stylish, creative edge, Robin Day by way of Zandra Rhodes.

I rub my tongue along my front teeth, smile into the window, then saunter over to the scruffy-looking door that leads up to the *Right On!* office, trying to ignore all the men in macs walking by.

'Evie!' says Nick, looking over as I walk in. He's sat *near* rather than *at* a desk, as if happy to have a bit of a fling with it every now and then but unwilling to commit to anything more serious. 'Morning!'

'Morning!' I say, hovering around the door.

He gives me a big smile. 'First day, then!' he says, walking over. 'Must feel a bit different to the BBC!'

'Oh, every office is the same, isn't it?' I laugh, a well-seasoned journalist kind of laugh (I hope). 'Just give me a typewriter and I'm happy.'

'Well, it's certainly nice to have someone with all your experience on board.' He pushes a hand back through his wavy blonde hair. 'I tend to make it all up as I go along!'

(I know the feeling.)

'To tell you the truth,' he goes on, 'I'm an actor. I'm between roles at the moment. I just do this on the side.'

An actor.

I suspected as much. It's his overwrought vowels and constantly upturned collar (a sure sign of luvviedom).

'Well,' he goes on. 'I say *make it all up as I go along* but I did read English at Peterhouse so I should be okay at chucking a few words on a page. In fact I'm writing a one-man play at the moment,' he adds. 'It's kind of Pirandello meets *The Golden Shot*.'

'Sounds wonderful,' I lie.

He beams, exhibiting the round, friendly face of a jolly medieval monk.

'I'm hoping to take it to Edinburgh, then maybe have it picked up by the BBC.' He winks. 'Anyway, enough about me – come on, let me show you your desk.' And he beckons me over to a small desk at the back of the room.

The desk is a faultless exercise in tidy minimalism, just a

few books (neatly piled), a couple of notepads, a typewriter and a mug.

'Perfect,' I say, hanging my shoulder bag on the back of the chair. 'Very neat!'

'Suzie, the girl before you, was manically tidy. Not like me, I'm afraid.' He points over to a messy desk by the window. 'And luckily for you, she was very organised too. She'd already made a start on this week's listings.' He takes one of the notepads from the desk, flicks it open and passes it to me. 'There you go! You've got an easy first week.'

'Oh don't worry, I'll make sure I add plenty to it,' I say. 'I know what's going down in London town!'

He smiles. 'Don't get too carried away. You've only got a page, remember, and some of it just runs over from one week to the next. Make life easy for yourself. Now then,' he says, picking up the mug, 'time for a drink, I think. Come on, I'll show you the kitchen.' And he walks over to the door at the back of the room, handing me the mug on the way.

As I walk through the door, I'm greeted by the flinty non-smiling face of the coffeepot. He's sitting on a sofa, smoking.

'Welcome to *Right On!*, Miss BBC.' He wafts his cigarettey hand around the room. 'We are *very* honoured to have you.'

The sarcasm in his voice is so heavy I'm surprised he doesn't fall through the floor and end up right in the middle of the sex shop.

'And I'm very honoured to be here,' I reply, making sure I sound as annoyingly cheerful as possible.

'I've just been showing Evie her desk,' says Nick.

'Hmm.' He has one last drag on his cigarette then stubs it out on a large ashtray on the coffee table in front of him. 'We need your copy by Tuesday, print is Wednesday, and then the magazine's out Thursday.'

He stands up and walks over to the kitchen units, rigid little steps that suggest he's got a stick shoved up his bum (which, funnily enough, is also how he speaks).

'You've got two months' trial.'

'Two months,' I reply, giving him the sunniest beam I can muster.

He frowns. 'Let's see how you get on.'

'Oh, I'm sure she'll be great,' says Nick, joining the uptight coffeepot at the kitchen units.

The coffeepot grunts.

At some point I'm going to have to stop calling him the coffeepot so I ask him his name.

'Nick,' he replies.

'Oh, like . . .' I gesture at the other Nick.

'Yes, like Nick,' he says.

'Two Nicks!' says the first Nick.

'Aren't you lucky,' says the second Nick.

'Very,' I reply, keeping tight control of my tone. 'And are there any more Nicks working here? Or is it just the three of us?'

'Oh, no more Nicks,' says the first Nick. 'Just Griffin.'

'Griffin?'

'Well, she's Janet really,' he explains, 'but she likes to be called Griffin because it makes her feel more arty.'

'She'll be here soon,' says the second Nick. 'She's not an early riser.' He flicks his fringe. 'I think the two of you will get along splendidly.'

The first Nick hesitates for a second then opens a cupboard door.

'Anyway, now for the important stuff, Evie. This is where we keep the tea and coffee,' he says, flourishing a hand in the direction of some spartanly stocked shelves. 'And there's the kettle,' he adds, pointing along the work surface with another little flourish. 'I'm tea, white, one sugar.'

'And I'm coffee, white, no sugar,' says the second Nick, strutting through the door back to the office.

'Thanks, Evie!' says the first Nick, following him. 'And help yourself, of course,' he adds, bobbing his head back round the door.

Waitress duties done, I settle down at my desk with a strong coffee (black, two sugars), watching steam from the mug curl through the bright beams of sunlight. Even though the desk is at the back of the office, it still – luckily – feels light and airy because of the lovely high ceiling. The walls stretch grandly up, great jigsaw puzzles of posters, pinboards, shelves and calendars (weekly, monthly, yearly). Lower down, next to my desk, is a mini-jigsaw of faded postcards, relics of another age (well, Suzie).

On the filing cabinet next to my desk is a pile of last week's *Right On!* I grab one and have a flick through. As far as I can make out, Nick with the collars does the reviews (theatre, music, dance) and Nick stick up bum seems to do everything else (politics, transport, vegetarians).

My job is to create a page of listings, which means about two hundred words on the latest films, gigs, art, theatre, shops – anything, in fact, that is 'right on'.

I put the magazine to one side and pick up the notepad given to me earlier by Nickwiththecollars. He was right when he said Suzie was very organised. The notebook is full of lots of neatly set-out information, page after page of it, each page a new week, with all the galleries, cinemas, theatres and so on clearly grouped.

A perfect template. My bible for the next two months.

I have a sip of coffee and crack on.

Half an hour later and I'm already feeling like a Fleet Street pro. I've whizzed through Suzie's notebook, completed quite a tricky doodle (Big Ben in dungarees) and started making a to-do list.

I've just stretched the list satisfyingly onto a second page when Nickwiththecollars comes over to my desk, announcing himself with a little cough.

'I've brought you a present,' he says, holding up a plastic desk tray.

'Oh, thank you.'

'Well, who doesn't love a desk tray? And I've brought you these to put in it,' he goes on, hoisting a bulging plastic bag onto the desk.

I peer into the bag and see a messy mix of cards and paper.

'They're press releases*,' he says, 'and private views. All that kind of thing. We get loads of them.'

'Fab! Thank you.' I look at the bag sitting Humpty-Dumpty-ish on my desk. 'That should keep me busy for a while.'

He smiles, nods, then has a quick foot shuffle. 'Er, Evie? Do you mind if I ask you something quickly while Nick's nipped to the loo?'

'Go ahead,' I say, smiling back (but sniffing trouble).

'It's about Glass.'

I nod.

'And Cage.'

I nod again.

He looks at me as though he's expecting me to say something.

My head is blank.

Glass.

And.

Cage.

And then I remember.

'Oh yes, the glass cage!'

'Exactly! It was a joke, wasn't it?'

I carefully study his scrunched-up face.

'Of . . . course!' I say, mentally crossing all fingers and toes.

'I knew it! Very good! Very droll.'

'Oh, glad you like it. The joke, I mean. The glass cage!' And I roll my eyes, aiming for a 'look-at-me-cracking-jokes' look.

'Brilliant!' he gushes, walking back to his desk and chuckling to himself. 'The glass cage! Wonderful!'

101

*

> Name: Quentin Porges–Watson
>
> From: Surrey
>
> Job: press officer at Rank films
>
> Seen for: two and a half weeks
>
> Appearance: a slightly more rugged
> Edward Fox
>
> Amazing: brilliant gossip, filthy jokes,
> extremely good tailoring
>
> Less amazing: narcissist, philatelist, bigamist

I put the bag of press releases on the floor and take a deep breath. What was all that about? I'm feeling exposed (not easy in a big floaty Liberty-print dress).

It's time for some Miss Marpling. I start working my way through Suzie's notebook again, scanning the pages for anything 'glass'- or 'cage'-related. Quite near the front, I come across a glass, a concert of classical music (*Music with Changing Parts*, which makes me think of car engines) by someone called Philip Glass, but have to work my way right to the end, almost to the last thing Suzie wrote, to find something with a cage: more classical music, this time by a man called John Cage, playing at the Roundhouse (*HPSCHD*, which looks like a particularly bad hand at Scrabble).

I tap my biro on the notebook. There's clearly a chink in my cultural armour.

I know just what I need to do.

And I grab my bag, tell Nickwiththecollars I'm nipping out for a few minutes, and race down the stairs into Soho.

I head straight for a phone box.

Phone boxes in Soho are particularly awful on account of:

1. The smell (pee)
2. The decorations (assorted postcards offering the services of Luscious Lucy, Busty Brenda and the like)

I jam my foot in the door to bring in some fresh air and have a rummage in my bag for the Apollo Gallery's business card. Then I get a 2p coin from my purse, rest it in the slot and dial the number.

'Apollo Gallery, Mayfair,' says Delphinia, sounding like the queen.

'It's me, Delphinia! Evie!' I shout, pushing the coin into the slot. 'Hullo!'

'Darling, hullo! How lovely. How's everything going?'

'Really well, thanks. I'm working for a magazine called *Right On!* I'm in charge of the listings.'

'You clever old thing,' she says. 'Well done!'

'I'll make sure you get a mention.'

'Thank you, darling. That'd be wonderful.'

'Actually, Delphinia, I'm phoning to see if you could do me a favour?'

'Of course!'

'Do you remember the guy from the BBC who came in for the painting of the naked men?'

'Yes, Mr Morgan. Lovely chap. Lives with Tarquin.'

'Yes, that's the one. Well, do you have his phone number? I need to ask him something for work.'

'Of course, darling. Hold on, I'll get it for you now.'

I hear her rest the phone on the desk and take the address book out of a drawer.

'Eames-Ward ... Hutchinson ... Lawrence ...' she says, flicking through the pages. 'Ah, here it is. Morgan. Have you got a pen?'

'Yes, fire away,' I say, taking a postcard of Saucy Sue and resting it on the dirty wooden shelf.

She gives me the number and I write it down on the side of Saucy Sue, carefully avoiding her sultry curves.

'Thanks, Delphinia, that's great. You're a star!'

'My pleasure, darling. Anything to help. It's funny, you know,' she says, her voice going all quizzical, 'he was in here yesterday asking after you.'

'Oh, really?'

'It's probably a BBC thing,' she explains. 'You're like the Freemasons, aren't you? Anyway, do pop in whenever you're nearby. It'd be lovely to see you again, Evie.'

'I will, definitely! Thanks again, Delphinia! Bye!'

I put the phone back on the hook and look at the number, trying to avoid Saucy Sue's eyes (as well as her various other bits). It's a west London number; Bayswater if I had to guess, or Paddington. Somewhere not a million miles away, anyway.

I glance at my watch. It's just coming up to quarter to eleven. Obviously most people will be at work at the moment but I know from experience that people who work for Radio 3 are not *most people*. Everyone there seems to work funny hours, on account of all the opera and poetry readings.

I give the number a try.

It rings a few times then ...

'Hullo?'

'Hullo,' I reply. 'Is that Lolo?'

'No, Lolo's out at the moment,' a voice drawls.

'Oh. Right. I see.'

'Can I help?' asks the voice.

'Er, could you just say Evie phoned, please. From the BBC. It's nothing important. I'll call back later.'

'Yes, of course. Bye then.'

And the line goes dead.

'Ah, here she is,' says Nickstickupbum as I walk back into the office. 'Miss BBC.' He's perched on my desk, arms folded. 'Welcome back.'

The room feels different. Harder. Sharper.

I look around. There's no sign of Nickwiththecollars but leaning against the bright sash window, outlined like a Hitchcock villain, is a woman.

'This is Evie,' says Nickstickupbum, holding out a hand in my direction but looking at the woman. 'And Evie,' he says, turning back towards me, 'this' – he swings his hand over to the window – 'is Griffin.'

The woman steps forward, no longer an outline but a fully formed person. Her clothes (Woodstock meets C&A) are a jumble of layers, tassels and beads, all of which are the colour palette of sludge.

'Hullo,' I say, with a little window-washing wave. 'Very nice to meet you.'

She glances over at me. Some parts of her mouth make an effort to smile but not all.

'Hi,' she replies.

'I was just telling Griffin that you're going to be with us for the next couple of months,' says Nickstickupbum.

'Yes, and hopefully even longer!'

'Hmmm,' grunts Griffin. I'm sure I see her roll her eyes but it's hard to say under her wonky fringe. 'So, you've done a bit of volunteering at the BBC, then?' she asks (with only the faintest hint of a sigh).

'Well, no, actually, that was my job. I worked there,' I explain. 'For almost ten years.'

She sniffs. 'Well, welcome to the real world.'

'Griffin runs the office,' says Nickstickupbum. 'She does the filing and handles all the paperwork.'

'As well as lots of other things,' she shoots back.

'Yes, of course.' He coughs. 'She writes too,' he adds, making it sound much lower in the pecking order than topping up the stationery.

'Great,' I say, trying Griffin with another smile. 'Always nice to meet another journalist!'

'Poetry,' she replies. 'Not journalism.'

'Yes, we sometimes feature it in the magazine,' says Nickstickupbum. 'When we have space, of course. Oh, and if you need to buy anything, go and see Griffin – she's in charge of the office kitty.'

'And the office tea and coffee!' says a beaming Nickwiththecollars, walking in and doing his jolly monk.

Griffin shoots him a Look that could flash-freeze a steaming mug.

'So expenses and that kind of thing,' says Nickstickupbum, 'are all Griffin's domain while I handle the bigger finances.'

The air crackles for a second, infused with sunlight and irritation.

'There, that's the introductions done,' he continues. 'Time to get on with some work.'

And we all traipse off to our desks.

The rest of the morning is an enjoyable romp through notebooks, lists and old editions of *Right On!* I'm having a great time, despite the odd hostile glance from Griffin and a wall of antipathy from Nickstickupbum, and am making excellent progress. I've been settling into my desk and have managed to dig out a few coloured pens from various drawers plus some pencils and a compass (just in case) and pop them all in a *Mexico 70* mug I found at the back of one of the kitchen cupboards.

I'm in the middle of finding out what's on at the Marquee when Nickwiththecollars lumbers over.

'You are allowed to eat, you know!' he says, munching a bag of crisps. 'It's lunchtime.'

'Is it?' I reply. 'Already! That's gone quick.'

He glances at the papers on my desk, a kaleidoscope of coloured underlining. 'Don't go getting overenthusiastic, you know, and putting the rest of us to shame.'

'Don't worry, I won't,' I say, putting down my green pen. 'Promise! And, actually, now you've mentioned food, I'm starving.'

For lunch, I pick up a sandwich from a baker's round the corner and then go back to the telephone box to give Lolo another try.

'Hullo,' answers the non-Lolo voice again.

'Hullo, I called earlier,' I say. 'For Lolo.'

'Yes, he's just got in. Hold on, I'll give him a shout.'

The voice puts the phone down as I'm saying *thank you* and then bellows, 'Lolo, darling. It's the BBC girl on the phone for you again.'

I half hear a muffled answer and a few seconds later the sound of the phone being picked up.

'Hullo,' says Lolo, a bit out of breath.

'Lolo, it's Evie. From the gallery. We met a few days ago. Sorry to bother you.'

'No, no bother at all, Evie. How's the chair swivelling going?'

'Oh, great thanks.' My eyes squeeze shut, embarrassed. 'I called earlier,' I go on, keen to move the conversation away from swivelling chairs. 'I was just wondering if I could ask you a favour?'

'Fire away.'

'Well, it's about my new job. I'm working for a magazine now doing the listings.'

'Oh, well done,' says Lolo.

'Thank you! Anyway, part of the job involves classical music, you know, concerts and opera. That kind of thing.'

'Yes, that kind of thing.'

'And it's come to my attention that I actually know next to nothing about classical music.'

There's a friendly chuckle down the phone.

'I see. Well, it sounds to me like what you need is someone who *does* know about classical music. Someone who works at Radio Three, for example.'

'Exactly,' I say. 'Do you know anyone?'

'As a matter of fact, I do. I've got the perfect person. He's an expert on concerts and opera and that kind of thing.'

Now it's my turn to laugh.

'Oh, thanks, Lolo. The new job's great and I don't want to mess everything up because of my stupid opera-phobia.'

'Don't worry, we'll soon have you knowing your cadenzas from your sonatas. I tell you what, how about the first lesson today after work? Are you free?'

'Oh, right. Lovely. Yes,' I say, sky-high loops of gratitude. 'That'd be great.'

'Marvellous. Shall we say half five by the empty plinth in Trafalgar Square, then?'

'Perfect. Thanks, Lolo!'

'No problem at all. See you later.'

And we both say *bye* and put the phone down.

As I walk back to the office, I replay the conversation in my head. It's very nice of Lolo to offer to help. Very supportive. Why is it that homosexual men are always so lovely?

Anyway, cadenzas and sonatas . . .

I smile. Mrs Scott-Pym would be proud of me.

Interlude – Winter 1971, Yorkshire

'Cancer?'

'Yes, I'm afraid so.'

Rosamund Scott-Pym's doctor swallowed. Here he was, in her home, perched on her armchair. Telling her she had lung cancer.

'I see.' She unclipped her silver hair grip, tucked her grey hair back around her ear then fastened the grip again.

They sat there for a moment, letting the words settle.

Outside, the day was already dark. Splashes of rain flecked against the large sash windows. The glass lamp on the side table flickered.

When he'd gone, she poured herself a sherry and put on Strauss's *Four Last Songs*.

So that was that, then.

She'd had a good innings but now it was time to get her affairs in order. A good death, she thought. To go with her good life.

CHAPTER 8

Summer 1972

The rest of the afternoon at the office was uneventful.

Nickstickupbum was out doing interviews and Griffin, with the exception of a minor incident involving me and a rogue teabag, kept herself to herself, happily scowling away at her desk before leaving early for yoga. That just left me and Nickwiththecollars, which was lovely. We bonded over a shared love of Bourbon creams and managed to get down to some very successful:

1. Work (lists, coloured pens, doodles)
2. Non-work (he told me a very funny story about Dame Sybil Thorndike)

As soon as it got to five o'clock he made a big show of downing tools (red felt-tip and a set square) then before I knew it we were both out the door and saying goodbye to each other on the streets of Soho.

*

And so here I am, next to the empty plinth in Trafalgar Square, a quarter of an hour early, surrounded by tourists and pigeons, waiting for Lolo. The sky is summer blue and, through the crowd, the National Gallery stretches out in the sun like a great dusty slab of wedding cake. Grandiose but slightly shabby, the perfect metaphor for London.

I have a look around, hoping to spot Lolo. The square is as full as a tin of beans. People taking photos. Men and women strolling arm in arm. Businessmen. Bohemians. And everyone in between. Near me I hear some children shouting. And the honking of some car horns. Suddenly there's a uniform whoosh of wing as a liquid mass of pigeons jumps into the air, opening up a lovely clean space like a drop of Fairy Liquid on greasy water.

And there, in the gap, is Lolo. He's looking round, clearly agitated, his head twisting and turning all over the place, shouting something. Shouting *someone*.

'Oscar! Oscar!'

(Oscar?)

As he's shouting, a joyous heft of basset hound bounds up to him and starts jumping up at his legs. Lolo, beaming, bends down to stroke the dog and is rewarded with a face full of licks and yelps.

'Lolo!' I shout, walking up to them both.

'Oh, hullo there,' he says, looking up. 'You're early.'

'Yes, I got parole for good behaviour.'

'Somehow I find that very hard to believe,' he replies, still giving the dog a good rub and taking the loose lead firmly in hand. 'I brought a friend to meet you.'

'I can see.'

'Evie,' he says, holding out his hand like a Tudor prince displaying his finest treasure, 'meet Oscar.'

I bend down and stroke Oscar, feeling his warm bristly coat between my fingers. 'He's lovely,' I say. 'An absolute sweetie.'

Oscar is solid and stout (a bit like Lolo). He's clearly enjoying the attention, stretching his head in the air and twisting it round so I get just the right spot. He makes a funny throaty rumbly noise (the basset equivalent of a purr) then leans over and licks my arm.

'Oi, Oscar!' says Lolo, pulling him away. 'Don't be so forward, young man.'

'It's fine, don't worry,' I say, tickling Oscar's neck. 'I'm a dog person. I'm used to being covered in slobber.'

Lolo gently pats Oscar's nose with a finger. 'Oh, you've got a dog, then?'

'No, it was back in Yorkshire. My neighbour, Mrs Scott-Pym.' (The sky glows as I say her name, a warm blush of baby blue.) 'She had a lovely dog. Sadie. An English setter.'

'A very noble hound,' says Lolo.

'Yes, that's what she always used to say. Daft as a brush, though!' I roll my eyes. 'Sadie, that is, not Mrs Scott-Pym.'

Lolo smiles.

'Actually, Mrs Scott-Pym was very wise,' I go on, thinking about her bright birdy eyes. 'She had books everywhere; she used to lend them to me.'

'Lucky you. Like living next door to a library,' says Lolo.

'Yes, I suppose it was. And she loved opera, too – it was always blaring away as I walked up her drive.'

'She sounds wonderful,' he says. 'Didn't she ever try and get you into opera, though? Take your musical education in hand?'

'No, I never took to it. It's all just a lot of orchestra and shouting, isn't it?'

'Shouting?'

'Yes. You know, plinky plonky music with the occasional scream.'

'Plinky plonky!' He puts a hand up to his face. 'The occasional scream! What have I got myself into?'

'Well, Delphinia said that us BBC types are like the Freemasons so you can't back out now. It's one for all and all for one.'

'Are you sure that was the Freemasons?'

We both smile. 'You know what I mean.'

'And correct me if I'm wrong,' he says, voice and eyebrows arching, 'but you're no longer at the BBC after . . .'

'Yes, yes, we know!' I bend down to give Oscar another stroke. 'Honestly, Oscar, what's he like?'

Oscar barks, an affable rumbling bass.

'He's a big floozy,' says Lolo.

'He's lovely,' I say, standing back up.

'He *is* a handsome chap, isn't he?' Lolo looks down and winks at Oscar, prompting another bark. 'And he's anyone's for a good rub.'

We laugh again.

'Shall we have a little walk?' asks Lolo.

'Yes,' I reply, aware of London opening up around us. 'A little walk would be really nice.'

*

'So, how's the new job going, then?'

A bus drives by, momentarily shading us from the late-afternoon sun.

'I love it,' I shout, trying to compete with its noise. 'Really love it. It's great to be doing something new, to be honest. It's all very exciting.'

'Better than the gallery, then?'

'Much better.'

'Even without a swivel chair?'

'Even without a swivel chair.'

'Good God. She really must love it, eh Oscar?'

Oscar glances up at Lolo, huffs, and keeps on trotting forwards.

'That's why I need your help,' I explain. 'Part of the job is to do listings for classical music and, well, as you've probably guessed, I know absolutely nothing about classical music.'

'Nothing?'

'Nothing.'

'Scale of one to ten?'

'Am I allowed minus something?'

He grins, tilting back his head and smiling into the sky.

'I'm worried I'm going to be found out,' I go on.

'Oh, come on, after all those years at the BBC, I bet you can blag your way through pretty much anything. You were doing a great blagging job at the gallery, by the way.'

'But art blagging's easy, isn't it? Anyone can do it. It's basically all just life, death, love, and the odd bit of war. Plus we've all seen lots of art, haven't we? It's everywhere – on the telly, biscuit boxes . . .'

116

'Place mats,' chips in Lolo.

'Exactly. Music's much harder, though. There's nothing for the blag to stick to. It's all a big plinky plonky fog. In fact I came a bit unstuck yesterday when I tried to blag about classical music. That's why I phoned you.'

'Really? What happened?'

'I'll only tell you if you promise not to laugh.'

'I suspect that won't be easy.'

'I could just buy a book, you know.'

'Sorry, yes, of course. I promise not to laugh,' he says, putting his hand on his chest and doing something saintly with his face.

I tell him about my Glass and Cage unsticking, trying to make it sound as reasonable a mistake as possible.

'The glass cage,' he says, stopping in the middle of the foot-path (Oscar immediately sits down). 'The glass cage?' He starts laughing, little bubbles at first but soon it's shooting out of him like a huge fountain. 'The glass cage! Oh, that's hilarious.'

'You promised not to laugh.'

'I'm ... sorry,' he says, struggling to speak.

He doubles over, clutching his stomach, filling the air with great Welsh booms.

This sets Oscar off barking. The two of them go at it like a room of double basses. Lolo tries to say something but fails.

And then I start laughing too.

Lolo looks over at me, his eyes red and watery, and mouths the word *sorry*. He's gulping down great buckets of air but still looks like he's struggling to breathe. Oscar's barks have turned into howls, deep whoops that echo down Haymarket.

'Oh, Evie,' wheezes Lolo. 'I'm so sorry.'

'You promised not to laugh,' I reply, trying to sound serious but failing.

'It's just so funny. Oh, it's brilliant.' He wipes his eyes. 'But you're right, you know. There absolutely should be something called *The Glass Cage*. It's a very good title,' he adds, just about regaining control. 'Very profound. It speaks to the human condition. *The Glass Cage*,' he booms, going all Richard Burton.

'Are we

outside

looking in

or

inside

looking out?'

As Lolo's portenting, Oscar cocks his leg (I'm very tempted to do the same).

I look across at him, serious face to serious face. For a second we're like gunslingers facing off outside a western saloon, and then mouths twitch, eyes narrow and we both explode into bright bursts of laughter.

'It was Virginia Woolf's favourite walk, you know.'

'What, shuffling past Hatchards?'

'No, the streets of London. All of them.'

We're making our way along Piccadilly and have managed to put the glass cage behind us. We're now onto general chit-chat.

'That's a very Radio Three thing to know.'

'I'm full of very good Radio Three things to know. Mainly music, obviously, but I can do books too.'

I've found out that Lolo studied at Cambridge then at the Royal College of Music and then got a job at the BBC. He's found out that I grew up on a dairy farm, can't stand celery, and once locked myself in the loo (unintentionally) at a recording of *Top of the Pops*.

'Books are much easier than music,' I say. 'At least classical music. Non-classical music is easy – you just let it take you. It does all the work for you, doesn't it?'

'Hmmm,' ruminates Lolo. 'This is going to be much harder than I thought. I might need some help, Oscar.' Oscar looks round but not for long, much more interested, as he is, in sniffing the pavement. 'I know, let's go to St James's Square,' he goes on. 'I suspect we'll need a park bench.'

'Why, do you think I'm going to fall asleep?'

'No, I just want you to focus. I don't want you being distracted by all these fascinating grey buildings like Virginia Woolf.'

'A park bench of one's own.'

'Exactly. Well, not quite. You're going to have to share with me and Oscar.'

'Point number one,' says Lolo, as the square opens up around us. 'Just like The Beatles, classical music has everything: love, hate, joy, grief, loss. It's all there.'

'But it takes so long to say it! The Beatles could do all of that and they only needed three minutes.'

'Ah, yes,' he replies, opening the garden gate for me. 'For the singles. But what about the albums? You should think of classical music as being all album, no single. Who wants just three minutes of The Beatles when you can have a whole hour?'

'Mmm,' I mutter, far from convinced. 'And what about point number two, then?'

'Well, you know you said books are much easier than music?'

'Yes.'

'You were half-right.'

'Really?'

'Or half-wrong.'

'Oh, just as I thought I was doing well!'

Lolo pauses and smiles. 'Shall we?' he says, gesturing at a nearby bench. Oscar has already flopped on the floor, sitting like the Sphinx, legs out, head up. We follow his lead and sit down.

'Back to point two,' continues Lolo, crossing his legs. 'You say classical music is much more *difficult* than books, but it's not. They're very similar really. Look, you can tell the difference between a novel written in 1810 and one written in 1910, can't you?'

'Yes, of course,' I say (hoping this isn't going to turn into a test).

'Well, it's the same in music. Music written in 1810 sounds very different to music written in 1910. It feels different, too, and it's speaking to different people. It might all be made out of the same plinky plonky stuff but what people do with the plinky plonky stuff changes – just like authors always use words but what they do with them, how they stick them all together, changes.'

I cross my legs, mirroring Lolo. 'Are you going to say "plinky plonky stuff" on Radio Three now?' I ask.

He laughs. 'Definitely. Anyway, have I convinced you?'

'Er . . .'

'I tell you what, pick a phrase and I'll show you what I mean.'

'A phrase?'

'Yes.'

'What kind of phrase?'

'Anything. Well, preferably something profound and beautiful.'

'Right.' I turn and look straight forward, facing the big statue in the middle of the garden (a camp man on a camp horse). Nothing comes. 'Profound and beautiful?' I repeat, checking.

'Yes, preferably. Infused with poetry.'

I feel under pressure. Lolo is very kindly giving up his time to help me with classical music so that I can keep the job I think I might actually love and all I have to do in return is come up with something profound and beautiful and infused with poetry.

I stare at the camp statue.

Nothing.

And then I see a man walking through the garden. He's probably in his sixties and is wearing a suit and carrying a briefcase and brolly. The perfect city gent. Except, of course, he's not wearing a bowler hat (who does?). And – bingo – it comes to me. Inspiration. Something profound and beautiful and infused with poetry.

'On Ilkley Moor Baht'at,' I say, triumphant.

'You're not making this easy for me, are you?'

'I thought I was helping!'

'Hmm, thank you.' He coughs. 'And now give me a year between 1066 and now.'

'Erm . . .' I poke around my mind to see what I can find. '1288.'

'That's very specific,' says Lolo. 'I didn't realise you were a scholar of the medieval world.'

'I'm not. They're two of my favourite bus routes: the twelve and the eighty-eight.'

Lolo laughs, shaking his head, then stretches his arms out in front of him, bending his hands backwards and linking his fingers as if he's warming up for a game of squash.

'Right, here we go then. 1288 . . .

```
o                                    ahhh T'aaa          aaat.'
O o                           ahhhh            aaa  aaa
    on Ill-kleeeey Mooor    orrrr B'ahhh                aa
                  orrr
```

When he sings, he really goes for it, belting out the notes as if he's on stage rather than sitting in a garden square in central London. Oscar joins in too, adding assorted barks and howls.

'What do you think?' he asks.

'Well it's hardly "Penny Lane".'

'To be fair, I'm hardly Paul McCartney.'

'True.' (Paul is my favourite Beatle.)

'But did you get the 1288ness of it?'

'Was that the syllables skipping around all over the place but taking for ever to get anywhere?'

'That's it. See, you're an expert. Ready for the next one?'

'Ready as I'll ever be.'

'Come on, then,' he says, radiating great waves of enthusiasm. 'Give me another year. And something a bit easier this time, please.'

'Okay . . . how about . . . 1875?'

'More buses?'

'No, I live at number eighteen and, well, seventy-five just sounded nice.'

'I'll never understand women,' says Lolo with another headshake. 'Anyway, well done, you've picked a good year.'

'Oh, have I. Why?'

'*Carmen.*'

'What, the rollers?'

'No, the opera. By Bizet. First performed 1875.'

'Only joking! Of course I've heard of *Carmen*. It's the one with the bullfighters, isn't it?'

Instead of an answer, he launches himself into *Carmen* by way of the West Riding of Yorkshire.

'On Il-kley-Moor

On Il-kley-Moor

On Il-kley-Mo or or or or Bah-t'at.

On Il-kley-Moor

On Il-kley-Moor

On Il-kley-Mo or or or oooooooooooooooooooor Bah-t'at.'

As soon as he finishes, Lolo stands up and does it all again,

this time stamping his feet and clicking his fingers like a flamenco dancer.

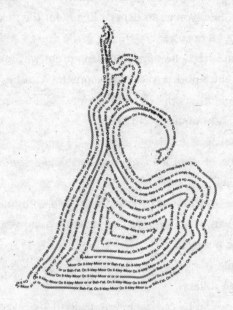

Oscar goes crazy, barking and howling and flinging his head
around, sending his prodigious ears flapping like tea towels on
a washing line. I sit laughing, unsure who looks the campest,
Lolo, Oscar or the statue of the man on the horse.

On the final Bah-t'at Lolo does a very elaborate bow.

'What do you think?' he asks, sitting down again, a bit out
of breath.

'Well, it's certainly a lot jollier than the last one,' I reply. 'At
least there's a tune. And I liked the dancing, of course.'

'I thought you'd appreciate that. We Welsh are famous for our
flamenco.'

'So you should be.'

He smiles. 'So, so you like 1875, then?'

'A very good year.'

'And can you see what I mean about the music? It's expansive, romantic, lush; full of energy, passion.'

'Oh, so that's what it was?' I say, as if unlocking a great mystery. 'I thought it was the same old plinky plonky stuff with a few extra clicky fingers.'

'Everyone's a critic, eh boy?' he says, leaning down and stroking Oscar. Oscar yelps and stands up, pulling on his lead. 'I think he's had enough,' laughs Lolo. 'And I think you probably have too.'

'It's been really good fun,' I say, breaking into a big smile. 'Thank you. The best music lesson I've had in a long time.'

'I'm glad it wasn't too boring.' He pushes a hand through a fading fringe. 'So does that mean you're up for another lesson, then?'

'Definitely. Will you be singing in every one?'

'Just try and stop me. And in the meantime, why don't you let me do the classical listings in the magazine? Just until you get a few more lessons under your belt . . .'

'Are you sure?'

'Of course. It won't take me long. We get to know everything that's coming up anyway. It'll be dead easy. I can just type it up for you.'

'Oh, that's really lovely of you! Are you *absolutely* sure?'

He nods. 'Yes, I'll enjoy doing it.'

'Thank you. You're the most wonderful *On-Ilkley-Moor-Baht'-at-singing-Welshman-who-works-at-the-BBC* I know.'

'That's extremely nice of you.'

'And, of course, you're friends with the most handsome dog in London,' I add, patting Oscar's bum.

'This is true,' says Lolo, nodding wisely. He looks at his watch. 'Oh, God, it's almost seven o'clock!' (He does a big Welsh tut.) 'Sorry but I'm afraid I'd better be heading home. Tarquin's doing supper tonight. He gets very prickly if I'm not there in good time.'

So we say our goodbyes and go our separate ways: Lolo home to Tarquin; me to the nearby delights of Fortnum's pastry counter and a queen-sized Chelsea bun.

CHAPTER 9

Summer 1972

It's eight-thirty the next morning and I'm late.

I walked home from Fortnum's yesterday, which seemed a really good idea initially (smugly eating my Chelsea bun on the banks of the Serpentine) but less so afterwards when my block-heel boots started playing up on Bayswater Road. I spent the rest of the evening with my feet in a bucket of warm water, a box of Radox in one hand and a Cadbury's Old Jamaica in the other. I slept like a log and woke up like one too, just ten minutes ago.

So I'm sprinting through breakfast (buttered toast and a glass of Rise & Shine) and, simultaneously, getting dressed. I did try putting on Radio 3 out of loyalty to Lolo and Oscar but it almost made me fall back to sleep and, what with running late, I needed something with a bit more oomph (Tony Blackburn and his many jingles).

My hair is brushed, my bra adjusted, my bow-belt tied.

I'm straightening out a particularly annoying twist in my tights when there's a loud knock on the door downstairs. I hover, mid-toast, wondering who on earth it could be.

The door knocks again, great rhythmic thumps.

'Coming,' I shout, racing out the kitchen and galloping down the stairs.

'Darling,' I hear back. 'It's only me.'

I open the door and see Caroline, a diaphanous flutter of cream and poppy.

'I'm sorry to come barging in at such an ungodly hour.'

'That's all right,' I say. 'I thought you were up in Yorkshire? Is everything okay?'

'Not really, darling.' She pushes her huge sunglasses up from her eyes, revealing two tired, cloudy smudges, red and soggy.

'I've been up all night,' she goes on. 'Driving. And crying ... look.' She points at her eyes. 'Digby and I had a big flare-up. It was awful.'

'Oh, I'm so sorry. Look, come in,' I say, gesturing up the stairs.

'Thank you, darling, but I can't. I've got a meeting at half nine at the Connaught*. Ossie Clark and bloody Lulu. That's why I had to drive down. I just wanted to drop this off for you first, though,' she adds, looking down and tapping an old suitcase with her foot.

'Oh,' I say, noticing the suitcase for the first time. It's scuffed and worn and very un-Caroline-like. 'What is it?'

'It was at Mummy's. In the study, tucked away under the daybed. We found it a couple of days ago, before all the upset.

Name: Ehsan Mobasseri

From: a suite at the Connaught

Job: international playboy

Seen for: four days.

Appearance: a young Omar Sharif

Amazing: beautiful fingernails, eyes like char-treuse marbles, had a farm (stud farm)

Less amazing: a definite show-off, didn't get my jokes, hair a bit like Dana's

Look,' she says, holding out a little label tied to the handle with string. On the label, in lovely looping handwriting, are the words *For Evie* and then three kisses underneath *xxx*.

I kneel down and run my hands along the dry veiny leather.

'It's lovely,' I say. The case is a rich oxtail brown, battered and bashed and hard to the touch.

I take the label in my hand, rubbing it between my fingers. And then I read it again. *For Evie xxx*. My eyes twitch and pull. Warm and tingling. I try to hold the tears back but I can't. Fat watery beads slip down my cheeks, making their way slowly but surely into my mouth. Salty little plosions of grief.

Caroline bends down and puts her arms around me.

'Hey, come on,' she says, rubbing my shoulder gently. 'It's okay.' She sighs, a deep, sad sigh, then tilts her head into mine.

129

'It's okay,' she repeats. 'It's okay.' I feel her head bob slightly. Up and down. Up and down.

And there we stay, on my doorstep, kneeling, hugging, crying, as, all around us, London goes off to work.

'Oh,' sniffs Caroline. 'Whatever would Mummy say?' She lifts her head from mine. 'The two of us out here blubbing like this. And you not even wearing shoes!'

This gives us a reason to smile again.

'I'm sorry,' I say. 'It was the label on the suitcase. It set me off. Mrs Scott-Pym's writing.'

'I know,' she replies. 'I know. It's the same for me, every time I find something up there. It brings it all back.'

She holds my hands and gives them a little squeeze.

'But the last thing she'd want is us both moping around. You know what she was like.'

'I really miss her,' I say.

'I really miss her too,' she replies. 'But just think what lovely memories we have of her. And what lovely suitcases.' She smiles and taps the suitcase. 'I've no idea what's inside, by the way,' she goes on, standing up. 'But it's quite a weight.'

'Really?' I stand up and wipe my face then put a hand around the worn leather handle and lift. 'Oh, it *is* heavy, isn't it? Heavier than I thought, anyway. I wonder what it can be?'

'Well, I'm sure you'll solve the mystery soon enough but I'm afraid some of us have very important meetings to get to.' She rolls her eyes. 'I'm sorry, darling, I'm going to have to dash.'

'I need to be in town, too. I don't suppose I could cadge a lift, could I?'

'Of course. Look, you go and grab your things and I'll put this' – she gestures at the suitcase – 'inside.'

I dash upstairs, grab my handbag, knock back the final few drops of Rise & Shine, give my teeth a quick brush and put on a pair of comfy (but stylish) sandals.

In less than a minute, I'm racing back downstairs, dodging the suitcase now occupying valuable space in my tiny hallway.

Caroline is in the car, top down and engine revving.

I jump in and off we go, rocketing into the day.

'The glass cage! That's hilarious, darling.'

We're bombing along Bayswater Road and I'm telling Caroline about my job (well, trial job) at *Right On!* She is full of enthusiasm and admiration and has said, several times, that I will be a *fabulous* journalist and that the magazine is *just right* for me and that it's *so lucky* to have me.

It's always quite hard to have a conversation with Caroline when she's driving, though, because she drives at the speed (and with the Highway Code awareness) of Apollo 16. We've already gone through two sets of red lights (*amber, darling, like the car*) and at one point she was powering past so many other cars that it looked like she'd invented her own lane.

All this speed has had a detrimental effect on my hair. It's all right for Caroline (Elnett in human form) – she looks magnificent, part Pre-Raphaelite muse, part Jackie Stewart. Her hair is still a perfect whorl of wavy bounce. My hair, which *was* neatly brushed, now looks like it's auditioning for a role in *Godspell*.

As we're coming up to Marble Arch, I ask her about Digby and the flare-up.

'Oh, it was awful, darling,' she says, swerving around one car and straight in front of another. 'It was after we'd found your suitcase. I decided to go through Mummy's drawers – I just haven't had the strength to do it up until now.' She shakes her head. 'All those memories. Anyway, I made a start yesterday and, in the bottom drawer, tucked away under acres of neatly folded bed linen, there was an old shirt box – it must have been one of Daddy's.'

(Mr Scott-Pym died in 1936, knocked down by a coal lorry outside King's Cross station.)

'So I took it out and opened it, of course. And what do you think was inside?'

She looks over at me (not the best way to drive down Oxford Street).

'All my baby clothes,' she goes on. 'Tiny little things. Booties. Caps. Cardigans. She'd saved them all.'

(A lone pedestrian wavers in the middle of the street, deterred from advancing further by Caroline's abundant use of car horn.)

'That's really lovely,' I say. 'What a wonderful thing to do, keep it all, I mean.'

'Yes, wasn't it? I had no idea. She never mentioned anything about it.'

We shoot over a still-sleeping Oxford Circus.

'It really touched me,' she continues, with a sad smile. 'I stretched out on Mummy's bed with the box and all the sweet little things around me and then the floodgates opened. I couldn't stop. And, of course, Digby heard me and came to see what was wrong. I showed her the baby clothes and she went very quiet. She just went round picking various things up, smelling them and holding them up to her cheek. And then she was off too. Crying. Great Scottish sobs.'

We lurch right into Berwick Street (no indicator) and almost knock a man off his bike.

'So there we were, the two of us, up to our necks in booties and shawls, crying our hearts out. Actually, do you know what, darling, it was quite nice in a way. Cathartic. A good cry every now and then works wonders I always think.' (A bald man wolf-whistles as we pass.) 'Anyway, eventually we stopped crying but then Digby said the strangest thing.'

She slams on the brakes as a delivery truck reverses.

'Bloody idiot,' she yells, darting round the truck (and yelling at the driver).

'What did she say?' I ask.

'That she wanted to have a baby.'

'Digby?!?!'

'Yes, that was my reaction too. She's far too old, of course. And I said as much. Not to mention the biological impossibility of it all. Talk about an immaculate conception. But then she said she didn't mean *her* having the baby. She meant me.'

'You?'

'I know! Yes! Me! Having a baby!'

'Have you never thought of it, though?'

'What, having a baby? No, not at all,' she says, pulling up outside the sex shop under the *Right On!* office. 'Well, there was a brief conversation years ago but I made it very clear I wasn't interested. I'm just not maternal. It's as simple as that.'

I turn round and look at her (feeling much safer now the handbrake's on).

'And so that's what the row was about, then? Digby wanting a baby?'

'Yes. Well, sort of. I don't know how it happened, to be honest, but before I knew it we were yelling at each other like fishwives. Shouting and swearing. It really was awful. She just wouldn't let it go. And then she let slip that she's been keeping something from me.'

'Oh, that doesn't sound like Digby. What was it?'

'Something important, darling, but I can't go into it now. It's all been such a shock. The two of us don't keep anything from each other, at least that's what I'd always thought. Well, I was furious so I jumped in the car and drove all through the night. I got home just after three. I tried to get some sleep but, of course, I couldn't. I just kept replaying the whole thing, over and over.' She closes her eyes and leans forward, resting her head between her hands on the steering wheel. 'And now I've got this damned meeting.'

'You must be exhausted,' I say, reaching out to her (the light silk of her dress is cold under my warm hands).

'Thanks, darling.' She sits back up and has a good sniff. 'Oh, I don't know what to do.'

134

'What do you mean?'

'After the meeting. Whether to stay down here or go back up to Mummy's.'

I look into Caroline's eyes. The unstoppable, unbeatable sparkle that's usually there is gone. She just looks tired and defeated.

'You need to go back up to Digby,' I say. 'It's no good letting things fester.'

'But she's in such a foul mood. And that gets me in one too. I might be better staying down here for a few days.' She tilts back her head and looks up to the sky. 'A baby. Of all things! Could you imagine me with a baby?' she adds, looking over and smiling.

'Well, no,' I reply. 'Not really.' We stare at each other for a second then burst out laughing.

'Go on,' says Caroline, starting the engine. 'Off to work. Show them how brilliant you are, darling.'

'Thanks for the lift,' I say, getting out of the car. 'And go back to Digby. You'll be able to sort everything out. She needs you up there.'

'And Lulu needs me down here!' shouts Caroline, driving off into London, a great spurt of engine rev and waving arm.

I wave back then saunter over to the sex-shop window, now my pre-work mirror of choice, readying myself for another day of *Right On!* fun.

Interlude – Autumn 1953, Dundee

The funeral had been awful. A dry and dusty affair. Desiccated, thought Catherine. With no tears.

They were in the car, driving home, sandwiched between flat open fields and the heavy, cheerless sky. She'd offered to stay for a few days but her father wouldn't hear of it. He was fine, he said, perfectly capable of looking after himself.

It had all happened so suddenly. Her mother had suffered a huge stroke in her sleep. She was dead by the time the ambulance arrived. Painless, said her father.

A numbed death for a numbed life.

Catherine closed her eyes. She would miss her mother. They'd never really been especially close, her father had left no room for it, but, still, a mother was a mother. In the background, quietly holding life together. Stoical. Invisible.

The service had been mercifully short, with just one reading, done by Muir. It had been her father's idea. She sat there, in the cold church, on the hard bench, listening to her husband reading in the same way she supposed he talked to his patients: clinical, impassive. Pompous.

She opened her eyes just in time to see the car passing a lonely phone box, an incongruous flash of red against the vast grey sky.

'We'll be home soon,' said Muir.

She nodded.

Home.

Is that what it was? Not really, not yet.

But soon.

She laid her hands on her belly. Inside was a new life. Something precious. Something so magical that at times Catherine struggled to believe it. Something she would pour her love into, endlessly.

This baby will be her family, she thought, rubbing gently.

It would be all she would ever need.

CHAPTER 10

Summer 1972

Listings checked: 58 (excellent)

Cups of tea & coffee made by me for me: 3

Cups of tea & coffee made by me for everyone else: 11

Doodles completed: 4 (two faces, a tall tower and
something zigzaggy)

Flickers of disdain from Nickstickupbum: 2

Times caught staring at Griffin's hair to see if she cuts
it herself: 5

Times sent out to buy loo rolls and other essential
supplies: 2

This last point is particularly contentious and springs from the
fact that Griffin is a very inefficient shopping-list maker.

Nickwiththecollars told her that we were running low on loo
rolls, clearly expecting either that:

1. Some loo rolls would magically appear, or
2. Griffin would go and buy some

(For some reason, men are unable to buy loo rolls. It's probably a brain defect of some sort, like not being able to empty bins.) Griffin came straight over to my desk and told me to go and buy a pack, which I did, and then when I got back she'd made a list of other things she wanted me to get (soap, Garibaldis, Brillo pads). This meant I had to go out – again – to exactly the same shop I'd been in a few minutes earlier, losing valuable listings-checking time. Normally I'd have been very happy to get out from work and have a wander (I was always doing it at the BBC) but here, at the magazine, I'm actually really enjoying work and want to make sure I do as good a job as possible. In fact, despite Griffin's rudeness and the arrogant twittery of Nickstickupbum, I love the job.

I think I may have found my calling.

I am a listings natural. Making lists is as instinctive to me as breathing (or bracketing). If making lists were an Olympic sport, I'd have so many gold medals I wouldn't be able to move.

I am Evie, queen of lists, master of listings.

'Evie?'

It's Nickwiththecollars. I think I may have been daydreaming.

'Are you okay?'

He's hovering by my desk again.

'Oh, fine, yes ... I was just ... thinking.'

'Jolly good,' he replies. 'I just came to check that you're on target for the deadline later. Nick's a stickler for it.'

'Absolutely.'

He smiles. 'I knew you'd be right for the job, Evie. Let me know if you need a hand with anything.'

'Actually,' I say, smiling back. 'I've been thinking about the listings and wondered about adding a little personalisation to some of them.'

'Personalisation?'

'Yes, you know, a bit of character, the human touch – something more than just saying where it is and what it is.'

Nick's smile drops. 'Oh, we haven't done that before. Do you mean like a review?'

'Oh no,' I say quickly. 'Nothing like that. You do all the reviews. It'd just be a bit of fun. A little comment every now and then to add interest. Just a few each week.'

'Well,' he says, tilting his head, 'I'm not really sure.'

'Just a bit of colour,' I go on. 'Sprinkled around very sparingly. Like a few hundreds and thousands on a lovely cream bun.'

'Go on then!' His smile returns. 'Let's give it a go and see what happens. You are the trained BBC journalist, after all.'

'Fantastic!' I say (dripping in shame).

'If people like it, we'll keep it. If not . . .' He gestures downwards with both thumbs and ambles off towards the kitchen.

Great. I think a bit of fun and chattiness is just what the magazine needs. There are lists and then there are **LISTS**. I need to do some Eviefying.

I want to start with something easy. Delphinia's gallery.

There's not much space to play around with – I've worked out

140

fifteen words is my absolute maximum, given all the other stuff I have to fit in (name, street, nearest Tube). I just need something that gives a taste of the place and at the same time raises a little smile. I get out my notebook, stare at it for a few seconds, then jot something down:

> *Wonderful friendly gallery with great art & great Chelsea buns – plus the best swirly chairs in Mayfair.*

I count the words. Sixteen. Well, that's close enough. And it is Delphinia. She deserves an extra word.

I sit and look at my handiwork. It might only be a sentence but it's my sentence. With a bit of me in it. And if it gets in the magazine, I'll be there too. For everyone to see. My first published words. A mark of my existence. For ever.

(Or at least until next week's edition comes out and this one gets chucked in the bin.)

I go back to my list, selecting, scribbling and crossing out, all accompanied by the sound of The Chi-Lites on the office radio and the silent roar of my smile.

I'm halfway through *Cinemas** when Nickstickupbum asks me to make a coffee (white, no sugar) and then the others chime in too. Off I traipse to the kitchen, again, to get the coffee plus a tea (white, one sugar) for the other Nick and another tea (black, no sugar) for Griffin. I make myself a coffee too and then, once all the drinks are delivered, get back to my desk. I have a quick read through what I've done so far, crossing out a few words here,

*

Name: Cosmo Wallingford

From: Oxford

Job: documentary film-maker

Seen for: a month

Appearance: bohemian Cary Grant

Amazing: good fun, well travelled, lovely embroidered Afghan (coat not dog)

Less amazing: fickle, flighty, always filming

adding in a few more there, then sit back and relax, sipping my coffee and watching the long shadow of the big sash window stretch across my desk and up the wall.

Mid-relax, a familiar face appears in the open office door. It's Lolo. In a plush burgundy suit. He stands and waves for a second then strides in, walking straight over to my desk. Everyone's head ratchets round, following him across the office floor.

'Hullo there,' he says, grinning. 'Sorry to barge in un-announced.'

'It's fine,' I say (hoping that it's fine). 'Don't worry.'

'I won't stop long – I just wanted to drop this off for you.'

He lifts a plastic bag up onto the desk. It makes a surprisingly solid thud when it touches down.

'Oh, what is it?'

'A present.'

'Aww, that's really nice of you. Thank you.'

'It's a musical present – part of your homework.'

'Oh.' It suddenly sounds less appealing.

'Are you going to take it out of the bag then?' asks Lolo, twinkling.

I gently peel the plastic bag away from its contents. When I'm done, I'm sat staring at a pointy wooden pyramid (tall and slim not solid and squat) with some numbers going up the middle of one side and a metal rod poised over them.

'It's a metronome,' says Lolo, as if that should mean something.

I stare at him, clearly in need of some help.

'It keeps time. Look.'

He reaches down and pulls the metal rod over to one side.

When he lets go, the rod swings back over to the other side and then back again. And again. And again. Each time making a satisfying *click* as it passes the middle.

'It's for musicians. It counts the beats. You can make it go faster, look.'

He slides a little weight down the metal rod and sets it going again. It zips backwards and forwards, brisk little jerks that make me feel quite anxious.

'It's lovely,' I say (using the word quite loosely).

Lolo beams. 'We had a spare one so I thought I'd bring it over. I hoped you'd like it – now that you're on your way to becoming a classical music aficionado, that is.'

'That's really lovely of you.' (Now using the word with laser precision.) 'Thank you.'

All this time Nickwiththecollars has been edging ever closer to my desk, carrying a notepad as a disguise.

'Hullo,' he says, finally getting within hovering distance. 'I'm Nick.' He holds out a hand.

'Lolo,' replies Lolo, shaking the hand. 'I'm just dropping this off for Evie.' He taps the metronome. 'Hope I'm not disturbing you all.'

'No, absolutely not,' he says. I glance over at the others. Griffin is blatantly scowling across at us whereas Nickstickupbum is being much more subtle, ignoring Lolo but still managing to emanate thick waves of disdain. 'Are you a musician, then?'

'Sort of,' replies Lolo. 'I play piano and do a bit of singing but these days I mainly talk about music.'

'Lolo's at Radio Three,' I explain. 'We were BBC colleagues.'

'Oh, yes,' says Lolo. 'We're *very* sorry you poached Evie. We're lost without her.' He glances down at me (there's a certain amount of eyebrow-raising). 'Practically running the place, she was. And she always kept us up to date with what was going on around town,' he adds. 'You're very lucky to have her, you know.'

Nickwiththecollars glows. 'Well, that's exactly what I thought when she walked through the door.'

'Well, I think *I'm* the lucky one!' I say. 'I'm really enjoying it here. And Nick is lovely,' I add, beaming a little ray of sunshine in his direction.

'Wonderful,' says Lolo. 'Well, anyway, look, I should really be getting going.'

'Oh, don't go on my account,' says Nickwiththecollars. 'It's fine. We're all very relaxed here.'

(I glance over again at Griffin and Nickstickupbum – two perfect dictionary definitions of not being very relaxed.)

'No, I really must get going, I'm afraid,' says Lolo. 'Nice to meet you, Nick. And I'll see you again soon, Evie,' he adds, turning to me. 'Don't forget your homework, will you?'

He nods at the metronome, winks, and then walks out the office, flashing an unreciprocated smile at Griffin on the way.

'He seems nice,' says Nickwiththecollars.

'Yes, he is. Really nice.'

'You know, Evie, if he ever mentions anything about the BBC looking for actors . . .'

'I'll put him straight in touch with you! Don't worry.'

'Thanks, Evie.' He gives me a jolly thumbs up then wanders back to his desk, leaving me alone with the metronome.

I have a good look at it. It's quite big and blocky, with stumpy feet, all finished in a dark brown, gravy-stain wood. I'm not entirely convinced by it to be honest so I move it against the wall, trying to keep it out of the way.

I sigh, open my notebook, have a quick swig of tepid coffee and then get back to my listings, throwing myself cheerfully into what's going down in London town . . .

'Who was that?'

It's Griffin. She has the ability to move with the silence of fetid air.

'It was a friend. From the BBC.'

She winces *almost* imperceptibly.

'Well, whoever he was, we don't like social visits during work hours.'

'Oh, sorry,' I say, out-breezing the breeze. 'It wasn't a problem at the BBC.'

Her eyes narrow *ever so slightly*.

'Well, *we* don't like it. What was he doing here, anyway?'

'He brought me this,' I say pointing to the metronome.

She pulls a face that could crack eggs. 'What on earth is it?' she asks. 'It's horrible.'

'It's a metronome,' I answer, suddenly finding it much more attractive than before. 'Look, it counts time.' And I set the metal arm swinging.

We both watch the arm for a few seconds. Left and right and left and right.

'Urgh, it's oppressive,' she says, shaking her head. 'Time should be free.' She wafts an arm in the air, sending the tassels on her blouse flying. 'It's an ethereal, spiritual thing, not something to imprison in an ugly wooden box.'

'Does that mean we can all leave early, then?'

She ignores me.

'It's very bad energy,' she continues, crossing her arms. 'But then I can't expect you to understand something like that, can I, Evie? It's only for those of us with an artistic soul.'

(My tepid coffee has more artistic soul than Griffin.)

'Anyway, you'd better get on,' she says. 'You've got a deadline, remember. You are going to make the deadline, aren't you? After all your little social activities.'

I flash her a thermonuclear smile. 'It's nearly all done.'

She grunts then slinks off, a botheration of patchouli oil and wonky fringe.

I sit for a moment, tapping my fingers on the Formica desk, contemplating the metronome. Then I carefully slide it away from the wall and over to the other corner of my desk, as near to the middle of the room as possible, inescapable, unavoidable. And right in Griffin's eye line.

Three-quarters of an hour later and I'm in the kitchen again making another round of drinks. Nickwiththecollars has left the office early (officially to review a show at the RA, unofficially to audition for a walk-on part in *Gypsy*), which means it's just two coffees and a tea. I'm adding a splash of milk to Nickstickupbum's coffee when he walks in.

'Hi,' I say, giving him a friendly little smile.

He makes a noise (more sigh than hi) and walks over to the brown corduroy sofa, flopping down with a groan.

I give his coffee a stir, thinking. The tinkle-clank of spoon on mug fills the room.

'Nick,' I start, my voice fluttering upwards, uncertain.

'Yes?' he replies, busying himself with a pack of Silk Cut.

'I was wondering, about the listings. I've had an idea.'

'Hmmm,' he says, not looking up.

'Well, I just thought I might try adding a few things outside London.'

I put his coffee down on the coffee table then stand back against the kitchen units.

He lights a cigarette, ignoring the coffee.

'I see,' he says, taking a big drag. 'I don't really think that would work, Evie.'

'What don't you think would work?' says Griffin, stalking in through the kitchen door, antennae bristling. (And inexplicably wearing a garland of silk flowers.)

Nickstickupbum wafts his cigarette in my direction. 'Something about the listings. Evie had an idea.'

'Really?' she snips. 'An idea?' She couldn't have sounded more surprised if I'd told her I'd married a Ford Anglia.

'Well, I just thought people might be interested in what's going on outside London, too, so we could add a few extra entries.'

Griffin sighs and pushes her hands through her hair.

(Her hair defies description. I think it might have started out as a bob but I can't be sure.)

'So,' she says, drenched in the drama of it all. 'Let me get this straight. You want to put some listings from *outside* London in a *London* listings magazine.'

'It was just an idea,' I say, deflated. 'I thought readers might like something different.'

'Would they *really*?' she snorts, an imperious ruffle of silk petunia and tassel. 'And what exciting things might be happening outside London, then? What will we all be dashing off into the shires to see? Cow gives birth! Ferret takes to the stage! Flat cap found in chip pan!' She rolls her eyes, two little smug white flashes.

'I'm just trying to help,' I say.

'Yes, thank you, Evie,' says Nickstickupbum, stubbing out his cigarette. 'But let's just focus on London for now. There's enough here to keep us busy.'

'More than enough,' adds Griffin, with a snarky glint of tooth.

148

'Speaking of which, I've put a few envelopes on your desk, Evie, and some flyers. There's an address list too – we need them all done by the end of the day. Now, if you don't mind,' she goes on, waving a mauve envelope she's been holding in her hand, 'I need the room.'

Nickstickupbum gets off the sofa and begins to make his way to the door.

'Oh, what's happening?' I ask.

'It's my chanting,' says Griffin, giving the mauve envelope another wave. 'You wouldn't understand. It lifts me to a higher spiritual plane. The kitchen's mine every day from twelve-fifteen to half past. It becomes a space of yogic healing and meditative energy.'

As she says this, Nickstickupbum walks past me on his way back to the office. I'm sure I see him frown but it's hard to tell because his face has the expressive quality of a Stickle Brick.

'Oh, I see,' I say, tucking into his slipstream. 'Lovely.' And we both exit the room, leaving Griffin to the nirvana-like joys of the corduroy sofa and a lotus-shaped serving of Om . . .

Back in the office, I see my desk has been covered in a messy pile of flyers and a big box of envelopes. I sit down, push the flyers and the box to one side and have a look at my to-do list. Luckily, the listings are nearly all done. I just need to finish *Shopping*, double-check *Theatre* and Eviefy a couple more entries, then that's that.

Nickstickupbum's office chit-chat is less developed than that of most houseplants, which means the room is silent except for

Griffin's *om-yoms* and *ting-tongs* coming from the kitchen and the *clicketyclack* of my buoyant typing. It doesn't take long for me to whizz through *Shopping* and, with the help of some Tipp-Ex, *Theatre* is soon high-kicking its way to perfection.

For the first of my special entries I choose a nice shoe shop on Church Street (excellent cork platforms and the Saturday girl's mum was once on Ready Steady Go!) then ponder what to do with the last bit of precious page-space. I stare at my desk, taking in some paperclips, a see-through ruler and a bright orange hole punch. And then it comes to me. Fabio's gallery. The Palace of Plastic. He really does deserve something special . . .

La Divinità: Sells spatulas, ladles, eggcups and art.

Concise, informative, and to the point. It's what good journalism's all about. I sit back and smile, admiring my handiwork, then tear the paper extravagantly from the typewriter (like they do in films).

'Here you are, Nick,' I say, handing him the listings. 'All done.'

He takes the sheets of paper, has a quick flick through then puts them in a tray on his desk.

'All done, indeed,' he says, glancing at his watch. 'And plenty of time to go, too.'

I stand in front of him, beaming like a two-bar heater.

'Which is just as well,' he goes on, 'given all those envelopes you've got to stuff.'

My filaments dim and I turn and walk back to my desk.

The rest of the afternoon is spent stuffing flyers into envelopes. I take a flyer, fold it, put it in an envelope then address it. Again and again and again. While I'm doing this, Griffin looks on from her desk, Whistler's mother in tassel form.

There are four pages of addresses, each page with thirty-four lines, and each line with one address, which means 136 addresses. And 136 flyers. And 136 envelopes. And 136 nasty envelope licks.

I'm getting quite near the end of it, when Griffin comes over. She's obviously trying to smile but her mouth can't quite manage it.

'How are you getting on?' she asks.

'It's been wonderful,' I lie, stuffing a flyer into an envelope.

'Good.'

I'm just about to seal the envelope when she holds out her hand.

'Can I have a look?'

I pass her the open envelope.

She takes the flyer out, turns it over in her hands and slowly unfolds it. She looks at it for a few seconds, rubbing her thumb along its edge. The rub turns to a tap. Tap. Tap. Tap. Tap. Tap. Her eyes narrow.

'It's the wrong flyer.'

'What?'

'This,' she says, giving the flyer a dilatory waft, 'is the wrong flyer. It's the *old* one. We need the *new* one sent out.' She drops the flyer in a bin.

'But those were the ones on my desk – the ones you'd left here.'

'I can't be expected to do everything,' she snaps. 'You should have checked. Detail, Evie. It's all about the detail. That's the thing about journalism, isn't it? I thought you'd have known that. Those,' she goes on, pointing to a cardboard box on top of a filing cabinet, 'are the new flyers. Now, luckily for you, the postbox round the corner has a six-thirty collection. You should manage to get them all done by then if you start now.'

And she slithers off, with a flick of wonky fringe and a tut the size of a sonic boom.

Interlude – Spring 1954, Dundee

Catherine looked out across the River Tay. She was in Balgay Park on her favourite bench, perched at the top of the hill.

This is where she'd bring the baby, she thought. Away from Muir and the stuffy house. Somewhere with a vast sky and trees as tall as an Edinburgh tower. She rested her hands on her beautiful big belly, thinking of the life that lay just under her skin.

Down the hill, children were playing. Some were on bikes, others were running, chasing. There was a boy with a kite, a direct line to God, and a group of girls skipping. All their voices swooshing and diving, chiming like church bells.

CHAPTER 11

Summer 1972

By the time I get the bus home, it's already late.

I've spent the last couple of hours taking old flyers out of envelopes and replacing them with new ones. The difference between an old flyer and a new flyer is minuscule (basically Jonathan Dimbleby versus David Dimbleby) so the whole exercise seemed pointless. Griffin left at five on the dot, with a smug shrug and a face like a pug. Nickstickupbum stayed a bit later and – very excitingly – gave me a spare key so I could lock up. It's not quite a foot in the door but it feels like a toe. Maybe two.

The bus trundles up Bayswater Road, stopping, starting, stopping, starting. When we get past Kensington Gardens, I give the cord a quick tug (*ding*) then head downstairs, tapping my shoe on the wooden stair-strips as the bus judders to a stop. I jump off and instantly feel at home, swapping the sleepy-smoky air of the bus for the exhaust fumes and clatter of Notting Hill Gate. I wander past the shops then up to the cinema, where I take a sharp left through a tiny cobbled cut-through.

And then I'm here, my street, quiet and calm, a squat row of different-coloured shoeboxes. Moments later and I'm standing outside the haberdasher's underneath my flat, our lovely corner spot bathed in early-evening sunlight. The shop is stuffed full of things, bursting at the seams (literally), squashed down under the weight of my flat and all its books, LPs and patent leather boots.

All the way home, I've been thinking about the suitcase. I'm dying to get it open and explore its Mrs Scott-Pymness. The closer I get to looking inside, the more desperate I feel (like loos and wanting to pee).

I bounce up the two steps to my front door, stick the key in the lock, twist and push. The door swings open, bashing against the suitcase squatting in my small, narrow hallway. I squeeze in, grab the case and lug it upstairs, depositing it in the middle of my living room.

This is my first chance to have a good look at the suitcase. It's a lovely warm colour and solid not squashy. It's about the same size as my old Dansette record player, just thinner and a bit wider.

The label (*For Evie xxx*) hangs down the side, tied to the handle with a loop of navy ribbon. I run my fingers along the ribbon and then down onto the label. I have a feeling this could all get a bit teary so, for moral support, I get up and put on some Joni Mitchell. The record player turns, the needle hisses and then the twangs and strums of 'All I Want' flutter into the room.

I'm ready.

On either side of the handle is a lock. I use my thumbs to push the two stubby pieces of metal outwards, sending both locks popping open, sharp cracks against Joni's gentle voice. Then I lay the case flat. Ready.

I rub my hands along the hard oxtail leather, imagining Mrs Scott-Pym's hands doing the same. And then I take a deep breath and lift.

It's like opening a treasure chest.

But instead of jewels and chains of pearls there are books, lots of books, and, dotted around the books, three fat bundles of material, all tied with navy ribbon. Lying on top, is a light blue envelope with just one word: *Evie*.

I sit for a moment, taking it all in, thinking of Mrs Scott-Pym packing everything in place. Moving things around so that they sit taut, no slack in sight.

I take the envelope. It's sturdy, substantial, quietly elegant. I bring it up to my nose and smell, hoping to find a trace of Mrs Scott-Pym. I think there's something there, something floral, woody, but I can't be sure. It's so faint it could just be a memory. A hope.

I untuck the top flap from inside the bottom one and slide the letter out. It's blue like the envelope and there's a single crisp fold. I open it, with shaking hands and knocking heart.

My dearest Evie,

All through your life, you have brought me many wonderful things, things that you will never understand or at least perhaps not until you are an old lady like me. You brought me strength, you brought me joy, and you brought me wisdom. You brought me friendship, just as your mother did all those years ago. You brought me my daughter, lost to me by my own stupidity for so many years. And you brought me life; a rich, fulfilling, happy life. I thank you for all this from the very bottom of my full and ancient heart.

I'm sorry I can't be there with you – but I will be watching you, I'm sure, and rooting for you whatever you do and wherever you are.

I have filled this case with books I think you may like and objects I feel should be yours. They are a small thank you for all you have given me.

Thank you, Evie.

You have meant more to me than you can possibly imagine.

With love, lots of love, always, Rosamund x

It's only short but it's still hard to get through because my eyes are full of tears, thick wet blobs that make reading really difficult. I can feel Mrs Scott-Pym in the letter, hear her voice, her clipped precise accent, her way with words. It makes me very happy but at the same time it makes me very sad.

A tear dithers at the end of my nose. Just as I'm about to wipe it away, it drops off, falling onto the letter. I brush at it with my finger, hoping not to damage the precious loops of ink. The damp stain spreads across the paper slightly, bleeding from word to word. I tut, annoyed with myself, and quickly put the letter back in the suitcase, out of harm's way. I wipe my eyes with my fingers and sniff loudly.

The room exhales. Everything is still. Out through the window, the sky is flecked with pink. On the stereo, Joni sings.

I think of my mother. How I'd love to have a letter from her. To be able to imagine her voice. To hear her tone and intonation. Hear her say my name.

And then it comes. Great sobs and snorts. Crying for everything I've lost, for everything so unfair, crying till my eyes hurt and my head hurts and my heart hurts. Crying till I'm empty.

Afterwards, I sit there for a bit, sobering up, and then go to the bathroom to blow my nose. The mirror isn't kind. I decide I need some food and The Beatles so I put on *Revolver* (side two, 'Good Day Sunshine') then make a quick omelette, eating it in the living room on the sofa, staring at the suitcase and humming along to Paul and John.

And here I am, revived and refreshed, tucking into a post-omelette Angel Delight (strawberry). I'm back on the floor, now, next to the suitcase, disgorging it of all its treasures. I've already taken out a few books – *Love in a Cold Climate* (which I've read), *The Old Man and the Sea* (which I haven't) and *South Riding* (which I haven't even heard of). There are lots of other books in the case but I decide instead to focus on the three fat bundles of material slotted in between them all, carefully wrapped and packed, mysterious clumps of Mrs Scott-Pym mystery.

I pick up the first bundle. It's about the size of a loo roll but much heavier. When I untie the navy ribbon, the bundle slackens. Once the ribbon is off, the thick fabric wrapping falls away. It's a Bolton Abbey tea towel – one of Mrs Scott-Pym's (I remember it well). Peeking out from inside the tea towel is Mrs Scott-Pym's old dark green pestle and mortar. I take it out, weighing its marble heft in my hand. I smile. It brings back lovely memories of being in her kitchen. The heat from her Aga. The delicious smells of her baking. The yelps and mumbles of Sadie, her wonderful dog, always on the lookout for food. Bent round the pestle is a small piece of blue paper. I unfurl it and find more writing: *A memento of our magical baking days*. My smile turns into a huge grin. Magical baking days. We certainly had some of those.

The other two bundles are much smaller. There's a tea-towel sausage and a tea-towel tennis ball. I go for the sausage first. The tea towel's quite dark (lots of greens and browns) and when I unroll it I'm greeted by the Brontë parsonage and assorted views of Haworth. Sitting inside, very fittingly, is a fountain pen. It's a lovely warm tortoiseshell colour with gold-coloured art deco fittings. It's beautiful. There's another note wrapped around it. *This is Edward's pen – it went all the way to the Spanish Civil War and back! It deserves to be in the possession of a wordsmith – and that's you, Evie*. Edward was Mrs Scott-Pym's husband. He was a journalist for the *Yorkshire Post* (noblest of newspapers). He died before I was born but I've seen many photos of him and even read some of his pieces and I feel like I know him. I take off the pen top and look at the elegant golden nib. Then I pop the top on the end of the pen, balancing it in my hand as if I'm writing. It feels perfect. As well balanced as a set of scales. Or Mr and Mrs Scott-Pym.

I put the top back on the pen then carefully place it on the coffee table next to the pestle and mortar. Is the pen a sign?

Career advice from the afterlife? A message from Mrs Scott-Pym letting me know that journalism's right for me, despite what Griffin and her non-smiling smile might think?

I ponder this for a moment then turn my attention to the tea-towel tennis ball. When I unwrap it, fold by fabric fold, it unveils two things, one grand and one not-so-grand. The grand thing is on the tea towel: York Minster bathed in light, a sight guaranteed to swell the heart of any Yorkshireman (or Yorkshirewoman). The not-so-grand thing is a cork from a champagne bottle. It's mottled slightly, a combination of nutty browns, and on the bottom, in a darker brown, there's a star and the word *Ruinart*. I turn it over in my hand, wondering why Mrs Scott-Pym has packed an old cork for me. And then I notice something else. Running up the body, in very faint pencil, is a date: 12th May 1945. Is it something to do with the war? My brain whizzes round, trying to think of battles or liberations or landings but nothing comes. Luckily, in the tea towel there's another slip of paper.

This is the cork from the champagne your mother and I had the day she told me she was pregnant with you. We drank outside, under a glorious blue sky, and toasted your life. I want you to think of the two of us there with you, toasting your life, every time you look up and see a glorious blue sky.

I put the paper down and pick up the cork again. It feels warm in my hands. Brittle but strong. As I hold it, I think of Mrs Scott-Pym and my mother sitting drinking champagne in the garden in the last days of the war. Raising their glasses and toasting an unborn me. The chink of glass on glass. The warmth of the summer sun. I look down at the cork, resting on my outstretched palm, feeling its insubstantial weight. How can something apparently so worthless at the same time be so precious?

I look up through the window, hoping to see a glorious blue sky but it's more pink than blue now, licked by giant swirls of orange, red and grey.

I place the cork next to the fountain pen and the pestle and mortar.

On the stereo, a song finishes. There are a few brief clicks of silence and then a sitar drifts in followed by a drumbeat looping round and round. John's voice reverberates across the room, accompanied by a thousand twangling instruments. 'Tomorrow Never Knows'. I stare at the three objects, pulled into their gravity, as the music swoops and twists around me.

Just as we get to the bit with all the backwards trumpets, the doorbell rings.

It takes a second for me to register.

And then it rings again.

I get up off the floor and head downstairs, wondering who on earth it could be at such an ungodly hour (just gone eight). When I'm near the bottom of the stairs, the doorbell rings again, longer, more persistent. I slide my Mary Janes out of the way and open the front door.

Standing there, a burst of smile and glittery eye, is a young girl, suitcase in one hand and poster-sized portfolio case in the

161

other, plus, rising up behind her like a Vegas showgirl's feathers, a giant sticker-covered rucksack.

'Great shoes,' she says, more bag than girl. 'Are they Quant?'

She nods at my slippers (backless leather slip-ons).

'Sorry?'

'Your shoes. They're very nice.' She nods again. 'Very London-y.'

I look down at my slippers, wondering if she's going to try and sell me something.

'I'm Geneviève,' she says, her smile almost as big as her rucksack.

'Who?' I'm utterly confused by:

1. The sudden arrival of an unknown girl on my doorstep
2. The sudden introduction of a French name in amongst an otherwise industrially broad Leeds accent

'Geneviève. Did Aunty Doris not say I was coming?'

'Aunty Doris?'

I look over her shoulders, convinced I'm being caught on *Candid Camera*.

'Yes, Aunty Doris. She said she'd spoken to you about it.'

My face must be as blank as a new notebook.

'Doris. Doris Swithenbank.'

'Oh, Mrs Swithenbank . . . I see.'

'Yes, she's my aunty. Well, great-aunty. She said she'd speak to you. About me staying for a few days. I've just come down on the train from Leeds.'

162

I'm only half listening because my brain is processing an important piece of information.

'Staying for a few days?'

'Yes, I've got some money,' she trills, enthusiastically reaching for her bag. 'Mum gave me some for board and lodgings.'

I look at her, just arrived in London, fresh from Yorkshire and King's Cross*, excitable and full of bounce, a human pogo stick, alive with dreams. And I look at the sky, already close to dusk, stars peeking through the darkening swirls of orange, pink and blue.

'You'd better come in,' I say. 'I think we both need a brew.'

'Oh, thank you.' She squishes herself and her bags through the door. 'Aunty Doris has told me all about you. She said you were lovely.' There's a fair bit of jostling as she inches past me and then she's in – leaving us both trapped in my tiny hallway.

'You'd better go upstairs,' I say, aware that the width of Geneviève plus bags is exactly the same width as my narrow staircase. 'There's a bit more room up there. Can I take a bag?'

'No, I'm all right, thanks.' She starts to wedge her way up. 'The bags keep me balanced. If I lose one, I'll be sent flying – like that donkey in Buckaroo.'

I look up the stairs. The suitcase and portfolio case are squashed against the walls and all the remaining space is taken up by the huge rucksack. There's no light, only shade. It's like watching a Tube train entering a tunnel in very slow motion.

'So has your train just got in, then?' I shout, starting up the stairs behind her.

*

> Name: Douglas McCrae
>
> From: Glasgow
>
> Job: British Rail engineer
>
> Seen for: nine days plus an interminable trip on the East Coast mainline
>
> Appearance: bearded Tony Jacklin
>
> Amazing: impressive knowledge of branch-line stations, Brontë fan, kilt-worthy legs
>
> Less amazing: wouldn't dance, grubby finger-nails, stray baked bean in beard

'No, I got to King's Cross a few hours ago but I've been beggaring around on the Tubes,' she shouts back, stopping mid-step. She attempts to turn round, fails, but scrapes a bit of paint off the wall trying. 'I think I got a bit lost.'

'You must be exhausted,' I say. 'And don't worry, everyone gets lost on the Tube at first. It took me ages to get used to it. Are you sure I can't take those bags for you?' I ask again, more for my sake than hers.

'No, nearly there now.'

She rolls her shoulders, making the suitcase and portfolio case bob up and down. There's a clatter here and a clobber there and then, suddenly, wonderfully, gloriously, she's out on the landing.

'Ooooh, wow, it's really lovely!' She drops the suitcase with a thud and rests her large portfolio against a bookcase.

'Very London-y. And look at all these books. Have you read them all?'

'Oh, no,' I say, coming up behind her. 'No one's ever read all the books on their bookshelves. Here, let me help you get that rucksack off.'

''Sall right,' she says, wriggling out of it. 'All done.'

Now that she's bagless, she seems tiny. I don't know how she managed it all – she's like one of those small insects that can carry five times their bodyweight in leaf.

'Come and sit down,' I say, shepherding her into the kitchen. 'Excuse the mess, though – it's been a busy few days.'

'Oh, isn't it lovely?' she coos, ignoring the kitchen-surface carnage and two days' worth of dishes in the sink. 'What a beautiful kitchen. I feel like I'm in a magazine.'

'Thank you. Here, sit yourself down,' I say, offering her a chair, trying to distract her. 'Now, let me get you a drink. Tea?'

'Oh, yes please, that'd be lovely.' She flops onto the chair with a little pixie sigh.

'Milk and sugar?'

'Three sugars, please. And a good splash of milk. Oh, and if you don't mind could you let it brew for a while, please?'

I smile, thinking of when I arrived in London all those years ago, policing the teapot every time someone offered to make me a tea.

'And what about some food?' I ask. 'Have you eaten?'

'Just a sandwich on the train.'

'You must be starving! How about an omelette?'

She looks unsure, like I'm speaking a foreign language.

'Or a Scotch egg, perhaps, and some Angel Delight?'

'That'd be smashing, thanks.' She reaches down and rubs her legs.

I look at her boots, forest-green platforms covered in glitter and stars. 'Take your boots off, if you like. Your feet must be killing you.'

'Oh, thanks.' She gives me a huge smile, mid-rub. 'They are a bit achy.'

I busy myself in the fridge. When I turn back round, I see Geneviève, bootless, wiggling her toes in a pair of stripy socks.

'Here you go,' I say, putting a Scotch egg and a bowl of butterscotch Angel Delight on the table. 'Do you want some bread and butter with it?'

'Oh, that'd be lovely, thanks.'

I'm reaching up to get a plate out of the cupboard when the phone rings.

'Sorry, I'd better get that. Help yourself to bread,' (I point at the bread bin) 'and the butter dish is just next to it.'

'Thanks, Evie,' I hear her reply as I skim out the room.

'Hullo,' I say, picking up the phone.

'Evie, love. It's Doris.'

'Doris!' A huge grin blooms on my face.

'Look, I won't keep you long, love – I know you're a busy young thing – but I'm ringing to ask a favour.'

'I think I might already know, Doris . . .'

'What? It's about Genevieve, our Julie's daughter, the one in Leeds.'

'Genevieve?'

166

'Yes, that's the one. Just a strip of a lass.'

'Not Geneviève?'

'Who?'

'*Zharn. Vee. Ev.*'

'Ooh no, love, she's not French. They've got an end terrace in Chapeltown. The nearest she'll have got to France is our Julie's soft spot for Sacha Distel.'

'Well, Genevieve or Geneviève, she's here now, sat in the kitchen.'

'She's what?'

'Yes, she got here just a few minutes ago.'

'She never did. Well, I'm right sorry about that, love.'

'It's okay, Doris, don't worry,' I say, thinking about the infinite number of times Mrs Swithenbank has helped me. 'Honestly, it's no trouble at all.'

'Oh, thank you, Evie, love. It'll only be for a few days, just till she gets settled. She's got ideas in her head about doing some-thing in fashion, although from what I've seen of her she knows as much about fashion as I know about space rockets.'

I laugh, thinking of Geneviève's glittery platform boots.

'It's fine. It'll be nice to have some company for a few days.'

'You won't know she's there, love. She's such a quiet little thing. And a proper grafter, too, from what our Julie tells me. Oooh, she's worried sick about her little lass being down in London.'

'I'll keep an eye on her, Doris. Don't worry.'

'Thanks, love. You're an angel. You deserve a medal the size of a dustbin lid.'

We have a quick chat about various other important things

(cod, hairnets, Engelbert Humperdinck), then say goodbye, with a big kiss and lots of *ta-ta*-ing.

When I get back to the kitchen, Geneviève is skating over the worktops with a dishcloth.

'Hey, don't worry about that,' I say. 'I'll do it later.'

'It's no trouble,' she replies. 'I was buttering my bread and thought I'd have a quick tidy-up for you.'

'No, sit down. You're the guest!'

She puts the dishcloth down and sits at the table, a perfect trio of Scotch egg, buttered bread and hungry mouth.

'That was Mrs Swithenbank on the phone,' I say, getting my tea and joining her. 'She says hullo and sends her love.'

'I hope everything's okay?' she asks, her voice suddenly as small as a five-pence piece.

'It's all absolutely fine.' I have a slurp of tea. 'She said you were called Genevieve.'

'Yes, but now that I'm in London I've decided to reinvent myself. Like David Bowie.' She points at her glittery eye make-up, thick streams of sparkle. 'Now I'm Geneviève, you know, like the foreign way.'

Zharn. Vee. Ev.

Just like that. A change. A new person. New possibilities.

I look at her, taking in her sparkly make-up, mullet hair, and brightly coloured lurex top. 'It suits you,' I say. 'Your new name. You make a very good Geneviève.'

'Thanks,' she says, reaching up and pulling at a long frond of hair. 'Aunty Doris has told me all about you, you know. Coming down to London in the sixties and working at the BBC, going to all those parties with pop stars and film stars and people off the telly. It sounds fab.'

'Yes, it really was fab,' I say, the room shimmering with bright little blasts of memory. 'And it still is, of course. You'll love it.'

'Oh, I can't wait. It's all dead exciting. A new start.'

The fridge does one of its sporadic shudders.

'I suppose that's what I'm doing, too.' I smile. 'Making a new start.'

The words linger in the air, like warm breath on a cold day.

'Oh, Aunty Doris said you worked at the BBC.'

'I did, yes. But I've left now – no one up north knows yet, though. It can be our secret.'

Geneviève makes a zippy-up gesture across her mouth.

'So, here's to a new start for both of us, then,' I say, lifting my mug up as if it were a glass of champagne. Geneviève lifts her mug too and we clink them together, a northern toast.

A pact.

A deal.

A spark of reinvention.

CHAPTER 12

Summer 1972

It's the smell that gets me first.

I'm lying on a beach under a beautiful blue sky. There are people walking around. People in swimming costumes. People in swimming costumes eating bacon sandwiches.

And then the sound.

The squawks and caws of the seagulls overhead steadily transform into the rhythmic stomp of 'Little Willy' by The Sweet.

One of the seagulls swoops down and lands on the beach. The next thing I know, it's turned into Tony Blackburn (thankfully not in swimming costume) carrying a huge portfolio case.

I open an eye.

I'm lying in bed. Wafting up the stairs from the kitchen are the smell of bacon cooking and the sound of Radio 1.

It's all very confusing.

And then I remember Geneviève.

I get up, pull on my dressing gown and poke my head round the corner to inspect the box room.

I'm met with the most incredible vision of orderliness. The

box room, pre-Geneviève, had been a thick forest of boxes, bags and unwanted furniture. It looks very different now. The boxes have all been piled into a corner behind the door, stacked up to the ceiling, all the different sizes put together like an extremely well-organised stack of Lego. The bags have been moved under the bamboo daybed, along with an unwanted floor lamp and two fold-up chairs. In the corner by the window, there's another chair (non-fold-up), home to Geneviève's clothes from last night, with her huge rucksack leant against it. And sitting neatly on the bed is her suitcase, open to the world, a masterclass in trim, efficient packing.

(Last night, when I suggested getting the box room ready together, Geneviève insisted on doing it herself and sent me off to bed, so up I came, leaving her with a blanket and pillow plus a large mug of Ovaltine. I did manage to have a quick once round the bathroom with some Vim, though, because it is a truth universally acknowledged that the bathroom is the only room people ever really notice is clean. Or not clean.)

'Morning!' shouts a voice from downstairs. I look down and see Geneviève's head popping round the kitchen door. 'Breakfast's nearly done.'

'Morning,' I shout back, giving her a little wave. 'Smells lovely!' And I skim down the stairs.

'There you go,' she says, putting a bacon sandwich down on the kitchen table. 'I nipped out to Dewhurst this morning for the bacon and used some of your bread. I hope you don't mind.'

'No, course not,' I say, taking a seat. 'Thank you.'

Geneviève must be the strangest-dressed cook in London. She's wearing bottle-green hot-pant dungarees over a blue sequinned blouse and orange tights. She told me last night that she'd love to be a fashion student. It came as no surprise.

Other things I found out include:

1. She's never had an omelette
2. She left school at fifteen to do an apprenticeship at a clothes factory in Leeds
3. Her favourite Beatles song is 'Yellow Submarine'
4. She does a very good impression of Glenda Jackson in *Elizabeth R*
5. She's been making her own clothes since she was eleven
6. She's obsessed with David Bowie

Perhaps the most surprising thing I found out (even more surprising than her favourite Beatles song) is that this is her first time in London. To be fair, though, she is very young. Just sixteen and a half. A baby.

I bite into the bacon sandwich. There's a satisfyingly crispy crackle. 'Mmm, very nice,' I say, between chomps. 'I'm not used to having breakfast made for me.'

'It's the least I could do,' says Geneviève. 'Are you sure I can't give you any money for board? Mum gave me some for you. I've been fretting about it all night.'

'No, don't be daft. I told you, keep your money. Just get some food every now and then and the odd bunch of flowers.'

'That's really nice of you,' she says, sitting down at the table. 'Thank you.' She smiles and tucks into her bacon sandwich. She reminds me of a squirrel, short and slender, with tiny, precise movements (albeit a squirrel with quite eccentric dress sense).

'It was dead exciting when I nipped out for the bacon,' she goes on. 'There were double-decker buses everywhere and people getting in and out of taxis. I felt like I was in a film.'

'I used to feel like that too,' I laugh.

'I even saw a man in a bowler hat!'

'Did you make a wish?'

A huge grin appears behind her bacon sandwich.

'They're a dying breed,' I tell her. 'There aren't that many bowler hats around. It must mean you're going to have a lucky day.'

'Oh, I hope so.'

'You'll be fine. London will love you. Are you still planning on going out all day with your portfolio?'

She nods.

'Very good plan. Oh, speaking of which, that reminds me, I've got something for you. Hold on a sec.' And I take another bite of bacon butty then nip next door to the sitting room.

'Here you are,' I say, returning with a pile of magazines. 'Hope they're useful.'

Geneviève's eyes inflate, two beautiful sparkly balloons.

'Wow! I've never seen so many magazines.'

'Well,' I say, putting them down on the kitchen table with

173

a thud, 'I just thought there might be a few useful contacts for you.'

'Oh, thanks, Evie.' She picks up the top magazine (June's *Honey*) and starts flicking through. 'I really hope I can find a job here. Fashion's the only thing I've ever been any good at.'

'Rubbish. You make *excellent* bacon sandwiches. Did you make all those?' I ask, gesturing at her hot-pant and sequin ensemble.

'Yeah, everything. Well, except for the tights.' She gives her orange legs a quick pluck. 'Tights are a nightmare to make. It's much easier to buy a pair.'

'I wouldn't know where to start.'

(And here I am living above a haberdasher's.)

'Oh, it's easy, really.' She shrugs. 'The main thing is having a clear idea what you want. I'm into Japanese design at the moment. *Basara*,' she adds cryptically. 'Like David Bowie.'

I take in her green hot-pant dungarees, blue sequinned blouse and orange tights. To me she looks 1 per cent Japanese, 99 per cent Tooty Frooty.

'I've moved on since I made these,' she says, clearly able to read my mind. 'I'm trying out a few new ideas. I'll show you later if you like.'

And with that we have a quick chat about fashion (tank tops, Ossie Clark, press studs) and then it's time for me to get ready for work and the joys of the number 94 bus, leaving Geneviève with a spare key, an *A to Z* and the *Right On!* office phone number (just in case).

An hour later and I'm sat telling Nickwiththecollars a story about growing up on the farm. His eyes are streaming and his cheeks are the colour of raspberry jam.

'Oh, brilliant,' he says, clutching his belly. 'With a cow! I can't believe it.'

We're sitting in the office kitchen having a tea. Nickstickupbum is out of the office all day, interviewing someone or other in Barnet. Griffin won't be in for at least another hour, so it's just the two of us. This is very good news because it means:

1. Much less nagging
2. Far fewer drinks to make

He gets a hanky out of his pocket and dabs at his eyes. He has outdone himself today with not one but two sets of upturned collar (a stripy rugby shirt over a stripy normal shirt). I, on the other hand, am collarless, resplendent in a duck-egg-blue jumpsuit, optical illusion in clothing form, helping me tower, ten foot tall, over Nick and, more importantly, Griffin.

He has a final slurp of tea then stands up.

'Right, better get on with some work, I suppose,' he says, walking over to the door (and leaving his mug on the coffee table). 'We should be getting the first copies through soon, by the way. The printer usually drops them off around now.'

'Fantastic!' (Today is publication day. It's very exciting.)

'Well, yes and no. It's when we find out how many typos the printers have slipped in.'

'Oh, I'm sure it'll be fine.' I shrug my shoulders. 'Anyway, I can't wait to see it. It's going to be really strange seeing something I've written being there on the page in black and white.'

'Oh, yes.' He nods enthusiastically. 'It's a real thrill seeing your name in print for the first time. Actually, not even just the first time. I still love it.'

'I'm going to save a copy for posterity.'

'Yes, you absolutely should. In fact you should frame a copy.'

'And stick it up in the loo!'

He laughs, two rosy-red cheeks joined by a broad extravagant smile, and walks out the room with a wave.

It's been a lovely morning.

Nags from Griffin: 0 (still not in)

Flickers of disdain from Nickstickupbum: 0 (ditto)

Amusing chats with Nickwiththecollars: 5

Lists made in preparation for next week's magazine: 8

Times caught singing along to 'Rockin' Robin': 1

Newly printed *Right On!*s delivered to the office: 500

Typos found (so far): 18

The typos generally aren't that bad. I've only spotted one in the listings (a new menswear shop in Chelsea that sells great *kipper pies*). Out of all the others, I have two clear favourites. One is from the letters page (*Dead Sir or Madam*) and the other is from an interview with a spiritual guru (obviously organised by Griffin) where the *m* and *w* got mixed up, meaning the guru goes on about the importance of having *quiet wind*.

The finished magazines were dropped off about half an hour ago, in big bundles. When I pulled out a copy, my heart was throbbing, like the moment you first hold a new Beatles LP.* I whizzed through to the listings pages and there I was. My words. In print. For everyone to see.

An announcement of intention.

A new start.

It's taken me a while to calm down but finally here I am, composed, happy and elbow-deep in next week's listings. I'm working my way through *Theatre* when in walks our very own Lady Macbeth. I put my head down and carry on working, happy to throw myself back into Theatreland and the vagaries of the Saturday matinée.

'Evie.' She's spirited over to my desk and is definitely looking more serpent than innocent flower.

I smile my best Macduffian smile. 'Griffin.'

She's wearing what looks like a brown tent with all the guy ropes hanging loose (more tassel than top). Under it, I glimpse a pair of trousers the texture and colour of loft insulation.

'Did you get the flyers in the post last night?'

'Oh, yes.'

'What, all of them?'

'Yes, all of them.'

Sunbeams shard across the halted room and the air hangs like daggers between us.

Outside, a scooter pootles by.

And then the phone rings. Nickwiththecollars picks it up with supersonic speed.

177

*

Name: Chuck Benjamin

From: America

Job: Soho record shop

Seen for: three days

Appearance: Jim Morrison meets James Dean by way of Al Pacino

Amazing: totally cool, lips to linger in, looked great in a leather pant

Less amazing: not much of a talker, not much of a reader, not much of a thinker

(Griffin narrows her eyes. I'm half expecting lasers to come shooting out of them.)

'Evie!' he shouts. 'There's someone on the phone for you.'

I go and take it from him.

'Hullo?'

'Hello, is that Evie?'

It's Geneviève.

'Hi, is everything okay?'

'Oh yes, everything's fine. I just wanted to let you know I'm having a great time.'

'Brilliant,' I say, aware of Griffin's corrosive glare (she doesn't like us using the phone). 'How are you getting on?'

'Well, I've been to two places already.'

'Oh, well done. Any luck?'

'They were quite busy and didn't really have time to

chat so I gave them your phone number – I hope that's okay?'

'Yes, course it is. Just think of it as home.'

'Aw, thanks Evie.'

'No problem.' I smile at Griffin, which has pretty much the same effect as smiling at mud.

Then the beeps go.

'Oh, my money's running out,' says Geneviève. 'Sorry for phoning but I just wanted to let you know everything's okay.'

'That's great. And don't worry – phone whenever you like,' I add as under-my-breath as possible so that Griffin can't hear.

'B—' The phone goes dead. You really don't get much for 2p these days (that's decimalisation for you).

'The phone's for work, Evie, not for personal calls,' says Griffin, crab-appleing her way back to her desk.

For a moment I consider telling her about Geneviève but then realise that the excitement of a sixteen-and-a-half-year-old girl on her first day in London would be lost on Griffin. So I just nod and get on with my listings.

Half an hour later, when I've moved from *Theatre* on to *Film*, the phone rings again. This time Griffin answers. I pause from my list of *Roxys* and *Ritzys* and earwig (of course).

'Hello. *Right On!* magazine. Griffin speaking.'

(Answering the phone is one of the few times Griffin manages to smile, although it always takes a few rings for her to engineer her mouth into the correct position.)

'Oh,' she says. The smile crumbles. 'Well, I'm afraid the phone isn't really for personal calls.'

She listens to the caller. Her face tightens, straining like it's on the losing end of a tug-of-war.

'And you're sure it's *absolutely* urgent?' she asks, tapping her finger against the headpiece.

Cue another pause. Then ...

'Evie,' she snaps. 'It's for you.'

I go and take the phone, doing my best to ignore the waves of vexation radiating from Griffin.

'Hullo?'

'Evie? It's Lolo.'

'Oh, Lolo. Hullo!'

'Who was that?' he asks.

I pause. 'Mozart.'

'Ha! She's standing next to you, isn't she?'

'Yes.'

'Well, whoever she is, she's got the social grace of Stalin.'

I laugh. 'Beethoven.'

(Griffin looks at me and taps her wristwatch with her finger.)

'You'll run out of names very soon.'

'I know.'

'Look, before you get sent to the nearest gulag I've got some more homework for you.'

'Oh?'

'I've just been given two tickets for Covent Garden tonight. I thought it'd be your perfect introduction to opera. It's something light and jolly. Only one death.'

'Well . . .'

(I've got Mrs Scott-Pym's suitcase to go through and then there's Geneviève.)

'Evie? Are you still there?'

'Yes.'

'Great! So, I'll see you at the main entrance at seven then?'

Griffin does a tut so big it could knock down a wall.

'Sorry, what, oh, yes . . .'

'And we're in the posh seats so no hot pants, I'm afraid.'

'Right, okay.'

'I can't even wear mine.'

I laugh, which clearly annoys Griffin as she leans over and puts her hand on the receiver.

'Bye!' I blurt out, just before the line goes dead.

She takes her hand off the receiver and attempts a smug smile but is only partially successful.

'Evie. The phone line is for business calls only. Especially on publication day.'

'We'd almost finished,' I say, putting the handset back on the receiver.

She bristles (an annoyance of tassels).

'Well, as I've repeatedly told you, the phone is *not* for personal calls. I should remind you that you are here on trial.'

'Yes, but—'

'Speaking of which, I'd like to have a word about this week's listings.' She picks up a copy of the magazine. 'You're adding things.'

'Only to a few of them,' I say. Fourteen to be precise but I don't say this as Griffin is going on about how the listings are just lists and how they only need arranging and checking and how they don't need any actual writing and that any fool can do it and it really isn't very hard and . . .

'I think Evie's done a good job,' says Nickwiththecollars, joining us at Griffin's desk. 'It's nice to see a bit of personality in the listings.'

Griffin shoots him one of her Looks.

'I just meant that writing is an Art, Nick,' she clips. 'It should be left to Writers. People who are Sensitive to Words. Creative People.'

'But I think Evie writes well,' he replies.

Griffin attempts another smile.

'Good writing comes to those of us touched by Calliope's gentle stroke,' she says, doing something with a tassel. 'Not someone who flicks through *Vogue* over lunch.'

(I glance over at the half-hidden copy on my desk. Nothing gets past Griffin.)

'Only people who read well, write well,' she goes on. 'What are you reading now, Evie? Apart from *Vogue*, I mean.'

I'm actually reading *Jacob's Room* but I say *Galahad at Blandings* because I know it'll annoy her.

'There you are,' she says triumphantly. 'I'm going to give you some writing advice now, Evie.'

(People who give advice without being asked for it are usually the same people who don't listen to advice when most in need of it.)

'You need to read Serious Literature,' she intones. 'With

a Meaning. And Sophisticated Vocabulary. And multiple Subordinate Clauses. Something esoteric and challenging. Something to admire, something to kneel before, not something to enjoy. That's how to learn about Good Writing.'

She pauses to get her breath; while she does this, her thick condescension spreads across the room like magma.

And then the phone rings again.

Everyone stares at it for a moment. Rrrring-rrring. Rrring-rrring.

Nickwiththecollars picks it up.

'Hello, *Right On!* Nick speaking.'

He listens.

He nods.

He smiles.

'It's for you,' he says, passing me the phone.

Griffin's cheeks turn the colour of turnips.

'Evie, it's Nick. I just wanted to let you know that the listings are not entirely terrible.'

'Oh, thanks, Nick,' I say, making sure I maintain eye contact with Griffin. 'That's really nice of you.'

'Yes, well, don't get carried away, BBC girl. I look forward to more of the same next week.'

'Absolutely.'

'Now can you put me on to Griffin, please?'

'Of course. Yes, thanks. Bye.' I pass the phone over to Griffin, making sure I show her what a smug smile really looks like.

And then I go and sit back at my desk, un-hide my *Vogue* and think about what to wear for the opera.

CHAPTER 13

Summer 1972

It's like being at a wedding, or the races, or a busy market just for very posh people.

I'm outside the opera house, dithering in front of the grand portico on Bow Street. Around me billow crowds of people, standing, walking, braying, talking, most of them looking like extras from *My Fair Lady*.

I'm ten minutes early. This is very surprising given what a mad dash the last hour and a half has been. Tube. Home. Geneviève. Chat. Clothes. Fish finger sandwich. Coffee. More clothes. Hair. Make-up. More chat. Tube. Brisk walk. Dither.

To pass the time waiting for Lolo, I'm doing a combination of two things:

1. Handbag checking (lipstick, hanky, fruit gums)
2. People watching

It's the best people watching I've done in ages. Bored middle-aged couples. Surreptitious lovers. A very grand man who looks like he's been on the telly. A tiara-ed old lady with the presence of a dreadnought. Someone in a kilt.

I'm deeply engrossed in a mother and daughter having a very middle-class row (few words, lots of eye) when I notice Lolo moving through the crowd. I give him a little wave and, when he's seen me, smile a big hullo.

'Evening,' he says, slaloming up to me. He's wearing a dinner jacket and a large, floppy bow tie. He looks quite dashing (homosexuals do tend to scrub up pretty well).

'Look at you!' I say, my voice sounding far more surprised than I meant. 'You look very smart.'

'Bugger. You beat me to it.' He breaks into a huge Welsh grin. 'I was just about to say the same thing.'

'What, how smart I look?'

'No, how fabulous you look.'

'What? This old thing?'

(I'm in one of Caroline's cast-offs: an Ossie Clark floaty dress with matching floaty cape – an airy summer spray of peony and cream.)

'You look really lovely. Just missing a swirly chair to show it off properly.'

'Oh, I don't need a chair,' I say, giving him a twirl.

Lolo laughs. 'I didn't realise you came with built-in swirl!'

'Very funny.'

'Sorry I'm a bit late,' he says. 'I got stuck at work.'

'What, you came straight here?'

'Yes, sprinted my way across London. I was like Nijinsky.'

'Horse or dancer?'

'I'd say a bit of both.'

This makes me laugh. For someone who works at Radio 3, Lolo can be quite funny.

'So is this what you normally wear for work then?' I say, gesturing at his bow tie. 'Or have they had you reading the news?'

He smirks. 'I keep it at work. It's like a uniform – I pop it on whenever they send me somewhere swanky. There's not much call for it at home. Speaking of which,' he goes on, 'Oscar sends his regards.'

'Oh, lovely. You should have brought him!'

'Well, Oscar's not much of an opera fan. Mind you, he's not the only one, is he?'

'Plinky plonky music,' I say. 'And a lot of shouting.'

Lolo laughs again. 'Let's see if you're still saying that in a few hours' time.'

'You'll be wishing you'd brought Oscar instead of me.'

'Well, it was a close-run thing but I thought your twirls are a smidge better than Oscar's.'

I do another one, giving the Ossie Clark a good shimmy.

'See? I don't think Oscar could compete with that.'

'Charmer.'

'Now,' he says, bowing slightly and gesturing towards the doors, 'shall we get this music lesson started?'

Inside is even busier than outside. It's much noisier too, with all the gossip and chit-chat trapped under the elaborate ceiling, bouncing between columns. The air hums. Lights sparkle.

Mirrors glisten. It might be my first time at an opera but I recognise the sense of expectation; it's exactly the same as before the start of any play or musical. The excitement. The buzz. Where are the actors going to take us? And what magic will they use to get us there?

We zigzag our way slowly through the crowd, easing past fur stoles, long gloves and gleam after gleam of diamond. Lolo leads, glancing back occasionally to beam a huge smile and check I'm still following. As we move, the chatter seems to rise and fall, swooping around like flocks of birds.

'Just up here,' says Lolo, gesturing at a very grand staircase. The staircase is tractor-wide, with furrows of people all edging upwards, step by sumptuous step. As we join them, I tilt back my head and take in the cavernous space, with great mirrors on the wall and a huge chandelier hanging at the end of a delicate glittering chain.

'It reminds me of Dad's farm,' I say to Lolo.

He grins. 'I thought you looked at home here. So is this how you dress on the farm, then?'

'Only for the very best cows.'

'Well, I just hope they appreciate all the effort.'

'They think I look moooooootiful.'

An old lady with a pink rinse gives me a Look.

'Well,' sighs Lolo. 'Yorkshire cows must have very good taste, that's all I can say. Here we are,' he adds as the stairs end and we step out into a room so swanky it makes the one downstairs look like an unloved porch.

There are more mirrors and more columns and, dotted around

like sales assistants in a Bond Street shop, large arrangements of flowers, lavish and assured.

'Very nice,' I say. 'What time does the queen arrive, then?'

'She's probably here already,' replies Lolo, guiding me over to one side. 'She works behind the bar most weeknights – it's a way for her to meet the hoi polloi.'

'The man on the street.'

'Exactly.'

He grins. 'Speaking of the bar, how about a drink?'

'Good idea.' I reach down into my handbag. 'Here, let me get them, though.'

'What! On your first visit? Don't be daft. You wait here,' he says, manoeuvring back into the crowd. 'Won't be long!'

And off he goes.

He's left me in prime people-watching territory. Standing by the staircase, I get to see everyone as they come up the stairs, wave after wave of dinner-jacketed men and helmet-haired women. Most look like they've travelled by time machine rather than taxi but there is the odd trendy couple here and there, standing out like daisies on a lawn. There are intriguing combinations of people too. Middle-aged ladies with young men. Middle-aged men with young men. Young men with young men. Someone with a shih-tzu.

I'd be amazed if the performance can compete with all this.

I'm busy watching another Ossie Clark (mint green and strawberry) make its way up the stairs when a glass of champagne magically appears in front of me.

'Here you are,' says Lolo. 'I thought we needed to celebrate the occasion of your first opera.'

'Oh, thank you.' I take the champagne, watching its bubbles twinkle like tiny diamonds between my fingers.

'Cheers then,' says Lolo.

'Cheers,' I say, clinking his glass. There's a bright sonorous ring, like someone playing the triangle. We smile and then take a gulp of champagne. It's cold and dry and hits the spot. 'Oh, that's lovely, isn't it?' I bring the glass up to my lips again and have another sip. 'Mmmm, this is the life.'

'Oh yes,' he says. 'Although, to be honest, at Radio Three every day's like this. We have champagne on tap.'

I grin. 'That doesn't surprise me.' I look over at Lolo. His cheeks have started to pinken, two warm friendly patches on a kind intelligent face. 'Funnily enough, somebody gave me a champagne cork this week.'

'What, just the cork?'

'Yes, just the cork.'

'Had you done something very bad?'

'Probably,' I laugh. 'It was from my old neighbour in Yorkshire, Mrs Scott-Pym.'

'Ah, the one with the books and the opera.'

'That's right.'

'And the one with the champagne, too, apparently.'

'I think she was more of a sherry fan, actually.'

'Was?'

'Oh, yes, sorry – I should have said. She died a few months ago.'

The lights dim momentarily and the room's many diamonds go dull.

'Oh, I'm so sorry, Evie,' says Lolo. 'I didn't realise.'

189

'That's okay,' I say, doing a sad smile.

Lolo looks at me, holding my gaze, and does a sad smile too.

'Anyway,' I go on, 'the reason I'm telling you all this is because her daughter, Caroline, has been up in Yorkshire clearing out her house. She came across an old suitcase with my name on and brought it down for me. When I opened it, I found the champagne cork.'

'Oh,' says Lolo, his eyes going as big as his bow tie. 'Why the cork?'

I smile. 'It's the cork from the champagne that she and Mum drank when they found out Mum was pregnant with me. They were out in the garden, apparently, *under a glorious blue sky*.'

'Well, Mrs Scott-Pym sounds absolutely bloody marvellous. I think we need to toast her.' He stands up straight and raises his glass.

I raise mine too.

'To Mrs Scott-Pym,' says Lolo.

'To Mrs Scott-Pym,' I repeat and then we *ting* glasses and have another slurp of champagne.

'I'm sure she'd approve of your being here tonight,' says Lolo.

'Oh, I'm sure she would! She loved opera. She had a huge stack of opera records and a gramophone as big as a cow. You could hear the music and shouting all the way down the drive.'

Lolo laughs. 'I think you'll find it's *singing*, not *shouting*.'

'We'll see.'

'Well, if it was good enough for Mrs Scott-Pym, it's good enough for me. I think this calls for another toast.'

'Another one?'

'Yes. To opera.' He lifts his glass in the air again.

I raise my eyebrows (not my glass).

'Come on,' he says. 'You might just enjoy it.'

I smile and slowly, very slowly, raise my glass.

'To opera.'

There's another quick chink then we both knock back our last drops of champagne.

'Okay,' says Lolo, putting his empty glass down on the balustrade ledge. 'I think it's time. Come on!'

Our seats are amazing. Smack-bang in the middle of the stalls. In fact pretty much everything about the auditorium is amazing. Walking in was like stepping into a giant Turkish delight – all deep red and soft and plush. As well as all the deep red there's also a lot of gold. On the balconies, on the ceiling, even on the thick heavy curtains that hang across the stage like the deluxe double doors on an advent calendar.

'It's not bad, is it?' says Lolo, leaning over.

'I've seen worse.'

I look around. The ceiling is cathedral tall and the room circles round us like a giant polo mint.

Lolo follows my gaze. 'I'm glad you like it. I love coming. In fact, it's probably one of my favourite places in London.'

'I can see why.' I have a quick test bounce on my comfortably plump chair (obviously made for a better class of bum). 'It's all very grand.'

'I've got my eye on the curtains,' he says, nodding over at the elaborate drapery. 'I think they'd look great in the downstairs loo.'

'Oh, yes, very nice.' (I bet Lolo and Tarquin have lovely soft furnishings.) 'I especially like the huge coat of arms.'

'I thought you'd like that,' he says. 'I bet you've got one just like it back at the farm.'

'Absolutely. In the barn with the cows.'

We're interrupted by a horrible discordant screechy, scratchy sound.

'Oh, God, what's that? Don't tell me we've got to put up with this for a couple of hours.'

Lolo laughs. 'It's just the orchestra tuning up. Although, to be honest, I've heard a few operas that do sound like this.'

I sense someone arriving at the empty seat next to me so I turn my head round to have a look. An old man with a pencil moustache is negotiating his way into the chair. I nod and give him an encouraging smile. He smiles back and then cranks slowly down. (I make a mental note to have my fruit gums at the ready – he looks a cougher.)

'So,' I say, turning back to Lolo and stretching the word across a fair bit of orchestral shenanigans. 'What's it about then, this opera?'

'It's *La Bohème*,' he replies. 'Everyone knows *La Bohème*.'

'I don't. Well, not really. I know it's about poets and Paris.'

'There you go. That's all you need to know.'

'No, come on.' I give him a good elbow prod. 'You'll have to tell me the story. I'll never be able to keep up when they're all shouting away in Italian.'

'Singing.'

'You know what I mean.'

Suddenly everyone starts clapping.

'What's going on now?' I ask.

Lolo nods at the stage. 'The conductor's just arrived.'

'Oh, I see. But what about the rest of the band? Don't they get a clap too?'

'At the end,' stage whispers Lolo. 'And they're an orchestra, not a band.'

When the clapping stops, there are a few seconds of silence, then the conductor lifts his arm in the air, has a quick glance round the orchestra and brings his baton down in a big elaborate swoop.

'Here we go,' says Lolo.

The music jostles in.

Bam-bam-baaam.

(Dim-dim-dim.)

Bam-bam-baam.

(Dum-dum-dum.)

Bam-bam-baam.

Di-di-dilidi-di-di-dilidi-di-di-di . . .

And then it's off. Sweeping up, soaring down.

There's an attractive man on stage, pretend painting. He starts singing – bullock low – to another man on stage (less attractive). It's all quite shouty at first but it soon begins to pick up a tune. Then the other man starts singing (more bull than bullock). They're half singing, half talking to each other – a bit like me in the kitchen when a decent song comes on the radio. I've no idea what they're saying but they seem to like each other. Then another man comes on stage. He seems to bring the mood down quite quickly (I know people just like that). There's a lot of man-shouting and quite a bit of singing. Sometimes the music disappears and sometimes it surges forwards; sometimes the music and the voices keep up with each other and skip along together quite nicely. While all this is going on, there are several toasts (now I know where Lolo gets it from) and then everyone leaves, apart from the attractive man, who faffs around on stage a bit, acting.

A lady (young, pretty, nice hair) arrives. The music immediately becomes more lush. They're speak-singing quite slowly and every now and then I recognise a word (*grazie, vino, quando*). The lights on stage dim a little and then – whoosh – the music goes *really* lovely. Up until now it'd been *quite* nice (like the theme tune to a costume drama on the telly) but this bit is wonderful. The attractive man is singing a lovely song to the pretty lady. She sits listening to him and doesn't interrupt once (you can tell it's a period piece).

Then the pretty lady starts to sing and it all gets even more beautiful. Her voice melts into the music, rich gooey flows of emotion. I think she's flirting with the attractive man – and he definitely looks interested. She sends her voice soaring up to the ceiling and the music pirouettes underneath, giving me goosebumps (just like The Beatles did at the Hammersmith Odeon).

There's a lot more singing after that, including some sitting-singing (which can't be easy) and another really good bit when the stage is full of people, all of them belting out a good show tune (with some excellent trumpeting). And then a crescendo, a flourish, a bottle of wine being waved in the air, a final blast from the band, and then silence. The stage goes dark. A huge roll of applause barrels up from the audience, with quite a few *bravos*, and then the lights come back on.

'Well?' asks Lolo, leaning over.

'Yes, well, I . . . yes, it was good. Some bits.'

'So you liked the shouting then?'

'Well, let's just say it was a better class of shouting.'

'And not plinky plonky?'

'There *was* a certain amount of plinky plonkiness but perhaps not *quite* as much as I expected.'

'So you're saying it's good, then?'

'Well, not Joni Mitchell good or "Bridge Over Troubled Water" good, but – yes – some bits were good.'

He grins, sending his rosy cheeks into two lovely pink squash balls.

'Come on, I think you need another drink to get you through the second half.'

And we head back to the bar, shuffling patiently behind the nice old man with the moustache.

'Cheers.' Our glasses *ting* and we both knock back a good mouthful of champagne.

The bar is heaving (again). We're in a thick fog of chit-chat, smoky and opaque. Every now and then I get a waft of nearby conversation (the singing, the set, strikes) but most of it's just a rowdy background hum. It all reminds me of a Soho pub at last orders but with more pearls and fewer beards.

'So there *is* a story, then,' I say to Lolo.

'Course there's a story!'

'Well, I knew there'd be some story,' I say, rolling my eyes, 'but I thought it'd mainly be lots of people singing and just doing the odd bit of acting in between.'

He grins. 'Actually, it's a really nice story. Taken from a book. *Scènes de la vie de Bohème,*' he adds in very good non-Welsh French.

'Oh, fancy!'

'Written by *Monsieur* Henri Murger. Published 1851.'

'Very clever. You're full of interesting facts, aren't you?'

'Stuffed to the brim. And bursting at the seams, too,' he says, patting his belly.

I laugh. 'Go on, then. Give me another interesting fact.'

'You first.'

I have a good think.

An interesting fact.

An.

Interesting.

Fact.

Suddenly I know nothing.

I look around the room for inspiration.

'Mmmmmm . . . .'

Lolo's eyebrows arch in suspended anticipation.

'Erm . . .'

I feel under pressure.

And then, from somewhere, my brain snatches a flicker of a fact and presents it to me. Triumphant.

'Elizabeth Taylor's first horse was called Betty.'

Lolo stares at me.

I smile.

'Betty?'

'Betty.'

'I see.' He has another sip of champagne. 'Well, you learn something new every day.'

'Come on, then, clever clogs – your turn.'

'Well, you know we're all made of stars.'

My eyes widen and I'm about to say how amazing that is when he stops me.

'That's not my interesting fact,' he says, shaking his head. 'Everyone knows that.'

'Oh, of course. Yes.' (Do they?) 'But not just stars, though? We must be made of something else.'

'Absolutely. And that's what I'm coming to. Any idea what?'

I'm under pressure again. This must be what being on *University Challenge* feels like.

'Erm . . .'

(I try to remember something from my school science classes but all I get is Bunsen burners.)

'Hopes and dreams?'

Lolo grins. 'Very good answer. I'm not sure how correct it is *technically* though.'

'Spoilsport.'

'I think what you were looking for is *water*.'

'Oh yes, that's what I meant. Hopes and dreams and water.'

'Exactly,' says Lolo. 'Now, the amount of water on Earth is

197

finite, it just keeps going round and round, which means that there's a very high chance that a few tiny drops of the water in *your* body was also in Cleopatra's.'

'Wow,' I say, properly amazed.

'And maybe even in Betty, Elizabeth Taylor's horse.'

'Oh, you've spoilt it now!' I say, laughing and having a sip of champagne.

'And the champagne you're drinking,' he goes on, 'is also made of water. Which means that some of it was probably drunk by Napoleon. Or Chaucer.'

'That's incredible, isn't it?' I hold my glass to the light, watching the bubbles fizz upwards. 'I'm drinking the same champagne as Elizabeth the First.'

'Or Puccini,' adds Lolo, having another sip.

'Or Puccini, yes,' I repeat. 'Or Katherine Mansfield.'

'Or Dickens.'

'Julius Caesar.'

'Emily Brontë.'

'Mrs Scott-Pym.'

We both smile.

And then I have another thought.

'Or my mum.' I look again at the champagne. 'I'm drinking the same champagne as Mum.'

Lolo gives me a lovely warm look. 'Yes.' He nods. 'Yes, you are.'

That's such a nice thing to know.

I stare at the glass, lost in its bubbles.

And then a very loud bell interrupts my staring.

'That'll be the end of the interval,' says Lolo. 'Are you ready for round two?'

'Do you know what? I think I am.'

Things go a bit unstuck in the second half (I knew it). The attractive man and the lady with nice hair fall in love and everything looks to be going great. But then she falls ill (probably tuberculosis – everyone seemed to have it in those days) and it all gets incredibly sad. There's quite a bit of sofa sitting and the man and the woman sing their lovely songs from the first part again (ish). But then the music slows down and her singing gets quieter and quieter until it just disappears, like a drop of blood fading in a glass of water, dissolving into nothing.

The auditorium is silent. Not London silent. A proper countryside middle-of-nowhere hear-a-pin-drop-from-ten-yards silent.

Tears trickle down my cheeks and I focus everything on crying as quietly as possible.

On stage, the handsome man shout-sings the dead woman's name. Mimi. He shout-sings from his stomach. From his heart. Broken. And then the lights go out.

I get my hanky from my handbag and have a good eye-dab (thank goodness for waterproof mascara). The lights come back on and everyone returns to the stage to take a bow, accompanied by a huge – and much deserved – applause.

'Well?' says Lolo. 'What do you think?'

I sniff, pause, gulp and finally manage to say one word.

'Amazing.'

*

It takes us a while to get out of the opera house (partly the fault of the nice old man with the moustache) but it doesn't matter because Lolo is a good chatterer. Before we get back out on Drury Lane we've covered:

1. Music (Puccini's other operas, our favourite Beatle, Art Garfunkel's hair)
2. Wales and Yorkshire (cheese, cows, poets)
3. Politics (power cuts, Hanoi Jane, Harold Wilson's mac)

I also discover that Lolo can do impressions. He does a very good Edward Heath, a passable Mick Jagger and even has a stab at Pamela from the BBC (each of which earns him quite a few Looks from the opera crowd).

'Oh, that's better,' I say as we eventually leave the building. 'It's nice to be out in the fresh air.'

'It was getting quite hot in there, wasn't it?' says Lolo, fanning himself with a programme. 'It's all right for you in your floaty summer dress – you should try being trussed up in a dinner jacket all evening.'

I'm just about to reply with a comment about being trussed up in strappy high heels all evening when I see Geneviève. She's standing on the other side of the road. She sees me and we give each other a wave.

'Oh, seen a friend?' asks Lolo, glancing round.

'Well, yes. She's staying with me for a while. I didn't realise she'd be here, though. Hullo!' I shout, as Geneviève walks over to us.

'Hi,' she shouts back, giving another wave.

'She works in fashion,' I say to Lolo.

'I can tell,' he replies, sotto voce.

She's causing quite a stir. Assorted furs and diamonds are staring at Geneviève's black and red Barbarella-meets-the-Magic-Roundabout outfit. She's wearing huge boots with big padded pantaloons that stick out below the knee then curve in at the hip. Her top curves in and out too, giving her the appearance of a walking Henry Moore sculpture.

'I was having a walk round London so thought I'd come and meet you,' she says, standing in front of us and suddenly looking very small and young. 'I hope you don't mind.'

'No, of course not! It's a lovely surprise. Lolo,' I say, turning to his smiling face, 'this is Geneviève. And Geneviève, this is Lolo.'

Lolo sticks out his hand. Geneviève takes it, a tiny curl in a big Welsh paw.

'Cool outfit,' says Lolo, sounding like someone's dad.

'Thanks,' says Geneviève. 'I made it myself. It's meant to be Japanese.'

'Oh.'

I can see he's floundering so I step in.

'How do you make it stick out?'

'Easy,' she replies. 'Armbands.'

'Armbands? What like when you're learning to swim.'

'Yeah, look . . .'

She untucks a fold of material from her boot and gives us a quick flash of inflated orange.

'Very clever!' I say, impressed by Geneviève's armband ingenuity.

Lolo nods. 'Who'd have thought.'

'It's easy, really,' says Geneviève. 'I'm going to try and make it better. More integrated. And less orange.'

This leads us into a brief conversation about the colour orange (pros, cons, use in Smarties) and then Lolo asks if he can walk us to the Tube. I tell him we'll be fine and that I'll take Geneviève the scenic route home (via Piccadilly to see the lights) and he smiles, bows, shakes Geneviève's hand again, and heads off to Holborn Tube.

'He's very nice,' says Geneviève. 'Is he your boyfriend?'

'No, Lolo's homosexual,' I explain.

'Really?' replies Geneviève. 'We had a homosexual man at the factory in Leeds. Lovely, he was. Very good with a cross stitch.'

I smile, take her by the arm and lead her off towards Long Acre and the bright lights of Piccadilly.

Interlude – January 1972, Yorkshire

Rosamund Scott-Pym stood by the French windows in her kitchen, looking out across her gravelled terrace and the garden stretching out behind it. It was a glorious winter day, crisp and bright, with Yorkshire resplendent under a rich Giotto blue. She was watching the birds, busy with their own lives. A robin on the lawn, pecking for worms. A chaffinch on the bird table, enjoying the leftovers from last night's supper. A couple of tiny goldcrests playing in the trees. Nature getting on with being nature.

She smiled, thinking of all the happy memories the garden had given her. Rich soil, indeed. It had become part of her, as vital as an organ, restorative and alive.

'Right, here we are,' said Caroline, getting a bottle of olive oil from a kitchen cupboard. 'Shall we start?'

It had been Caroline's idea. At breakfast, she'd noticed her mother had a dry patch on her scalp, red and angry under her fine silvery hair. The olive oil was a trick she'd picked up in Italy, a comforting piece of magic that delivered soothed skin (as well as polished shoes).

Rosamund pulled a towel closer round her shoulders.

'Well, if you're quite sure,' she replied. Her hair was damp, freshly washed, giving off a faint smell of roses.

'Absolutely. It'll really help, Mummy. You'll feel much better.'

Caroline was at the kitchen table, decanting some of the olive oil into a ramekin.

'Would you mind if we did it out on the terrace?' asked Rosamund.

'What?' shot Caroline, looking up. 'You'll catch your death.' She put the bottle down with a tut. 'Honestly I won't make a mess. Promise.'

It wasn't the mess Rosamund was worried about. Who's afraid of a little mess? She just wanted to be out there, in the garden. Soaking up the precious drops of life.

'Oh, the midday sun will have taken the edge off it,' she said. 'It doesn't look at all cold.'

'It's January! Of course it's cold. And you're not getting any younger, are you?'

Digby was now in the kitchen too, tapping a folded *Times* against her thick winter cords.

'I think you could probably say the same for all of us,' she said, winking at Rosamund.

Rosamund beamed back.

'Oh, but Mummy's got this crackpot idea about sitting outside while we do her hair.'

'Well, it sounds like an *excellent* idea to me,' said Digby.

'Vote carried,' chuckled Rosamund.

Caroline drummed at the table with her fingers. 'Oh, I see, so now I'm the sensible one, am I?'

'Well,' said Rosamund, holding out her hand to her daughter. 'If that's the case, dear, then I think we're all in trouble.'

She had decided to have one last Christmas free of all talk of cancer. Free of sad faces. One last innocent Christmas. The X-rays had suggested it was quite far on. Too far on, really, for treatment. There was the operation, of course, but it was brutal and, the doctors freely admitted, all very uncertain. Next Christmas would probably be her last. She'd tell them in the summer. Or spring, perhaps. Bad news always seemed much easier to cope with in the spring. For now she just wanted to enjoy this precious, unspoilt time.

'There you go,' said Digby, putting an old woollen blanket over Rosamund's knees. 'That should keep you warm.'

'Thank you, dear.'

They were outside on the terrace now. The sun was overhead, doing its level best to warm the winter air, unhindered by cloud or breeze.

Caroline combed a parting in her mother's hair, put the comb into her apron pocket then took the ramekin of olive oil from a nearby bench.

'Are you ready, then?'

'As I'll ever be.'

Caroline dipped her fingertips in the ramekin and then, gently, tapped her fingers along the parting. And then again. Dip and tap.

(*Is that okay?*

Perfect, dear. Thank you.)

When she thought there was enough oil, Caroline began to move her fingertips in small circles, no bigger than a ten-pence piece, easing the oil across her mother's scalp, massaging, smoothing. When she came to a particularly dry patch, she dabbed her fingers back in the ramekin and then slowly worked her way through it, bathing the flakes with oil and lightly rubbing them away.

Rosamund closed her eyes.

Somewhere, in the distance, she heard a bird sing.

Digby tapped Caroline on the shoulder then gestured inside and walked back to the kitchen, gravel crunching softly underfoot.

Caroline carried on. Dipping. Rubbing. Easing. She leant in, just a breath away from the fine grey hair that twisted under her fingers. Here they were, after all these years, their differences long forgotten, growing into each other.

'You will look after Evie, won't you, when I'm gone?'

(Where did that come from, wondered Caroline.)

She kept rubbing. 'No, I'll put her in a box and send her off to Cuba. With only a Battenberg cake and a few Adam Faith LPs for company.'

Rosamund smiled. Caroline was so close that she could smell her scent, fresh and woody.

'Of course I'll look after her,' whispered Caroline, leaning forward and kissing her mother on the cheek. 'And I'll look after you, too, you silly old thing.'

Rosamund peeked open an eye and saw Caroline looking straight at her. They held each other's gaze for a moment. A loud silent eloquence.

And then the music started. Jaunty looping strings and horns that raced out from the house, romping their way down the terrace.

'I thought we needed some *Norma*,' shouted Digby, stepping out through the French windows and carrying a tray. 'And some tea.'

She crunched her way over to Rosamund and Caroline. 'Oh, and I thought I'd bring the last of Rosamund's delicious shortbread, too. Scottish central heating.' She put the tray down on the gravel and handed a mug to Rosamund then offered her the plate of shortbread.

'It's all gone, has it?' said Rosamund, taking a piece of shortbread. 'Well, I'll make some more, dear, after lunch. A big batch this time, I think, so you can take some back to London for Evie ...'

Chapter 14

Summer 1972

'Sublime. Electrifying. Isn't it just glorious?'

That's Nickwiththecollars. He's been gushing over my opera trip for the last ten minutes. He's talking about the bit when Mimi (the lady with the nice hair) dies on the sofa.

'Well, it wasn't that glorious for her,' I say. 'Or the nice chap she'd just shacked up with.'

We're in the office, having our (Evie-made) morning coffee. Nickwiththecollars is hovering at my desk, coffee in one hand, biscuits in the other. It turns out he's a Big Fan of opera, probably a combination of all the drama mixed with the comfy seating and better class of catering. Nickstickupbum is doing his best to ignore us, which can't be easy.

'I tried to get a press ticket,' says Nickwiththecollars, craning round and speaking to the other Nick. 'But they didn't get back to me.'

'Mmm,' he replies, not looking up.

Nickwiththecollars turns back round to me. 'I bet the staging was marvellous. They always do *such* a good job at Covent Garden. I saw a wonderful *Don Giovanni* there,' he adds, gesticulating with the Bourbon cream.

'Yes, it was all lovely. I really enjoyed it. Much more than I thought I would, in fact.'

'Oh, it's such a good night out,' he says, giving the Bourbon cream a good dunk. 'The singing, the drama, the music, the sets. Total spectacle, that's what they say, eh, Nick?'

Nickstickupbum ignores us and carries on doing something editorial with a red pen.

'And the audience!' I say. 'They were definitely all part of the show too.'

'Ah, you've been reading your Debord,' replies Nickwiththecollars.

Have I? I have no idea what he's talking about but I smile and nod and try to look as though that's exactly what I've been doing.

'Commodity fetishism . . .' he goes on.

(My mind jumps to the PVC suit in the sex-shop window downstairs.)

'. . . that's what it's all about. *The Society of the Spectacle*. Brilliant, Evie. Hey, I've just had an idea,' he says, having another dunk. 'Why don't you write a review?'

'Me?'

'Yes, you. I think you'd really bring something fresh to it. The readers would love it. That'd be okay, wouldn't it, Nick?'

'Mmm,' he grunts again (the oral equivalent of a cow swatting flies with its tail).

'There you go,' says Nickwiththecollars. 'Agreed.' He does his jolly monk smile and has a sip of coffee. 'Oh, actually,' he goes on, having a final dunk, 'if you've got a minute, Evie, you couldn't nip out for some more Bourbon creams, could you? This is the last one.'

When I get back from the shop (Bourbon creams, fly spray, pack of dishcloths), the post has been. One of my jobs is to go through the post and put it on the appropriate desk. This is fairly easy as it mainly fits into three clear categories:

1. Anything addressed to the editor – Nickstickupbum
2. Anything that feels like it's got tickets in – Nickwiththecollars
3. Anything that looks like a bill or an invoice or a Buddhist chant – Griffin

I get to open whatever's left, which usually isn't very much other than the odd slightly mad letter (*the pub you referred to on page 20 DOES NOT sell cheese & onion crisps*) plus the occasional Jiffy bag from an anonymous man who likes to send naked drawings of himself in various office scenarios (he's very good with shelving).

Today's pile is average, about as tall as a Wimpy burger. As usual, most of it is for one of the two Nicks or Griffin but, very excitingly, a small sliver of it is for me (well, for 'the listings').

Two postcards.

A black and white one of Christina Rossetti looking poetic and a colourful art deco-style one of Brockwell Lido.

Christina is quite formal (*To whom it may concern, I congrat-ulate you on your new listings format. It brings a refreshing note of personality into something that could otherwise be fairly dry*) whereas the Lido is short and to the point, albeit a little excessive with its use of exclamation marks (*Really diggin' the listings!!!!!*).

I put the two postcards next to each other on my desk and smile. How lovely of people to write in and say they like the list-ings. To take time out of their day just to say something nice to someone they've never met and probably never will. To bother doing anything at all like that when the world is full of plane crashes and bombs and wars and power cuts.

I look at the wall next to my desk. The faded postcards left by Suzie are still there. Little windows into someone else's world. Memento mori of another life. I take them down, one by one, slowly, respectfully, carefully removing each drawing pin so that I can use it again. I put Suzie's postcards in the bottom drawer of my desk and then pin my new postcards in their place. Christina and the Lido. A happy pair.

Nickwiththecollars looks over and smiles. His desk is by a large sash window and the bright morning sun haloes around him so that he looks like a chubby medieval saint. I smile back and an enormous feeling of contentment wraps around me.

I pick up Mr Scott-Pym's pen, open my notebook and start to jot down a few notes about *La Bohème*.

I'm still deep in operatic thought half an hour later when I sense someone hovering over the desk. I look up

211

expecting Nickwiththecollars (king of hoverers) but, unfortunately, it's Griffin.

'Moving in, are you?' she says, pointing at the two new
postcards.

She's obviously just arrived – she's carrying her tasselly bag
and wearing a large floppy hat that looks like it's suffered some
kind of major trauma.

'They're from readers,' I say, beaming gloriously. 'Saying how
much they like the listings.'

Griffin's mouth twitches, an uncontrollable blur of
Yardley brown.

'There's no point getting comfortable. You're only here on a
trial, remember.'

'Well, I just thought . . .'

'It's probably best if you leave the thinking to us,' she snaps,
wrestling with the hat brim. 'You just stick to the listings.'

'Thelistingsthatpeoplelove,' I mutter, looking down and
straightening an imaginary fold in my skirt.

'What was that?'

'Nothing,' I say, flashing Griffin a smile so bright it could power
a small town.

She gives me a Look.

'What are you doing now, anyway? That doesn't look like the
listings.'

'Oh, no, it's something I'm doing to help Nick. Just a little
review of La Bohème.'

'La Bohème?'

'Yes. It's an opera.'

'I know what *La Bohème* is, Evie. I've got a diploma in Cultural Studies.'

She bristles, a quick irritation of tassels.

'Why are you writing a review?'

'Because I saw it last night. At Covent Garden.'

'Hmm,' she grunts. 'I see.' Her top lip curls so much it looks like a cocktail sausage. '*La Bohème* is an opera for people who know nothing about music. It's all very lightweight.'

'Well, I enjoyed it.'

'Yes, of course. You would, wouldn't you.'

(Griffin is an intellectual snob. She'll only read a novel if it's set in Russia or north London.)

'I thought the music was lovely,' I say. 'It had some really nice tunes.'

'Tunes?' repeats Griffin, making them sound as appealing as venereal disease.

'Yes, and the story was good too.'

She tuts. 'It's a sugary confection of meaningless sentiment. Real opera should be challenging and intellectual.'

'Oh, I don't need opera for that,' I say. 'I've got Melvyn Bragg.'

She tuts again then walks off into the kitchen, eyes rolling and mouth mumbling.

I sit back in my chair and have another look at the two new postcards.

And then I glance over at Griffin's desk. It's by the wall opposite the main door, in front of lots of shelves filled with books and folders plus a couple of macrame wall hangings and a feathery dreamcatcher. Her chair is slotted between the wall and the desk, meaning she looks out over the whole office (a brooding flower-powered lighthouse). Over the chair is a badly tie-dyed throw and on the desk itself, as well as various desk tidies and a typewriter, are a lava lamp and a (thankfully unplayed) tambourine.

A sixties desk in a seventies world.

I drum my fingers gently, a little taken aback by being old enough to see the wheel of time turning (or at least the wheel of office-furniture fashion turning).

And then I realise there are no postcards.

No wonder Griffin's so annoyed. She's very much a zero-sum-game kind of person. She must be a terrible hippy. Always worrying that if someone gets a bit more yin, she'll get a bit less yang.

I add a few more drawing pins to Christina and the Lido, smile, then get back to *La Bohème*.

An hour or so later and I'm beginning to flag. I'm trying to write about the bit in the opera when everyone comes on stage and belts out the huge song but a Battenberg cake has just flashed into my mind and is busy sucking up all focus. I put Mr Scott-Pym's pen down on the notepad and close my eyes for a second. When I open them, instead of the massed ranks of the Covent Garden chorus I see a smiling glittery face peeping round the open office door. Geneviève's smiling glittery face.

'Hello,' she mouths, waving from the door.

'Hullo,' I mouth back and beckon her in.

She unfurls round the door and shuffles her way into the room. For someone so hesitant, she makes quite an entrance.

She's wearing a skin-tight black-satin all-in-one with big puffy shoulders (definitely involving armbands) and, below the knee, swishy flares that jut out with the rigid poise of a tail fin. In her hair, tucked behind an ear, is a black satin flower, buoyant and blooming. All this plus huge platform boots (which still only make her about five-foot-five).

Nickwiththecollars and Griffin stare, mouths open, as she makes her way over to my desk; even Nickstickupbum has a surreptitious gawp.

'Hiya,' she says, her eyes two glittery arcs. 'I hope you don't mind me popping in.'

'No, course not,' I reply. 'It's lovely to see you. Everything okay?'

She shrugs, which can't be easy when you're carrying a portfolio case that almost comes up to your armpit.

'Yeah. I've been taking this round town' – she gives the portfolio a quick waggle – 'but no one seems interested. I was just round the corner so I thought I'd say hello.'

'Well, I'm very glad you did. Welcome to the office!'

She looks round, sending three pairs of eyes darting quickly back down to their respective desks.

'Oh, it's great, isn't it?' she coos. 'Very London-y.'

I smile. You can practically see the excitement radiating off her like a Ready Brek glow. (I remember the feeling well. When everything was new and fabulous and cool. When everything was so thrilling I thought I'd burst.)

'Yes, I suppose it is,' I say. 'Very London-y. Have you had lunch yet?'

'No, just a jam doughnut and a cup of tea.'

I glance at my watch. Twelve-ten. Five minutes to go before Griffin's lunchtime chant-a-thon. Perfect timing.

'Right, come on, it sounds like you need some proper food, then,' I say, standing up. 'I know just the place.'

And I grab my bag and lead her out the office, six beady eyes burning into our backs.

A few minutes later we're sat in a lovely little Italian just round the corner. It's cheap and cheerful and stuffed-full of bushy moustaches (a sure sign of authenticity). It's one of the many places Caroline introduced me to when I first got to London, a list so big I'd struggle to squeeze it into Geneviève's huge portfolio case.

Our table is criss-crossed with red gingham. In the middle, next to a glass salt cellar, is an empty bottle of Valpolicella* with a candle stuck in (unlit) and drops of dried wax caught mid-dribble on the neck.

A waiter (small, tanned, pristine shirt) comes and asks for our order. Geneviève looks to me for guidance so I jump straight in and go for a classic. Spaghetti al pomodoro.

'Is that spaghetti?' she whispers, bending forward.

'Yes, it's very good here,' I reply, smiling up at the waiter.

'What does it come with, though?'

'Tomatoes.'

'Just tomatoes?'

'Yes, and cheese.'

'Not on toast then?'

'Oh no, it's not that kind of spaghetti,' I say, going all sotto voce.

216

Name: Miles D'Arbly

From: Home Counties

Job: wine merchant

Seen for: starter and half a main course

Appearance: annoyingly good-looking

Not amazing: white trousers, pretentious, much unnecessary jewellery

Amazing: didn't come after me when I sneaked out halfway through meal

The waiter smiles, pen hovering over pad.

'Does it come with chips?'

'No, just on its own. It's really nice.'

The waiter coughs. 'And for you, signorina?'

She looks at me, her glittery eyes wide and unsure.

'Err . . . I'll have the same, please.'

'*Bene*. Two spaghetti.' And off he struts.

'You'll love it,' I say, giving her my best reassuring smile.

'Oh, I hope so. I really want to love it.'

'Well, if you don't love it, we'll get you another jam doughnut.'

We share a flash of grin, and a quick sparkly eye.

'Right, come on then,' I say, leaning across the red gingham. 'I want to hear all about these fashion designers. What have they been saying?'

Geneviève's head goes down for a second so that I find myself staring at the black satin flower in her hair. When it comes back up, her eyes are flush and teary.

'Hey, what's wrong?' I ask, reaching out and holding her (doll-size) hand. 'Don't worry. Everything'll be all right. It just takes time to get used to London.' I give her palm a gentle stroke with my thumb. 'Everyone feels a bit lost at first. You'll be fine.'

She sniffs and tries a smile.

'All the fashion people must love this,' I go on, enthusiastically tapping the portfolio case (currently leaning against the table like a barn door).

She untucks a hanky from under the sleeve of her all-in-one and dabs at her eyes. 'They don't even want to see it,' she says, attempting another smile. 'I go in and introduce myself and they normally just look at me as if I'm speaking gibberish.' (She has another eye-dab.) 'Maybe they're just not interested in a stupid young girl.'

'Oi,' I say, giving her a friendly prod. 'Less of that. Come on. Number one, you're not stupid; you've got Doris Swithenbank's blood coursing through your veins, remember, so you can't be stupid.'

She smiles (a proper smile).

'And number two, you're not a young *girl* – you're a young *woman*. A clever, brave and very talented young woman.'

There are a few big sniffs followed by a *thanks, Evie*.

'Hold on, there's more. Number three . . . look at you! You look amazing! They're mad not to want to have a look in here.' (I tap the portfolio case again.) 'They're all missing the next big thing.'

'Do you really think so?' she says, little bubbles of hope.

'Absolutely. You'll be in Paris next, with your own fashion show.'

'Oh, I wish!'

'Or Tokyo.'

Her eyes gleam. 'Yes, with David Bowie! Or New York, maybe.'

'Absolutely. Or Milan, surrounded by models and pasta. There'll be no stopping you.' As I speak, I notice the waiter weaving his way towards us with a basket full of bread rolls. He pulls up to the table, smiles and offers the basket to Geneviève.

'Oh, no thanks,' she says, smiling back up at him. 'I didn't order soup.'

The waiter looks confused for a second and then offers the basket to me. I take two, one for each of us.

'It's for the spaghetti sauce,' I say to Geneviève as the waiter makes his way back to the kitchen. 'It's too good to waste – the bread mops it up.'

'Oh, right, I see.'

She picks up the bread roll.

'Maybe I'm too northern to get a job in London. Maybe they're only looking for sophisticated southerners – people who know how to behave in an Italian cafe.'

'Rubbish. I'm northern and I'm the height of sophistication,' I say, ripping a chunk from the roll and stuffing it in my mouth.

Geneviève laughs and does the same.

'You're very sophisticated,' she says, chomping through the bread. 'I wish I were more like you.'

(More like me. Is that what I'm trying to be too?)

'Sophisticated and cool,' she goes on. 'Like your office.'

I laugh. 'That's not sophisticated and cool!'

'Well, all those books and papers – that's a sign of being sophisticated. And the metronome on your desk is pretty cool – David Bowie's got one.'

'Oh, really?'

'Yes, and the coloured typewriters are cool too. And the big old windows.'

'And my Hayward Gallery pencil,' I add, counting on my fingers. 'And the creaky old Georgian floorboards. And my Beatles mug.'

'Yes, I spotted that on your desk. Very funny!'

'Funny?'

'Yes, like from an antique shop.'

(An antique shop?)

'Two spaghetti al pomodoro,' says the waiter, doing a Griffin and sneaking up on us. He puts both plates down and then shoots off.

Geneviève eyes the bowl of spaghetti. 'Oh, it's not what I was expecting,' she says. 'And why have they put it in a soup bowl?'

Before I can answer the waiter is back. He's got a big chunk of parmesan and a grater. He hovers both over my dish and gets to work. I sit back, watching the little curls of cheesy snow melt onto the pasta. He does the same for Geneviève and then, with a quick *enjoy!*, he's off again.

'Wow,' says Geneviève. 'You don't get this in Leeds.'

'All part of the service. I told you you'd like it.'

'He's forgotten to bring me a knife, though. I've only got this,' she says, holding up her fork.

'That's all you need. Look . . .' And I show her how to fork a few pieces of spaghetti, then twist them round against the bowl until you're left with a lovely slippery knot of pasta.

Geneviève copies me. There's a fair bit of splashing, lots of twisting, and quite a few straggly ends but – after a lot of laughing – she finally gets some spaghetti into her mouth.

The gingham clenches. The table tenses. The cafe holds its breath.

Geneviève's mouth goes round and round and up and down and round and round and up and down.

And then her glittery eyes open wide and when I look inside them I see pure joy.

'Oh, that's delicious,' she says, already twisting another forkload.

My job is done.

Forty minutes later and I'm walking up the stairs on my way back to the office. Geneviève, buoyed by the spaghetti and a quick limoncello, is off taking her portfolio round more factories and workshops. I'm buoyed too, by the limoncello and by a particularly good hair-spruce in the sex-shop window downstairs.

My buoyant mood doesn't last long.

'Ah, there you are,' says Griffin, the hunchback of marjoram. 'I wondered what time you'd be getting back.'

She looks at her watch in an exaggerated manner, as if she were in a silent film.

'Well, I'm back now,' I chirp.

Griffin makes a noise, like a grunt mating with a tut.

'Both Nicks are out having lunch,' she snaps, 'so I've been

running this place on my own. Not that I don't practically do that anyway, of course ...'

There's an eye-roll and a huff.

'... and as if I didn't have enough to do, I've been fielding more calls for you. The phone's for magazine use only. Not personal. How many times do I have to tell you?'

'Sorry,' I chime, two (hopefully annoying) syllable clangs. 'Who was it?'

'Someone from the BBC.'

(Another eye-roll.)

'Oh, did they leave a name?'

She lets out a space-hopper-sized sigh.

'Yes, it was something funny ...'

(This is rich coming from someone called Griffin.)

'... something like Lolly.'

'Lolo?'

'Yes, that's it. Lolo.'

I look over at the big, blocky metronome on my desk (*pretty cool*) and smile.

Interlude – Spring 1954, Napoli

Walking out of the station was like walking into a different country. A different continent, even. Car horns blared, people shouted, scooters fizzed and purred.

She was in Naples – *Napoli* – a teeming, gleaming bolt of life.

'*Pensione Cachiotolli, per favore*,' said Catherine, carefully pronouncing every syllable.

A wall of words came back at her.

She shrugged and showed the taxi driver the piece of paper with the *pensione*'s name and address. '*Non parlo Italiano*.'

The driver smiled and beckoned for her to get in, spraying words like notes from a bugle.

She'd lost the baby.

Her precious baby.

Gone. A cold, hard word that understood nothing.

Life had burned around her. Brightly lit hospital rooms, hard metallic glints, starched white uniforms, the vivid sheen of her own blood.

But all Catherine felt was darkness. A black, blank space.

When someone died, a mother, a father, a husband, a child, you were allowed to mourn. It was expected, an essential passage that would help heal the loss. But no room was given for mourning someone who hadn't yet been born. No room for the sadness, guilt, denial, confusion. No room for the rage. She had locked herself away in a world of her own making, a silent world, a dead world, a world with no sunshine or beauty or hope.

She stayed in hospital for almost three weeks. And then home. But, of course, it wasn't really home. Not now.

Nell, lovely Nell, had moved away just before it happened – to Glasgow, living with an aunt, working as an office girl at a shipyard. There had been a few visits by women from the church and the WI, but their polite words and sympathetic smiles offered no consolation. Her father had visited too. Awkward little moments of frigidity. Catherine was unsure which of them found the visits more uncomfortable.

And Muir? He'd been a cold, wet fish. Detached, practical, prescribing tinctures and pills but offering little else. She could hardly bear to be in the same room.

So she had planned.

Muir agreed to a bank account of her own. For the church, she said vaguely. A flower committee. She'd always had a secret cache of banknotes, tucked into a boot, growing month by month. And now, after what had happened, there was more money. Her father agreed to pay for some time away at a hotel in the Highlands. An aunt sent her kind words and a cheque (*for something pleasurable*). Muir, on asking, provided money for new clothes. There were other things too. She took cufflinks, valuable but unworn, from her father's house and added them to her jewellery. Altogether there was quite a collection, rings, necklaces, brooches, all filled with pearls and precious stones, from generation upon generation on both sides of the family. And there were the first editions too. Not many but, still, useful pots of money, portable and secure.

One day, when Muir went out to work, she packed a small suitcase, layering clothes with jewellery and books, and filled her handbag with various rings, sovereigns, documents and her passport (a relic from their French honeymoon). Then she took half the money from the pot in the bedroom where Muir stored his petty cash and got a taxi to Waverley station in Edinburgh. There she bought a ticket to London. She planned to stay in a hotel for a few days and then contact an old school friend who now lived in Hampstead – hopefully she'd help her get a room in a shared house somewhere. And then she'd get a job, an office girl, perhaps, like Nell.

But when she arrived at King's Cross, a poster on the concourse caught her eye. An Italian tourist poster. Colourful and inviting. She stood in front of it, intrigued, transfixed by its potential. It made her think of Forster and blue skies and a great emotional thawing. If she was going to do this, she told herself, she might as well do it properly. A new start meant just that, didn't it? So she made her way across London to the BOAC office in Paddington, where she bought a one-way ticket to Rome. Before she knew it, she was walking across the tarmac at London Airport, shoes clicking and heart pounding, carrying her future in an Antler suitcase and heading for the plane.

She stayed in Rome for a few days, selling the books and a couple of rings, and then, on finding out her money would last longer further south, she took a train to Naples.

And here she was.

The streets of Naples glided by like the opening credits of a wonderful technicolour film. Every now and then the taxi driver would point and say something in Italian; she replied with a nod or a smile, feeling ashamed her Italian didn't stretch far beyond yes or no.

The back windows of the taxi were half-open. She shuffled over so that she sat right next to one, letting the warm Neapolitan air skim her face. She breathed in, taking the air deep into her lungs.

They swung round a corner and then, suddenly, just like that, there was the sea, a long sweep of glistening blue.

'*Guarda!*' said the driver excitedly. '*Il mare! Bella Napoli, no?*'

She smiled.

'*Si, bella Napoli!*'

Beautiful Napoli, indeed.

CHAPTER 15

Summer 1972

The day whizzes by.

I crack on with various things (the listings, the *La Bohème*, the washing-up) and feel super-productive and businesslike. By four o'clock, we've lost Nickstickupbum to a Barbara Castle press conference and Griffin to a chakra reading in Belsize Park, leaving just me and Nickwiththecollars in the office. It only takes him two minutes to suggest clocking off early; a few minutes after that and we're waving goodbye to each other outside on the street, our reflections bobbing along beside us in the sex-shop window.

I decide to make the most of my extra hour by going to Caroline and Digby's to water the plants. This is something I always do whenever they're away but I've neglected it slightly in the last few days because of suddenly finding myself tending a far more consequential bloom (Geneviève).

We've had keys to each other's place ever since I got my own flat. For Caroline and Digby it's so that I can water the plants and deal with any emergencies when they're away (usually Caroline forgetting to turn off her Carmen rollers) but with me it's mainly for when I lock myself out (a not uncommon occurrence). The key swapping works really well. It gives Caroline and Digby a porter on tap and it gives me a sense of feeling settled, connected, part of something, a safety net spread out under my blustery London life.

I walk down the cobbled mews (all hanging baskets and barrel planters) until, right at the end, Caroline and Digby's house looms into view, a very modern grid of oversize windows and Lego angles.

When I see the house today, I'm surprised. In front of the slate-grey bricks, parked at a jaunty angle, is Caroline's Alfa Romeo. This means they're back from Yorkshire. Well, at least I hope it means that. Perhaps they've had another row and Caroline's back on her own.

I give the doorbell a ring and wait.

Inside the house there's music. Loud music. I put my ear to the door and have a good listen. It doesn't sound like opera or someone shouting. It's far more rhythmic and drummy and I'm sure I get a blast of trumpet. This is a good sign. Rhythmic, drummy music probably means it's . . .

'Evie!'

It's Digby, looking terrible, standing in an open doorway, all bloodshot eye and Breton stripe.

'Oh, come here, dearrrrrrrrrr,' she says, wrapping her arm and Rs round me like a lovely tartan scarf. 'I've missed you.'

'I've missed you too,' I say, folding my arms around her. 'When did you get back?'

228

'Not long ago.' She steps back and has a good look at me, cupping my cheeks with her warm hands. 'We've had an awful time. You'd better come in.'

'So where's Caroline, then?'

We're in the sitting room, on the first floor. At the end of the room a wall of glass frames the mews, giving the impression of a large chocolate-box painting plonked in the middle of a very modern gallery.

'Out,' replies Digby. 'Gone for a quick walk.' She goes and sits in an armchair, a huge upturned scoop of plastic and velvet (I'm on the sofa, a modern plump of orange bubbles that snakes around the room). 'She wanted some fresh air.'

She stares out through the chocolate-box window, tapping her finger on the side of the armchair.

'Oh,' I say, nodding slowly. 'I see.'

Digby sighs, like a wind gusting or a dam breaking. 'We had a blazing row in the car, Evie. Another one. It's been one row after the other over the last couple of weeks. I suppose she told you about the baby?'

'About you wanting her to have one, you mean?'

She nods, wiping an eye.

'But wouldn't it be . . . difficult? You know . . .' I'm at a loss how to phrase it so I try moving both hands around as communicatively as possible but that just seems even worse.

'Oh, where there's a will, there's a way,' she says, trying a smile. 'We've got lots of friends who've done it. It really isn't difficult at all. The *way* is there – Caroline's just lacking the *will*.'

'But couldn't *you* have the baby, then? Rather than Caroline.'

'Well, it's all a bit complicated, dear. Medically complicated.' She looks away, just for a moment, staring at an inconsequential spot of wall. 'And, anyway, I'm too old to be having a baby – I'm forty-two; I'll be forty-three soon. Approaching grandmother age.'

(Digby would be a wonderful gran. Kind and funny and wise.)

'So *you*'d better hurry up!' she goes on.

'Me?!'

'Yes, so that I can be a glamorous granny.'

'Ha! I'll be a while yet – I need to get a boyfriend first.'

'Och,' she says, a quick flutter of dismissive hand. 'You must have them throwing themselves at you, a beautiful girl like you.'

'Not quite.'

(Although I do have my moments.)

'I always seem to end up getting bored of them.'

'Bored? Oh, that's no good. You need someone who's going to keep you interested, dear.'

'It's not easy, though, is it? At first you think they're interesting but then you realise they're just a pretty face stuck onto a flatulent lump of self-absorption.'

The corners of Digby's mouth flicker upwards. 'Life's long, Evie – you need a partner, not a poster.'

(I should have a badge with that on.)

She sits back in the plastic and velvet armchair and crosses her arms, looking like a sad and sombre Bond villain.

'What exactly does Caroline say about not wanting a baby?' I ask.

There's almost-silence for a few seconds, just the sound of us both breathing. Then she rolls her head, putting her hands through her thick, greying hair.

'Oh, it's the same thing every time. She keeps saying she's just not maternal.'

'Yes, that's what she said to me too. But it's not true, is it?'

Her hands work their way down to the back of her neck. 'Not true? What do you mean?'

'Well, she is maternal, isn't she? Very maternal. She's done a wonderful job looking after me all these years.'

Digby smiles, a tiny little plaster for a heart-sized gaping gash.

'Yes, I suppose she looks after us all, dear, in her own funny way.'

There's a few more seconds' silence, long enough for Digby to reach over and get a packet of cigarettes from the coffee table. Then she pulls a thin elegant lighter out of her pocket and lights the cigarette, closing her eyes and taking a big, slow drag.

'Anyway,' she goes on, sending hazy swirls of smoke out across the room. 'She's her own boss, as you know. There's no point arguing with her.' She flicks a bit of ash into a marble ashtray. 'I just wish she'd try and understand this time, though. It's not some silly little whim. It's coming from somewhere deep inside me. I can't ignore it. It's there, like air, all around me. Running through me.' She lifts her cigarette hand and dabs an eye with her ring finger. 'Oh, I don't know,' she goes on, dabbing the other eye.

I sit there for a moment, letting the room breathe. And then I walk over to Digby and kneel on the floor beside her, burying my legs deep in the sheepskin rug around the armchair. I lay a hand on her knee and my head on my hand and sit there, head on hand on knee.

'It'll all work out,' I say. 'You two always work it out.'

'Maybe we won't this time,' she replies, stroking my hair. 'Maybe it can't be worked out. It's a mess. An absolute bloody mess.' She sniffs and has another drag of cigarette. 'And here I am, meant to be getting some food ready ... Look, why don't you stay for supper tonight? It might help pull us out of these foul moods.'

'I've got a better idea,' I reply, lifting my head from Digby's knee. 'Why don't you both come round to me? I'll be cooking for Geneviève anyway.'

'Who?'

Ding-dong.

My doorbell rings, marking the arrival (hopefully) of Caroline and Digby.

'They're here,' I shout to Geneviève, busy laying the table in the next room.

She rushes into the kitchen clutching a rattan tablemat.

'I'm really nervous,' she says. 'I'm bound to say some-thing stupid.'

'Don't be nervous,' I reply. 'They'll love you. They're really down to earth,' I add, not entirely truthfully, as I slip past her and head down the stairs to the front door.

I pull open the door and . . .

'Darling!' It's Caroline, a lush rush of smile and kiss. 'You're just what the doctor ordered! And food too!'

'Well, I thought it'd save you cooking after that long drive. And I wanted you both to meet Geneviève.'

'Oh, yes,' she says, edging past me in the tiny hallway. 'Digby's told me all about your new friend.'

Digby is patiently waiting on the doorstep. 'Hullo again, dear,' she says, giving me a little wave.

'Shall we go up?' asks Caroline, already on the stairs.

'Of course! You know the way.'

As we walk into the sitting room, I'm sure I see Geneviève do a little curtsey.

'And *you*,' says Caroline, holding out both hands, 'must be Geneviève. Darling, you look wonderful.'

This is true. Geneviève has outdone herself. She's wearing a red satin kimono-style jumpsuit. Her sleeves are so baggy that when she holds out her arms the satin droops down like a giant pair of sunglasses. There's a hot-water-bottle's worth of satin tied extravagantly round her belly. Various shades of orangey red meld and fade around her eyes. In fact the only non-red is her boots, which are black and platformed (of course).

A huge smile beams across Geneviève's face, like when the sun comes out from behind a cloud.

'Thank you,' she says, her little voice fluttering. 'You too. Is that *Kenzo*?'

Caroline glows, a surge of grandeur (making her well above six feet).

'It is, darling. How on earth did you know?'

'Geneviève's our resident Japanese design expert,' I explain. 'And our resident fashion expert.'

'Well, you look fantastic, dear,' says Digby, nodding enthusiastically at Geneviève. 'Where did you get your outfit from?'

'Oh, I made it myself,' she replies.

The room fills with lavish bursts of surprise and praise (mainly from Caroline and Digby but I join in too) and there's a clear consensus that Geneviève is Very Clever Indeed.

'She's brilliant, isn't she?' I say, winking at Geneviève. 'Now, who'd like a drink? I've made a jug of Pimm's.'

'Ooh, yes, please,' coos Caroline.

'Me too,' adds Digby.

We all look at Geneviève.

'Er, I've never had it before,' she says. 'What's it like?'

Caroline grins. 'It's lovely, darling. Very summery.'

'I'll get you a small glass so you can try,' I say.

'No, I'll go and get them,' says Geneviève, edging towards the door. 'You stay here and I'll bring them through.'

'The jug's in the fridge,' I shout as she disappears out the room. 'And there's some fresh mint, too, on the draining board. Just a sprig for each glass.'

'Okay,' shouts a sprite-like little voice from the kitchen.

We all look at each other and smile.

'Isn't she wonderful?' says Caroline (keeping her voice low).

'She's lovely,' I reply. 'An amazing little dynamo.'

(This is true. Geneviève has the compact energy of a bicycle bell.)

'She did all this,' I go on, pointing at the smartly set table, 'and we've divvied up the cooking too. You'll see!'

'Well, I like her,' says Digby. 'Making her own clothes *and* helping to feed us wrinklies.'

'Less of the wrinklies,' clips Caroline, giving Digby a Look (no smile).

'You should see some of the things she's made,' I say, sending out my syllables as bouncily as possible. 'They're incredible.'

'She's *very* good, darling. Heaven knows how she made what she's wearing tonight but it looks fabulous.'

I begin to tell them about some of Geneviève's other outfits and how she's out every day with her portfolio, touting for a job, but before I've had chance to say much she re-appears at the door.

'I hope I've done it right,' she says, a tray-carrying whirl of red satin. 'I've never put mint in a drink before. I've only ever had it on lamb.'

'They look perfect,' I say. 'You're a natural!'

'One Pimm for you,' she says, carefully passing a glass to Caroline, 'and another Pimm for you.' She passes another glass to Digby.

'Thank you, darling,' says Caroline, smiling then flicking her eyes over at me.

(The flick is quick but eloquent, communicating the important job I need to do.)

'And a Pimm for you, too,' says Geneviève, offering me a glass as if it were the Blessed Sacrament.

'Oh, lovely, thank you.' I take the glass and give her a big smile. 'Actually, you wouldn't mind giving me a hand with something in the kitchen, would you?'

'I just wanted to have a quick word about this,' I say, standing by the kitchen window and holding up my glass.

'The Pimm? Is it okay?'

'It's perfect, it's just that we don't say Pimm. It's Pimm's. With an S.'

'Oh, even if there's only one of them?'

'Yes, it's always Pimm's. One Pimm's. Two Pimm's.'

'Like hovercraft.'

'Hovercraft?'

'Yes, one hovercraft, two hovercraft.'

'Exactly.'

Walking back into the sitting room is a bit like walking down the chilled-food aisle in a supermarket. Caroline is sat on one end of the sofa with Digby down at the other end. Between them, greedily sucking up space, sits a great hulking lump of froideur.*

'Almost ready,' I say, turning my breeziness levels up to full. 'Hope you're both hungry.'

'Famished, darling,' says Caroline, almost managing a smile. 'So, what are we having then?'

'Well, I won't spoil the surprise by telling you what we're having

236

Name: Dr Glenn Adams

From: Bristol

Job: marriage guidance counsellor

Seen for: two weeks (in my head), three and a half weeks (in his)

Appearance: louche Dr Kildare

Amazing: attentive, lovely neckerchiefs, tandem bike

Not amazing: sandal botherer, sesquipedalian, jazz

---

but I can say that Geneviève's done the starter and pudding and I've done the main course. So it's an Evie and Geneviève sandwich.'

'Sounds delicious,' says Digby, steadfastly not looking at Caroline.

Caroline cranes back her long neck and rolls her sylphlike shoulders.

'How's the job hunting, Geneviève?' she asks.

Geneviève sighs. 'Well, to be honest, it's not going great.'

'It's a funny old business, darling. Makes no sense at all most of the time. What do they say when you turn up?'

'Not much.' She shrugs. 'Most of them can't be bothered to talk to me. And even the ones who do aren't really interested. I've got loads of experience but I'm sure they just think I'm too young.'

'Hmmm,' says Caroline. 'That's the thing with fashion. You're either too young or too old.'

'Or perhaps they think I'm too northern? That I'm not sophisticated enough?'

'Rubbish,' says Caroline.

'Or maybe they're looking for a Pimm's,' she goes on, 'and all I've got is a Pimm?'

Caroline grins. 'Well, more fool them, darling.' She lifts her glass. 'It's a bloody good Pimm.'

A few minutes later and we're sat at the table waiting for Geneviève's starter.

'Do you want a hand?' I shout, happy to leave the chilly foothills of Mounts Caroline and Digby.

'No, I'm okay, thanks,' shouts Geneviève from the kitchen. 'Just finishing it off.'

We all smile at each other, politely.

'Oh, I didn't tell you about the suitcase, did I?' I say.

Caroline's face brightens. 'The suitcase! No, what was in it, darling?'

'Well, books mainly but there were a few other things, too. Your dad's pen, Mrs Scott-Pym's old pestle and mortar, and a champagne cork from the day Mum told Mrs Scott-Pym she was pregnant.'

'How lovely!' says Digby.

'Good old Mummy,' says Caroline. 'I'm glad it was more than just a suitcase of old books.'

'Not that there's anything wrong with a suitcase of old books,' jumps in Digby.

Caroline ignores her. 'And I'm glad you got Daddy's pen, too. It just feels right, doesn't it, now that you're at the magazine? Mummy really was a clever old thing.'

'She was that,' says Digby. 'The cork's such a beautiful thing to have, Evie – a memento of a very special day.'

'Yes, and do you know what's really strange? When I hold it, I feel like I was there.'

'Well, you were there, darling,' says Caroline. 'A tiny precious Evie, no bigger than a thumb.'

'It must be such a magical moment,' says Digby, 'telling someone important to you that you're carrying a child. No wonder Rosamund kept the cork.'

Caroline's jaw sets.

'And the pestle and mortar brings back lots of lovely memories, too,' I say, radiating bonhomie. 'I'd spend hours in Mrs Scott-Pym's kitchen watching her cook and bake.'

'That's lovely, dear,' says Digby. 'Maybe Rosamund leaving you the pestle and mortar was her way of saying don't let yourself get ground down by things.'

'Uuhhh,' huffs Caroline, filling one syllable with the dismissive punch of a year's worth of *Private Eye*.

Digby glances at Caroline then looks away, numbing the room into silence.

'Here we go,' says Geneviève, breezing back into the room, a flurry of kimono sleeve and cheese-and-pineapple hedgehog.

She puts the hedgehog down on the table.

It's magnificent. A silvery body of scrunched-up kitchen

239

foil with row after row of cheese-and-pineapple cocktail sticks.

Caroline and Digby stare at it, united, briefly, in awe.

'You can eat it all,' says Geneviève, proudly wafting a sail's worth of sleeve at the hedgehog. 'I used chocolate buttons for the eyes and the nose is a glacé cherry.'

'Very resourceful, darling,' says Caroline. 'It looks wonderful.'

And she reaches over and plucks a cheesy spine.

Ten minutes later and I'm in the kitchen again.

I'm getting the main course ready, which only really consists of taking a ready-made quiche and some ready-made potato cro-quettes out of the oven (Mrs Scott-Pym would not be impressed) and mixing up a quick salad.

It's a relief to get away from the table. The temporary ceasefire caused by the appearance of Geneviève's cheese-and-pineapple hedgehog didn't last long. In fact the bad feeling escalated, rumbling on pretty much until we'd stripped the poor hedgehog bare. Before long, the only prickly thing left in the room was the atmosphere.

I give some lettuce leaves a quick whizz in the salad spinner then decant them into my chunky wooden serving bowl. Then I chop up some spring onions and radishes and throw them in the bowl, too, plus a few sliced tomatoes.

As I'm plating up the quiche and croquettes, I hear the strangest thing.

Little bursts of laughter coming from the other room.

Very odd, given the arctic chill when I left.

I can't work it out.

I'm straining to hear what's going on when Geneviève walks in carrying the tray.

'Everything okay?' I ask.

'Oh, yes. They're lovely aren't they?'

'Well, yes ...'

'I just brought this in for you,' she goes on, giving the tray a red-satin tap. 'I thought you'd need it.'

'Great, thanks ... They're not arguing then?' I ask, taking the tray.

'No, they were a bit moody at first but they soon warmed up when we got chatting.'

Ah. I see.

'Bugger. I forgot the bread.'

I'm back at the table. I'd bought a crusty baguette to have with the quiche but it's still balancing on the bread bin: forgotten, unloved and unsliced.

'I'll get it,' says Geneviève, jumping up.

She's out the door before I can say *boulangerie*.

'Oh, she's great, isn't she?' whispers Digby, over-mouthing every word.

I smile. 'Yes, she's lovely. I knew you'd like her!'

'Darling,' says Caroline, 'she's absolutely marvellous. Such a sweet little thing.'

'And such good fun,' says Digby (still over-mouthing).

'I can't believe she's so young,' says Caroline.

'And I can't believe she made that outfit,' adds Digby.

'Doesn't she look wonderful, darling?' Caroline goes on, turning to me. 'You should see if she can make *you* something.'

'Me?'

'Yes, why not? She's *very* good.'

Digby looks like she's about to comment when Geneviève walks back in with the bread. She's cut it up and put it in a little basket (like in the Italian restaurant earlier).

'Here we are,' she says, putting the basket on the table.

'Thanks, Geneviève. Now come and sit down – there's nothing worse than a cold croquette.'

'Oh, you've led a very sheltered life, darling,' says Caroline, giving me one of her winks. 'Anyway, look, how's the job going? Are you all set for Fleet Street?'

'Oh, not quite. But, it *is* going well. I *think* I might have found my calling.'

'That's wonderful, dear,' burrrrrrrs Digby.

'Certainly is,' says Caroline. 'So you're queen of the London listings then?'

'Absolutely! And not just the listings. They've asked me to write a review too. For an opera.'

'An opera?' exclaims Caroline. 'You, darling? But you hate opera!'

'Well, hate might be a little strong.'

Caroline spears a croquette.

'So, which opera are they sending you to, then?' asks Digby.

'*La Bohème*. And I've already been.'

'Already been!' The forked croquette hovers near Caroline's

242

mouth, a mini breadcrumbed Zeppelin. 'Well, I can't believe it. You'll be telling me you've gone off Battenberg next.'

'Very funny.'

'Who did you go with?' she asks, jabbing the Zeppelin in my direction.

'Lolo.'

'Lolo?'

'Yes, Lolo. He invited me. He's helping me with the classical music listings because I'm so hopeless.'

'Oh, I see,' says Caroline, putting the croquette back down on her plate and resting her chin on her beautiful long fingers. 'Lolo.'

'No, it's not like that!' I say. 'Don't be silly. Lolo's homosexual. He works at Radio Three.'

Digby and Caroline both sigh and nod.

'But he's quite tall to be homosexual, isn't he?'

We all turn and look at Geneviève.

'Well,' she goes on, doing something artistic with a drop sleeve. 'It's just that all the ones in Leeds seem so much shorter.'

Interlude – Summer 1954, Napoli

It had become her morning ritual.

Coffee and a pastry in the bar at the end of the street. The coffee was a rich frothy soup of milk, a *cap-pu-cci-no*, and the pastry, a *cor-ne-tto*, always flaky but somehow deliciously moist too. She loved saying the Italian words, clanging every syllable with the enthusiasm of an apprentice blacksmith. Her Italian was improving. She'd been in Naples two months now and was beginning to piece together phrases, sometimes even a basic sentence or two. It made her feel part of the city, a drop of Scottish blood running through its wonderful chaotic veins.

The bar wasn't anything fancy but she liked that. It was a rough and ready affair that suited the *quartiere*. Photos of the Napoli football team shared a wall with a framed picture of the pope and various adverts for Campari and Aperol. A coffee machine hissed on the counter, always in use, and the chinking of crockery and glass offered a percussive beat under the orchestral sounds of the spoken – or shouted – Italian that swooped constantly round the room. Patterned Formica tables filled the floor, one of which, in a corner looking out onto the street, she was sat at today.

She took a sip of the cappuccino and then went back to her *Times*. She bought the paper once a week, from a kiosk near the train station. It was ridiculously overpriced but it made her feel connected – just enough – to home. Every day she'd read a couple of pages, every article, no matter how dry or uninteresting, the adverts too, eking the paper out for a full week.

There'd been letters home and a couple of disagreeable phone calls. She'd said, very clearly, that she needed some time away. Muir didn't understand, of course, and her father was downright threatening. They conspired together – even to the extent of a visit one day from the British consul in Naples, a ridiculous act that made her even more determined. She had no intention of going home, not to Muir, not to her father. She was happy here, slowly piecing together a new life, grief layered with hope.

She'd found a job teaching English to private students. It brought some money in, more than enough to pay for the small flat she rented, plus she still had money in the bank and most of the jewellery. She would take her time; there was no rush. Naples suited her.

She finished off the *cornetto* and had another sip of coffee, dabbing her mouth afterwards with a folded paper napkin. Then she returned to her *Times*, peering through its long telescope to observe home from afar.

She was in the middle of reading a review of the new Rattigan when she sensed the atmosphere in the bar change. The Italian chatter calmed; espresso cups were left on saucers. Heads turned.

She looked up.

A beautiful young woman had walked in, tall and princely, with a Roman nose and lush red hair.

Catherine watched as she walked over to the bar and started chatting to the *cameriere*. Hands flew, smiles grew to laughs, heads rocked back, elated. All in fluent Italian. And yet, despite the Roman nose, she didn't look Italian. It was the hair, perhaps, but there was something else – the navy pedal pushers, maybe? The loafers?

The young woman turned round and caught Catherine staring.

Catherine dived back into the paper, folding it around her like a windshield.

A few seconds later the woman was standing at her table.

'Hullo,' she said, in a crisp English accent. 'I see we're stablemates!'

Catherine looked up. The woman had sparkling eyes and a smile a mile wide. She looked a little younger than Catherine, early twenties perhaps.

'Sorry?' said Catherine.

'The paper,' said the young woman, gesturing at the *Times*. 'We're two Brits abroad. Although I think that was a Scottish accent, wasn't it?'

Catherine put the paper down on the table and smiled.

'Yes, Edinburgh.'

'Lovely,' the woman replied. 'Well, I say lovely – I've never been! But I'm sure it *is* lovely. It always sounds such a nice place.'

Catherine laughed. 'Yes, it is lovely. In a very different way to here, though. The sea isn't *quite* so blue – or the sky either, for that matter!'

'It's marvellous, isn't it?' the young woman replied. 'I love it here. I really do feel at home.'

'And where is home?' asked Catherine.

The young woman faltered for a second.

'Well, I'm not really sure any more.' She flicked down her eyes. 'I'm from York, though,' she went on, flicking them back up with a gleam. 'Well, Yorkshire. I'm Caroline, by the way. Caroline Scott-Pym.'

'And I'm Catherine . . .' She hesitated, unsure of which surname to use. 'Catherine MacLeod.'

Caroline pulled out a chair and sat down.

'Catherine and Caroline – we can't have that!' she said, grinning, her face as beautiful as the Bay. 'It sounds like a team at the local gymkhana. One of us will have to change. I'm going to call you . . . Digby.'

Chapter 16

Summer 1972

It's Sunday morning. My favourite morning.

I'm striding across Kensington Gardens. The sun is shining, the sky is blue and my legs are out.

The world is good.

I'm a Quant summer queen, Boadicea in a romper suit, a goddess in shorts. Hera. Juno. Twiggy.

I'm on my way to meet Lolo. He's agreed to have a look at my review of *La Bohème* before I give it to Nickwiththecollars. I spent practically all day yesterday writing it, give or take a few phone calls, a whites wash, several blasts of Radio 1 and a trip to the cinema with Geneviève. I'm hoping the review strikes the right note between enthusiastic amateur and seasoned professional but I worry that it actually just comes across as being written by someone whose only acquaintance with classical music is the Old Spice advert.

Dotted around the grassy stretch of parkland are people lying on big towels, catching some summer colour (blancmange pink). Most are on their own with a book but there are a few couples too, usually accompanied by a picnic basket and a smug, relaxed air. And, of course, there are dogs. Lots of them. Running, barking, sniffing, larking. I love it.

I'm meeting Lolo at a little cafe on the bank of the Serpentine. As I get near, I hear the constant hum of talking punctuated by the occasional clink of teaspoon on china.

A few more steps and a big fat sausage of a dog lollops up to me and gives me a good slobber. It's Oscar.

'Sorry!' shouts Lolo, waving from a table. 'Oscar, come here!'

'He's fine,' I shout back, bending down and making a big fuss of him. 'I don't mind at all.' Oscar reaches up and tries to lick my nose, sending out long spurts of drool. I have a quick hanky wipe (always tucked up a sleeve) and make my way over to Lolo's table, Oscar in tow.

'Hullo there,' beams Lolo, now standing.

'Hullo,' I beam back. 'You managed to get a table then. Well done!'

'Well, we've been here since seven this morning.'

'What?'

He grins.

'Oh,' I say, with a big sigh. 'You had me then for a moment.'

'I did get here early, actually – just not *that* early. I wanted to bagsy a table next to the water.'

'You're spoiling me!'

(It's true – the table is right next to the Serpentine, our nearest neighbours a couple of ducks.)

'Well, not quite. I might have got you a chair with a view but I couldn't find you one with much of a swivel.'

'I wish you'd stop going on about that chair,' I say, sitting down. 'It's embarrassing! I must have looked a right idiot.'

'Well, I wouldn't say a *right* idiot,' replies Lolo, smirking. 'Actually, I thought it was rather charming.'

'Charming?'

'Yes, charming,' he repeats, sitting down too. He slips Oscar's lead under a chair leg. 'There, that's got *you*, boy. There'll be no chasing off now.' He runs a friendly hand down Oscar's back and then looks up at me. 'It'd take much more than a basset hound to shift a chair with *me* sitting on it.'

'I'm sure! How about a shire horse?'

'Oh! Thank you very much! And here I am doing you a favour!'

'Only joking. Perhaps just a Shetland pony.'

'Sorry, what was that I was just saying about you being charming?'

'It's a compliment! They're only tiny.'

Lolo smiles.

'I've got another compliment for you now.'

He braces himself, grabbing the arms of his chair as if preparing for a crash.

'You've had your hair cut,' I tell him. 'It looks good.'

He reaches up and rubs a hand self-consciously over his shorn head.

'Yes, I had it all cut short.' (I think he's blushing.) 'It was just about ready to leave by itself anyway so I thought I'd help it on its way. No more long wispy bits blowing in the wind.'

'It suits you – you look younger.'

'Oh, thank you.' (He's definitely blushing.)

'Anyway,' I go on. 'My turn to get you a drink – what do you fancy?'

'Oh, I don't know. Anything. Surprise me.'

'Here we are ...' I say, standing over the table and contending with an ample tray.

Lolo looks up.

The sun streams over my shoulder, lighting up his face.

Somewhere, out on the water, a duck quacks.

And that's when I notice his eyes.

A soft, warm brown.

Like freshly poured tea.

(How have I never noticed them before?)

'What have you got there?' he says.

'It's a surprise. Like you said. One vanilla milkshake,' I say, sitting down and carefully decanting the tray. 'And one strawberry tart.'

'Oh, this looks smashing. You might be right about the shire horse after I get through all this.'

Oscar pokes his nose in the air, catching the summer smells wafting from the tray.

'No, this is for me, boy,' says Lolo, giving Oscar a quick tickle under the chin.

'He's a big fan of strawberry tarts, then, is he?'

'Who isn't? Actually he's a big fan of more or less anything.' Lolo looks down at Oscar. 'Hold on ... I've got something for you.' He reaches into his pocket, pulls out a dog chew and gives it to Oscar, who promptly flops down on the floor in chewy heaven.

'Cheers then,' I say, raising my (very full) glass of milkshake in the air.

'Cheers,' says Lolo, carefully chinking glasses.

We both set to with the straws, sucking up the thick sweet creamy goo and steering our way round the rectangular block of vanilla ice-cream floating in each glass.

'Excellent choice,' says Lolo.

'I thought you might like it.'

'Are all your surprises this good?'

'Of course!'

Lolo laughs, causing him to cough into his straw. A little splodge of milkshake splashes out, narrowly avoiding his sky-blue slacks.

'Oops!' he says, wiping the milkshake off his chair with a hanky. 'That's your fault.'

'My fault? Why?'

'For making me laugh.' He refolds the hanky and puts it away.

I have another slurp of milkshake. 'I can't help being so funny. It just comes naturally.'

'Hmmm,' says Lolo, sipping. 'We should get you on TV with Mike Yarwood.'

'*Silly billy!*' I say, doing my best Mike Yarwood doing his best Denis Healey.

'There – told you!'

We both smile. Out on the Serpentine, a swan lands with a graceful flap of wing.

'Thanks again for taking me to the opera, by the way,' I say. 'It was a really lovely evening.'

'Yes, it was, wasn't it?' he replies. 'I really enjoyed it.'

'I can't believe I actually like opera after all these years saying what a racket it is!'

'Well, hold your horses. Some of them *are* a bit of a racket. You were lucky. *La Bohème*'s a good one to start with. I think we'll do something a bit more challenging next time, though, see how you cope.' He puts his milkshake down on the table. 'That's if you want a next time, of course.'

'Oh yes,' I say, bubbling away enthusiastically. 'Definitely. Speaking of which, would you mind having a quick look at my review before you tuck into your tart?'

'Hmm?'

I nod at the strawberry tarts on the table.

'Oh, I see – yes, of course. Hand it over, then.'

I reach down and get the review out of my bag, feeling like I'm back at school, handing in homework to a favourite teacher.

Lolo takes it, sits back in his chair and starts to read.

'I hope you like it,' I say, a tiny voice (huge in doubt).

There's an almost indiscernible nod.

His eyes are trained to the page. He makes a little grunt . . . and then another . . . then a quick flash of smile followed by another grunt . . . then a serious face and a nod . . . then another grunt and smile . . . a nose scratch . . . and then a chuckle . . . a nod . . . a sniff . . . another grunt . . . another nod . . . and – finally – a big broad smile.

'Excellent!' he says, putting the review down on the table.

'You liked it?'

'Yes, a lot.'

'You're not just saying that to be nice?'

'What, to the woman who said I need a shire horse to get me off my chair? No, it's *very* good. I'm not sure it'd find its way into *Gramophone* but it's perfect for *Right On!* I think you've found your voice.'

'You're *absolutely* sure?'

'Yes!' Lolo cries. 'It's great. The essence of Evie.'

'Thank you.' Now it's my turn to blush. 'And it's funny, but a really good friend said exactly the same thing to me once. The essence of Evie.'

'Well, there's definitely something there. It's unmistakably you. And that's a very good thing.'

He puts a hand on the table and starts tapping his thumb on the shiny metal surface.

'I ... really did enjoy going to the opera with you, Evie,' he says. 'It was a ... lovely evening.'

'Yes, it was fun, wasn't it!' I say, bright as a spinning top.

Lolo's thumb stops mid-tap.

'Yeah, it was lots of ... fun. Anything else?' he asks, half looking up.

'Well, it was interesting,' I reply, thinking of Lolo's water stories. 'And I mean properly interesting – not just interesting when you don't know what else to say.'

'Fun and interesting, then?'

'And exciting too, of course, but mainly fun.'

'Oh.' Lolo smiles but his face isn't smiling and his lovely kind eyes aren't smiling.

'Well, you're funny, aren't you,' I say. 'Like me, I mean.'

'Am I?'

'Yes. It's a good thing. Being funny.'

'Right.'

He attempts another smile then looks down at Oscar.

I'm trying to think of something amusing to say when a seagull suddenly swoops onto the table, gunning for the strawberry tarts.

I scream.

Lolo lunges forward, a whirlwind of Welsh arm.

The bird shoots off but so does Oscar, taking Lolo's chair with him, something that Lolo doesn't realise until it's too late.

His bum goes down, his arms go up, his head goes back, and a leg juts out for balance. Instead of balance, it finds the table, smashing it from underneath and knocking the whole thing over towards him. Lolo hits the floor with an *ooof*, immediately followed by an *aargh* as the table topples onto him, covering him with industrial amounts of vanilla milkshake and strawberry tart.

'Oh, God, Lolo,' I shout, darting off my chair. 'Are you all right?'

'It's fine,' he says, wiping a big pile of strawberries and cream off his pants. 'I'm fine.'

I've got my hanky out and am busy dabbing at Lolo's milkshake-and-ice-cream-covered shirt.

'Is this what you meant by funny?' he says, looking down and flicking a rogue strawberry off his belt.

He's covered in food and milkshake. The dabbing's doing no good at all. My hanky is sodden and I think I'm just making it worse. It's like being a stone and trying to stop a stream.

'Oh, you poor thing,' I say, squeezing the hanky out (a cold, creamy slop oozes through my fingers). 'Are you sure you're okay?'

'Yeah, I'm fine. Honestly. Just embarrassed.'

(Everyone, quite understandably, is gawping.)

Oscar, still dragging the chair, saunters back and starts licking Lolo, more for the cream, I suspect, than for any notion of loyalty.

'Thanks, boy,' says Lolo, giving Oscar a sloppy stroke. 'Talk about kicking a man when he's down.'

'Or licking a man when he's down,' I say (and immediately wish I hadn't).

Lolo ignores me. He just looks down and lets out a sigh so deep it must leave him empty.

'Let me help you up,' I go on. 'You can rinse it all off in the loo.'

He scoops a clot of cream from his shirt and shakes his head.

'Rinse it all off?' he repeats (still not looking at me). 'No, I need to go home and get changed. I'm covered.' He plucks at his wet and sticky shirt. 'I feel ridiculous.'

'It's just an accident,' I say, 'they happen all the time.'

'I'm an embarrassment. An absolute bloody clown.'

He brushes off another strawberry, leaving a long red smear across his pants, then lifts himself up off the floor.

'I think I just want to go home, Evie. Sorry.'

'I'll come with you, then,' I say, righting the table. 'We could get a taxi.'

'Thanks, but I'm fine. Really.

'No, come on, let me help.'

'No, I'd rather you didn't, thanks,' he says, wiping his face with a hanky.

He picks up Oscar's lead.

'At least let me walk with you for a bit, then.'

'No, honestly, sorry, I just want to be left alone. I feel like such a damn idiot. Look, I'll give you a ring.'

'But I feel terrible.'

'You shouldn't. I'm the one who's ruined it all.'

'Ruined? Don't be silly. Come on, let me help.'

'No, please don't come. I just need to get cleaned up and have some time on my own. That's all. Really.'

And he puts his head down and walks off, not smiling, not waving, not looking back.

I stand there for a while, watching him disappear into the crowd.

And then I turn round and start walking home, feeling low, like it was somehow all my fault, like I've somehow broken something.

I'm still feeling out of sorts when I get home.

I obviously feel very sorry for poor old Lolo, covered in milk-shake and ice-cream and strawberries. And I'm definitely sad about him not wanting me to help. Plus knowing he's upset is making me upset.

But there's something else.

As I walk past all the different coloured doors down my street, I think about Lolo and his dented pride and warm-tea eyes. I

257

hope he's got home okay. I'm sure Tarquin will be there, ready to help him get his clothes in the wash, putting some new clothes out on the bed while Lolo has a bath.

I try to picture Tarquin but it's difficult. I can't get past Lolo and his affable hearty smile. I hope Tarquin's nice. Lolo deserves someone nice. Someone as nice as him.

I drift down the street. Past the lovely old couple who live at number thirty-six. Past the man at number thirty-two who we suspect is a nudist. Past the lady with all the cats at number twenty-four. And, propping up my flat, past the haberdasher's on the corner and its window crammed with stuff.

Even before I put my key in the door, I know Geneviève's in because David Bowie is coming full-tilt through the kitchen window (directly above my front door).

Good. She's just what I need.

'Hi,' I shout as I walk into the kitchen.

She jumps up and turns the cassette player down a bit, fading out the Starman's tuneful rockets.

'Hiya,' she replies, a smiling fashion chipmunk in hot pants and spangly vest. 'Nice morning?'

'Well, yes and no. Lolo liked the review' – (Geneviève raises her hands in the air victoriously) – 'but then something strange happened.'

'Something strange? Oh, hold on,' she says, reaching over for the kettle. 'It sounds like this calls for a brew.'

While she's making the tea, I tell her about the milkshakes and the strawberry tarts and Oscar and the seagull and the chair and the mess and my sodden hanky and poor Lolo's face as he walked away.

'Oh, that's awful,' she says. 'Poor Lolo. He's so nice, too.'

'Yes, he's lovely, isn't he?' I reply, sitting down. 'Really lovely. I hope he'll be okay.'

'He'll be fine. He's got his boyfriend to look after him, hasn't he? They're probably sat at home right now having a good laugh about it.'

'Yes, probably.'

'Wearing silk pyjamas and listening to Barbra Streisand.'

I smile. 'Maybe. Yes.' (I struggle to picture this.) 'Anyway, enough about my morning. What about yours?'

She joins me at the kitchen table, complete with a tray filled with assorted tea accoutrements.

(Geneviève is meticulous. Tea is always served from a pot and accompanied by cups and saucers, a sugar bowl, milk in a jug and a plate of biscuits. Despite being very modern in many ways, when it comes to tea, she's like the Queen Mother.)

'Well, it's been quite a morning, really,' she says, pouring the tea. 'I was working on a few things' – she nods at a sketchpad on the table – 'trying out some new ideas and then the doorbell went and it was Caroline with a sewing machine. She said she'd bought it for me. Just like that! I couldn't believe it.'

'Oh, good old Caroline!'

'I know! She's lovely, isn't she?'

'She's brilliant,' I say, putting a splash of milk into both cups. 'Was Digby with her?'

'No, it was just Caroline.'

'Oh, I see.'

'The machine's in the front room,' she goes on, scooping sugar into her tea. 'It's fantastic. Dead fancy.'

She looks as though she's just been given a million pounds.

(I knew she'd cheer me up.)

'I've got an idea,' I say, having a sip of tea.

'Ooh, what?'

'Why don't we make Caroline and Digby a thank-you cake?'

Her face lights up. 'Yeah, that'd be ace! Are you any good at baking?'

'Not really,' I reply. 'I can do savoury okay but I'm much better at eating cakes than making them. What about you?'

'I'm no good, either. I always used to get out of domestic science so I could practise my needlework. But there is *one* thing I can make, though . . .'

Ten minutes later and I'm balancing a glass bowl on a saucepan of boiling water.

The front door opens, followed by a quick *I'm back* and the sound of Geneviève's platforms hammering up the stairs.

'Ta-da!' she sings, waving a couple of bars of chocolate in the air as she bursts into the kitchen. 'I got Bourneville because I know they're both posh.'

'Oooh, very nice.'

'And I got these too.' She holds up a jar of glacé cherries, giving them a quick maraca shake. 'I thought I'd jazz up the recipe. You know, make it a bit more sophisticated, like Fanny Cradock.'

'Good idea.' (Nothing says sophistication like dark chocolate and glacé cherries.) 'This is boiling by the way,' I add, pointing to the saucepan.

Geneviève takes up position next to the pan and starts breaking the chocolate into the glass bowl. There's a lot of simmering and stirring (Geneviève) plus a fair amount of cupboard rummaging (me) looking for my jelly mould. Eventually I find it: a bright orange plastic affair that looks like a curvy sandcastle bucket. I pass it up to Geneviève and she pours the melted chocolate into it, demonstrating excellent spatula-ing skills and getting the chocolate into all the bulbous nooks and crannies.

(I am forever destined to be Johnnie to someone else's Fanny)

'There,' she says, putting the mould in the fridge. 'Right, time to do it all again now.'

And she does another round of chocolate melting but this time stirring in some butter and Golden Syrup. When it's all melted, she takes it off the heat and adds the *pièce de résistance*: a few good shakes of Rice Krispies plus some glacé cherries and half a tube of Smarties for good measure. Then she takes the jelly mould out of the fridge, fills it with the Rice Krispie mix and re-fridges it – all while I'm making another brew.

There's a lively blast of kitchen tidying accompanied by some bowl-licking, tea drinking and chit-chatting (acrylic fabrics, Barbara Cartland, Brussel sprouts). Then it's time to take the mould out of the fridge again, carefully ease out the cake, and – the finishing touch – add the remaining glacé cherries (a nipple for every peak).

It looks magnificent.

A pert glistening delight of chocolate curve and cherry.

'What do you think?' asks Geneviève, her voice nervously snap-crackle-and-popping.

'They're going to love it,' I reply. 'It'll be the best cake they've ever had.'

She sighs, visibly relaxing, sending out a smile that fills the room.

'Fab! Shall we take it round now?' she asks.

(My mind clicks round, engineering an idea.)

'Actually, would you mind taking it by yourself? I've got *loads* of really boring stuff I need to do for the magazine.' I roll my eyes, in full acting mode. 'It all needs to be done by tomorrow.'

'Oh, right, okay. Are you sure?'

'Yes, sorry. You'll have a great time, though. And try and make a big fuss of Caroline – she's in need of a pick-me-up, I think.'

The moment she's out the door, I phone Caroline and Digby.

Digby answers. After a few hullos and a quick conversational cul-de-sac about cystitis, I ask about the Big Freeze.

'Well,' she says, lowering her voice, 'we're still not really talking but at least we've managed to avoid any major flare-ups for a few days – since supper at yours, in fact. I think spending some time with you and Geneviève was just what we both needed.'

'Actually,' I go on, 'it's about Geneviève that I'm ringing. She's made a cake for you both to thank you for the sewing machine.'

'Och, it was nothing.'

'Well, she's on her way round with it now and I wondered if you could do me a massive favour and keep her there for a

while? I've got to finish something important for the magazine,'
I explain (lie).

'Of course, dear. Look, why doesn't she stay here for supper?'

'Are you sure?' I ask, trying to sound as un-Machiavellian
as possible.

'Yes, it'd be no trouble at all. We'd be delighted. She and
Caroline can have a good natter about fashion while I'm beggaring around in the kitchen.'

'Oh, thanks, Digby. That's a huge help – I really appreciate it.'

(I am an evil, manipulative only child.)

'It's our pleasure, dear. You just get on with your magazine
work. And don't worry about Geneviève – we'll drop her off in
the car tonight, well fed and watered.'

And we say our goodbyes.

An hour or so later I'm spread out on the sofa with a Cadbury's
Flake and an oversized snowball.

I've been thinking about Lolo.

I hope he's okay.

I hope he's snug on a sofa with a clean change of clothes and
a warm glass of beer and a comforting arm around him. There
was something in his eyes today, in amongst all the chestnutty,
treacly warm autumnal shades. Something sad.

I should speak to him, shouldn't I? Make sure he's all right.
Make sure he's not embarrassed in any way by the agonising
spectacle he made of himself in front of a cafe terrace full of
strangers.

I pick up the phone and begin to dial his number, circling my finger round, number by number, watching the rotating holes rachet back into place each time.

Every number, I think about Lolo. I think about him lunging for the seagull. About him crashing to the floor. About him being covered in mess. I think about his embarrassment. His hurt. And I think about the look on his face when I told him he was fun.

The strange, disappointed look.

I put my finger in the five, ready to dial the final number. I hesitate, not really sure why. And then I click the handset back down on the receiver and sit staring at the phone.

Wanting it to ring.

Interlude – January 1972, Yorkshire

It had been snowing heavily since breakfast. There was a deep covering now, blotting out the familiar lines and contours around the house. A new geography, vague and unexplored.

It was a day to stay inside.

Rosamund Scott-Pym tried to make herself comfortable on the sofa, arranging and rearranging cushions. Her back throbbed, little swells and eddies of pain.

It will pass, she thought, as she savoured the muffled silence outside.

She reached out – carefully – and took her afternoon glass of sherry from the coffee table, sipping it, welcoming its familiarity on her lips. Then she put down her glass and picked up a copy of *Country Life*. On the cover, a stream bent gently round somewhere flat. Suffolk, probably, or perhaps Essex. She flicked through a few random pages in the middle. A short article on fly fishing, 'A Countryman's Notes', something about Impressionism. She shifted her back, searching for more support. None came so she stretched out again and had another sip of sherry.

It had been wonderful having the girls to stay. They always made such a fuss of her. Seeing them together, their loving ease, made Rosamund very happy. It meant the world to her that they had each other. It gave her peace.

She would have to tell them soon, of course, and Evie too. Maybe at Easter, when they'd all be up again. She had time, her doctors assured her. The best part of a year, one had said. It wasn't really so much a question of when to tell them, but of how ...

Back in *Country Life* she skipped over an article about quince and sought out one of her favourite regular features, 'In My Garden'. Just before it was a feature on the food and drink of World War Two. Rosamund glanced through the accompanying photographs. Woolton pies! Oh, she remembered them well. There was a sliced National Loaf there too, grey and unappetising. She turned the page and was surprised to see a table set with champagne and lobster. It was at the Dorchester, apparently. They kept quiet about that, she thought. Rosamund couldn't remember seeing many lobsters around during the war. Or much champagne, either, for that matter. And then her mind took her back to a morning she hadn't thought of for years: a spring morning in the last few weeks of the war. Here in the garden. With Diana, Evie's mother. And a bottle of champagne. The day Diana told her she was pregnant.

Rosamund sat there for a while, her pain sedated by memories. Muffled without and within.

*

She'd saved the cork, she was sure. It had to be somewhere, but where? She eased herself up off the sofa and made her way over to the sideboard. The bottom few drawers were full of knick-knacks and all sorts of things that had probably not been touched for twenty-odd years. She pulled up a chair and began to go through each drawer, fumbling around between old pens, paperclips, a few marbles and various pieces of stationery. As she fumbled, her mind clicked round. Where could she have put it?

She was in the third drawer down when it came to her.

The back bedroom was little more than a store cupboard. It was the fourth bedroom and had never actually been used by anyone to sleep in. There was a single bed and, opposite it, an Arts and Crafts wardrobe that had belonged to her parents. Rosamund opened the wardrobe door and – very steadily – eased herself down onto the floor. Inside the wardrobe was a wall of shoeboxes and the occasional hatbox. She moved a few of the boxes round and – with a sigh of delight – found what she wanted.

A battered and worn leather suitcase.

She lifted the suitcase onto the bed and then sat for a few moments, gently rubbing her back, exhausted by the effort of it all.

Opening the suitcase was like opening a time capsule. It took Rosamund right back to the war. Ration books, a *Dig for Victory* leaflet, her National Identity card, and quite a few slimmed-down copies of *The Times*, their front pages shouting out key wartime events: Dunkirk, Paris, the Normandy landings ...

And there, underneath a Civil Defence leaflet, was the champagne cork.

It felt warm. Hard but soft. She smelled it, hoping to catch a hint of champagne but there was nothing. As she lifted the cork up to her nose, she noticed something written on it. Something faint. She brought it closer to her eyes, slowly moving it backwards and forwards, allowing her eyes to focus.

It was a date: 12th May 1945.

She smiled. Her head awash with memories.

CHAPTER 17

Summer 1972

Monday mornings are strange, aren't they?

You know they're coming. They don't try and sneak up on you. In fact they jump up and down waving at you for most of Sunday night.

But even after all that warning, they still somehow manage to throw you right off kilter.

Luckily, I've now got Geneviève, the best anti-Monday-morning magic anyone could ever have. When I got down to the kitchen today, she was already there, complete with three other lovely things:

1. Tea (in the pot – brewing)
2. Bread (in the toaster – toasting)
3. Music (in the air – Don McLean-ing)

All of this was accompanied by a constant stream of sunshine and lots of good breakfast chat (Jean Marsh, France, hair tongs).

Geneviève's back upstairs now and I'm eking out the last drops of tea from the pot. I add a splash of milk and sit back, easing my way into the day. Beside me on the table is a stack of magazines, with last Friday's *Evening Standard* perched on top. The paper is folded open at the crossword – we had a go at it on Saturday morning but gave up, defeated by three down (*First man to believe in pop* – nine letters). As I'm pondering, the phone rings. It's still only half past eight (before the nine o'clock rule), which means it can only be Dad or . . .

'Darling!'

Caroline.

'Morning!' I say, curling the phone cord round my finger. 'This is a nice surprise. Is everything okay?'

'Yes, everything's fine.'

'Ah, good. And how are things with you and Digby?'

'Well, darling, she's still sulking but I think she's slowly coming round. It was lovely having Geneviève here last night, actually – she buoyed us both up marvellously. Is she around?'

'Yes, she's just upstairs.'

'Oh, good, I'm going into town later for a new outfit and I thought I might borrow her young eye. I don't want to start getting old and frumpy.'

'Don't worry, there's no danger of that!' I say, having a sneaky tug on my tights. 'Anyway, I'm sure she'd love to come shopping. She's been going on about what a good time she had with you both yesterday.'

'Really? She doesn't think we're old and boring?'

'No, don't be daft! Completely the opposite, in fact. She thinks you're exciting and glamorous.'

(The phone purrs.)

'She really looks up to you,' I go on. 'It's the fashion connection, I think. She sees you as a role model. Magnificent and refined.'

(More purring.)

'That's very sweet of her, darling. She's such a tonic, isn't she?'

'She's great. Hold on, I'll give her a shout.'

I yell upstairs to Geneviève, telling her Caroline's on the phone. She's downstairs before I know it, shooting into the sitting room like a supersonic Dinky Toy.

I say bye to Caroline and pass the phone to Geneviève, then slink out the room, smiling a crafty smile and giving my tights another good yank.

Half an hour or so later, I'm skipping into the *Right On!* office.

I have an extra little spring in my step. This is not because of my carrot-and-rust Biba tea dress or my strappy cork-sole sandals but because I've got the opera review tucked neatly away in my bag.

'Morning,' says Nickwiththecollars, hovering at a filing cabinet near the door. 'Oh, you look very bright-eyed and bushy-tailed. It's Monday, you know, not Friday.'

'But a very special Monday,' I reply with suitably special smile.

'And what's so special about it, then?'

'I've written the review,' I say, tapping my bag. 'For *La Bohème*.'

'Really?' He gives his upturned collar a bit of a thumb. 'I tell you what, why don't we go through to the kitchen so I can have a read while you make some tea?'

*

271

'Oh, it's *very* good,' he says, chortling.

We're in the kitchen. I'm beggaring around with a split teabag and Nickwiththecollars is sitting on the sofa reading the review.

'Marvellous!' he goes on. This is followed by a long chuckle, a sniff and two increasingly rosy cheeks.

'So you think it's okay, then?' I ask, putting a mug of tea down on the coffee table for him.

'Okay? I think it's wonderful!'

'Really?' I join him on the sofa with a box of Huntley & Palmers. 'We can put your name on it if you like?'

He tuts and takes a custard cream. 'Don't be silly.'

'Well, you're the reviewer, aren't you? It just seems right. I don't mind at all.'

'Absolutely not,' he says through a mouthful of biscuit.

'Well, if you're sure ...'

'Of course I'm sure. I've never been surer.'

I smile and dunk a digestive, happy in my new role of bona fide journalist, like Ludovic Kennedy or Tintin.

Then the kitchen door swings open and Nickstickupbum struts in with the relaxed air of a dressage pony. 'Morning,' he snips, clip-clopping his way to the sofa. 'Coffee, please, Evie.'

(This is an improvement – at least I get a *please*.)

'What's that?' he says, pointing at the opera review.

'It's a little something Evie wrote,' replies Nickwiththecollars. 'A review. The one I told you about. Remember?'

'A review? Evie?'

'Yes. A BBC friend got the tickets – isn't that right, Evie?'

'That's right,' I reply, standing back at the kitchen cupboards,

272

busy with the Maxwell House and trying to make myself invisible. 'Lolo. He's at Radio Three,' I add, attempting gravitas by association.

Nickstickupbum holds out his hand. 'Let's have a look, then.'

He takes the review, clears his throat and starts to read. His face is expressionless; I have no idea what he's thinking. But then – finally – when his eyes get near the bottom of the page, there's the faintest glimmer of a smile, like when a tiny slit of light first cracks through at sunrise.

'Not bad,' he says.

I stop stirring his coffee. Amazed.

'Of course, it needs some tweaking here and there. Proper editing. But in the grand scheme of things, in its own funny little way, it's actually quite readable.'

'Oh, thanks, Nick,' I say, putting his coffee down on the table with a huge smile.

'Well,' he huffs. 'I suppose it's only to be expected from a trained BBC journalist, Evie. Now, would you mind nipping out? We need a couple of lever arch files and some blotting paper.'

'Ooooh, and could you get me a Crunchie while you're out?' adds Nickwiththecollars. 'I'm starving.'

While I'm out I decide to give Lolo another ring. Despite leaving several messages with Tarquin and various BBC people, I haven't heard from him since Sunday's horrible milkshake incident and I'm beginning to fret. I've been thinking about him quite a bit, actually. His kind, smiling face and big Welsh hands. His in-depth knowledge of water and who's drunk it. His freshly-brewed-tea eyes. Plus I'm now dying to tell him about both Nicks liking my *La Bohème* review.

I nip into a phone box (taking care to avoid the puddle in the corner) and call Lolo at home. It rings and rings and rings but there's no answer. So then I try the BBC switchboard, ask to be put through to the Radio 3 office and leave a message with a man who sounds like Kenneth Williams.

Back in the office, I put away the lever arch files and blotting paper, give Nickwiththecollars his Crunchie and then go and sit at my desk. I'm working my way through this week's listings and am almost at the end of *Cinemas*, one of my favourite categories because it reminds me of Dad taking me to see *Lady and the Tramp* six times at the Leeds Odeon. (I was obsessed with the film. It had the magical combination of Disney and dogs. Dad always used to joke about how the film was like him and Mum – one of the few times he spoke about her – and I'm sure I spotted him going damp of eye several times.)

No Disney in this week's listings though. Or dogs, either. It's all horror, sex and European art (often in the same film). The radio is tinny-ing away in the background, providing musical accompaniment to all my *Roxys* and *Regals*. I make fast work and, thanks to Jimmy Young and his top pop picks, I've soon finished *Cinemas* and am ready to move on to the next category: *Classical Music*.

I stare at the blank page.

It stares back at me.

For the past few weeks, Lolo's helped with the classical

music listings, slipping me a typed-up sheet that makes sense of all the various symphonies and adagios going on across London. Without him I'm lost.

The blank page screams, a sweeping expanse of nothingness.

I pick up a pen and decide to skip on to the next category (*Fashion*) but, as I do, something catches my eye. The metronome. Lolo's metronome. The ugly desk adornment that perhaps isn't so ugly after all. I look at it for a few seconds, taking in its reassuring heft, and then pull back the pendulum and let go.

The pendulum ticks left and right, left and right, moving one way then the other like a clipped robotic cradle. Backwards. Forwards. Backwards. Forwards. When the metal arm clicks right, it catches the light from the windows and there's a quick little gleam. On, off, on, off.

It's hypnotic.

Click. Click. Click. Click. Cli—

A tasselled hand swoops down and stops the pendulum.

'Daydreaming again, Evie?'

'I was just thinking, actually, Griffin,' I reply, struggling to take in the full *Hey Nonny Nonnyness* of her outfit (oversized tasselled waistcoat, bell-sleeved tassel top, patchwork tasselled loons).

She makes a short deep noise, like a hillock getting thwacked with a spade.

'Thinking? You're not here to think. You're here to write lists.'

She whips out a copy of last week's *Right On!* from her tasselly bag and throws it on the table.

'Preferably grammatically correct lists too,' she huffs, quickly flicking through to the listings page. 'Look!' She jabs a finger at the magazine.

I look down at the page.

She's pointing at the listing for Delphinia's gallery:

Wonderful friendly gallery with great art & great Chelsea buns - plus the best swirly chairs in Mayfair.

It looks okay to me. No demonic apostrophes or fanny spellings. Griffin gives the listing another jab (accompanied by a loud tut) so I read it again, more slowly, parsing every word just like Mrs Weston, my old Latin teacher, taught us.

'Wonderful

friendly

gallery

with

great

art

& great

Chelsea

buns -

plus

the

best

swirly

chairs

in

Mayfair.'

Nothing.

I look up at Griffin, defeated.

Her eyes roll (two blank bingo balls rattling round a demoni-cally coiffured basket) then something appears on her face that could almost be a smile.

'Well, I'm surprised someone like you can't spot it,' she says. 'Someone with all that journalistic experience. Someone from the BBC.'

We hold each other's stare for a moment, eye to tassely eye.

'Here,' she goes on, filling the four letters with enough smug-ness to keep Edward Heath going for a year. 'The hyphen.'

'What's wrong with it?'

'Well, it shouldn't be there, should it?'

'Shouldn't it?'

'No, of course not.' (Another tut.) 'It should be an en dash.'

'A what?'

'An en dash. Which is different to an em dash, which is dif-ferent to a hyphen.'

She stands back, awash in grammatical glory.

'Aren't they just all the same?' I ask.

Griffin snatches a pencil from my desk and draws three little lines.

'There,' she says, the corners of her mouth curling upwards, venturing into unknown territory. 'That's an em dash' – she points to the first little line – 'that's an en dash' – she points to the second little line – 'and that's a hyphen' – she points to the third little line.

The three lines are microscopically different lengths. Together, they look like they could be saying something deeply unimpressive in morse code.

'Oh,' I say, a syntactic deflation. 'But isn't life too short to worry about things like that?'

The sides of her mouth droop downwards, back to familiar territory.

'No,' she snaps. 'It certainly isn't. People need rules. And they should stick to them.' She bristles (quite an impressive sight given all the tassels). 'Now, can you go and get some files and blotting paper, we've run out.'

'I've already got some,' I reply, trying to sound as helpful and grammatically in control as possible. 'I nipped out earlier.'

Her eyes narrow and she does something unattractive with her nose.

'Well, go and get some paperclips then.'

(Another eye-roll.)

'And while you're out,' she adds, putting the magazine back in her bag, 'could you get me some fig rolls . . .'

(I take a very dim view of fig rolls – they are not proper biscuits.)

'. . . a couple of Kit Kats and a Britvic orange.'

And she lords off into the kitchen in a state of hyphen nirvana.

While I'm out, I give Lolo another ring. There's no answer at home (again) but when I try Radio 3, I hit jackpot.

'Hullo, Lolo speaking.'

'Lolo, it's Evie!'

There's a moment's silence.

'Evie.'

'I keep missing you!'

'Sorry?'

'On the phone, I keep missing you. I've called a few times and at home, too.'

The moment's silence stretches.

'Yes, sorry. It's been a busy few days.'

'Oh. Right. I see. Well, I just wanted to check that you were okay after Sunday – you know, with the ice-cream and everything.'

I hear a little sigh, a tiny puff of air.

'Yes, all okay. Just fulfilling my role as court jester.'

'Sorry?'

'Nothing. I'm absolutely fine. The clothes went straight in the wash. No harm done. I put your listings in the post, by the way. Have they arrived?'

'No, not yet,' I answer, aware something's not quite right (like a skew-whiff sock in a shoe). 'That's why I was calling, actually. To see if you wanted to meet. Well, not just for the listings obviously. I was going to—'

'I'm sorry, Evie, but I'm a bit tied up over the next few days,' interrupts Lolo. 'That's why I put the listings in the post.'

'Oh. Right.'

'It's a busy time for us. Lots on.'

'Yes, of course.'

'Sorry.'

The silence ticks, then tocks.

'Not even a quick thank-you coffee? For doing the listings, I mean.'

'It's just that ...'

'Please, Lolo, it'd be lovely to see you.'

I hear him breathing down the phone.

'Just a really quick coffee,' I urge.

He sighs.

'Lolo? Hullo?'

'Yes, I'm here. I was just thinking. Perhaps Wednesday afternoon? Would you be able to finish work early and meet about four-thirty?'

'Oh, yes, I'm sure that'll be fine,' I reply (not at all sure).

'By the empty plinth again?'

'Of course! Where else?'

'Okay. Look, Evie, I'm afraid I've got to go.'

'Yes, yes, you're busy. Sorry!'

'See you Wednesday.'

'Yes ... okay ... bye, Lolo.'

'Bye, Evie.'

And the phone goes dead.

The rest of the morning is spent finishing off the listings, tidying out my bottom drawer and avoiding Griffin and her evil grammary tassels. I've also spent quite a bit of time thinking about how I can bunk off early on Wednesday to go and meet Lolo. At the moment my mind is blank but I'm sure I'll think of something – an only child is never far away from a good sneaky plan – plus Lolo's definitely worth bunking off for (despite his oddness just now on the phone).

I'm in the kitchen adding water to the kettle (and thinking about all the famous people who've already drunk it) when Nickwiththecollars walks in.

'Evie!' he sings, shimmying his way over to the kitchen cabinets. 'I come with good news.'

'Oh, cool! Have you won the pools?'

He laughs. 'No, silly, that's just a northern thing. It's much better than that!'

'Come on, then,' I say, passing him his tea. 'What it is?'

'A party!'

'A party?'

'Yes, at Dotty's.'

(Dotty is his girlfriend – Dorothea – jolly, curvy, arty).

'Oh, fantastic – you lucky thing. That'll be great.'

'Well, you're coming, too, of course.'

'Am I? When is it?'

'Wednesday.'

'This Wednesday?'

'Yes, it's all a bit short notice, I know, but that's Dotty for you.'

(Wednesday's when I'm meeting Lolo – this means:

1. I won't be able to hang around too much, which isn't really a problem because he always seems to be dashing back to Tarquin.

2. I won't be able to use an excuse *too* medicinal to
   bunk off work because soon afterwards I'll be bopping
   around at the party.)

'There'll be lots of eligible men for you too,' Nick goes on, giving his collar an excited little rub. 'Dotty's friends are all on the prowl, apparently. We'll have you shacked up by Thursday.'

'Oh, really? Is that a promise?'

'Absolutely. They'll love you. Painters, poets, musicians, actors ...' (He does an appropriately theatrical little flourish.) 'And I've not even told you the best bit yet.'

'Are John and Yoko coming?'

'Better,' he says, smirking. 'It's fancy dress!'

'Really?'

(Fancy dress parties are on my list of Things I Really Do Not Like. Other items on the list include celery, dry sponge and Malcolm Muggeridge.)

'Yes, and there's a theme.'

He says this as though it's a good thing. Which it isn't.

'Look,' he says, reaching over to the fruit bowl, grabbing a banana in each hand and holding them up to his head. 'Fancy dress!' He has a little wiggle of banana and hip. 'Who do you think I am?'

'Carmen Miranda?'

'No, a Viking. These are my horns, look,' he adds, having another little wiggle of banana.

'Oh, is that the theme then, Vikings?'

'No! It's *come as your favourite place in Europe* – now that

282

we're all Europeans, you know, with the EEC and all that. So a Viking is Scandinavia. You can be as creative as you want.'

'Right, I see.' I grab the quilted tea cosy and stick it on my head. 'And who am I then?'

'Er ... Spanish bullfighter?' he says, pointing at me with a banana. 'One of those funny Greek soldiers?'*

'No, it's a beret! I'm a sophisticated *Parisienne*.'

'*Très* sophisticated,' he says, arching an eyebrow.

Then he lifts the bananas back to his head, giving them another good wiggle, and starts singing.

'*Last night*

I heard my mama

singing a song ...'

'*OooOooEeee*,' I sing back. '*Chirpy chirpy cheep cheep ...*'

And we dance round for a bit, two banana-wiggling, tea-cosy bobbing, chirpy-cheeping sophisticated Europeans.

'What on earth are you doing?'

It's Griffin. Walking into the kitchen with a face like thunder and a voice like lightning.

'Oh, just getting in some practice for a fancy dress party,' says Nick, quickly putting the two bananas back in the fruit bowl.

'Fancy dress party?' repeats Griffin.

(Fancy dress must be easy for Griffin. Every day is pretty much fancy dress for her. Today she's dressed as a curtain pelmet.)

'Yes,' says Nick. 'You can come if you like.'

(What?!)

Griffin's eyes narrow; her pupils flick from Nick to me, from me to Nick.

283

> Name: Nikos Eliopolous
> From: Greece
> Job: military attaché to Greek embassy
> Seen for: a week and a day
> Appearance: Adonis
> Amazing: (see appearance)
> Less amazing: snoring, ouzo-pouring, boring

'Well, maybe.' She does something with her lips that makes them look like Lego bricks. 'We'll see.'

The morning air hangs still for a moment.

'Right, better be getting back to work,' chirps Nick. He picks up his tea, flashes me a quick smile and then walks back into the office, leaving me with Griffin (coward).

'Are you going to wear that all day?' she says, pointing at my head.

Bugger. I forgot about the quilted tea cosy.

'Perhaps,' I reply, striking a quick pose.

'Hmmm,' Gollums Griffin. 'It suits you. Actually, I wanted to have a word with you about something. It's your expenses. You haven't filled the form in correctly.'

'Oh,' I say, with a droop of shoulder. 'Sorry about that. What's wrong?'

Her mouth smudges into position.

'Well, where do I start?' she asks, knowing, I suspect, very well where she'll start. 'First, there's your name.'

'My name?'

'Yes, the form clearly asks for your *full* name and you only put E. Epworth.'

'But that's my signature.'

'You weren't asked for your signature, though, were you?' She folds her arms, causing a great chafing of tassel. 'And then there's the postcode.'

'What's wrong with the postcode? I put it all down, even the new bit.'

'But you didn't do it properly, I'm afraid,' she says, as apologetic as a blitzkrieg commander storming his way across France. 'You forgot the full stops.'

'What full stops?'

'The full stops between each character.' She sighs. 'I think you'll find that's still the right way to do things, despite the recent modifications. Anyway, all these mistakes mean I can't process the form.'

'What? So I don't get any expenses? Because of a few missing full stops?'

'It's the details, Evie. Surely as a professional journalist, BBC-trained no less, you understand these things.'

'But it's not fair.'

'It's got nothing to do with "fair", Evie. It's just the rules. What did I say earlier about sticking to rules?'

'I'm not even sure you're right about the full stops. I can't—'

'Don't argue back,' she interrupts. 'You're still on trial, remember? I'm sure you'll do it properly next week. And then you'll get your expenses. Now, I suppose this must be mine,' she says, taking a mug of black tea from the Formica then smugly *Hey-Nonny-Nonny*ing her way out the kitchen.

I pick up my tea, have a good slurp, then slide the tea cosy off my head, plotting.

For the next hour or so I keep myself busy (listings, daydreams, fruit gums). Every now and then I glance over at Griffin and send surreptitious waves of unruly em dashes, but she's had her head constantly stuck in a ledger and seems impervious.

When the postman comes with the second post, he puts a small pile of letters on my desk (as usual), gives me a wink (as usual) and exits immediately (as usual) on his way upstairs to the lava-lamp importers. I pick up the letters and start organising them by recipient, grouping them together like a little game of snap.

And that's when I see it.

A mauve envelope.

The mauve envelope that Griffin's chants come in every week.

My evil only-child mind whizzes around like a Kenwood Chefette.

I reach down into a desk drawer and take out this month's *Cosmopolitan* ('Be the Successful <u>Extra</u> Woman') then carefully, nonchalantly, secretly slide the envelope into it. Then I take a blank postcard from another drawer, quickly write something on it, and slide it into the magazine as well. Then

I take the *Cosmopolitan* to the kitchen, boil the kettle, hold Griffin's envelope in the steam for a bit, and head for the loo. In the loo, I carefully peel open the envelope, teasing the edges gently with my fingertips. Inside, just like every week, there's a postcard and a few flower petals. I take the postcard out, making sure I don't spill the petals, and then replace it with the one I've just written. I put the envelope back in *Cosmopolitan*, rip the old postcard up into tiny pieces and flush it down the loo. Then I go back to my desk, check everyone's busy doing officey things and quickly Pritt Stick down the flap of the envelope, making a wish.

I place the mauve envelope on the pile with Griffin's other post, wait a few minutes, then take all the post to everyone's desks, getting a lovely smile from Nickwiththecollars, a nod-ette from Nickstickupbum, and a huge blank from Griffin.

I return to my desk and wait.

The envelope sits on Griffin's desk, a jack-in-the-box waiting to go off.

After a bit, Griffin picks up her post. She flicks quickly through the envelopes, pulling out the mauve one. She opens it, reads the postcard, pops on her dusty garland of silk flowers and transcendentals into the kitchen.

Twelve-fifteen.

It's showtime.

'Do you mind if I turn the radio off for a bit?' I say to the two Nicks. 'I've got a headache coming on.'

There's a flurry of head-shaking and Anadin-offering and Nickwiththecollars gets up and switches off the radio.

(I picture Griffin in the kitchen, garlanded, crossing her legs on the sofa and holding out her arms, two little washing lines strewn with tasselly pegs.)

And then the chanting starts.

OOOOOOOOOO ...
     WAAA ...
          TA ...
               NARRRRRRRRRR ...
                    SIAM.

And again.

OOOOOOOOOO ...
     WAAA ...
          TA ...
               NARRRRRRRRRR ...
                    SIAM.

And again.

OOOOOOOO ... WAAA ... TA ... NARRRRRRRRR ... SIAM.
OOOOOOOO ... WAAA ... TA ... NARRRRRRRRR ... SIAM.
OOOOOOOO ... WAAA ... TA ... NARRRRRRRRR ... SIAM.
OOOOOOOO ... WAAA ... TA ... NARRRRRRRRR ... SIAM.

Over and over.
Again and again.

For a couple of minutes.

At one point Nickwiththecollars looks up and cocks his head to one side. Listening. Pondering. Smiling. He glances over at me.

I muster up the most innocent look I can manage and get another fruit gum.

Interlude – Spring 1956, Napoli

She poured an inch or so of Campari into each glass.

It was her favourite time of day. Work had been put back in its box and the pleasures of a Neapolitan evening stretched out in front of them.

She added a large measure of soda to the Campari, smiling to herself.

Che bella è la vita. She couldn't believe how happy she was; couldn't believe her luck. Muir and her father and Scotland all felt like another life. Could she really be the same person? Her once-pale skin now glowed, sandcastle brown. Her hair was short; her clothes transformed. Even her organs had changed, her lungs pumped full of Neapolitan air, her heart thumping – roaring – alive.

Digby reached into the freezer box and pulled out the ice tray, popping a handful of cubes into each glass. The kitchen was only small, tiny in fact, *piccolissima*, but it was big enough for them. Most of the time they ate out – cheaply – at local pizzerias or trattorias or, if they weren't hungry, they just stayed at home for cheese, *antipasti* and a glass of wine – nearly always followed by a *passeggiata* and a *gelato* from a nearby bar.

Outside, the noises of the city swooped and soared. Bells, shouts, car horns, song. A grand orchestral score.

She took an orange, halved it then cut one half into slices. A few slices were dropped into each glass and everything given a good stir.

Perfect.

'Thank you, darling,' said Caroline, taking the Campari.

She was on the balcony, as small as the kitchen and hardly big enough for the two chairs they had out there. The view, though, was far from small.

It was immense.

Over the rooftops, the Bay of Naples curled round and out to infinity, all watched over by Vesuvius, a majestic, brooding lord. The sky swelled above, as vast as an ocean, glossy and diffuse.

'What a lovely evening,' said Digby, sitting down.

'Isn't it just?' replied Caroline. She took a sip of Campari and threw back her head, letting her long red hair brush against the wall. 'Oh, this is good!' she said, jangling the glass. 'Maybe you should give up teaching and get a job in a bar.'

'I'll leave that to you!' said Digby. She put the glass up to her lips and drank, feeling the bitter icy kick give way to something sweet. *Delizioso*. A deep, luscious calm opened up around them. She looked over at Caroline, staring out to sea, taking in her profile, shapely and proud, a line of aquiline beauty. Behind her, the faint moon hung like tracing paper in the still-blue dusky sky.

She didn't think she'd ever been so happy.

Instinctively, they leant into each other, locking together like a perfect jigsaw.

Bliss.

Time passed. Honeyed drips dropping into space.

The view from the balcony softened. The burnished sky began to dim; the sea took on an inky sheen. The moon – now bright – stood guard across the Bay.

Downstairs on the street, children's voices fizzed and popped.

Digby craned her neck. 'They're having fun tonight!'

Caroline made an indeterminate noise.

The voices swirled, bubbling up past window and washing line. Digby drank them down, bittersweet. She paused for a moment, lost in thought, then bent her head into Caroline's. 'Do you ever think about having a family?'

'Hmmm?'

'A family. Wouldn't it be lovely?'

Caroline sat up.

'We're each other's family, aren't we?'

Digby ran her hand gently along Caroline's thigh.

'Yes, of course, but I meant children, a little boy or girl.'

'Well, there are certain biological difficulties.'

Digby couldn't tell if Caroline's tone was joking or annoyed.

'There's always Dino,' she said. 'He's a handsome Neapolitan. Good genes. Kind. And about as likely to marry as we are.'

'Don't joke,' said Caroline, taking a large gulp of Campari.

'I'm not joking. It happens all the time. We wouldn't be the first women to do it. And I'm sure Dino would help. There are ways ...'

Caroline sat rubbing her finger round the rim of her glass.

'So *I'm* not enough, then?' she said, dropping a stone into the silence.

The air rippled out around them.

'Of course you are – I didn't mean it like that. I just meant, well, don't you ever want children?'

'No. I *don't* want children. I don't want to be responsible for someone else. Definitely not yet,' she added, standing up. 'And I don't think I ever will. I'm just not maternal.'

'Oh, I'm sorry, I just—'

'It's a ridiculous idea,' snapped Caroline. 'We're lucky to be here – together – and now you're saying that's not enough.'

'No, I didn't mean that at all.'

'Well, that's what it sounded like.'

'No, I just thought how lovely it'd be to be here, together, with each other, and with a child. *Our* child. A perfect family.'

Something fell between them. Something invisible but clear.

'I see.'

Caroline breathed out slowly then looked down at her half-filled glass. She brought the Campari up to her mouth and gulped it down.

Digby looked on. Unsure.

Was now the time? To explain what had happened. To share with Caroline the bottomless, pitch-black hole she stared into every day.

For a few seconds, silence consumed them.

Then Caroline's glass came smashing down onto the floor.

'Aren't we enough?' she yelled. 'And isn't all this enough?' (She gestured across the Bay.) 'And me, I suppose I'm not enough, either, then? That's what you're saying, isn't it?'

'No!' cried Digby. 'Of course not. Don't say that.' She lifted Caroline's unresponsive hands and kissed them.

The two were still for a moment, facing each other, love blistering with pain.

'You know how I feel about you,' Digby went on, aware she had something to save. 'I love you more than I've ever loved anybody. It's just—'

'Just stop, please,' interrupted Caroline, pulling her hands away. 'I'm going out.'

'I'll come with you.'

'No – on my own. I need some air.'

A few seconds later, there was the sound of the front door slamming shut.

Digby looked out across the Bay, punctuated by boats and stars, bright pinpricks of light on a darkening stage. She stayed there, standing, staring, who knows for how long, and then she dropped her head into her hands and wept.

CHAPTER 18

Summer 1972

It's Wednesday morning at the *Right On!* office.

I'm super-excited because:

1. It's editorial day
2. It's party day
3. It's Lolo day

Editorial day is when Nickstickupbum finalises the layout of this week's magazine, meaning I should find out very soon if my *La Bohème* review is in or not. I'm currently in his good books because I finished all my copy yesterday (I am fast becoming the Jackie Stewart of the listings world) and have been helping him with the *Contents* page and *Personals* ever since.

At ten o'clock, Griffin arrives.

(She has – so far – completely failed to spot my fake chant. Hopefully it will be my lunchtime treat for the whole week. People who take themselves very seriously often have no idea other people might not take them quite so seriously.)

She makes quite an entrance. This, for once, is not because of what she's wearing (she's head-to-toe in murky tie-dye, a walking sheet of blotting paper) but because of what she's doing: waving around a dangly rubber funnel which looks very similar to something my dad would use to get medicine into a cow (both ends).

'Oh, hi, Griffin – what's that?' asks Nickwiththecollars, bravely.

'It's for toxic karmas,' she replies, glancing at me. 'I got it from my swami.' She gives it a little wave in my direction. 'It helps promote an atmosphere of peace, love and spiritual reflection. The toxic karmas go up and get trapped here' – she points at the brown funnel attached to the end of the rubber pipe – 'and get here.' She points to a bobbly thing at the other end of the pipe, which looks suspiciously like a painted Jif lemon.

'Lovely,' he replies, mustering up a surprising degree of enthusiasm (you can tell he's an actor).

Griffin parades over to her desk, shaking the rubber funnel around like an altar boy equipped with a very modern incense burner. She has a good shake over the desk, a quick once round under the desk, a bit of theatrical detoxing near a sash window and then, accompanied by some excessive *ommmm*ing, really goes to town with it around her office chair. Eventually, she hangs the dangly rubber funnel from a shelf, gives it another wiggle, and sits down, a great whirl of karmic brown.

A few minutes later, Nickstickupbum is at my desk.

'Could you get me a coffee, please, Evie?'

(No smile but my second *please*, so I'm happy.)

'Of course,' I reply, flashing him my best Susan George. 'Anyone else fancy a drink?'

'Ooh tea, please,' Tiggers Nickwiththecollars.

'Coffee,' Eeyores Griffin. 'Black.'

I get up, making my way to the kitchen. On the way, I notice Nickstickupbum heading for Griffin's desk, his back ramrod straight and his eyes sharp and narrow.

'Whaaaat?'

A noise full of pain and fury comes from next door.

'Whaaaaaaaat?'

Luckily the drinks are made so I can go and have a good nosy.

'Whaaaaaaaaaaaaaaaat?'

I rush the mugs onto a flowery tray and bolt back into the office.

Griffin is shouting and screaming, definitely not promoting an atmosphere of peace, love and spiritual reflection.

'I can't believe you're printing that idiotic review instead of my poem.'

She slams a hand down on her desk.

'Well, it's just that the review is more timely,' says Nickstickupbum, remaining preternaturally calm.

'Timely?' spits Griffin.

'Yes, the opera ends in a few days' time. The poem doesn't.'

Griffin makes a noise like a Friesian giving birth.

'As I said,' he carries on, 'we'll print the poem next week.'

'Next week? Where have our standards gone?' howls Griffin.

'We're not writing for intelligent adults any more. Evie's trite little piece will be one-dimensional and overdrawn. Crammed with anachronisms.'

'It's very well written, actually,' replies Nickstickupbum. 'A pleasure to read. Oh, coffee, thank you,' he adds, turning to me.

He holds out his hand, as if the coffee will magically appear in it. I help it on its way by walking over to him and offering up the tray. He takes his coffee, completely unflustered (he has the remarkable ability to cut himself off from all emotional under-currents, like a BBC newsreader or the Queen Mum).

I turn to Griffin (a horrible swirl of sludge) and offer her the tray too.

She looks at the tray then at me. Her eyes are fiery, brimming with toxic karma.

'Actually,' says Nickstickupbum, serenely sipping his coffee. 'I think you'd enjoy the review, Griffin. There's something quite poetic about it.'

Griffin lets out a scream Genghis Khan would be proud of.

Her arms whiplash through the air, delivering a noisy uppercut to the tray. The tray shoots out of my hands, sending the remain-ing three mugs flying.

One mug hurtles off to the left, delivering its contents all over a sash window.

One mug veers to the right, pebble-dashing the wall.

And one mug comes straight at me, covering me with tea (milk, two sugars).

'I've had enough of this,' she shouts, grabbing her tassely bag and making for the door. 'It's ridiculous. The barbarians are at the gates, Nick, and you're letting them in.' She jabs a tasselly finger at Nickstickupbum. 'Some of us still have integrity. Some of us don't pander to the trite modern world. Some of us still know what real journalism is and that's exactly what I'm going to show you.'

And she storms out, an apoplectic drab of tie and dye.

An hour later, I'm back at home.

Both Nicks were lovely. Nickwiththecollars made me a tea (incredible) and Nickstickupbum told me to take the rest of the day off. The best way to deal with Griffin, they said, is to ignore her because she always calms down after a flare-up. They'll have a word with her this afternoon when I'm not around and maybe try to squeeze a couplet or something onto the *Classifieds* page. I thanked Nickstickupbum for printing my review and he said that it was a very easy decision, magazine-wise, because the review was much better than Griffin's poem, which, surprisingly for him, was exactly the right thing to say.

My tea-soaked navy smock is in the washer. I'm very relaxed about it because, from experience, I know navy is the perfect colour to repel tea stains. They'll just wash out. Which is exactly what I plan to do with Griffin and her vicious swirls.

The one good thing about it all (apart from getting the afternoon at home) is it solves the puzzle of bunking off to meet Lolo. I've now got a free run all the way through to meeting him and can relax without having to think of an elaborate plan (otherwise known as a lie).

Caroline has taken Geneviève to Brighton for the day (with

Digby) to see one of her well-connected fashion friends*, which means I've got the flat to myself. I'm in the kitchen, enjoying a bowl of tomato soup and flicking through the *Standard*, all accompanied by the stereophonic sounds of Radio 1 and the gush and churn of the washing machine.

Every now and then my eyes wander over to Mrs Scott-Pym's pestle and mortar, staring at me from the worktop, a beautiful green memory made real. I wish I could remember which bit's the pestle and which bit's the mortar. I always get them mixed up (like *The Two Ronnies*). Pestles and mortars just go together, separate but one. A perfect little pair. Which must be nice. Maybe we're all pestles looking for our mortar? I wonder when I'll meet mine? All I've managed to find so far are a few whisks, plenty of spatulas and the odd tin-opener.

I finish my soup and sit back in my chair, relishing being back at home at lunchtime. 'Ooh Wakka Doo Wakka Day' skips out from the radio and I find my head gently swaying left and right as the music bounces along. And then, right in the middle of a particularly long *Doo-di-doo*, Gilbert O'Sullivan falls silent. As does the washing machine.

Bugger.

I get up and try the kitchen lights.

Nothing.

Then the ones in the hall.

Nothing.

I don't understand how we can get men on the moon but everything else seems to be moving backwards. So far the seventies have been a bit of a disappointment. Instead of flying cars

300

Name: Christopher Barry

From: Hull

Job: fashion photographer

Seen for: two Cinzanos and a bag of chips

Appearance: Carnaby Street in human form

Amazing: lovely cheekbones, stylish gait, generous with his Maltesers

Less amazing: hypochondriac, espadrilles, overly windy

and helpful robots all we seem to have are acrylic bed-sheets and power cuts.

I give the lights another try.

Still nothing.

Someone somewhere is trying to tell me that it's time for a nap . . .

Waking up after a nap is always a very good thing. You feel like you've had a bonus, a treat, an extra little something in the day. It's the equivalent of being given two flakes in your 99 or a free mini pot of face cream by the nice ladies in the Biba beauty hall.

It takes me a few seconds to focus. My brain fast-forwards through the morning's events (tie-dye, karma, spillage) bringing me right up to date with power cuts. I reach over and try the bedside lamp. Still nothing. (It never used to be like this when Barbara Castle was in charge.) I sigh and roll over onto my back.

As I lie here, I ponder the clothes draped across my lovely wicker chair. My costume for tonight's party. My favourite place in Europe. I spent last night getting it ready – trying on various things and rummaging through cupboards and drawers in search of appropriate props. I've plumped for something quite low-key and comfortable, something not very technical and – crucially – something quick to put on (there won't be much time to spare between getting back from meeting Lolo in town and going out to Fulham for the party).

Geneviève's coming to the party too. I think she's expecting it to be like a scene from *Performance* (quite possibly with Mick Jagger) and I don't have the heart to tell her it's far more likely to be a cross between a school disco and cricket-club tea. She spent all last night in her room getting a costume together. We're keeping what we're wearing as a surprise for later but I suspect hers will be the polar opposite of comfortable, low-key and not very technical.

I get up, go to the loo, and am just about to go downstairs when I have an idea. I could have a sneaky peek at Geneviève's costume for tonight. A quick glance at my watch confirms there's still plenty of time before I meet Lolo so I edge towards her room and push open the door.

The dour utilitarian box room has been transformed into a world of wonder.

There's colour everywhere, flashes of it popping up all over the place. Postcards on the wall. Fabric swatches along the windowsill. Half-finished clothes hanging off the wardrobe. Even Caroline's sewing machine, perched on a tiny table by the bed, is decorated with magazine clippings and a spray of colourful stickers.

I step inside.

The room is immaculate, much neater than anything I could manage. On the bedside table I notice two photo frames – one strawberry red (Geneviève with her mum and dad) and the other bright orange (Ziggy Stardust in a catsuit). I smile, thinking of the signed Adam Faith photo I used to have on my bedside table, a magnificent teenage treasure. I wonder what happened to it? One day it was priceless and meant the world to me; the next it had gone, replaced by thoughts of four young men from Liverpool.

I turn my attention to the wardrobe and its colourful adornments.

A pair of bottle-green leggings hangs lopsided from a hanger. One leg droops down, flaccid and uninteresting, but the other is girdled by an inflated band that blooms out from the thigh. The calf has another bloom, shaped like a sail, an air-filled flare.

Amazing.

I give the flare a squeeze. It's plasticky and squishy and makes me think of beach balls.

There's a top there, too, with inflated bulbous arms: a PVC Charles Atlas.

Incredible.

Next to them both is a long stretch of plastic, limp and empty of air. It hangs down, blocks of black hoops sandwiched together with thin strips of red. I think it's a dress.

Each of the black hoops has an air nozzle jutting out. I take the one at the bottom and start blowing, great lungfuls of air that make short work of it. Soon the hoop has expanded into a fully inflated ring. Shapely. Firm. I pop the top on the air nozzle and get going with the next one and then the next. Ring by ring. Nozzle by nozzle. Working my way up. A growing tower of air-filled black hoops. When I've done a few, I take the dress off the hanger and stand it on the floor. It sits there, the bottom half of a very stylish Dalek, supporting itself and calling out for more.

I crack on with the other hoops, watching the dress take shape. The arms are particularly impressive, jutting straight out like inflatable little cranes. The dress commands the floor in a great bounce of sculptural glory. I've never seen anything like it before.

I stand back and admire my handiwork (well, Geneviève's handiwork).

It is deeply impressive.

I'm going to have to try it on.

This is easier said than done. I'm not quite sure where to begin. It's a bit like trying to get into a stack of hula hoops. I lift the dress off the floor, swing it on the bed, and then, arms first, like diving into a pool, push myself inside, wriggling up its dark plastic tunnel.

My arms pop out the sleeves and my head pops out the neck.

I ease myself off the bed and back onto my feet and then navigate round to have a look in the mirror.

It looks stunning.

A catwalk Michelin Man, chic and shapely.

A living work of art.

Geneviève is a genius.

I stand there, taking it in.

A different Evie stares back at me. Someone sci-fi. Future-facing.

Then I realise I can't move my arms – they're wedged in the inflated hoops, stuck out at right angles from my body. I try to wriggle them around, just a bit at first, gently, and then more vigorously but it's impossible. There's no movement. They're stuck. Rock solid.

I try again, jabbing my arms up and down, but there's virtually no give. It's the fully inflatedness that seems to be the problem. Rather than telling me interesting stories about water, Lolo should have focused on the sartorial dangers of air.

I have a manic squirm, hoping to dislodge myself somehow, but it's no good. The dress comes down to my thigh, an inflated tubular cage that delivers the heavily restricted movement of an *It's a Knockout!* costume. I can wiggle my hands and below the knee is fine but anything in between is held rigidly in place like a set of medieval stocks.

I have another manic squirm, this time accompanied by a frustrated wail.

Nothing.

The fully blown dress has the structural integrity of a nuclear bunker.

I take a deep breath (which is how I got into this mess in the first place) and try to think what to do. A childhood of Guides and the Brontës does not prepare you for moments like this.

I shuffle over to the wall, a stumbling Yorkshire geisha, and press myself up against it, face first, hoping to force out some air. I push as hard as I can, but nothing really happens – with my arms out of use, my shoulders are left to do the majority of the work and it's hard to get any traction. The rings hold solid and the only outcome of the whole thing is a pair of achy boobs.

I carefully manoeuvre myself round and try again, this time pushing against my back. It's the same. Nothing. Not even a little leak. I try bouncing harder and harder against the wall but all this produces are a few squeaks and a sore head.

The air nozzles in each ring are holding everything very firmly in place. Maybe I could knock the top off a few and release some air like that?

With my mouth, I have a quick go at a nozzle on a sleeve but it's just out of reach and I end up flailing around open-mouthed like a seal at feeding time.

I'm getting tired now. And stressed. I could really do with sitting down but it's impossible: everything from my upper legs to my shoulders is as rigid as an ironing board (I've turned into Nickstickupbum).

And then the phone rings.

Happy *tring-trings* of potential rescue.

I shuffle sideways over to the bedroom door, manoeuvre carefully through it and emerge onto the landing.

The phone is still ringing, a cavalry of *trings*.

I look down the stairs. Suddenly they seem very narrow. And very steep. I swing myself round to the side again and start making my way down, one step at a time. Left foot. Right foot. Left foot. Right foot. Clomp. Clomp. Clomp. Clomp. Clomp.

I'm halfway down when the phone stops.

Bugger. I hover for a second then carry on, deciding I've got more chance of freeing myself downstairs than up.

When I get downstairs, I shuffle around, thankful of more space but increasingly aware of all the things I can't do:

1. Get a drink
2. Unwrap a Twix
3. Go to the loo

I'm also increasingly aware that I'm going to be late for Lolo. I picture him waiting by the empty plinth, looking at his watch, surrounded by the teeming crowds and feeling very alone. I don't want to let him down, especially because, in a way I can't quite put my finger on, I feel that I let him down already on Sunday at the Serpentine.

Lolo. I say his name and it makes me feel happy but then, just a few moments later, it makes me feel sad.

And then the phone goes again. I pivot-lunge for it, scarecrow-armed, but end up stumbling and knock the handset onto the floor.

'Hullo,' I shout. 'It's Evie. Hullooooo.'

There's a click followed by a long flat tone.

Brrrrrrrrrrrrrrrrrrrrrrrrrrrrrrrrrrrrr . . .

The handset lies on the floor, mocking me.

I need to get it back on its base in case it rings again so I lower myself down as much as possible and reach out, very gingerly, the handset almost at my fingertips. Then knees shake, arms wobble, legs give and I topple over backwards, unable to move and utterly defeated, face up, spirits down, arms jutting out like a horizontal Christ the Redeemer.

I've got no idea how long I've been lying here – when you're trapped in an inflatable dress you tend to have a flexible notion of time. I've made several attempts to get up but it's impossible. It's only when you're stuck with scarecrow arms that you realise how useful bendy arms are. The nearest I've got to actual movement is when I shuffle-bounced a few inches across the floor to prop my head against the beanbag. At least I'm relatively comfy now, my head snugly beanbagged and the inflatable dress acting like a built-in Lilo.

Outside, the hum and hoot of traffic is getting louder. It must be getting on for rush hour. I really hope poor Lolo isn't hanging around at the plinth. I feel terrible. Maybe he'll just stay ten minutes then leave. Quarter of an hour at most. I wonder if he's been trying to ring? (I strain a look at the evil handset on the floor, still smugly brrrrrrrrrrr-ing.) I'll take him out and buy him lunch. Or a pint, maybe, at a nice pub. It'll be nice to spend more time with him. Clear the air. Laugh a bit. Talk.

I stare up at the ceiling. Trapped. Am I my own living metaphor? I was definitely a bit trapped at the BBC, doing something I just fell into and carried on with because that was the easiest thing to do. But now, at the magazine, starting out a new life, a new career (perhaps), I don't think I'm trapped. And then I think of Griffin and her tassels and tambourines, trapped in the sixties. Or maybe trapped *by* the sixties. Is that me too? Perhaps it's all of us. Trapped by the weight of it all. The expectations. And by the huge come-down of what happened next.

Time passes, languidly bending its way to nowhere in particular. Then – all of a sudden – I hear the click and whoosh of the washing machine, closely followed by the smiling, happy lilt of Johnny Nash. The power cut. It must be over.

About time too.

I lie here for a bit, listening to the washing machine chase the radio. In the middle of a David Cassidy-spin cycle duet, a key rattles in the door downstairs, followed by an emphatic swinging *hiya*.

Geneviève. My cavalry.

Interlude – January 1972, Yorkshire

The suitcase was downstairs now, on the sofa, its lid resting open against a cushion.

Rosamund had had an idea.

It was going to be for Evie. A surprise gift from the other side. She didn't want to make it mawkish or ghoulish – just a few things and some books and a note or two. A selection box wrapped in an epilogue.

She'd already started to put a few books in alongside the champagne cork. Books that were special to her or books that she thought would help Evie in some way, keeping her company on whatever lay ahead. There was no rush, though – she didn't plan on going anytime soon. The suitcase could live alongside her for a while, giving her something to do now that the snow had penned her in.

She was in the kitchen getting supper, yesterday's chicken and ham pie with a few boiled potatoes. The potatoes were on the range, simmering, and Rosamund was up in a cupboard getting the mustard. She closed the door and put the mustard down on the work surface. Behind the mustard, lined up against the wall like soldiers on parade, were her kitchen gadgets. Scales, clocks, egg-timers, trivets. And there, too, was her pestle and mortar. She smiled. The pestle and mortar always made her think of Evie, with its memories of magical buttons. Bliss it was in that dawn to be alive.

Evie must have it, of course.

She picked it up. It was made of marble – sage green – and was a fair weight, durable but somehow also fragile (aren't we all, she thought). She'd need to wrap it in something to protect it from itself and stop it rattling around. Her eyes ranged over the kitchen, alert for inspiration. A tea towel lay folded over the back of a kitchen chair, offering intimations of Bolton Abbey. Perfect. Soft swaddling postcards from Yorkshire. She was going to have fun doing this.

CHAPTER 19

Summer 1972

The middle-aged man two seats in front has another surreptitious glance. It's his third already and he only got on last stop.

A sour-looking elderly lady across the aisle from us, meanwhile, has given up all pretence of subtlety and is openly gawping. Other gawpers include a young mother (with chubby gawping child), a couple from the Sally Army and three kids carrying pogos.

Possibly the reason for all this gawping is my outfit (wellingtons, flat cap, piece of straw tucked behind my ear) but I suspect it has more to do with Geneviève.

She is Starman meets Michelin Man, gleaming in a black plastic catsuit with red and gold flashes. The catsuit balloons out from each leg like two giant protractors and at the end of each arm is a series of thick blow-up doughnuts. Her hair, bright red, bristles skywards, held in place by nearly half a can of Elnett.

She is an alien, a work of art, a star. A queen atop London Transport's best burnish'd throne.

Her throne has been causing her hassle all journey as the inflated protractors have the practicality of an eighteenth-century court mantua. They are not happy at being crammed behind the seat in front. Sharing a seat with Geneviève's party outfit is like sharing a phone box with a hot-air balloon.

('What are you meant to be?' I asked, when I'd got over the initial shock of her stepping out of her bedroom.

'Mars. I'm one of Ziggy's spiders.'

'But you're meant to be your favourite place in Europe.'

'I am.'

'Oh, right,' I said, reminding myself that she'd just rescued me from death by an inflatable dress.

'What about you?'

I gave her a twirl. 'Yorkshire.'

Of course.)

Geneviève flaps a squishy protractor out of the way to let a man in a cravat get by.

'It's a shame you missed your coffee with Lolo,' she says, letting it flap back again once he's passed.

'I know, I'm so annoyed.' (The bus judders to a halt). 'I was really looking forward to meeting him. Especially after Sunday and, well, you know, all the awkwardness.'

She nods knowingly as the bus pulls off again.

'I just hope he didn't hang around for too long,' I add.

'Did you not get hold of him in the end, then?'

'No, there was no answer. Work or home. He'll have been out doing something musical.'

'Or in a bar with Tarquin sipping gin.'

'Gin?'

'Yes, that's what all the homosexuals in Leeds drink.'

'Oh, I see.' (That's Leeds for you.) 'I'll give him another try tomorrow. I definitely owe him a drink. Gin or otherwise. Come on, this is us.'

And I pull the bell and guide Geneviève down the bus, watching her inflated legs catch on every seat.

I give the front door a good knock.

We're standing outside Dotty's house, a red-brick terrace, squat and sensible, on the Fulham–Chelsea borders. Pink Floyd oozes through an open window and, behind the stained-glass panels in the door, blurry shapes divide and tangle.

'I'm nervous,' says Geneviève, glancing up.

(How can someone wearing an inflatable plastic catsuit be nervous?)

I flash her my best reassuring smile.

'Don't worry, you'll be fine. Everyone'll be really friendly. And you look fab,' I add, topping up the smile with a wink.

The door swings open, revealing Nickwiththecollars's beaming face.

'Evie!' he cries. 'You found us then?'

'Yes, easy. All roads lead to Fulham, don't they? This is Geneviève, by the way, the friend I told you about.' I gesture at my glamorous Martian sidekick.

'Oh, I love your costume,' coos Nick to Geneviève. 'Don't tell me, let me guess ... Belgium?'

'Belgium?' we both chime.

314

'Yes, it all looks very ... Belgian. Or at least how I imagine Belgium – I've never been.'

Poor Geneviève looks crestfallen.

'What about you, Nick?' I ask, a quick diversionary tactic. 'Where are you?'

(He's wrapped in a white sheet with another sheet – purple – slung over a shoulder and tucked into a thick golden waistband. It's all topped off with a gold headdress and a tuft of chest hair.)

'I'm a Roman emperor!' (He gives us a quick twirl). 'So I'm Rome. *La Città Eterna*. Dotty helped me make it – she's such a clever old thing. Look, *this'* – he points to the waistband – 'is an old curtain and *this'* – he points at his headdress – 'is a few leaves we glued together and sprayed with gold car paint.'

'Impressive,' says Geneviève (no doubt getting ideas).

'You look great,' I say. 'Very noble.'

He gives the curtain a quick preen.

'Oh, here's some wine, by the way,' I go on, passing him a bottle of Valpolicella.

'Aw, thank you. Anyway, don't hang around on the doorstep all night – come in.'

As I walk in, he puts a hand on my arm.

'Are you okay?' he asks. 'After Griffin this morning, I mean.'

'Oh, I'm fine. It was nothing.' I wave a dismissive hand. 'I'll just keep out of her way for a few days.'

'That's my policy too. Makes life much easier! Actually, she phoned just after you'd left saying she'd be out for the rest of the day. Joy, gentle friends! Joy and fresh days of love!' he emotes, going all theatrical (never that far away with him). 'Anyway, come

315

through, let's get you both a drink. Oh, and I think the Scottish outfit's great, Evie – who doesn't love the Highlands?'

He leads us down a hallway (flowers, nice tiles, Japanese prints) and veers off into a room just before we hit the stairs. The room is full of people: some are dancing, swaying around like a smack of jellyfish; some are standing chatting, drink in one hand, cigarette in the other; and some are sat on the various sofas, beanbags and chairs pushed right up against the walls (as if the seating had been arranged by a giant Moulinex blender).

As soon as we walk in, everyone turns and looks. Geneviève is, understandably, quite an attraction but the stares don't last long. This is probably because at least half the people in the room are wearing something just as strange. A man in a full ski suit. Another dressed as a mermaid. A woman head-to-toe in bunches of lavender (must be v itchy). The costumes seem equally divided between those who've really gone for it (Geneviève, ski-suit man, lavender woman) and those who've taken the easy option (me, two men in berets, a woman carrying a tulip).

Nick guides us through the room and takes us to a table covered with food and various bottles and glasses.

'What can I get you?'

Geneviève glances up át me, her Martian eyes searching for guidance.

'Red wine, please,' I say.

'Oh, me too, please,' she echoes.

'Two red wines. Perfect.' And he busies himself with a bottle.

'It's a lovely house,' I go on, taking in the paper lampshades and the long peacock feathers curving out from a large vase.

'Oh, Dotty's got a great eye. She comes from a very arty family. Her father's got an auction house in Devon.' He passes us the wine. 'And you should see what her mother can do with a crochet hook. Help yourselves to food, by the way,' he adds, giving his purple sheet a quick tug.

The table is covered with party food, piped, primped and carved to perfection. A couple of cheese hedgehogs. A fan of cocktail sausages and pickled onions. Indeterminate vol-au-vents filled with something brown and creamy. In the middle of the table sits a pineapple, circled by ring after ring of finger sandwiches, like a giant culinary sun on the BBC weather map.

We tuck in. There's some good small talk with Nick (Shirley Bassey, the north, shaving rash) plus a very quick work chat (staples) then, midway through a discussion on the pros and cons of tartan, there's a loud knock at the front door.

'Ooh, better go,' says Nick. 'I'm on door duty. See you both later!' And he bobs his way back into the crowd.

'He seems nice,' says Geneviève, nibbling on a potato puff.

'Yes, he is. Really nice. He's good fun to work with, too.'

'Oh, I wish I had someone who was good fun to work with. Or even just someone to work with.'

'Hey,' I say, 'don't worry. Something'll turn up soon – it always does.'

A thick-set man in lederhosen interrupts us.

'Don't mind me!' he says, reaching over for some vol-au-vents. He's got hairy knees and a fringe like Friar Tuck. 'I *love* the costume,' he says to Geneviève. 'Are you Berlin? I went to a club there once and everyone was dressed like that.'

He winks and walks off.

Geneviève sighs and flicks an airy protractor.

'Do you fancy a dance?' I ask.

We look down the room. The crowd of dancers is top-heavy with beardy men in Terylene flares (possibly a result of back-to-back Jethro Tull).

'Not really,' she replies.

'Me neither. Well, not yet anyway.'

She puts her empty plate down on the table.

'Come on,' I say, putting mine down too. 'Let's go and find the kitchen. I should say hullo to Dotty, really, and the kitchen's usually where you'll find all the interesting men ...'

As we enter the kitchen, a flamenco dancer is doing something creative with a side of ham.

'Evie!' says the dancer, turning round. 'Lovely to see you again. I hope Nicky's been taking care of you?'

It's Dotty, a heaving crescendo of green and black ruffles.

'Oh, hi, Dotty! Yes, he's been as lovely as ever.' I give my glass of red wine a little jiggle, the results of *Nicky's* loveliness. 'We just came to see if you needed a hand with anything. This is Geneviève, by the way – she's staying with me for a bit.'

They say hullo and shake hands; Geneviève does a little bow, thrown somewhat off track, I think, by Dotty's operatic bosom.

'I *love* your costume,' Dotty says to Geneviève.

318

'Aw, thanks,' she replies, opening out the inflated protractors to maximum capacity.

'Are you somewhere in Scandinavia?' Dotty says with a huge smile. 'You know, one of those Nordic pixies? I've never been,' she adds, turning to me. 'But I hear it's wonderful. Stuffed full of hunky Vikings!'

Geneviève lets go of the protractors, letting them flop back.

'Speaking of Vikings,' I say (queen of the non sequitur), 'what can we do to help?'

'We're all okay, thanks, Evie. Jenny's giving me a hand.'

A lady with a plastic Eiffel Tower on her head waves at us from a nearby pine table.

'She's famous for her savoury nipples, aren't you Jenny?'

Jenny smiles and gives the Eiffel Tower a quick nod.

'They're delicious,' Dotty goes on. 'Just salad cream and ketchup in a piping bag, quick swirl on a Ritz cracker and finish off with an olive.'

'Oooh, lovely,' says Geneviève, clearly impressed by Dotty's culinary sophistication.

'Jenny's piping's legendary,' Dotty goes on. 'She's a vet, you see, so very good with her hands.' She has a slurp of wine. 'Anyway, look, we're absolutely fine in here, thanks. You two go and enjoy yourselves – there are lots of nice men out there who need keeping company. Off you go . . .'

Back in the party room, we have a game of 'guess the place'. With most people it's easy (clogs, Viking horns, bowler hat) but a couple of people throw us:

1. A woman wearing an upside-down plastic potty
   on her head
2. A man wrapped in flowery curtains

We end up having to ask. The woman's the Queen, apparently, at Prince Charles's investiture (Wales) and the man claims to be the Von Trapp family (Salzburg).

Quite a few people are thrown by Geneviève's costume too. She gets various guesses (a couple of Ruhr Valleys, Vienna, Preston) but nobody comes close. My costume is obviously much easier and, apart from Nick plus a man in a Breton top who looks like Debbie Reynolds, everyone guesses Yorkshire, which is quite satisfying.

We try a bit of flirting, mainly for Dotty's sake really, but it isn't entirely successful. A Roman centurion tells me I look good in wellies then spoils it by talking about trout fishing. Another Breton top (more Henry Cooper than Debbie Reynolds) has a lovely smile but also halitosis and wandering hands. Geneviève fares no better. She chats to a large man dressed as Marie Antoinette for quite a while but is obviously keen to get away, so I rescue her with a trip to the loo. Then she gets stuck with a man in a kilt, which is a rite of passage for us all. Best to get it out of the way sooner rather than later.

That's not to say there's an absolute dearth of handsome men here. One of the Vikings is very good-looking, as are a bullfighter, a priest and Charles de Gaulle. I just don't think either of us is in the mood. Geneviève's quite disappointed because there are no pop stars or film stars here – nobody remotely famous, not even someone from ITV. And me? What's wrong with me? Normally I'm the chatty type and like nothing more than flirting with a handsome artist or sophisticated European (or a combination of the two) but, for some reason, it doesn't feel right tonight. My heart just isn't in it.

The music isn't really helping. There's been quite a lot of guitar solo-ing, long stretches of testosterone that swank around the room, plus the Terylene flares are hogging the best spot in front of the speakers; around them little groups of people swing and sway (complete with the occasional arm wave).

'I wish they'd stop playing all this old music,' says Geneviève, halfway through a mini-roll.

'Old music?'

'Yes, you know, the Moody Blues and whatnot.'

Oh.

I look at Geneviève. Her spiky hair. Her striking suit. Her sparkly eyes locked towards tomorrow. I sometimes picture myself as a great wave roaring towards the shore, packed with energy and clearing all before it. But I've never really stopped to think there might be other waves behind me, racing to catch up, crashing and curling in a new and different way.

'Why don't you go and see if there's any other music?' I say, gesturing over to the stereo. 'I'll wait here and guard the drinks.'

She slinks off cautiously through all the swinging and swaying.

For us the sixties were all about music and freedom and fashion and life but for Geneviève, I suppose, they were really just school playgrounds and *Jackanory*.

When The Beatles split up everyone talked about what was

going to happen next. Where would the sixties take us? What would all those years grow into? What future will we make? Perhaps, though, we were looking in the wrong place. Perhaps it's not the sixties that'll get to decide. Perhaps the future will be decided somewhere else. And by someone else.

'There's *loads* of old-man music,' says Geneviève, returning with a great roll of eye. 'And no Bowie.' (Her little face drops.) 'But, the good news is I *did* spot a couple of T. Rex singles near the bottom of the pile.'

'Well,' I say, putting my hand on Geneviève's plastic shoulder and looking her straight in the glittery eye. 'What are you waiting for? You know what you have to do.'

There's a twang of guitar, the ba-bum of a drum, a keyboard shimmers and slides ... and then BANG! The music jabs and twirls as Geneviève sweeps over to me and pulls me into the middle of the swaying crowd.

It's time to

Get.

It.

On.

Geneviève shimmies and pops across the floor, a rhythmic blur of inflated limb, stabbing and stomping her way through the first verse. I abandon my usual one-two side-step and have a go at Gen-y-fying my moves, a quick kick here, a little frisk there. When the chorus comes I'm ready for it. We stand head on, shaking our shoulders at each other, bobbing backwards and forwards like a pair of well-oiled pistons. The other dancers give us plenty of space, clearly aware that they are in the presence of greatness (Geneviève) and madness (me). Geneviève flaps her protractor with the passion of a torero while I high-clap my way across the floor. We are Pan's People. Unstoppable and Irresistible. In comparison, most of the other dancers look like dinosaurs, swaying their way into extinction.

Geneviève, the quiet little mouse who'd never had pasta or Pimm's, has turned into a roaring rhythmic lion, beamed down from the future in a blaze of *Get It On* glory.

By the end of the song, quite a few people are joining in and there's a real bounce to the room. Even a few of the Terylene flares are having a go. Whoever's in charge of the stereo makes the wise decision of repeating the song so, after a short clicky hiss, we do it all again.

We get through the first verse and are just about to launch into another thumping chorus when a gondolier sidles up to me and starts gyrating. Normally I would be very pleased – he's just my type (swarthy and sparkly of eye). He distracts me for a second (*ciao, bella!*) but then I realise I really can't be bothered and turn back round to piston-shimmy with Geneviève.

And that's when I see it. Geneviève is in the middle of some major protractor flapping. She sends three inflated doughnuts up in the air (*Get it on*) . . . the doughnuts hit a man in the face (*Bang a gong*) . . . the man drops his glass of red wine (*Get it on*) . . . and the wine goes all over his white suit.

'What the hell do you think you're doing?' shouts the man. 'Have you lost all bloody control?'

'I'msorryI'mreallysorryI'msosorry,' Geneviève says, over and over and over again.

I step in.

'Look, don't worry. I can fix this.'

'Who are you?' he shouts. 'Mary bloody Poppins or something?'

His face is fiery red (a bit like his suit).

'Don't worry, I know how to sort it,' I say, taking his arm and trying to sound calm and helpful. 'We need to be quick, though.'

I lead him away from the dancing and take him to the table with the food and drink; Geneviève follows a few steps behind, deflated in soul if not in body. At the table, I grab a couple of bottles of Blue Nun, tell Geneviève to wait here, and coax white-suit-man up to the bathroom.

'So who are you meant to be, anyway?' he says, sitting on the edge of the bath.

He's calmed down a bit, thanks to my mollifying staircase chit-chat, and has moved from apoplectic to just angry and sullen.

'I'm a farmer.' I gesture at the flat cap. 'A Yorkshire farmer.'

'Oh, northern,' he groans. 'I should have known.'

I pour more Blue Nun into the basin and keep dabbing the jacket into it, rubbing it with a flannel.

'Is it working?' he snaps.

'Oh, yes, don't worry – it always works really well,' I reply, splashing the wine over the stain, desperately hoping that it does indeed work really well. 'What about you?'

'Eh?'

'Where are you meant to be?'

'I'm the Riviera, of course. Playground of the elite.' He has another swig of the Blue Nun. Between my scrubbing and his drinking, we've burned through one bottle and are already almost halfway through the second.

'Look, could you just go easy with that?' I say, taking the bottle and pouring more wine over a sleeve. 'We might need it.'

He snorts.

'I hope that stupid little bitch hasn't ruined my jacket.'

'It was an *accident*,' I stress, rubbing hard, wine on wine. 'And don't call her a stupid little bitch.'

He takes the bottle again, accompanied by various sighs and tuts, and has another swig.

'The stain's coming out,' I tell him. 'You won't be able to tell after a dry-clean.'

I glance over at him, perched on the edge of the bath, an arrogant soaked sponge of hauteur.

'Pass me your shirt,' I say. 'Looks like some wine's got splashed on it too.'

He looks down at the shirt (*'oh, shit'*) and begins to unbutton it, fumbling slightly over the byzantine complexity of a button. While he's doing that, I take the wine again and give the flannel another good drenching.

'Here you are,' he says, peeling his shirt clumsily through an arm. He tosses the shirt in the basin and takes back the wine before sitting down again on the edge of the bath.

I set to with shirt and flannel.

Suddenly I feel a pair of hands grab my bum.

'Oi,' I shout, twisting round, my hands still in the basin. 'What do you think you're doing?'

'Come on,' he says, kneading me like a lump of dough.

I let go of the shirt and push him away.

'Get off. You're drunk. Sit still and be quiet.'

'Come on. You know you want to.'

I've had enough. I turn round and, mustering up the strength of a Hereford bull, shove him into the bath. He plops down, arms and legs flailing, then lies there, squirming around, startled and sweary. Quick as a flash, I throw his wine-soaked jacket and shirt onto him (there's a satisfactory splat as they hit his face) then turn my attention to the shower taps, sending a storm of cold water raining down as he slips and slides his way to nowhere.

'Idiot,' I say, charging out the room.

Geneviève's just inside the party room, pressed up against the wall and almost making herself invisible (quite a skill in an inflated plastic catsuit).

'Are you okay?' I ask.

'Yeah. I'm really sorry, Evie.'

'You've got nothing to apologise for.' I give her a sisterly shoulder-squeeze. 'Do you mind if we go?'

'Oh, yes. I've had enough – I feel like I've let myself down. Sorry.'

'Don't keep saying sorry. It was an accident. That's all. Anyway, he deserved it.'

As we're talking I see a face in the dancing, drinking, smoking crowd.

Lolo's face.

He's in full rugby kit (nice legs) with his arms round a man, swaying, stumbling and singing along to the music. I'm on the verge of going over and saying a very quick hullo when the man with Lolo lunges across to another man. A woman in hot pants and stripy top (plus onions) immediately grabs Lolo. She says something to him and he laughs. She dances. He sways. She rubs her hand over his head. He smiles. She puts her face close to his. He closes an eye and says something. She kisses him.

What?

She kisses him again.

What?

Her fingers flutter up and down his neck.

He tilts his head back and smiles.

'Evie? Are you okay?'

It's Geneviève, looking up at me, her glittery eyes dimmed.

(The room begins to spin, great baffling, unsettling swirls.)

'Come on,' I say. 'Let's go.'

Back in the flat, I sit for a while, staring out my sitting-room window, bathed in the dim orange glow of the street lights.

Geneviève has gone up to bed. On the way home, she indulged me in a long Lolo chat, the two of us going round and round in circles about whether he's homosexual or not (plus a quick conversational detour into moustaches – Lolo's grown one and it really suits him).

I wonder who the man was with Lolo? It must have been Tarquin, surely. But then what was Tarquin doing lunging at another man? And, more importantly, who was that woman with Lolo? The one with the onions and the fluttering fingers.

I lie back on the beanbag and close my eyes, chasing the hazy shades beneath my eyelids.

Something's pulling at me – a heaviness – something from inside.

A doubt, maybe. A fear.

I burrow into the beanbag, pushing down into its comforting folds.

Hiding. Searching.

Cradled.

A trundling car outside softens the silence.

When I open my eyes, the room seems smaller.

I trace its edges, from door to sofa to bookcase to window and back to the beanbag. On the floor next to me is Mrs Scott-Pym's suitcase, still packed with books. I open the suitcase and take a book at random.

It's a copy of *Emma*, worn and well read. I open it, hoping to see Mrs Scott-Pym's writing – a date, maybe, or her name. But there's nothing. Just printed page after printed page. I flick through, looking for signs of Mrs Scott-Pym but there's nothing until I get right to the end, inside the back cover. *Rosamund Elizabeth Rose, October 1912, York*. I didn't know her middle name was Elizabeth. Or that her maiden name was Rose. I wonder how many other things I don't know about her? How many things did she choose to keep secret or just forget to mention? Do we ever *really* know someone else? Even when we think we do . . .

I flick through the book again, this time lifting it up to my nose and smelling as I flick. The smell immediately takes me back to Mrs Scott-Pym's house, sitting in a sun-filled room with Sadie and cake and Mrs Scott-Pym. I close my eyes, savouring Mrs Scott-Pym's presence. Not being alive doesn't stop someone from being part of us. I smile, rubbing the book between my palms.

After a bit, I put the book down and take another. This time it's Emily Brontë's *Collected Poems*. I open the first few pages, again on the lookout for signs of Mrs Scott-Pym. Nothing. But when I start flicking through, the book falls open midway – wedged into the crease of the spine is a folded sheet of blue paper, crisp and inviting. I take it out and read.

My dear, wonderful, unlucky-in-love Evie,

I write this fresh off the phone from you. Another man has melted away, burnt by the heat of your sun. You know I think of you as a daughter – and so, as a daughter, I am going to offer you some important advice about men, something you may think I know very little about . . . but you'd be wrong. Old as I am, I was young once and I learnt three important lessons about love, lessons whose essential truths have been confirmed over time, through experience and observation.

Knowing that young women very rarely listen to the advice of old women (I am, of course, thinking of my darling stubborn daughter here) I am giving you the advice in a form that I know you will enjoy, in the hope of sugaring the pill as it were . . .

To be happy in love – for that is what we all want – you will need to find:

1. A funny man, someone who makes you laugh.
2. An interesting man, someone open to ideas, someone who wants you to think.
3. A kind man, someone to share the load, an equal, a peer.

All these three points can be summarised, of course, in one word: friendship. And a friend is exactly whom you must try to find. I'm sure your mother would agree – so very happy, as she was, with your wonderful father.

Whomever you choose is a lucky man indeed, Evie. Remember that.

With all my love,

Rosamund x

PS extra points, dear, for a man who likes dogs – generally a very good sign.

I rub the letter between thumb and forefinger, touch on faded touch. And then I read it again, smiling when I get to the list (she knows me well).

A funny man.

(I think of Lolo and the swirly chair.)

An interesting man.

(I think of Lolo and his ancient water.)

A kind man.

(I think of Lolo and his listings and his opera and his smile.)

When I get to the PS, something pulls at me again inside. Something good. Something lost. I glance down at the book of poems, still open at the page where I'd found the letter. The poem there is short.

But still I don't manage to get to the end before the tears arrive.

Interlude – January 1972, Yorkshire

Rosamund Scott-Pym put the phone down and smiled, shaking her head.

Oh, Evie. Would she ever learn?

Yet another boyfriend had been sent packing. A French one this time. Hugo.

She seemed to go after the most unsuitable young men. It was always the same. Fireworks to start with, great bursts of enthusiasm lighting up her world. But then the poor girl seemed to get bored of them almost as soon as it had started.

Maybe this was the way now? She reached over for her sherry and took a sip. Maybe this is what the sixties had been all about? Rosamund wasn't sure it was progress. It was very different in her day, of course. And in Evie's mother's day, too. Poor Diana. She rested her glass on her knee and thought of Evie's mother. Sad thoughts, very sad, but tempered with light. What advice would she have given Evie?

Rosamund had tried her best. A gentle steer here and there. But she didn't like to interfere – she'd learnt her lesson with Caroline.

Still, she should try and help.

Her eyes flickered shut, the night's restlessness catching up with her. She stayed there for a few moments, released, lost in the comfort of rest, and then the muscles round her spine squeezed and her body flexed, taut in pain.

She opened her eyes. Cushions were moved and a new position found. She glanced down at the suitcase next to her. Evie's suitcase, as she'd come to think of it. Maybe a voice from the grave might carry more weight when it came to advice? Something written down. Evie had always valued the written word.

She took another sip of sherry, thinking. And then it came to her. She knew just what she had to do.

When the letter was done, Rosamund wondered where to put it. She was desperate not to appear to nag or hector and wanted to make everything about the advice as playful as possible. She thought a little game, a treasure hunt if you like, might work. She'd hide the letter in a book, a book that would in itself act as an extra piece of advice, underlining the sentiments of the letter.

She eased herself off the sofa and walked slowly over to her bookcase. The greats of world literature were there, sitting alongside the not-so-greats. Her eyes jumped along the shelves, taking in a lifetime of reading. Dickens? Plenty of lessons to be found there, although perhaps not so many on finding suitable boys. Shakespeare, maybe? Surely he must have something to say on how best to find love? Rosamund's head was blank, crushed by the enormity of it all. But, then again, was a man really the right person for this kind of thing? Surely what Evie needed was some sisterly advice, woman to woman. And then she remembered something. A poem, not by Shakespeare but by Emily Brontë, a poem that she was sure said what Evie needed to know.

She went to the *Collected Poems* and started flicking through, scanning the first couple of lines on every page. About halfway, she found it – the words feeling as warm and familiar as a comfortable old slipper.

Love is like the wild rose-briar,
Friendship like the holly-tree
The holly is dark when the rose-briar blooms
But which will bloom most constantly?
The wild rose-briar is sweet in spring,
Its summer blossoms scent the air;
Yet wait till winter comes again
And who will call the wild-briar fair?
Then scorn the silly rose-wreath now
And deck thee with the holly's sheen,
That when December blights thy brow
He still may leave thy garland green.

Yes, this was the one. Advice from Rosamund would be fairly easy to ignore but advice from a Brontë much less so. She folded the letter, pressing its crease between finger and thumb, and then placed it in the book next to the poem.

Back on the sofa, she had another sip of sherry. It had been a job well done. How she'd love to see Evie's face when she found the letter! She ran her hand across the book, happy that the next hand to do this would be Evie's.

Somewhere in the distance, down some village lane or other, a dog barked.

And then she had another idea.

She took out the letter, smiling, and added a postscript.

There, she thought. Perfect.

CHAPTER 20

Summer 1972

'Have you been down here all night?'

That's Geneviève, dressed in a zebra-print nightie, her red hair sticking out like a Rorschach test. She's standing in the sitting-room doorway and has clearly not been awake very long (just like me).

'Oh, I must have nodded off,' I groan, still slouched on the beanbag. I try to move but my body has the pliancy of Ryvita.

'You look dead rough,' she says, helpfully. 'Stay there, I'll go and make us a brew.'

She's back in a few minutes, complete with tea and custard creams.

I still haven't moved. The beanbag is toying with me: part cot, part instrument of torture.

'Thank you,' I say, taking a mug and a couple of biscuits. 'What a night.'

'Have you been thinking about Lolo?' she asks, sitting down on the floor opposite me, wedged up against the sofa.

'Lolo? No . . .' I give my head as solid a shake as I can manage at the moment.

She doesn't reply, unless raising an eyebrow and dunking a custard cream is a reply (which it is).

I have a long slurp of tea.

'I've been really stupid, haven't I?' I groan. 'I don't know how it happened – he's just sneaked up on me without me knowing. One minute he's homosexual and helping me with the listings and the next he's got beautiful tea-coloured eyes and a lovely sweet smile.'

'Just speak to him,' says Geneviève, her face suddenly adult and wise.

'I can't – it's too late now, isn't it?'

'What do you mean?'

'Well, that woman he was kissing last night.'

'It looked more like *she* was kissing *him*. And it was a party, anyway; everyone kisses someone at a party.' She has another dunk. 'Well, everyone except me and you.'

An hour later and I'm trudging through Soho on my way to the magazine.

The Lolo chat with Geneviève continued over breakfast and all the way through getting changed. We kept going round in circles. I'm still not convinced he's not homosexual (a double negative that would push Griffin over the edge). Geneviève thinks I'm wrong and cites his height, his girl-kissing and his Welshness as evidence. Even if he isn't homosexual, though, it's still very confusing. It's all a bit bird-in-the-bush-ish. At the moment I have my one bird (Lolo as a friend) but do I want to risk that for two birds? (Lolo as more than a friend.)

The combination of Lolo, the party and the beanbag has left me feeling pretty flat so to try and bolster my way through the day I've armed myself with happiness in dress form: my flowery silk shirtdress, big bold tulips of various shades of green tumbling over a field of inky blue, all bottomed off with emerald tights and navy-and-green strappy sandals. The dress works its magic momentarily but by the time I reach Soho I'm just left thinking how nice it'd be to be somewhere sunny and tulipy with Lolo.

As I walk down the dusty, messy Soho streets, the occasional crisp packet wafts gamely along and cigarette stubs eddy and flow. It's all a far cry from a few years ago, when everything seemed shiny and new. We seem to have gone from *white heat* to obsolete in no time at all. It's like the sixties were a big 9-volt battery, sparking up the world and shocking us into life. But now, in the seventies, the battery's run out, drained of all power, dead. The Beatles are gone. And The Doors. Jimi Hendrix. Janis Joplin.

Maybe it's time for something new.

I turn a corner and lumber down the street. Crowds of people mill around me, sitting in cafes, setting up stall, going in and out of shops buying pasta and linen and sex. I pass one of my favourite pubs: The York Minster. It always makes me think of the real Minster, stately and proud, a magnificent galleon. I smile (my first of the day). And then, just like that, another magnificent

Yorkshire galleon comes to mind: Mrs Swithenbank. Stately and proud and full of good advice.

I wander over to a nearby fragrant phone box (eau de urinal), carefully step inside and dial her number. There are a few rings and then:

'847225. Doris Swithenbank speaking.'

'Doris, it's me, Evie,' I say, pushing 2p in the slot.

'Oh, Evie, love. I thought you might be a man from the council – I'm having trouble with my drains. Is everything all right? You sound as flat as the fens.'

'Man trouble,' I say, twisting the phone cable round my finger.

'Well, that's about the only thing worse than drain trouble, love. What's the problem? Are you bored again?'

'No, completely the opposite. This one's a friend. A really lovely friend.'

'But isn't that a good thing, love, him being a friend? He's less likely to be a crackpot, surely – although from what you tell me, London's full of crackpot men. He's not a cockney, is he?'

'No,' I smile. 'He's Welsh.'

'Welsh? I don't know why you can't find yourself a good Yorkshireman, love, although you could get a lot worse than the Welsh, I suppose. What are you fretting about, anyway? If he's a friend, then you're halfway there already, aren't you?'

I pause, unsure whether or not to go into the details of Lolo's byzantine complications (men, women, Radio 3).

'Listen, love,' she goes on. 'Does this friend make you happy?'

(Does he make me happy? Does thinking about him, even in this stinky, dirty, graffiti-strewn phone box, make me happy?)

'Yes, he makes me very happy.'

'Well, people who make you happy are few and far between, that's what I've found. Look love, I know it's more awkward with a friend. There's more to lose. But there's more to gain, too, remember. I was once close to a very nice young man called Albert. There was no courting, mind – we were just friends. We'd sit and talk and we walked out a few times together, too. He went off to France in 1915 and it was only then – when he'd gone – that I realised I was sweet on him. I wrote a letter telling him but I was too shy to post it and, anyway, I was worried about spoiling things. So the letter just sat there. And then one day I heard that he was dead – just like that. Not even a grand battle. Shot by mistake in training. Pointless. Like so many things back then.'

I can hear her breathing down the phone. Deep breaths. Deep and meaningful.

'So,' she goes on, 'you speak to this friend of yours and tell him Doris Swithenbank says if he's got any sense at all, he'll snap you up.'

'Oh, I'd love to be snapped up, Doris,' I say, staring out onto the street through the smudgy panes of glass.

'You will be, love, don't worry. In fact, go and phone him now. Never mind talking to an old lass like me.'

'Now?'

'Aye, now, love. There's no time like the present. Off you go.'

A couple of big sloppy kisses come flying down the phone and then the line goes dead.

I hold the phone in mid-air. I'm aware of the dialling tone's steady drone but my mind is elsewhere. Lolo-land, to be precise.

Should I call him? What will I say? Will I make a complete fool of myself? Will I spoil everything? Or should I get in quick before he succumbs to friendly fire (in stripy-top-and-onions form) like Mrs Swithenbank's Albert?

I put the phone down and then immediately pick it up again. The dialling tone clicks and whirrs. I wait for a few seconds, then start to dial Lolo's home number. It rings and rings but there's no answer. So I try his office at the BBC but it's the same. No answer.

So much for there being no time like the present.

Bugger.

I carry on walking to work, glum little steps that meander and drag. Eventually I find myself outside the *Right On!* office, where I give my hair a perfunctory primp in the sex-shop window and head upstairs.

'Evie!' chimes Nickwiththecollars as I walk in.

'Morning,' I reply, a downbeat little jangle.

'Oh, you sound blue. Everything okay?'

'Yes, just a little flat today, that's all.'

'Oh no.' He's back in his nine-to-five outfit, an upturned navy collar replacing last night's purple robes. 'I hope it isn't anything to do with the party?'

'No, the party was great. Thanks for inviting us, Nick.'

'Aw, it was lovely to see you there. You were a brilliant Scotland, Evie. And your little friend is *so* cool.'

I flash him a smile, more on Geneviève's behalf than mine.

'Actually,' he goes on, 'we did get a bit worried about you. You just disappeared! Where did you get to?' He does a pantomime wink. 'You're a bit of a dark horse, aren't you!'

'Who's a dark horse?' asks Nickstickupbum, strutting in from the kitchen.

'Evie – she scarpered early from the party last night.'

'Evie?'

'Yes, we couldn't find her. And we looked *everywhere*,' he says, as if they'd searched the entire Russian steppe rather than a two-up, two-down in Fulham.

Both Nicks turn to me, eyebrows arched.

'No, it wasn't like that!' (I feel stirrings of a blush.) 'My friend Geneviève knocked some red wine over a guy's suit when we were dancing – it was a white suit, too, so you can imagine what a mess it was.'

'Terrible,' sniffs Nickstickupbum.

Nickwiththecollars starts doing something theatrical with his eyes (a pretty common occurrence). I ignore him and carry on telling them both about white-suit man: the wine, the groping, the shower. Everything.

'So,' says Nickstickupbum when I've finished, 'this guy was horrible, then?'

'Oh, yes, *really* horrible. Such a creep.'

'And arrogant?'

'Oh, God, yes. Honestly, I've never met *anyone* so arrogant.' (Current company excepted, obviously.)

Nickstickupbum narrows his eyes.

'He's my brother.'

The room judders for a second, like when the telly's on the blink and needs a good thump to get it working again.

'Sorry?'

'He's my brother. The horrible, arrogant man in the white suit.'

I scrutinise his face, searching for evidence of a joke but find nothing. It's like staring into the face of an Easter Island statue.

'Right, okay, I see . . .' (Could today get any worse?) 'I had no idea, Nick.'

He sniffs.

I see my job, the job that I think I may love, shrivel and shoot off into nothing, like a deflating balloon. All because of some idiot man and his stupid bloody suit and arrogant groping hands. 'I'm really sorry, Nick,' I say. 'Honestly, I didn't mean—'

Suddenly, there's a loud clatter out on the stairs leading up to the office.

'Stop everything,' shouts Griffin, shooting through the door like a poor man's W. H. Auden. 'I knew something was wrong. I just *knew* it. I'm never wrong. Not *ever*,' she adds (tautologically), slamming a hand down on the nearest desk.

She stands there, panting, a sour combination of lank hair and fury.

'Are you all right?' asks Nickstickupbum, clearly just as confused as the rest of us.

'All right? Yes, of course I am,' she spits, red of face and feisty of eye. '*I'm* all right but perhaps you should be asking *her*.' She points a yogic finger straight at me. '*She*'s the one who's been lying to us all this time.'

'Look, Griffin,' says Nickwiththecollars. 'It's pretty obvious you don't like Evie but I think accusing her of lying really is going too far.'

'Oh, do you, Nick? Do you?' she says, moving from tautology

to simple repetition. 'Well, let me tell you that I spent yesterday afternoon at the BBC. I thought one of us, at least, should do some proper journalistic investigation into *this one*.'

She's pointing at me again, jabbing her finger manically. Her ratty hair is girdled in a velvet tassel headband, giving her the appearance of an angry Victorian lampshade.

'And it turns out that Evie here,' she goes on, dousing the floor with spittle, 'didn't actually *leave* the BBC. She was *fired*.'

Nickwiththecollars gasps and his eyes grow as big as Wagon Wheels; Nickstickupbum surveys the scene, impassive.

'Her old manager told me *everything*.' She pauses dramatically (two, three, four). 'Including Evie urinating in Princess Anne's mug.'

This produces major eye action from both Nicks.

'It was *my* mug!' I cry. 'And it was an accident.'

The room creaks; the air bristles. London holds its breath.

'She's right, though,' I say, with heavy heart and downturned eye. 'I did get the sack from the BBC. And I lied when I came for the job. I'm sorry. I wasn't a journalist at the BBC – I was a junior assistant producer.'

Griffin shoots a triumphant look around the room.

'I've been stupid, haven't I?' I go on. 'Really stupid. But I only did it because I wanted to work here so much. It just seemed like the perfect place to be.'

'You see!' roars Griffin. 'What did I say? Get rid of her. We can't trust a thing she says.'

'No, we can't get rid of Evie,' says Nickwiththecollars. 'She's doing a wonderful job.'

'Oh, shut up, Nick,' snaps Griffin.

Nickstickupbum is perched on the edge of his desk, a silent, inscrutable slant. His arms are folded and he's looking down at the floor, swaying slightly.

'So you lied to us then, Evie?' he asks, looking up.

'Yes, I did, Nick. I'm *really* sorry,' I reply, looking straight into his face and apologising for the second time in less than a minute. 'It was stupid. *I* was stupid.'

His head bobs down, almost a nod.

'Get out, Evie,' spits Griffin. 'You're not welcome here.'

I look over at my desk, with the postcards and Lolo's metronome, with my notebooks full of listings, with the typewriter and the flyers and the ...

'Well, the thing is, Griffin,' says Nickstickupbum. 'Evie's a good writer.'

Griffin flashes him a Look that could lay waste to half of London.

'That's a matter of opinion.'

'Yes, I know,' he replies. 'And it's my opinion that she's a good writer.'

'Don't be ridiculous,' shouts Griffin, all flapping cloth and wonky fringe. 'She can't write. It's rubbish. Just throw-away rubbish, that's all. It's not *real* writing. *I'm* the creative one here. I write poetry. I read the *New Yorker*.'

'But can't we both just be good in different ways?' I pipe up. 'Does everything always have to be win or lose?'

She spins round to look at me. 'Yes, Evie. It does.'

(So much for Griffin's wonderfully balanced chakras.)

'It's either me or her,' she goes on, spinning back to face the two Nicks.

'Look, Griffin, let's all calm down,' says Nickstickupbum. 'Evie made a mistake by lying . . .'

'Which I am *very* sorry about,' I chip in.

'And I'm sure she wouldn't dream of doing it again,' he goes on, accompanied by vigorous nodding from me. 'But getting a good story often relies on a little subterfuge – so you could say that she did the *wrong* thing in order to get the *right* result.'

'The right result?' yells Griffin, turning a nasty shade of puce. 'What on earth do you think is the *right* result? You have to get rid of her, Nick.'

Nickstickupbum calmly leans over his desk and pulls some letters from a drawer.

'I've been receiving these ever since Evie started,' he says, tapping them in his hands. 'Just a few at first, nice comments about the listings, but when we published her opera review, lots more.' He's tossing the letters one by one onto the desk. 'All of them saying how much they enjoy Evie's writing.' He puts down the last one and folds his hands. 'We haven't had one letter about your poems, Griffin. Ever.'

'What?' she gasps, all open mouth and bulbous eyes, like one of those funny fish no one wants to eat. Her mouth jerks back into shape and, with a quick flick of straggly headband, she lets out a gruesome scream (aural napalm). Mid-scream she flings her hands across a nearby desk, sending everything on its surface (pens, notebooks, mug of cold tea) onto the floor.

'**You.**

Are.

Nothing.

Without.

Me,' she bangs, going from flower power to Baader-Meinhof in less than a minute. '*I'm* the writer here; *I'm* the artist.'

'Don't talk rubbish,' says Nickwiththecollars, enunciating every syllable with full theatrical luvviedom.

She screams again, with even more power, seemingly in stereo until I realise that the scream's merging with a car horn outside, (un)harmonising like a mangled Beach Boy. The car horn is very loud, very insistent. I'm standing near the window so have a sneaky look.

The noise seems to be coming from an Alfa Romeo Spider.

A dark orange Alfa Romeo *Spider.*

With Digby and Geneviève squeezed into the tiny slip of space behind the seats.

What's going on?

Griffin, meanwhile, still screaming, is going around grabbing things from various drawers and shelves and shoving them in her tasselly bag.

'I'm leaving,' she spits. 'I've had enough. That's it. When *I* go, all the creativity goes. And all the good karma. You won't last two minutes without me.'

'Oh, I think we'll be all right,' says Nickstickupbum calmly.

There's another scream. She grabs her dreamcatcher from a shelf and hurls it across the room like a Polaris missile. 'You have *no* idea. No idea at all. This place is just a squalid din of tatty bourgeois dialectic.'

(I want that on a badge.)

'You're all philistines,' she goes on, taking her dusty silk-flower garland off a shelf and shoving it in her bag. 'Philistines.'

Nobody is trying to stop her. Nickstickupbum looks on like a Whitehall mandarin and I get the feeling Nickwiththecollars is loving the drama of it all.

'You'll be begging me to come back.' She snatches her bag from the desk and storms towards the door. 'Begging me. Just you see. But I won't. No way. You've had your last drop of blood and sweat from me, Nick.' She turns and jabs a finger at Nickstickupbum. 'You're nothing but a jumped-up little boy, playing at being an editor. And you,' she says, jabbing at the other Nick, 'are just a pathetic out-of-work actor. And as for you' – she turns to me, a seething flurry of tassel and spit-tle – 'you're exactly what's wrong with this world: lightweight bubblegum froth.'

(I wonder for a moment about explaining the non-frothy nature of bubblegum to Griffin but think better of it.)

'Mark my words,' she goes on, turning back towards the door with a final surge of suedette. 'This is it. Goodbye.'

She stomps towards the doorway but, just before she gets there, it's filled by a figure from the staircase. A familiar figure. A flame-haired Amazonian warrior. Caroline. She's wearing something inflated, Japanese-y, and has the silhouette of a very modern table lamp.

Griffin falters.

'Excuse me, darling,' says Caroline, looking about eight feet tall.

They stand there for a second, two alien worlds facing off, then Griffin reverses, accompanied by a monumental tut and an irritated flick of headband. Caroline inches through the doorway with all the majesty of Cleopatra and her court arriving in Caesar's Rome.

Griffin huffs and puffs and – as soon as there's enough space – bolts through the doorway, squeezing behind Caroline. There's a brief squeak of suedette on plastic and then, suddenly, grubbily, wondrously, she's gone.

'Was that her?' asks Caroline.

'Yes, that was Griffin,' I say. 'Sorry.'

'Don't worry, darling. I know the type. All the leaves are brown and the sky is *very much* grey.'

She smiles over at the two Nicks. The two Nicks stare back, dumbfounded.

'Hullo,' she says, unleashing a neutron-bomb-powered twinkle. 'Look, I know this is *really* very cheeky of me but I'm afraid I need to borrow Evie for a *tiny* bit of time.'

'What's wrong?' I ask. 'Has something happened?'

'No, nothing to worry about, darling. I'll tell you in the car.' And she gestures towards the door.

The two Nicks are still staring, open-mouthed.

'Would that be okay?' I ask. 'I'll make up the time later, honest.'

'Of course,' says Nickstickupbum. 'But I want the inside scoop about Princess Anne and the mug.'

'It's yours!' I shout, running out the door with Caroline.

I get halfway down the stairs then remember something and nip back up.

'Oh, and Nick, I am *really* sorry about your brother, by the way,' I say, poking my head round the door.

'Oh, that's okay,' he replies, still looking fairly stunned. 'You did exactly the right thing. My brother's a prat.' He flashes me his first smile. 'A sleazy, arrogant prat.'

Interlude – Spring 1956, Napoli

Caroline still wasn't home.

It was gone three in the morning, Digby saw, checking her watch for the umpteenth time that hour.

She'd stayed in the flat at first, her fingers tapping and fumbling around cigarettes. More drinks were poured, whisky now, solid and reliable. Time ticked slowly round, unsympathetic. Hostile.

Then she'd grown tired of waiting so she slipped a shawl round her shoulders and went out. She didn't stay out long, didn't venture far. Didn't break the invisible thread that tied her to the flat and their life together.

She'd just got back to the flat after her fourth trip out and was busy spooning Illy into the little espresso pot, mound after sobering earthy mound, when the front door clicked open.

She swung round and saw Caroline walk in, head bowed.

'Oh, thank God,' she said, dropping the spoon and surging to the door. 'I thought you'd gone.'

Caroline looked up and, instinctively, lovingly, threw her arms around Digby.

'Gone? No, of course not.' They held each other, squeezing, a mess of tears and hair. 'I'm sorry,' whispered Caroline. 'I've been selfish, I know, but it's just how I am.'

'No, I'm the one who should be apologising,' replied Digby, losing her fingers in Caroline's ample curls. 'I was stupid. We're a perfect team, of course we are – just you and me, together.'

Caroline held her tight. 'You're my family – I want you to know that.'

Digby's eyes swelled, heavy with tears. 'And you're mine. You're all I ever wanted,' she whispered. 'All I'll ever need.'

CHAPTER 21

Summer 1972

'Reykjavik!?'

'Yes, darling,' shouts Caroline, trying to make herself heard over the noise of the open road. 'For a whole bloody year.'

We're rocketing through Soho in the Spider on an urgent mission. Apparently when I left the flat this morning, Geneviève phoned Caroline and Digby to tell them about the party, particularly the bit about Lolo not being homosexual (perhaps) and me (perhaps) somehow managing to fall in love with him without ever really noticing. They made a few phone calls (*It's the lesbian mafia, darling*) and found out two very important things:

1. Lolo's broadcasting live from Wigmore Hall for today's lunchtime concert
2. Lolo's leaving London straight after the concert to go and live in Reykjavik

'What?' I shriek. 'A year!'

'Yes, that's why we had to come and get you,' Caroline goes on. 'We need to put a stop to it.'

'You need to tell him how you feel, dear,' yells Digby from behind. 'You can't let him go off to Reykjavik without knowing.'

(I'm up in front with Caroline. Squeezed behind in the non-seat space, on account of their diminutive leggage, are Digby and Geneviève.)

'But I can't believe he didn't say anything about going away,' I shout. 'And for a whole year, too.'

'Maybe he was going to tell you yesterday,' chips in Geneviève, cupping a hand to her mouth as a makeshift megaphone.

(We're all in need of a megaphone. Caroline's driving makes it feel like we're heading into a force 10 gale. My hair is in full anarchic mode, buffeted by the equivalent of a thousand Clairol dryers.)

'Yesterday?'

'Yes, you know,' she goes on, 'when you stood him up for coffee.'

'But I didn't stand him up!' I shout. 'It was an accident. I was stuck in one of your dresses.'

The car jolts to the right. 'Bloody idiot!' yells Caroline, waving a perfectly manicured hand at a C&A van. Thankfully the other hand is still attached to the steering wheel (not always a given with Caroline's driving).

'What am I going to say?' I shout.

'You'll think of something, darling. You always do.'

'He'll think I'm mad, just turning up in the middle of his work.'

'Nonsense, he'll love it,' she replies, speeding past a black cab (bowler hats on wheels). 'Who wouldn't love being chased? The thing is to get in there quickly, darling, before he leaves.'

'You need to convince him to stay,' shouts Geneviève.

'But how?' I howl (inside and out).

'Just tell him how you feel,' shouts Digby, giving me a little shoulder-squeeze. 'It's as simple as that.'

'Yes, it'll be easy,' shouts Geneviève. 'He thinks you're ace, it's obvious.'

The car swings round a corner, turning left, sending us all flying to the right.

'If you think you might love someone, darling,' shouts Caroline, looking at me and not the road, 'they really do need to know. And preferably quickly, before they go off and live in bloody Reykjavik for a year.'

She turns back and slams her way through the gears. We're speeding down Wigmore Street like Evel Knievel.

'But I don't want it all to go wrong,' I shout. 'I don't want to risk spoiling things.'

Suddenly I'm back in the phone box speaking to Mrs Swithenbank, her wise words shooting through time. *People who make you happy are few and far between.* I smile, emboldened, as the words burst around me.

'People who make you happy are few and far between,' I repeat.

'Exactly, darling,' shouts Caroline, almost clipping a parked car.

'And if he does turn out to be gay,' shouts Digby, 'at least you'll have a lovely pen pal, dear. Perfect for a holiday.'

'Very funniiiiiiiiiiiiiiiiiiiiiiiiiiiiiiiiiiiiiiiiiiiiiiiiiii,' I yell, thrown around the car as Caroline swerves across the road, ignoring all notion of lanes. One wheel mounts the pavement and she slams on the brakes.

We all lurch forward, like a troupe of contemporary dancers.

'Here we are,' says Caroline, switching off the engine. 'Wigmore Hall.'

Wigmore Hall looks out at us, stately and assured. There's a Victorian heft to it except for a fancy glass awning, dripping with culture and curlicue; it's exactly the type of fancy glass awning that could lead from this life into a magical new one. Potentially.

We're parked (I use the term loosely) behind a BBC van, like an ice-cream van but far less interesting. A bundle of cables runs from the van across the pavement and into the hall but apart from that there's no sign of BBC life, not even a dry canteen sandwich.

We all start getting out of the car (never easy in a low-slung convertible).

'Okay, darling, you know what to do,' says Caroline, giving me a nod.

I stare up at the fancy glass awning.

'You'll be fine, dear,' says Digby, coming over and giving me a hug. 'Just one word is enough to start. Then another will come. And another after that. Before you know it, you'll have said everything that needs to be said.' She takes a step back and beams, holding both my hands. 'It's all *much* better out than in, as they say.'

This makes me smile.

'Right,' I sigh. 'Here I go, then.'

'Er, darling,' says Caroline. 'Haven't you forgotten something?'
She points to her hair.

Oh God. My hair. It probably looks like the Wreck of
the Hesperus.

Where's a sex shop when you need one?

Luckily, there's a clothes shop just next to the entrance so I
have a quick primp in the window, followed by another hug from
Digby, a thumbs up from Geneviève and a beautiful encouraging
wink from Caroline. Then I dash under the fancy glass awning
and head inside, following the bundle of BBC cables like Dorothy
starting off on the yellow brick road.

I've decided to say, if anyone asks, that I'm from *Woman's
Hour* doing a feature with Radio 3 so I make myself look as BBC-
like as possible (inform, educate, entertain) and stride quickly
through the entrance lobby.

There's nobody around. I speed up, rushing through a couple
of doors. There's a swanky staircase, which I race up, bringing
me to a balcony and a few seats but no Lolo. I have a quick look
round the auditorium below but all I see are some chairs on the
stage and a few dangling microphones. I'm getting worried now
so I dash back downstairs and try another set of double doors.
Behind them is a little room with more stairs, this time going down
to the basement, so I run down and come across a bar (empty)
and a cloakroom (ditto). I chase back upstairs and notice that the
BBC cables meander discreetly round the wall and through yet
another set of double doors at the far end of the room.

I bash through the doors, bringing me back to the auditorium,
but the stalls rather than the balcony. I have a quick look around

but can't see Lolo (or anyone) so dart down an aisle that leads to the stage, hoping to find signs of life. As I'm darting, I scan the stage but it's all very quiet. Maybe I've missed him? Maybe he's already set the recording up and left? Maybe he's on his way to the airport? Or in the air, rocketing towards Reykjavik and a new life? Maybe he's ...

'Eeeevieee?'

I hear Lolo shout my name. I spin round and see him walking towards me from a dark corner at the back of the stalls.

'Lolo! Oh, thank goodness!'

He cocks his head to one side and smiles.

'What are you doing here?'

'Oh ...' I pant, relieved, breathless and treading water, searching for the elusive starter word that Digby mentioned.

'Is everything okay?' he asks.

'Yes, fine. Absolutely. I'm sorry for barging in. I ... er, just wanted to ... to ...'

There's a raising of a Welsh eyebrow. 'To?'

'I just wanted to see you.'

'Oh, very nice.'

'Well, talk to you, actually.'

'Talk to me?'

'Yes ... talk to you.'

'I see.'

'Before you go off to Reykjavik.'

He stops smiling.

'I know all about it,' I rattle on. 'About you leaving today. And about you staying there for a year. A whole year! Why didn't you tell me, Lolo? Fancy going away for a year. To Reykjavik! Without saying anything. How could you?'

His looks pained. Guilty. Confused.

He turns away and sighs. Then he takes a piece of paper out of his pocket, unfolds it and passes it to me.

'What's this?' I ask, in full grumpy mode.

'Read it,' he replies, looking down.

I look at the paper. 'Janáček, String Quartet No. Two. Look, Lolo, I haven't come for another classical music lesson,' I snap, moving from grumpy to annoyed. 'This is serious. I want to talk to you about it.'

'Not Janáček,' he replies. 'The one underneath it.'

I huff and tut and look down at the paper again and read:

'Thórarinsson – "A Year in Reykjavik".'

'What was that you were saying about me going to live in Reykjavik for a year?' beams Lolo, fighting a losing battle with the world's biggest smirk.

'Oh.'

(Oh. Oh. Oh. Oh. Oh.)

'So . . . this is your year in Reykjavik?' I say, giving the paper a flutter.

'Yup.'

'Oh, God . . . bloody classical music. What a stupid name for a song! I thought you were going away for a year without saying anything. Just disappearing.'

His eyebrows arch and his mouth curves upwards. His whole face, in fact, is heading north so quickly it's in danger of catapulting into the sky.

359

'And you came here to see me?'

We stand looking at each other. Two lighthouses, still and shining, beam to glorious beam.

'Ready for the sound check, Lolo?' shouts a plummy voice from the back of the stalls.

Lolo pauses then, with mouth and willing eye, says *sorry* quietly, before booming out a reply.

'Yes, but come and say hullo to Evie first.'

'Oh, lovely, coming!' And a heavily corduroyed man comes out from behind the outside-broadcast desk and makes his way towards us.

(*Aubrey. Sound engineer*, whispers Lolo, by way of explanation.)

'Well, Evie, I must say it's very nice to finally meet you,' says Aubrey, a banquet of sideburn and Aramis. 'I've heard a *lot* about you.'

'All good, I hope!'

Aubrey high-kicks his eyebrows. 'Oh, yes.'

Lolo gives him a semi-Look. 'Actually, Aubrey, Evie and I need to have a quick chat so would you mind giving us a minute, please?'

'Of course, I'll go outside for a smoke. Leave you two alone for a "chat". Give me a shout when you're done.' He flashes us both a film-star smile and, with a stylish chafe of corduroy, he's off.

'He seems nice,' I say.

'Yes, he is. Very nice.'

We stand there for a moment, shuffling feet and thoughts.

'Oh, I like your moustache, by the way!' I blurt out, needlessly pointing to the non-moustache space on my face.

'Really? Thank you.' He has a quick moustache groom. 'I just thought I needed a change. You know, something a bit more modern.'

There's a mutual smile and more shuffling.

Silence booms around the room.

'Look . . . Evie,' says Lolo, quietly, hesitantly. 'I . . . actually *did* feel like running off to Reykjavik for a year yesterday. You didn't turn up for our coffee.'

'I know. I'm really sorry, Lolo. I was stuck.'

'Stuck? What, in a meeting?'

'No, physically stuck. In a dress.'

'What?'

'A blow-up dress,' I explain, as if it's something completely normal.

'A blow-up dress?' repeats Lolo, all scrunched face and mystified eye.

'Yes, it was one of Geneviève's. I was home early and had loads of time before coming to meet you so I thought I'd try it on. But then I got stuck in it. I couldn't move my arms. It was horrible. I couldn't phone you or anything.'

'Well, I did try to phone *you*, actually, but it was engaged.'

'Yes, that was me! I knocked the phone off when I was trying to answer but then I couldn't put it back because my arms were locked.'

'Hold on, let me get this straight. You didn't meet me for coffee because you were stuck in an inflatable dress?'

'Yes – it was awful. I toppled over and ended up on my back all afternoon. I was just lying there, stranded. I couldn't get up.'

Lolo's lips quiver.

'I was stuck like a turtle on its back waiting for Geneviève to come home.'

'I thought you'd stood me up,' he says. 'I thought you didn't want to meet me.'

'No! Not at all. Completely the opposite, in fact – I *really* wanted to meet you. I'd been looking forward to it all day.'

'Really?'

'Yes, well, we hadn't spoken for a couple of days and I . . . I missed you.'

'Oh.'

'And then last night,' I go on, 'I saw you at the party.'

'You were at the party?' (The scrunch returns.)

'Only briefly – we didn't stay.'

'We?'

'Yes, I went with Geneviève.'

'Oh, of course, yes. Well, it's probably just as well I didn't see you because I was *very* drunk.'

There's a quick clatter out in the lobby and then the door swings open. Two elderly ladies walk in.

'Morning,' they say, walking past us (a shuffle of coordinated hat and bag).

'Morning,' we both reply, dropping swiftly from one world into another.

'We always get a few early starters,' Lolo whispers, cocking his head over at the two elderly ladies. 'Grabbing the best seats.'

362

'Well, it must be nice for them being here without anyone else. It's quite exciting, isn't it, having the place to yourself? It's like the stage just belongs to you.'

Lolo smiles. 'Come on,' he says. 'I'll give you a quick tour.'

'No, we can't – aren't you busy?'

'We've got time.' He starts walking towards the stage. 'Come on then,' he says, looking back. 'You'd be up there like a shot if you thought there was a swivel chair waiting.'

'Very funny,' I say, quick-stepping after him. 'It all feels much smaller than I thought. The hall, I mean.'

'See what you think when you're up there. It's a funny thing being on a stage – it plays tricks on you. It's like walking into an optical illusion.' We get to a little set of steps tucked away at the side of the stage. 'Here, let me give you a hand up.'

I take his hand (warm, solid, dependable) and trot up the steps.

'Well, what do you think?' he says, following me up.

'You're right. It does feel bigger now.'

'Told you!'

I look out across the hall. The seats line up beyond us like a tightly ploughed field. The two elderly ladies are still busy settling in, faffing with buttons and bags.

'Here's our handiwork,' says Lolo, sweeping a hand at a group of microphones ranged round four chairs. 'And this is where the musicians will sit, taking all the glory while we beaver away in the background.'

'There aren't many of them, are there? It's not like the band at the opera.'

'Well, I think four's quite enough for a string quartet, don't you?'

'Oh, yes. Thanks, smartypants. Anyway, look, you were saying ... about you being very drunk.'

'Ah ... yes. Shall we sit down?'

I lower myself onto a chair; Lolo sits down next to me, a symphony of burgundy pant and serious face.

'I was very drunk,' he starts, leaning in. 'Very, *very* drunk. I'd been in the pub all afternoon because I was so upset about being stood up. I thought it was a message.'

'You thought *what* was a message?'

'You not turning up. Or phoning. I thought it was your way of letting me know that you weren't interested. Like the Serpentine but clearer.'

'The Serpentine?'

'Yes, when you tried to brush me off gently, making it clear I was just a friend. A funny friend.'

'Well you *are* funny!'

'I was hoping you might see me as something more than funny, though. I was hoping to woo you.' He smiles. 'And then I made a complete fool of myself with all the damned food everywhere. No wonder you think I'm nothing more than a performing clown.'

'You're not a performing clown. But you are funny. And interesting. And kind. The thing is, though,' I go on, squeezing out the words like toothpaste left at the end of a tube, 'I thought you were ... homosexual.'

'What? Homosexual? Why on earth would you think that?'

'Well, Tarquin . . .'

'Tarquin! He's my cousin! We share a flat – well, actually, I share his flat. He's homosexual, yes, but I'm not.'

'Oh, but what about the painting with all the naked men at the beach?'

'It was for his birthday! We were in Portobello one day and he saw it and liked it so I bought it on the spot – he's always so hard to buy for. It was dirt cheap. It cost more to get it cleaned than to buy it in the first place.'

'Oh, I see.' I'm beginning to feel I have the psychological insight of a soggy dumpling.

'You really have thought about this a lot, haven't you?'

'Well, yes, I suppose I have.' (Although clearly not enough.) 'To be honest, it was Radio Three that really threw me,' I say. 'Everyone's homosexual there.'

'What! Red-blooded chaps like me and Aubrey? Are you mad?'

I can't tell whether he's joking or not. And then I realise that this is exactly why I like him.

'Well, I did start to wonder after last night, actually. I saw you – at the party – kissing a woman. The one with the stripy top and the onions.'

'Ah, I see.' There's a quick rub of burgundy pant. 'Look, Evie, I have no idea who she was. One minute I was dancing with Tarquin, the next she's there, bopping around all over me. It was all very awkward – you must have seen me trying to wriggle free?'

'We didn't stick around. I saw you kissing and we left pretty much straight after that.'

'Right. Well, it was probably just a matter of seconds. And *I* wasn't kissing *her* – *she* was kissing *me*. You must have seen that.'

I shrug, staring down at the tulips on my dress.

Lolo takes my hand. 'Look, Evie. Whatever you saw really was nothing. A stupid nothing, something that means nothing, counts for nothing, will amount to nothing, and has absolutely nothing to it. But you're *not* nothing.'

(Another double negative – there must be something in the air today.)

'You're very much something,' he goes on. 'Something very special. Something . . . magical.'

I look up. He's looking straight at me, his lovely hearty face blushing slightly. Behind him, the room stretches out. Endless.

'Over the last month or so, well . . . I've really enjoyed spending time with you. I've enjoyed it a lot. It's been wonderful, actually. Really wonderful.'

His thumb gently brushes my hand.

'I wasn't sure whether to say anything, though, because I didn't want to spoil it.'

'Oh, I've been just the same,' I say, word tumbling over word. 'I didn't want to mess things up. I didn't want it all to go funny and end.'

'Well . . .'

(Out of the corner of my eye, I think I see Geneviève pushing through the door at the back of the room.)

My head flicks to the left slightly.

'Evie, it sounds like we both . . .'

(I'm sure I see her tiptoe towards the sound desk but it's difficult to tell as the room is full of shadows and shade.)

'Evie?'

'Sorry, Lolo, I just thought I saw . . .'

I stand up and look out across the seats.

Lolo stands too.

He steps towards me and takes my hands again.

The stage lights flash, on and off, on and off.

'What's that?' I say.

'Oh, just a power surge or something. It happens all the time.'

He moves his head close to mine.

'Evie?' he says, his soft Welsh vowels making my name as warm as sunlight.

'Yes?'

I look into his eyes and see chestnuts and caramel and freshly brewed tea.

'I think you're funny . . . and interesting . . . and kind . . . and on top of all that you're the most beautiful woman I've ever met.'

And, like two separate train tracks merging into one, we lean into each other and kiss.

A few seconds later the music starts.

Even with my very limited knowledge of classical music, I know it's not a string quartet.

There's some tentative piano plinging, with strings oozing in the background. The piano gets a bit more confident, definitely on its way somewhere, and then someone shouts *oh yeah* and it all takes off.

babaBABAbabaBABA

plingplingPLINGPLINGplingplingPLINGPLING

We both look round, mid-kiss.

There's no sign of any musicians (or instruments, for that matter).

'What is it?' I ask.

He shrugs. 'It's coming from the speakers.'

Then a voice comes in. Alien. Sharp. Fragile.

Lolo pulls me close, takes my hand and starts swaying to the music. We're here, on stage, at Wigmore Hall, rocking gently from side to side.

And then the music speeds up.

Ch-ch-ch-ch-changes ...

Lolo speeds up too and before I know it he's twirling me around the stage, great swoops of joy, *ch-ch-changes*, round and round, beaming, spinning, laughing.

I catch a glimpse of Geneviève at the back of the room, behind the decks, thumbs in the air. And then I see Caroline and Digby burst through the doors and start dancing down the aisle, arm in arm, gliding, twisting, eye to gleaming eye.

'I could get used to this,' shouts Lolo, curling me round.

'Me too!' I shout back, laughing, full of music and life.

By now Caroline and Digby are clambering up the steps to join us on stage. Geneviève is here too, a joyous blur of flinging limbs.

'Darling!' shouts Caroline. 'What did I tell you!'

'I know,' I shout back. 'Are you ever wrong?'

'Never!'

The music swings and loops, insistent.

Ch-ch-ch-ch-changes ...

Out in the stalls I glimpse the two elderly women on their feet, holding each other arm in arm and shuffling along to the music.

Here, now, on the stage, with my friends, with Lolo, I feel an overwhelming sense of something being just right. Of everything being just right.

I know who I am and who I want to be.

Lolo pulls me close, still swirling. The music slows, the piano PLINGS, drums *ratatatatat*, a saxophone slinks in – smooth, assured – we look into each other's eyes and we kiss again, holding the moment.

Something new.

Something different.

Something wonderful.

As the music melts to silence, a door slams.

'Well, congratulations, everyone,' shouts Aubrey, stomping down the aisle. 'You've just been live on Radio Three. What an absolute fucking mess.'

Interlude – January 1972, Yorkshire

Rosamund watched Mr Hawkes walk down the snow-covered path and get into his Volvo. Then she closed the door and turned the key, locking the cold air out.

Mr Hawkes was her solicitor. He'd been visiting to talk about *arrangements*. She wanted to make sure that everything was in place for the girls; to make sure that, when it came, everything was as easy as possible for Caroline. Thank goodness for Digby, she thought, smiling. Yes, Digby would take care of it all. Should she think of Digby as her daughter-in-law or her son-in-law? Rosamund didn't know. And didn't really care. She'd somehow found herself part of a very modern family – it had brought her tremendous joy and she wouldn't have it any other way.

She was back in the sitting room now, easing herself down onto the sofa. Death would come soon. She felt it. She'd been told it, too. Months, possibly just weeks.

The house was silent, just the occasional gurgle of a radiator. Outside, snow muffled the village. Life passed quietly by.

She looked down at the suitcase sitting next to her. Evie's suitcase. She would put it in the study somewhere. There was no point lugging it back upstairs now. Would it work? Would Evie listen to her words?

She turned her head to look at the sideboard. On it stood a great choir of photographs, all different sizes and in different frames. Her girls were there. Caroline in her Brownie uniform. Digby on a horse. Evie smiling from a car. The four of them together, last summer, on Skinningrove Beach, ice-creams in hand. And there were the other photos too. Faded memories. Ghosts. Her mother and father, standing next to a country church. Her young husband, Edward, in Madrid, handsome and smart. Sadie, her faithful setter, a noble hound. And Diana, Evie's mother, sat under a tree, her eyes bright and her smile warm.

I'll be with them soon, thought Rosamund. Wherever they are.

She looked up at the ceiling and beyond.

'I did my best, Diana,' she said, resting her hand on the suit-case. 'We all did. It's up to Evie now . . .'

CHAPTER 22

Spring 1973

I am the wind. Swooping, swirling, whooshing, blasting. An excited gale of delight.

I'm going home. Yorkshire. Back to the farm. Dad's farm.

Fields slant past me as I speed, bombing up the A1 in Caroline's Alfa Romeo. The roof is down and I feel alive.

London is far behind.

It's eight o'clock on a glorious Saturday morning. The road is empty, a great expectant slash of space just for me. An arrow flying north.

I look in the driver's mirror and see myself reflecting back, sunshine glinting all around me. I move my head and the mirror fills with great folds of cheek flapping around like bedsheets drying on a gusty day. It's Oscar. Lolo's basset hound.

Our basset hound.

Lolo is next to me, in the passenger seat, smiling, laughing – radiant and warm, a funny, interesting and kind Welsh bear.

'I quite like having a glamorous chauffeur,' he shouts over the roar of the wind. 'I could get used to it.'

'And I quite like having a glamorous assistant,' I shout back.

'Don't you mean a glamorous co-pilot?'

'Co-pilot? Second navigator, maybe, if you're lucky.'

'Oh, you're power mad! Put a woman in charge for a minute and she just wants more.'

'I know,' I shout, glancing over to see Lolo's beaming face. 'We'll be running the country soon.'

'Steady on,' he says, bending in towards me and landing a kiss on my cheek.

It's been nine months since our first kiss, on stage in Wigmore Hall, broadcast live to the nation.

Nine lovely months.

A joyful flickering reel of films, pubs, restaurants, walks, trips to the seaside and a long weekend in Rome.

We've been to lots of concerts, too. I took Lolo to see Elton John (wonderful); he took me to see John Cage (not so wonderful). We've been to pop, rock, baroque, string quartets and lots and lots of opera, mainly thanks to Lolo's new job at the Royal Opera House, his dream job – something, he says, he's had his eye on for a long time. He was sacked by the BBC (snap!) after the Wigmore Hall incident, a result of Geneviève beggaring around with the outside-broadcast mixing desk when putting in her *Hunky Dory* cassette.

And me? I'm a full-time, permanent, completely un-temporary, pen-swinging, pad-carrying, shorthand-bothering journalist at

Right On! I love it. Nickstickupbum is actually quite friendly now and, if the wind's blowing in the right direction, he could almost be classed as nice. He has me writing more or less anything and everything: interviews, columns, features. I do most of the reviews now, too, because Nickwiththecollars has gone back to acting (he's currently to be found touring the northwest in a double Pinter).

Griffin, the walking frown, has not been seen since the day she stormed out of the office. Apparently, she's doing something involving yoga (or goats) in Camden (or Hove). Wherever she is, I hope her tassels are happy and her fringe is behaving.

Life, for me, is good.

I feel like I have become the woman I want to be. I have a career (as Mrs Scott-Pym would say), wonderful friends (a full range), a car (well, Caroline's car), a boyfriend (nine months now, practically a lifetime), half a dog and a fondue set.

We're almost there. I turn down a country lane, all hedgerow, cow and bridlepath. The engine revs, Oscar yelps and Lolo sings. I grab his ample leg and give it a loving squeeze. We are the three musketeers, the three kings, the three stooges. A perfect little team. Crosby, Stills and Nash. Snap, Crackle and Pop. Freeman, Hardy and Willis.

Soon we reach the village, driving past scenes that suck me back in time. Immediately familiar but strangely distant. Part of me but alien.

Home. But, then again, not home.

There's the pub and the butcher's and the grassy bit of land where three roads meet then the telephone box and the flowery strip of cottages and the church and finally, set back from the road, Georgian and grand, Mrs Scott-Pym's house. I turn, taking the car down the narrow rustic driveway that runs past Mrs Scott-Pym's and down to the farm.

'Here we are,' I say, in my best sing-song voice as the car potholes down the drive.

'Looks like we've got quite a welcome party,' replies Lolo.

He's right.

In front of us, spread out across the courtyard like a grand Renaissance tableau, are Arthur (my dad), Élise (his lovely French lady friend), Caroline, Digby, Mrs Swithenbank and Geneviève, all jumping up and down and looking very jolly; each of them is waving something (flag, handkerchief, tea towel), shouting something (welcome, *bienvenue*, *benvenuti*) and wearing something on their head (I have no idea why).

'Hello, love,' shouts Arthur (flat cap). 'Welcome home!'

'Hullo,' I shout back, waving with one hand and parking the car with the other.

'And welcome back, Lolo,' Arthur adds. 'It's lovely to see you again, lad.'

Lolo (on his fifth visit) is already out of the car, closely followed by Oscar. There's a lot of hand-shaking (Arthur and Lolo), a lot of hugging (Lolo and everyone else) and a lot of giddy howling (Oscar).

'We wanted to give you both a proper Yorkshire welcome, Evie, love,' says Mrs Swithenbank (knitted tea cosy), squeezing me to her Crimplene chest as soon as I get out of the Alfa.

'And *I* wanted to make sure you were looking after my car,' says Caroline (tiara), ambling towards us, a floaty swirl of maxi-dress and bump.

(Caroline is six months pregnant. She realised, with a little gentle nudging from Geneviève, that she does have a maternal streak after all. Digby is euphoric, a constant blaze of wonder and pride. The mechanics of it all elude me but I know it involved Lolo's lovely cousin Tarquin, a turkey baster and lots of brandy.)

'Of course Evie's looking after the car,' roars Digby (large sombrero). 'She's the best driver in the country. Isn't that right, Lolo?'

Lolo looks over at me and grins.

'Oh, definitely.'

'Well, actually, Lolo,' says Arthur, arm around Élise (stylish beret), 'there was the time . . .'

'Dad!' I shout. 'We can very easily go straight back to London, you know!'

'Oh no we can't,' says Lolo, glancing over at Arthur (was that a wink?). 'I'm really looking forward to this weekend.'

'Yes, you can't go now,' says Élise, her silky French accent oozing onto the day like cream over strawberries. 'I've made you some *patisseries*.'

'And I made some shortbread,' pipes up Geneviève (part hat, part living sculpture). 'Some real Scottish shortbread,' she adds, looking over at Caroline and Digby.

'Aye, come on in, everyone,' laughs Arthur. 'Time for some tea, I think. Are you putting the kettle on, love?' he asks Élise, taking her hand.

'*Oui, ma petite théière,*' she replies (beautiful bursting French bubbles).

As they walk inside, Élise lifts Arthur's hand to her lips, giving it a tender kiss.

I smile, flush with love, and follow.

'Top up, Doris?'

That's Élise, teapot in hand, doing the rounds again.

'Oooh, go on then, love. Don't mind if I do.'

We're all on our second cup now, sat around the big wooden table in the kitchen. In the middle of the table is a Victoria sponge the size of a tractor tyre (made by Mrs Swithenbank), Geneviève's shortbread and various buttery delights made by Élise. There's been lots of breakfast chat, some of it serious (EEC, VAT, TUC) and some less so, all interspersed with a good helping of village gossip (the new vicar, Wendy Fox's triplets, Mr Doughton's bunions).

Lolo's busy polishing off his second helping of cake, his face fixed in a visual purr. 'Oh, this really is delicious, Doris,' he says, smacking his lips.

'Thanks, love. But my cakes aren't a patch on Rosamund's,' she says, turning to Caroline. 'Your mum was the best baker in the village.'

We all agree, warm waves of memory and bonhomie.

'In fact,' says Digby, rubbing Caroline's arm, '*everything* Rosamund cooked was wonderful.'

Mrs Swithenbank nods. 'Aye, love. She could have baked an old boot and it'd still taste bloomin' marvellous.'

'I wish I'd met her,' says Lolo.

'Oh, she would have loved you, darling,' says Caroline.

'She liked opera, didn't she?' he asks.

'Liked it? She loved it. Brought me up on it too, like mother's milk. She had it blaring out every day, isn't that right, Evie?'

'Oh yes, she definitely loved her shouty music.'

Lolo smiles.

'Darling,' Caroline goes on, waving a beautifully manicured nail in Lolo's direction, 'you should see the size of her old gramophone. It's as big as a bull. Lord knows where we're going to put it.'

(Caroline and Digby are keeping Mrs Scott-Pym's house. They'd originally planned to sell it but they couldn't – it's just too much like home. They'll be spending a lot of time up here because Caroline wants the baby to grow up a Yorkshireman (*or Yorkshirewoman*, corrects Digby). So Geneviève's moved into a spare room in their house in London, *to help us keep an eye on things*, says Caroline. She's got a bedroom (much bigger than my box room) and another room, which she uses as her studio. She's working for one of Caroline's fashion friends but still makes her own clothes too, a line of inflatables that I appreciate from afar. I miss her, of course, but she's only round the corner. Plus my flat is now almost permanently full of Lolos and Oscars.)

'Och, we'll find somewhere,' says Digby, still stroking Caroline's arm. 'We're hardly stuck for space, now, are we?'

'You're certainly not, love,' says Mrs Swithenbank. 'Space and class are two things Rosamund had in bucketloads.'

I'm mid-slurp of my tea when an idea comes.

'I think we should toast Mrs Scott-Pym,' I say.

'Oh,' eyebrows Arthur. 'Don't you think it's a little too early for champagne?'

'Or sherry,' adds Caroline, under her breath.

'No, I meant with tea!'

'Good idea, love,' says Mrs Swithenbank, pushing back her chair and standing up.

We all follow, a mass scraping of chair on tile.

'To Mrs Scott-Pym,' I say, lifting up my teacup.

Various voices bounce back at me (*to Rosamund; to Mrs Scott-Pym; to Mummy*) and we all raise our cups.

The room is silent for a moment, a long luscious blink, then there's a soothing clatter as all the cups go back down on their saucers.

'God bless her,' says Mrs Swithenbank.

Caroline smiles and dabs at an eye with her hanky.

Digby squeezes Caroline's other hand then bends down and kisses her swirly silk bump.

The warm air softens.

Everything connects.

The grandfather clock in the hallway chimes midday.

'Right, well, I suppose we'd better be off,' says Mrs Swithenbank, tapping a hand on the table. 'I expect you Londoners have plenty to be getting on with.'

'And we'll be going too,' says Caroline, manoeuvring off the chair.

'Yes, busy day ahead,' says Digby, giving her a hand. 'Although we might pop back later.'

'Oh yes,' says Geneviève. 'Just to see how you're getting on.'

'Aye, you know, if we're passing,' says Mrs Swithenbank.

'That would be lovely,' says Élise. 'If you're passing, of course.'

(Knowing looks are bouncing round the room like a set of rubber balls. It's all very strange.)

Caroline, Digby, Mrs Swithenbank and Geneviève are at the door now, not so much the three wise men as the four cryptic women. There's a lot of waving and *bye*ing and then, in a final surge of Crimplene, they're gone.

'Oh, that was all a bit odd. Do you think everything's okay?' I ask, sitting back down with Arthur, Élise and Lolo.

'Oh yes,' says Arthur. 'They're probably just excited about seeing you, that's all.'

Half an hour later and I'm upstairs unpacking.

Our sleeping arrangements are the same every visit, carved in stone by the god of farmhouse propriety.

Lolo's in 'his' room, the big spare room formerly known as the *Pink Palace* (thankfully Élise has given it a thorough de-pinking and it's now very swish, like a Habitat shop window). And I'm in my room, archive of my teenage self. It's like stepping into an old photo. On the walls are my Beatles posters, fading slightly and beginning to curl. On my bed is my soft flowery eiderdown (flying carpet, den and fort). Next to it is my bedside table, with a photo of Mum, Arthur and me when I was four months old, an ample mass of wool and lace with a tiny beaming face (one of two copies – the other is in London; Arthur has the original in his study). The table has a drawer, once keeper of all my earthly treasures but now home to a long-dry mascara, a bag of Opal Fruits and a 1969 *Vogue*.

The room feels smaller now. Inched in. In fact everything feels smaller ... the bed, the wardrobe, the lamp, the windows. Only the view is still big, stretching out across the countryside, field after field, a giant rug of green that unfurls until the horizon.

My weekend bag is on the bed and I'm busy in the wardrobe, hanging up a heavily creased cheesecloth smock.

There's a knock at the door, quickly followed by Arthur's smiling face poking into the room.

'Hullo, love,' he says, coming in. 'All unpacked?'

'Almost,' I reply, closing the wardrobe door.

'You know we can do the room up if you like, don't you? Make it a bit more modern.'

'Thanks, Dad, but I like it like this. It brings back lots of lovely memories.'

He smiles. 'It certainly does.' He walks over to the bed and sits down, tapping his hand on the eiderdown, an invitation to join him.

'Well, I must say, he's a very nice lad, Lolo, isn't he? You've done well there, love.'

'Oh, thanks, Dad!'

'No, I mean, *he's* obviously done well too, of course. There aren't many men who are good enough for my little girl.'

'I'm glad you approve,' I say, turning to catch him smirking. 'I'll let him know he gets the Arthur Epworth *Certificate of Recommendation*.'

'Aye, you do that. He makes you happy, doesn't he?'

We look at each other, every silent atom between us saying something.

'Yes.' The sunlight dapples in his bright blue eyes. 'Lolo makes me very happy.'

'Well, that makes me very happy, then,' he says, putting his arms around me. 'And I think your mother would like him too, you know. She'd be proud of you, love.'

I press my head deep into his chest and smile.

'Will this do?' asks Lolo, gesturing at a grassy bank that slopes down to the stream.

We're out on the farm, later in the day, looking for somewhere to have a picnic.

'Yes, perfect. It's my favourite spot!'

'I know.'

'How?'

'Ah, well, there's not a lot we Welsh don't know.'

Lolo's made a beeline for the bend in the stream. A weeping willow stands guard to one side and, down in the narrow trickle of water, a solitary stepping stone sits squat and firm.

'I used to come here all the time when I was little,' I tell him. 'Usually with a book and some of Mrs Scott-Pym's cake.'

'Aha!' he says, giving the picnic basket he's carrying a little shake. 'I think I can help out there.'

The shake sets Oscar off barking. He's been shadowing the basket ever since we left the kitchen.

'Don't worry, boy, I haven't forgotten you. It's not just cake in here.'

Oscar's tail flops left and right and a long strip of drool dangles down from his prodigious cheeks.

'I still don't know how you managed to magic up a picnic basket,' I say, unfolding a blanket and throwing it out across the sloping grass.

'Ah, well, I might have had a little help.' He puts the basket down and flicks back a corner of the blanket, making a perfect square. 'A little French help, shall we say?'

I laugh. 'I knew it! I could tell you'd all been planning something.'

'Well, it was meant to be a nice surprise,' he says, sitting down.

I join him on the grassy bank, nature's armchair.

'So that's why Dad and Élise went out for lunch, then? It's all part of your elaborate picnic plan.'

'I am an evil genius,' he replies, passing me a Scotch egg. 'Ooh, I almost forgot.' He puts his own egg down and dives back into the basket, pulling out a bottle of dandelion and burdock (my guilty pleasure).

'Ha! Now it's a real picnic,' I say, mid-egg.

He passes me a bright green plastic cup and fills it with a bubbling fizz of liquid caramel.

'What else have you got in there?' I ask, craning over and trying to look inside the basket.

Lolo snaps down the lid. 'Never you mind.'

'It better not be any plinky plonky music,' I say, leaning back. 'I'm having a good time; I don't want it spoiling.'

'Well, I can't promise that' – he's got the basket open again and is rummaging around inside – 'but I can promise the finest sandwiches this side of Paris. *Voilà!*' He pulls out a magnificently crusty stick of bread. '*Un jambon-beurre.* Élise made the bread this morning, apparently, she and your dad went to Leeds yesterday for the French ham and butter.'

'Oooh, very swanky! I see you've charmed them both, then.'

'Charmed them?' (He does his best '*beurre* wouldn't melt in my mouth' face.) 'Well, it's just my natural sparkling charisma.'

'Very funny,' I say, taking the sandwich. 'They *do* really like you, though.'

Lolo rips into his *jambon beurre* and smiles, a splodge of French butter on his lip.

'I really like them, too. They're great. And it's wonderful being up here with them at the farm; it reminds me of home in Wales.'

'It's beautiful, isn't it?' I look around, taking in the stream and the weeping willow and the cows and the farmhouse and the endless rolling blue sky. 'It was the perfect place to grow up, you know. I had everything: Dad, the farm, Mrs Scott-Pym, everyone in the village.' I turn back to Lolo. 'The only person missing was poor old Mum.'

He leans over and kisses me. I savour the saltiness of the butter on his lips.

And then a barrage of barks breaks out around us.

We look round to see Oscar playing in the shallow water, his short stubby legs almost submerged.

'He's on his holiday,' says Lolo. 'It'll be buckets and spades next.'

I laugh, gulping down the day.

'You see that stepping stone,' I say, pointing towards the stream. 'I used to stand on it and pretend I was a giant striding across the oceans, stepping from one continent to another.'

'Hmmm,' says Lolo, chewing on his *jambon-beurre.*

'I thought I was invincible. A god down from Mount Olympus. Leaping across the world.'

'That explains a lot,' he says, swallowing. 'Has anyone ever talked to you about your overactive imagination?'

I give him a pretend slap and finish off my sandwich.

Lolo sprawls across the blanket, his feet slanting out towards the willow and his head resting on my outstretched legs. The air is warm and the sky cornflower blue. We laugh and talk and laugh and talk, our voices splashing together like water in the stream.

At some point, Lolo rolls over and looks up at me.

'Right, Athena, do you fancy some pud?'

'Oh, yes,' I reply, clapping my hands. 'You've said the magic word!'

'Well, I'm afraid I don't have any ambrosia or nectar,' he says, back in the picnic basket. 'But I do have some rather special cakes . . . Ta-daaa!'

And, with a flourish any television magician would be proud of, he pulls out two fairy cakes.

One blue.

And one pink.

I burst out laughing.

'Oh, those bring back memories!'

'Yes, I thought they might.'

'Bagsy the blue one.'

'No!' cries Lolo. 'The blue one's for me. Celery flavour.'

I make a yucky face and take the pink fairy cake.

'And what flavour's this one, then?' I ask.

'Fruit gum and opera,' replies Lolo, beaming.

'Oh, delicious,' I say, lifting it up to my mouth.

'Hold on, greedy guts, these are special French cakes. You have to eat them like this . . .'

And he breaks his fairy cake in half and has a good bite.

'Right, I see. Well, now we're all in the EEC together, I suppose I'd better do it the right way, hadn't I?'

As I'm breaking the cake in half, Lolo inexplicably starts to get on one knee.

And then I look down into the halved cake and see a glint of something, shiny and crystalline.

'Evie Epworth,' says Lolo, 'would you make me the happiest slightly overweight balding Welshman in the world and marry me?'

Time stops. I think of Dad saying earlier how much Mum would like Lolo . . . I think of Mrs Scott-Pym's advice about finding someone *funny, interesting* and *kind* . . . I think of the wonderful feeling I have when I'm on my way to meet him and how I feel a lush, balmy warmth whenever he's nearby. I think of all this – and more – and my mouth says something before my brain can even begin to ponder.

'Yes.'

He hurls both halves of fairy cake high in the air and throws his arms around me. I hold him tight, arm locked round arm, and we kiss.

'Are you sure?' he whispers.

'Almost.'

'That'll do.' And he kisses me again.

A minute or so later and I'm wearing a beautiful, crumb-ridden engagement ring. Lolo's standing on the grass, dandelion and burdock bottle in hand.

'We won't be needing this,' he says, turning the bottle upside down and emptying it all out.

'Oi, we need that to toast the good news.'

'Don't worry,' he says, grinning. 'It's all in hand.'

He twists the empty bottle into the ground and then nips back to the picnic basket.

'What are you up to?'

'You'll see.'

He pulls something out of the basket. Something that belongs to dark, winter nights rather than beautiful summer days.

A firework. A large rocket.

'What's going on?'

'Just a bit of magic, that's all.'

He puts the long wooden stick into the bottle, pulls a box of matches out of his pocket and lights the blue touchpaper.

'Here we go,' he shouts.

The rocket whooshes into the air, a fizzing mass of sparks and flare. A couple of seconds later, colours burst against the bright blue sky and the air crackles with noise.

'Are you going to do this every time I say yes to something?' I ask.

'Maybe.'

Oscar is on the rampage, running round and round, lifting his head to the sky and sending out great barrels of howls.

And then, in the distance, I see a group of people. My people. All running, waddling, panting, waving. Arthur and Élise bookend the group, each holding the end of an unfurled banner.

CONGRATULATIONS!!!

Under the banner totter Caroline, cradling her bump, and Digby, waving a magnum of champagne. Skipping along next to them is Geneviève, each hand fully occupied with a bouquet of glasses. And, just about keeping up, there's Mrs Swithenbank, a stately battlecruiser, majestic and proud.

They're all shouting. Cheering. Whooping. A wonderful booming of joy.

I look up into the glorious blue sky and think of Mum and Mrs Scott-Pym, watching over us, toasting my life. Toasting all our lives.

And that's how this new chapter begins.

With a toast, the odd tear, an abundance of cheer, and lots and lots of love.

ACKNOWLEDGEMENTS

The thing about acknowledgements is once you start, you might never end. I could easily fill an entire second book thanking everyone who has helped me in some way while I've been writing this one. It would be a long book (and possibly a bit dull) but if it were a bit stream-of-conscious-y with some jaunty punctuation, it may well pick up a prize. Instead I'll say an enormous general thank you to everyone who has been so supportive of me and Evie over the last couple of years – all the brilliant bloggers and wonderful booksellers, many of whom are now firm friends; all the archivists and librarians who've helped with research, events and F&M care packages; all the friendly authors who've provided a much-needed support network; all the graphic design-ers, copyeditors, reps, page setters, font wizards, and marketing & PR ninjas who've helped put this book together; and all my long-suffering work colleagues, who've had to put up with me not knowing one end of a Microsoft Teams from the other. Extra thank yous to: Sue McGregor, Veronica Jordan, Tessa Moore, Val White and Janice Simeone for sharing their 1972s with me; Dr Emily Mayhew for her extensive knowledge of 1972 food (always delicious); and my mate Chris for his daily displays of 1972 fashion (always suspect). Thank you to all my lovely family and friends for being so understanding about me being as present as a gold unicorn when in writing mode. Thank you to my agent, Alice Lutyens, for keeping an eye on everything. Thank you to my editor, Chris White, for being so patient, clever, and kind. Thank you to my dad, for being the best grumpy old Yorkshireman this grumpy young Yorkshireman could ever wish for. And finally thank you to Lindsey, now one tick further on with the bucket list.